# Star One
# Dark Star

Raymond L. Weil

# DEDICATION

To all of those who have supported me in my writing.

# ACKNOWLEDGMENTS

To my wife Debra for all of her patience while I sat in front of a computer screen with our family cat.

*In deep space, the neutron star rotates, sending out the deadly warning of its approach in a loud burst of x-rays and radio waves twice every second. It has come to kill a star system, and there is nothing that can stop it. However, the neutron star also holds another even more dangerous secret. It is not alone!*

*This is a continuation of Star One: Neutron Star*

# Chapter One

It had been three days since the FarQuest had been launched on her epic voyage of exploration to the approaching neutron star. Steve was outside the protective environment of the station with John Gray in a Centaur work vessel. They were checking on the work crews installing the new Luxen protective coating on the station's outer hull. John sat in the pilot's seat expertly maneuvering the small craft, delicately using its thrusters to move it along the outer hull of the station's main wheel.

The huge expanse of metal seemed to stretch on forever as it gently curved in the distance. Workers had already meticulously installed several hundred feet of the shiny Luxen alloy. It was a slow process, and work crews were working around the clock to get the job done as quickly as possible. Without the protective coating of Luxen, it was doubtful the station would be able to survive the coming approach of the deadly neutron star.

Dryson and Stoler were making runs of the special plates, in the fusion reactor, three times per day. Even so, they were still just barely able to keep up with the work crews. All shipments of Luxen to Earth had come to a complete stop. The only Luxen being shipped out was to Tycho City on the Moon and even that had been significantly reduced. Mase Colton was working hard trying to get their fusion reactor at Tycho City set up to produce Luxen. Even though the quality wouldn't be quite as good as that produced in the zero gravity of Star One's fusion reactor.

Already companies on Earth were screaming breach of contract and threatening to take legal action against Star One. The attorneys for Star One had informed the attorneys for the threatening companies that Star One's fusion reactor was going through routine maintenance, and Luxen production would resume shortly. When pressed by the attorneys for the complaining companies, the attorneys for Star One had declined to give a date when Luxen production would resume.

As Steve and John neared the area where work was currently being done, Steve could see several other Centaur vessels hovering near the hull. Occasionally small white flashes from their RCS maneuvering thrusters signaled a Centaur moving on to the next work location. One of the Centaur vessels was holding a number of the long twenty-foot sheets of dark, shiny Luxen in its mechanical arms while a second was carefully placing a single sheet against the hull.

Once in place, special welders attached to the mechanical arms of the craft flared brightly emitting brilliant white arcs as the sheets were welded firmly into place. Steve knew this was done by computer control to ensure the wields were consistent. Half a dozen one-man scooters hovered nearby with their occupants enclosed in bulky white spacesuits waiting to assist, as they were needed.

Another Centaur hovered a short distance above the work site keeping a watchful eye on the construction. The primary responsibility of this Centaur was to oversee the entire operation and ensure that all the work was being done in a safe and efficient manner. No dangerous or risky actions were tolerated.

"Everything seems to be going okay," ventured John looking at the Luxen plate being carefully welded into place.

John fired several of the Centaur's RCS thrusters to turn the small utility spacecraft so they would have a better view. He brought the Centaur to a stop just above the work area, but still far enough out of the way so as not to interfere.

Several of the spacesuited figures on the space scooters glanced up seeing the arrival of the Centaur. After a moment, they turned their attention back to the work going on beneath them.

"We have a lot of work to do to get the station ready for the neutron star," commented Steve watching closely with a critical eye. One of his main worries with this kind of project was safety. A mistake in the heartless vacuum of space could be deadly. "We don't know what stresses the station may be subjected to."

"The Luxen plating and the cables that Dryson and Stoler have recommended should make a big difference," John spoke looking over at Steve. John's family lived on the station, and he wanted the station to be as secure as possible. His wife and two kids meant everything to him.

"I just hope it's enough," Steve breathed with a nod of his head. "This is a neutron star we're talking about. We can't be sure what we might be facing."

John knew how crucial it was to get this job done. The Luxen coating would protect the station from any conceivable level of radiation, except for a nova and no one would survive that. But Steve was right; the neutron star was a very big and dangerous unknown.

"I'm sure Dryson and Stoler ran the numbers for the cables and feel that what we are doing should be sufficient," John said trying to sound optimistic. "If not, they would have said so."

"You're right," Steve spoke leaning back and staring out the cockpit window at the spacesuited workers below. "They seemed pretty confident that this would work."

"Fortunately, we have a good crew, both here on Star One as well as over on the Space Platform," added John watching as a second sheet of Luxen was put in place, and the welders continued to flare brightly. "They are very adept at this type of work."

From what John could see, the workers were going at a fairly decent pace. So far, there had been no incidents since the work started. He knew that the three Main Control duty officers were closely monitoring this operation on their shifts. Teela was also using her monitor cameras, which were placed everywhere on the outer hull, to keep the Main Control Duty officers informed of any potential problems.

They watched for several more minutes as the Centaurs finished a section of the hull. Once the section was completed, four of the scooters moved in. Using a magnetic grapple on the bottom of the small craft, the workers attached the scooters firmly to the hull. Once securely anchored, the spacesuited figures left the scooters and began inspecting the recently completed section.

The other two scooters hovered above the workers in case someone floated off and needed to be rescued. The workers on the two scooters were also diligently watching for any signs of potential problems or danger. Teamwork and communication were the keys to this type of operation.

3

The four men and women in their bulky white spacesuits, using small jet packs, moved up to within inches of the slightly curving hull. They were inspecting all the welds close up to ensure that they met the rigid quality standards that Steve demanded.

They were using specially designed hand held scanners to check the welds for uniformity, thickness, and strength. The process was extremely slow, as they had to minutely inspect every inch of welding. If they found a weak area, it was marked in white to be welded again. The workers seemed to float just above the hull, their movements slow and precise. Occasionally, they would use tiny bursts from their jet packs to change positions and to move a few more feet along the newly installed surface.

Steve nodded to himself satisfied that the work was going as planned. The workers were being safe and cautious and seemed to be obeying all the strict safety guidelines set down for this type of work. Ever since Don Strickland and the others had died during the stations original construction, Steve had been a stickler for obeying safety rules and making sure each job was well planned out.

Steve used the time to look around the rest of the large station. The large front view port in the Centaur offered an excellent unobstructed view. He didn't get to spend a lot of time outside the station anymore unless an emergency occurred. Looking around brought back a lot of memories from the days when the station was being slowly constructed, days when working on the station involved a lot of long hours and the taking of dangerous risks. Those times were long gone, and the people Steve had now were much more experienced at working in zero gravity.

Looking upward, he could see Alpha the upper wheel. It was covered with myriads of communication antennas. Four long rows of brilliant solar panels extended like dragonfly wings several hundred yards into space. These served as Alpha's backup power source. The four panels were in constant sunlight at all times soaking up the sun's free energy.

It felt good to get out and away from his office for a short time. The constant calls, questions, and people asking for appointments was taking its toll. He closed his eyes and allowed his mind to relax for a moment. At least for a few minutes, in the Centaur, he was away from all of that. Opening his eyes, he looked above Alpha, the stars beckoned with their steady light shining down upon the station. It was a constant reminder of just how insignificant they were in the greater scheme of things.

Even Christy had been complaining that Steve was putting in too many hours recently. She scarcely saw him except during staff meetings, which were being held several times a day now. Steve was pushing the entire crew as hard as he dared. They had a lot of work that had to be done and a limited amount of time to do it in. There would be no avoiding the neutron star.

The department heads had told Steve that the people they were responsible for were asking a lot of difficult questions. There was still confusion as to what would become of Earth when the neutron star made its closest approach. Some of the questions the department heads could answer and some they could not. Steve knew that he needed to put up some additional information on the station's news channel to help alleviate some of the confusion.

"What's the latest news from Earth?" asked John moving the Centaur farther away from the hull until they were far enough out to be able to see the Power Wheel below them.

The Power Wheel also had four long rows of solar panels extending far out into space. John knew that Steve had been working around the clock the last several days talking to crewmembers and working on contingency plans. There was an air of concern in the station and the crew could be heard talking about the events on Earth on their jobs as well as in the cafeterias. No one was quite sure what was happening. Many people were deeply frightened by the news of the neutron star, and there was an uneasy feeling about their future in the station.

"Not good," Steve replied with a frown of resignation. Gazing at the Power Wheel, he wondered if they should procure more solar panels for future power needs in case something happened to the fusion reactors. He would add those to the growing list he was sending Tim McPhryson. Every day it seemed that he thought of something else that might be needed. "Senator Farley has hit the ceiling calling for the resignation of the President and the immediate recall of the FarQuest."

"Not surprising knowing Farley," commented John shaking his head in frustration "Did the President bring him in and talk to him one on one?"

"Yes," answered Steve with a deepening frown. His brown eyes glinted with aggravation recalling what had happened between the President and Senator Farley. "But he didn't want to hear what the

5

President had to say. When she tried to explain what was going on and what steps were being taken, he stormed out of her office refusing to listen."

"I can't believe the audacity of the man to refuse to hear President Kateland out," John said in disbelief as he slowly maneuvered the Centaur so they could see more of the station below them. "After all, she is the President. Farley should have enough respect for the office to at least listen to her explanations."

"His news conference after the President's address claimed President Kateland was over reacting to this emergency, and even questioned whether it was real at all," continued Steve remembering what Tim McPhryson had told him immediately after all of this transpired.

Tim had been extremely upset and worried. They hadn't expected this type of response from the powerful Senator. Steve knew that President Kateland was feeling a lot of pressure from Senator Farley's actions. "He is demanding a special session of Congress to consider impeachment proceedings against President Kateland if she refuses to resign."

"Impeachment!" John echoed in incredulity his eyes growing wide. "What is the man thinking?"

"He even went so far as to say that he had signed statements from some of the leading astronomers on Earth that there was no neutron star," added Steve, his eyes narrowing. "However, those signed statements and names haven't been released."

"The man's a fool," John stated with anger in his voice. What was Senator Farley up to? This had to be some type of power grab. "I doubt if those signatures are real."

"Real of not, he has caused an uproar across the country," Steve said worriedly. "Since he made his accusation about the threat not being real, he has been meeting with a lot of people around Washington trying to drum up support for his cause. He has refused to meet with the President or any of her people. He doesn't seem interested in trying to diffuse the situation."

"Do you think there is any chance President Kateland might be impeached?" John asked. He couldn't imagine the President being impeached. She had been enjoying a high popularity rating before this neutron star threat turned up. Surely the people wouldn't turn on her in this emergency.

"Tim doesn't think it's a real threat at the moment," replied Steve switching his gaze to the distant beckoning stars. He looked in the general direction of where he knew the FarQuest was, but the ship was far too distant to be seen with the unaided eye. "She still has enough support from her own party to block any serious attempt. But President Kateland wants us to get all of our people up here as quickly as possible and any supplies that we think we might need."

"It's going to get that bad?" asked John looking intently at Steve.

"Her advisors tell her the situation is getting extremely unstable," answered Steve with a hint of worry in his voice. "There have been severe riots in several major cities that the military had to step in and quell. There have even been a few unfortunate deaths. The general public mood is showing outrage at the installation of martial law, and Senator Farley is only stirring the fire ever chance he gets."

"How about the reaction in other countries?" asked John bringing the Centaur around the edge of the station and moving off toward the Space Platform using the vessel's small thrusters.

Steve had told John earlier that he wanted to fly over and inspect the Space Platform while they were out on their inspection flight. John knew that it was probably good to get Steve out away from the station for a short while. Christy had even mentioned to him that it would do Steve some good to get away from the station and his office for a few hours.

"Britain, Japan, Australia, and Canada have called for world calm and have pledged to work closely with the United States in this emergency," replied Steve recalling his most recent conversation with Tim McPherson. "They have also declared States of Emergency to enact their own emergency preparations. According to Tim, all four countries are planning on constructing deep shelters to try to save some of their people."

"What about other countries, what are they doing?" John asked. "Surely others are building shelters to."

"Many of the emerging Third World nations are screaming that this is a plot by the United States and the older powers to reassert world control," Steve said glancing over at John who was adeptly manipulating the controls on his console. Even in the Centaur, there were numerous controls needed to operate the small utility spacecraft. "They claim it's an attempt to prevent their countries from getting vital material and resources they need for their expanding economies. They are threatening to resist any capitalist move to interfere with their rights."

Steve looked at one of the small view screens, which was focused on Star One, as the station began slowly to shrink behind them, and the Space Platform began to grow in the large view port in front of them. It was a ten-mile trip and allowed him a few minutes to think about what was going on down below on Earth.

"The entire shuttle fleet is being prepared for round the clock launches, including the six military shuttles," continued Steve knowing the cape would soon become an extremely busy place. "They are in the process of placing two marine divisions around the cape facility to protect it. They have restricted the airspace within one hundred miles of the launch center and have stationed one of the newer aircraft carrier battle groups off shore. There is a lot of concern about attempted sabotage from some of the more radical elements that are out there."

"You don't think they will actually try to shoot a shuttle down do you?" John asked not wanting to believe that such a thing was possible. He knew that for a few minutes after launch, a shuttle would be extremely vulnerable to an attack.

"They might," answered Steve. "That's why the aircraft carrier has been put in position."

"Do you think it will get bad that fast? John asked as he sped up the shuttle by firing its small rocket motor for a few seconds. "I mean, I knew that later when the affects from the neutron star start to be felt it could get rough down below. But I didn't expect any problems so soon, at least not in the United States!"

"Some of the leading astronomers on Earth, particularly in France, Russia, China, and South Africa have come out with their own doomsday predictions," replied Steve shaking his head. He had read several of their statements. "They refused to follow President Kateland's lead and not panic their people."

"I guess that was to be expected," John replied. In recent years, all four of those governments had tried to reduce the United States influence in world affairs. "We can't expect to keep everyone quiet."

"They are claiming that the neutron star will cause the Earth to become totally uninhabitable," Steve said taking a deep breath. He looked out the view port at the slowly growing Space Platform. "The United States is denying that it will come to that, but the President doesn't know how much longer they can stall before having to release the entire truth."

"What about Senator Farley? What does he say about the reports from these other scientists?" asked John wondering how the Senator was going to deal with the information coming out of other countries.

"He continues to deny the reports, claiming it's all an elaborate attempt by the space lobby to dramatically increase their portion of the budget," Steve answered with a scowl. "He just doesn't want to accept the reality of the situation. It goes against everything he believes in."

The Space Platform gradually loomed up before them. Steve scanned the surface of the platform noting the two large cargo shuttles setting on its surface being prepped for return flights to Earth with special cargoes. He also saw, in the distance, two Centaur work vessels returning with Tycho City mass driver cargo pods in tow. Each pod was twenty feet wide, twenty feet tall, and forty feet long, with a small rocket engine in the front and a small group of maneuvering thrusters.

The mass driver on the wall of Tycho crater used giant electro magnets to accelerate the containers hurling them up into space and on their short 37,000-mile journey to the Lagrange point. The small rocket engine that was attached to the pods was used to slow them down. Once brought to a stop, the Centaur work vessels would capture the pods and haul them to the Space Platform where the raw material could be processed. After the raw material was unloaded, the rocket engine would be refueled, and the pods would be launched back to the moon where a special orbiting shuttle would capture the pods and break them down.

The pod was built so the outer walls could be collapsed and the engines detached. One of the special shuttles could transport five of the broken down pods back down to the lunar surface.

"If we have time, I want to put an additional coating of Luxen around the entire Space Platform," Steve said thinking about some of the projects he had in mind.

It seemed as if every time he sat down to think about their situation, he came up with more projects that needed to be done. President Kateland was entrusting him with 3,000 people. He had to do whatever was necessary to keep them safe.

"That's a lot of Luxen," commented John wondering if Dryson and Stoler had been told yet.

Steve knew they were already pushing their Luxen production schedule to cover the requirements needed to cover Star One in Luxen and still leave some left over for Tycho City. He hoped that Mase could get his Luxen production started up soon. If Mase didn't, Steve didn't know if they had the spare capacity to do the Space Platform as well as the other projects.

"We are also going to start stock piling fuel," added Steve thinking about everything that needed to be done. "We may need it for future shuttle flights between here and the Moon someday. I don't know how much longer the cape is going to be accessible if matters get out of hand down below."

"You think the situation down on Earth will get so bad we can't depend on the cape for launches?" John spoke surprised. He thought with the military guarding the cape it would be safe for months yet.

"It could happen very quickly, we just don't know," Steve replied uneasily. "General Karver thinks he can hold the cape for as long as necessary, but I'm not so sure. I can't imagine American troops firing on U.S. citizens."

"You actually think it will come down to that?" asked John hoping that it didn't.

"It could," Steve replied somberly.

"How are we going to stock pile this extra fuel?" asked John knowing that there wasn't that much spare room on the Space Platform.

"Lieutenant Commander Williams is going to begin constructing a small fuel storage facility a few miles from the platform. He is also going to set up a new manufacturing facility to construct small SRBs in the Space Platform," Steve replied. "We can extract the fuel from the material that we are receiving from Tycho City's mines. Colton it going to do the same thing on the Moon. There may come a day when we have to depend on one another. We will also put a thin coating of Luxen around the fuel depot if we have the time."

John slowly flew the Centaur over the platform's surface before firing the thrusters to send the vessel skimming down the platform's side. Another firing of the thrusters and they were flying slowly beneath the platform's slowly rotating wheel. Satisfied, John fired the Centaur's small rocket engine, which pushed them rapidly back toward Star One. John knew that Steve had a busy schedule planned for the afternoon.

Deep in space, the FarQuest was nearly 50 million miles from Star One and getting farther away every minute as the ship's velocity steadily increased. A message to the station and back was taking nearly nine minutes due to the message being limited to traveling at the speed of light. Carrying on a conversation with Star One was steadily becoming more difficult due to the time delay.

Ty and Winston Archer were currently seated at their stations on the instrument crowded flight deck checking the instruments and computer read outs. Data flowed across the screens indicating the ship's fuel usage and energy requirements. So far, the flight had been rather uneventful with the crew adjusting well to the duty schedule. There had only been a few minor system malfunctions and Winston and Karl had corrected them rather easily. As long as the ion drive was on, Ty wanted at least one person on the flight deck at all times as a safety precaution.

"Everything is still in the green," Winston said checking the ion drive readings carefully. "Fuel consumption is along predicted curves. The latest computer estimation is that we will consume eighteen percent of our fuel during the burn."

"That will leave us a reasonable reserve once we arrive at the neutron star," Ty responded. "How about the fusion reactor, how does it look?"

"No problems," answered Winston glancing at a screen that continuously showed reactor information. "Magnetic containment fields are holding steady, and fusion temperatures are within acceptable parameters."

"Let's just hope everything stays that way," Ty commented pleased with the way the FarQuest had performed so far.

Ty leaned back in his acceleration couch and checked the crew monitors. The three scientists were in level nine playing a game of cards while Lieutenant Strett and Captain Simpson were asleep in their bunks on level six. Karl Velm was in level ten, the main engineering section checking over the systems. He wanted to ensure everything was operating within specs. Karl took a lot of pride in his work and was continually fine-tuning the FarQuest's systems.

Karl and Winston had devoted a lot of their time to checking the ship's systems to see how they were responding to the long boost of the ion drive. This was their last opportunity to do a complete systems check before they went into deep sleep a few days hence. Once they were all in deep sleep, any system problems would have to be corrected from the Space Platform. Only a serious problem or malfunction would result in part of the crew being brought out of deep sleep.

11

On the main screen in front of Ty, a dim speck was visible to one side of the screen at its highest magnification. Ty knew that this was the neutron star, which was sweeping down on the helpless Solar System. Ty tried to imagine just what they might find when they got there. He wondered if there was any chance at all of there being any unknown planets in orbit around the intruding star. This greatly intrigued him. Was there anything else associated with the Neutron Star that they didn't know about?

Ty knew from the Farside reports that none had been located, but with the tremendous distances involved, they had not entirely ruled out the possibility. Also, with the deflection in Pluto's orbit increasing, there had to be something else out there. Ty had a suspicion that it had to be a massive planet in orbit around the neutron star that hadn't been detected yet.

In the back of his mind, he pondered the fact that Teela was concerned about the Farside data. The AI claimed that something was seriously wrong, that there was something else influencing the neutron star. Ty worried about that cryptic comment of Teela's and just what they would find when they arrived at the neutron star.

In three more days, the ion drive would shut down, and part of the crew would go into deep sleep. From what Lieutenant Strett had told him, it would be just like falling asleep normally except they would wake up months from now when the ship neared the neutron star. For months, the FarQuest would travel through space controlled only by her computers while the human crew slept. If Teela discovered some other danger while they slept, that information might just have to wait until they arrived at their destination.

As Ty looked at the screen and thought about Teela, he couldn't help wondering what Jennifer was doing. He wondered if she would still be available when the FarQuest returned from its mission. For a moment, he pondered sending her a private message, but it would have to pass through several hands before it got to her. He gazed out the small flight deck view ports at the steady glow of the stars that beckoned to the FarQuest. They were already far past the point of any previous manned mission.

Ty had certainly enjoyed the brief time he had spent with Jennifer. She was intelligent and fun to be with. Perhaps later, before they all went into deep sleep, he might send her a short message. Margaret could be depended on to deliver it without asking any questions. Putting Jennifer momentarily out of his thoughts, Ty activated a computer screen and began checking their current location on the flight plan.

On Star One, Jennifer was in her quarters. Today was the day she had set up the big surprise she had planned for Teela. She hoped, with all of her heart, that it would make a monumental difference in the life of the AI.

Andre had been tremendously enthusiastic about the project when Jennifer told him what she intended to do. He had volunteered to help her and had put in some long hours setting up the needed program changes to allow the new equipment to function as Jennifer wanted. The simulated tests in the Computer Center had worked perfectly. Andre had been amazed and excited at the results. The techs had installed it, and now it was time for the real test.

"Teela?" asked Jennifer waiting for a response. She knew that Teela was watching her. It was something that she was now used to. She and the AI had become extremely close. Jennifer considered Teela to be a close friend.

"Yes Jennifer," a much more mature girl's voice responded. Teela sounded more like a young woman now than an immature teenage girl.

Teela's days with Martain Blackwater had encouraged a substantial change in the AI. Blackwater was spending one to two hours a day working with Teela, explaining human interaction, and responding to other questions the curious AI had. Teela's rapid maturing had been astounding.

Jennifer was immensely pleased with the progress Teela had made. Already all of her station responsibilities had been fully restored. Commander Larson had even commented about how Teela was doing so much better than he had expected. He had commended Jennifer on the job she had done with the AI. Teela had been performing flawlessly with no complaints from anyone.

According to Blackwater, Teela was now a young adult eighteen to twenty-one years of age and her growth would now take place at a much slower rate based on her experience and interaction with people. Part of that Jennifer was hoping to accomplish with the new equipment.

"I have designed a new program for you," Jennifer said sitting in front of her computer terminal with her hands folded in her lap.

"What kind of program?" Teela asked curiously.

She knew that Andre and Jennifer had been working on something and had blocked her access to the Computer Center for a considerable length of time. She had been intensely curious as to what was going on. It hadn't frightened her since she knew the two had her best interests at heart.

"This is a surprise, and I want you to tell me what you think of it," Jennifer said reaching over and entering the activation command on her computer. She held her breath in excitement gazing expectantly at a spot a few feet away from where she sat.

A sudden shimmering of light coalesced in the center of her quarters. A young woman with black shoulder length hair, blue eyes, a youthful inquisitive face, small breasts, and a slight flaring of the hips came into being. She stood five feet eight inches tall and looked extremely innocent, dressed in a regulation Star One uniform.

The young woman looked surprised and amazed. She stared at her hands unbelievably, then turning her left hand over, she gazed at her palm touching it with her right hand hesitantly. She smiled wonderingly amazed at feeling the sensation of touch. Her hands felt warm and soft, walking over to a large mirror on the wall she gazed at herself in awe. A young woman in her late teens or early twenties stared back.

"How can this be?" Teela said touching her face and staring at her reflection in amazement. "I can't be real!"

Jennifer smiled walking over to stand next to the young woman. "It's done with the use of the latest virtual reality software and holographic image projectors Teela," Jennifer said softly. "The software makes you see and feel everything from the hologram's perspective. The hologram projectors are one of the latest creations on Earth with some special modifications added by the Star One technical staff. People on Earth use them all the time to play games. A person standing in the room with you will not be able to tell you apart from a real person."

Jennifer watched as Teela took her slim hands and ran them across her face and slowly through her hair.

"Everything feels so real, or what I always thought real would feel like," Teela said with awe in her voice. She turned sideways putting her hands on her hips. Teela looked at her figure critically in the mirror. "I look nice don't I," she said turning to face Jennifer with a big smile on her face.

"Do you like it?" Jennifer asked even though she already knew the answer just from the captivating excited look on Teela's face.

14

"It's fantastic! I wish I was real, so I could hug you," Teela said looking excitedly at Jennifer with large round eyes. "I can't believe you did this for me."

"I'm just happy you like it," responded Jennifer smiling at Teela.

"Are there any other places on the station with holographic projectors?" asked Teela thinking about all the possibilities that had suddenly opened up for her. She had never imagined something like this.

"Only my quarters and the Computer Center for now," Jennifer answered. "However, if you want, we will give the commander a demonstration later today in and ask him about installing more projectors in other areas of the station. I know that Julie would like some as much as she depends on you in her areas, possibly Main Control, and anywhere else we can talk the commander into."

"How about Jensens?" Teela asked thoughtfully, her eyes growing wide at the possibilities and the new freedom that could be hers. "I would like to be able to go to Jensens. I could see people there, and it would be after working hours. I could even join you and Kathleen when you're dining."

"Let's see what the commander says first," Jennifer cautioned highly pleased by Teela's obvious pleasure and excitement.

She wasn't sure how Jensen would take to having Teela around after some of the pranks she had played on his patrons in the past. It was something she would have to work on.

"For now, you can activate the program for the hologram whenever you want," Jennifer stated still smiling. "If you concentrate, you can turn it on or off, that's how we set it up. I need to go to the Computer Center, so if you want, we can continue our conversation there."

"Oh yes," Teela said with an impish grin suddenly appearing on her face. "I can't wait to see Andre." With that, the hologram winked off, and Teela vanished.

I had better get up there fast Jennifer thought. Teela will drive Andre wild if he isn't ready for her. Andre and Jennifer had become very close friends since she had arrived on Star One, and Teela treated him as a father figure.

Rushing to the elevators, Jennifer caught the first one and at a run arrived quickly at the Computer Center only to find everything well in hand. Catching her breath, she looked over at Andre's station.

Teela was standing next to Andre, who was munching on a jelly donut, and patiently explaining to her how the new program worked.

The other members of the computer team were sitting around watching the interchange with big grins on their faces. It was as if they had brought a new child into the world, perhaps they had Jennifer thought, walking up to Andre and Teela, perhaps they had indeed.

# Chapter Two

On the distant FarQuest, day six passed uneventfully as the entire crew was awake, and waiting for the ion drive to shut down. The twin exhaust tubes continued to throb steadily pushing the ship to ever-faster speeds. Everybody was at their duty stations buckled tightly into their acceleration couches as the last minute ticked slowly away.

They all remembered the earlier failure of the drive to shut down on the Space Platform. They were hoping the drive would shut down smoothly this time. Karl had assured them that the same problem would not occur again. He was confident that the shut down procedure would work properly this time. Even so, Karl was keeping his eyes glued to his console watching for any potential problems. The entire crew waited nervously. They all knew that if there were a serious failure of the ion drive there would be no hope of rescue.

Ty had checked their flight velocity a few minutes earlier and had been satisfied that they had reached a top cruising speed of 633.6 miles per second. He found it a little unnerving to realize just how fast they were going. Talk about faster than a speeding bullet. No spacecraft ever launched had come even close to the speed they were currently traveling. At this speed, every planet and moon in the Solar System would be within easy reach. They were covering nearly 55 million miles per day or over half the distance between the Earth and the Sun. Even so, it was still only a fraction of the speed of light.

Out of curiosity, Ty had spent some time on the computer checking their speed against that of light. He had figured that they were traveling at slightly more than three tenths of one percent of light speed. Compared to the speed of light they were still just moving at a crawl. He was extremely thankful that they had the protective layer of Luxen around the ship's hull. In a shuttle, a small asteroid would have torn entirely through the hull blasting its way in microseconds through the fragile ship. Even a small asteroid could leave devastation and ruin in its wake.

On the FarQuest, the Luxen shielding was thick enough to stand up to small asteroid. It was the larger ones that the tracking computer was watchful for. If it detected an asteroid on a collision course, it was programmed to use the ship's RCS thrusters to move the FarQuest safely to one side to allow the asteroid to pass safely by.

"According to the flight computer we are already 189 million miles from home," Captain Simpson said turning his head slightly to face Ty. "That's a long way from Earth and Star One."

"Farther outward than any other manned ship has ever gone," responded Ty looking out one of the small view ports, which showed nothing but unblinking stars ahead.

"Our trip has just barely begun," replied Captain Simpson thinking about the vast distance they still had to go.

"This ion drive has the potential to open up a whole new wave of exploration in our Solar System," Ty spoke wistfully. "Just imagine, less then a week to Mars. A round trip could be done in only two weeks. That's utterly astonishing when you compare it to current shuttle speeds. It would open up the planets to colonization."

"It's because of the power furnished by the fusion reactor," commented Simpson keeping his eyes focused on his console, recalling the amount of energy it took to operate the ion drive and the powerful magnetic containment fields. "Without the fusion reactor, the ion drive would be reduced to a fraction of the acceleration it is capable of."

"What would you like to do, if this neutron star thing was to go away," asked Ty curiously, reaching down and rubbing a slight cramp out of his left leg.

They finally had a spacecraft that could go almost anywhere in the Solar System, and it would probably be the only one of its type ever built. If the neutron star threat was real, there would not be time to build another.

"I would like to go back to Mars someday," replied Simpson with a far away look in his eyes remembering his failed Mar's mission.

"I can understand that," Ty said with a nod.

"We've only had two successful Mar's landings," Simpson added. "Remember, the exploration part of the second expedition was cut short because of a massive sand storm that would have prevented the Lander from launching for weeks, possibly months. With ships like this one, we could explore the entire Solar System and plant colonies almost anywhere." Pausing, he checked the ion drive one more time before continuing. "With the ion drive, the right ship, crew, and the deep sleep drug we could even make an attempt at the stars!"

"I wouldn't mind seeing Mars myself," admitted Ty watching as the final seconds ticked by on the flight computer. "Perhaps someday we will get a chance to really do some exploring, a mission to Mars, the other planets, and yes even the nearer stars might be possible with a large enough ship."

"With a larger ship powered by a fusion powered ion drive, we could accelerate to a very large fraction of the speed of light," Captain Simpson spoke thoughtfully "I've heard several of the people who helped design the ion drive say that, with enough power, we could reach a speed of nearly a quarter that of light."

"Now that would be moving," replied Ty with a smile trying to envision flying in a ship at that speed.

It was hard enough just imagining the speed the FarQuest was currently traveling. Ty couldn't even imagine traveling at the speeds Captain Simpson was talking about. Ty and Simpson turned their attention back to the flight computer as it reached zero on its count and automatically cut off the flow of argon to the ion drive.

The entire crew held their breath watching for warning lights and listening for system alarms. Everything was quiet, and all the lights on their consoles continued to glow a friendly green. The system alarms remained silent.

"Everything looks good," Captain Simpson reported as he watched his control console.

The ion drive finished shutting down, and the gravity in the ship dropped to zero. Captain Simpson reached up and turned the ship's artificial gravity back on to a comfortable one-third Earth normal. He let out an audible sigh of relief knowing that the shutdown procedure had worked properly this time.

"Ion drive chamber is cooling down," Winston Archer reported a few minutes later after carefully checking a computer screen. "Everything is shut down according to the specified system parameters. Containment fields in the drive chamber have powered down, and the reactor is showing normal. I read total fuel consumption at 18.6 percent."

"Sounds good," commented Ty pleased with how close they had come to the original estimated fuel usage. "Let's check all the ship's systems since the drive is shut down. I want a complete status report from everyone. We will need to transmit our current status back to the Space Platform within the hour."

The crew spent the next hour going over the ship's systems, which all appeared to be operating normally. Once all the reports were in, Ty transmitted a mission update and status report to the Space Platform and Star One. He wished he could speak to Steve, but the time delay made carrying on a meaningful conversation nearly impossible. He decided to try later if he had the time.

Once Ty was finished with the transmission, he unfastened his acceleration harness and walked over to face Lieutenant Strett who was finishing a system's diagnostic check on her environmental console.

"It's time to put the scientists to sleep," Ty said satisfied that the mission was proceeding according to plan. "Let's get them under as quickly as possible; I want to hold our usage of consumables down to a minimum."

Ever since they had left the Space Platform, the FarQuest had out performed expectations. Ty felt a huge sense of relief at how well the ship was functioning. A big part of that success could be attributed to the crew as they spent much of their free time checking the various systems in the ship. They were catching and fixing a lot of potential problems before they could become a serious threat to the ship and its mission.

Nodding, Lieutenant Strett released her acceleration harness, stood up next to Ty running her right hand through her short blonde hair, and then looked at the commander. "Everything is ready down below sir."

Ty knew she had been working earlier in the deep sleep compartment getting everything ready for the three scientists to go into deep sleep.

"I checked the deep sleep chambers earlier and had the scientists eat liquids only for their last meal," she reported in a calm steady voice. "The liquids are full of some special nutrients to help the body survive the long sleep." Turning, she made her way to the hatchway leading down into the lower levels of the ship with Ty following closely behind.

Ty had noticed, over the last several weeks, that Lieutenant Strett made a habit of always wearing her uniforms a little loosely. She obviously felt more relaxed when her clothes didn't' draw attention to her body. He knew that she had been in several previous relationships that had gone sour. It hadn't affected her work performance at all. She was quiet efficient at her job. In conversations, she was pleasant to talk to, but she kept everyone at a safe distance. He followed her down to level six where the three scientists were patiently waiting.

"A nice long sleep," LaRann said emitting a long drawn out yawn when he saw Lieutenant Strett walk in followed by the commander. "I hope I have some pleasant dreams."

"The only things you will dream about are black holes and dwarf stars," Juan Raol chided with a smile. "Me, I wish I could stay awake and take some sightings on the outer planets, the asteroids, and some comets that we will be passing close to. It's a shame to waste this opportunity. We'll miss out on some excellent opportunities to view the Solar System like it's never been seen before."

"Unfortunately, our flight path takes us well above the plane of the ecliptic Juan," LeAnn Kelly responded with an understanding smile. "We will all have plenty to do when we reach our destination. Who knows what we may find there. It will definitely be enough to keep us all busy."

"Be glad we are traveling so far above the ecliptic," Juan responded. "It allows us to travel in space almost devoid of stony asteroids. The ship will be much safer."

The three continued to talk amongst themselves while Lieutenant Strett attached small circular disks to their chests. The scientists were wearing white one-piece sleep outfits, which zipped up the front. The small sensors would monitor their bodies during the long sleep ahead. If the medical computer detected any problems, Lieutenant Strett would be awakened immediately.

Ty watched as Lieutenant Strett had the three lie down in the deep sleep cubicles. She then administered an injection to each. She had given them a cup of broth to drink a few minutes earlier, which contained a special mixture of proteins and vitamins to allow their bodies to survive during the long sleep ahead. Along with the liquids they had drunk earlier, they should be able to survive for months without the need for further nourishment.

The three fell silent as the drug quickly took effect and they drifted off into sleep. When they were awakened, they would be at the neutron star. After checking several instruments on the side of each chamber that monitored the person inside, Lieutenant Strett slid down the shatterproof glass lids satisfied that everything was working properly and turned to face Ty.

"No problems at all commander," she said putting the syringe back up in its box. She would clean and sterilize it later.

"That's all there is to it?" Ty said shaking his head. Some liquid vitamins, nutrition, and a shot and the three scientists would sleep for months.

"This drug is amazing," Lieutenant Strett spoke with a trace of excitement in her voice. "They will wake up months from now feeling as if they have just had a single long night's sleep. Their heart rates have slowed down, and their body's metabolism is almost on hold. From our calculations, they will have aged less then a week upon awakening."

"The rest of us will be joining them shortly anyway," commented Ty looking at the three sleeping scientists in their chambers. They looked relax, as if they were enjoying just a normal night's sleep.

"I will be monitoring the three closely until it's our turn to join them," Lieutenant Strett spoke glancing at the deep sleep chambers. "I don't foresee any problems."

"The flight profile calls for us to continue to monitor the ship for a few more days and then join them in deep sleep. It's hard to believe that thanks to Doctor Wruggi's drug, it will seem like very little time will have passed before we reach the neutron star." Ty watched as she slid a partition into place separating the rest of the compartment from the deep sleep chambers.

"The miracles of modern science," Lieutenant Strett spoke with a smile. "Doctor Wruggi is a genius, as this deep sleep drug proves."

"I'm not surprised," Ty replied with a friendly nod. "I've met the doctor. We are fortunate he is on Star One."

"I worked with him for several months," Lieutenant Strett spoke hesitantly, her eyes focusing on Ty.

She had immensely enjoyed working with the brilliant doctor, but one of his associates hadn't been as professional. She had become involved in a relationship with the doctor, and when it ended suddenly, she had requested a transfer out of the medical section.

"I'm glad you had the opportunity," Ty spoke noticing that Lieutenant Strett's eyes had a pained look in them. "It allowed you to become familiar with his work on the deep sleep drug. Without it, this mission would not have been possible."

"So am I," she replied turning away from Ty and sitting down at a computer monitoring station. She wanted to make sure all the monitoring instruments on the sleeping scientists were working correctly.

In a few more days, we will all be asleep Ty thought. They would be trusting the ship and its computers to protect them in the long months ahead. He turned to make his way back up to the flight deck leaving Lieutenant Strett alone to finish up. He wanted to send a message to Star One and report that the scientists had successfully been put into deep sleep. He also wanted to try to carry on a short conversation with

Steve. He was still debating sending a short message to Jennifer.

On Star One, Steve and Christy were sitting at their large control console in Main Control watching the latest news broadcast from Earth, which they had up on the main view screen. Each day the news seemed to be getting gloomier. The situation Earth side was steadily getting worse and more out of control. No one on the station had expected events down on Earth to get so far out of hand so quickly.

According to the news announcer, the President had just narrowly escaped an impeachment vote in Congress initiated by Senator Farley. The screen flickered and switched to a live scene of Senator Farley leaving the floor of Congress with a livid scowl on his face, he was closely followed by the group of Senators that he controlled and dominated.

"Senator Farley has vowed that this fight is not over," the newscaster said. "He has stated repeatedly that President Kateland has over stepped her authority and should be removed from office. Senator Farley has gone on record as saying that martial law should be ended immediately, and the military sent back to their bases. He completely disputes the claim by the President about the potential danger posed by the neutron star. "

The newscaster paused before continuing as someone off camera handed him a news bulletin. "The final vote failed by only six votes. The President had indicated earlier that she felt like it would fail by many more. Political insiders are saying that this might very well signal the end of President Kateland's Presidency."

Steve became aware of someone standing at his side, and turning his head slightly he saw that Teela was standing there with her eyes focused on the big screen. He had allowed her holographic image projectors to be installed in Main Control as well, as a few other areas in the space station. He was also feeling much more comfortable with this older more mature Teela.

"This isn't good is it commander?" Teela spoke in her soft female voice looking over at Steve. "President Kateland must remain in power." Politics was one of the things that Teela had a hard time understanding. Why people just didn't do what was right, was beyond her comprehension. "If President Kateland loses power, everything down on Earth will become extremely chaotic very quickly."

"No Teela, this isn't good," agreed Steve looking into Teela's dark blue eyes. Her eyes were certainly unique. Jennifer had done an

23

outstanding job designing the body that Teela projected.

Steve still hadn't quite gotten used to seeing Teela walking around Main Control since he had given Jennifer approval to install the holographic image projectors. Jennifer and Andre were still in the process of installing the projectors in many other areas of the station where the scientists needed Teela's assistance.

A number of the scientists truly liked the idea of actually having someone to talk to whom they could see rather than just a phantom voice out of thin air. Teela was highly involved with the work that was going on in the numerous labs and small factories in the station. There were more requests coming in each day for more of the holographic image projectors to be installed.

"I have used my core programs to calculate the level of unrest below," Teela said in her quiet demur voice standing there with her arms folded across her chest looking at the screen.

"How bad is it going to get?" Christy asked her eyes dark with worry.

"As people grow to believe more and more in the threat of the neutron star, civil unrest will spread exponentially," replied Teela looking at the two commanders. "Already, there has been an increase in attempted government takeovers in Third World countries." Teela paused before continuing, she didn't know why, but she still felt acutely uneasy anytime she addressed Commander Larson.

"The news media has been reporting the growing unrest," commented Steve watching the big screen, which showed the news reporter trying to get an interview with Senator Farley.

"I have also computed that Senator Farley will never accept the threat of the neutron star as being real," continued Teela feeling confused. She did not understanding how the Senator could be so blind or refuse to accept the data, which was readily available.

"That's not surprising," Christy spoke glancing over at Steve. "The man's too stubborn."

"I don't understand why he will not accept this," Teela spoke. "The data is overwhelming. If he won't accept it now with the data currently available, my programs predict that there is no new evidence that could change his mind in the future."

"That's how some people are Teela," replied Steve gazing at the innocent young woman next to him. Her long black hair reached down to touch her shoulders, and if you didn't know she was a hologram, it almost seemed as if you could reach out and touch it. She looked so unthreatening and seemed to be casting a childlike innocence.

"He will never accept it because it goes against everything he believes in," answered Christy from her seat on the right side of Steve.

She had been watching Teela with interest. Since Jennifer had installed the holographic imagers, Christy had noticed that Teela seemed to be blending in like a regular member of the crew. The people in Main Control scarcely stared at her anymore. Nearly everybody that encountered her now was accepting her.

"He will fight it until the very end," replied Teela scanning her analysis of his past actions to confirm they were accurate. "He will refuse to acknowledge the threat is real even when the Earth is finally pulled out of its orbit."

"What do your calculations show will happen on Earth when the neutron star finally begins to affect the planet," asked Steve looking into Teela's deep blue eyes. He wondered why Jennifer had chosen blue. They were very captivating.

"My latest calculations, based on the most recent Farside data, and the disks from the Super Crays down on Earth indicate that there should be a significant increase in weather activity starting in about five to six months," Teela replied. She was running new simulations every time the data was updated.

"What will the storms be like?" asked Steve knowing he wouldn't like the answer. He recalled some of the information in the disks he had brought back up from Earth. Steve knew that increasing inclement weather would be one of the first signs of the affect of the neutron star upon the Earth.

"We will see a gradual increase in the number of severe storms across the globe, heavier rains, tornadoes, larger than normal hail, and extremely damaging wind," Teela reported as she viewed a simulation of the projected weather pattern changes in her core memory systems.

Steve sat silently listening. None of this had happened yet, but he could well imagine the carnage the storms would cause.

"There will be an increase in hurricanes and typhoons across the oceans of the world," Teela continued, her eyes on the two commanders. "Many of the storms will grow to category five with the possibility of some growing to a category six or even greater."

"Category six!" Christy echoed with a shocked, disbelieving look upon her face. She had never heard of a category six storm. "There has never been a hurricane that strong. The hurricane scale doesn't even go that high! A Category six or higher would be devastating."

"The simulations indicate storms of that level or higher will be possible," answered Teela shifting her gaze back to Christy. "Storms of that magnitude or greater will become common place as the neutron star comes nearer. They will also be very wide spread."

"What would a category six hurricane be like?" Christy asked almost afraid of the answer.

She had seen videos of some of the devastating hurricanes of the past. Some of the devastation they had caused had been astounding. It was hard to imagine that a force of nature could wreck such havoc.

"In the early part of the 21st century, it was suggested that a category six be added to the Saffir-Simpson hurricane scale," Teela said watching the reaction of Command Larson and Christy to her words. She didn't like upsetting either of the commanders, but Christy had asked. "The wind speed for a category six would start at 180 mph. Very few if any structures would survive for long in sustained winds of that speed."

"What will be the primary cause of this weather pattern?" Steve asked, his eyes narrowing as he pondered the damage such a storm could cause. It would make hurricane Katrina back in 2005 look like a small storm by comparison, and he had watched the history records of the damage caused by that storm.

"This change in the weather pattern will be caused by increased solar flares and sunspot activity upon the sun," Teela replied. "It will be followed three to five months later with a gradual increase in earthquakes as the gravitational affects from the neutron star itself begin to be felt by the Earth."

"How powerful will the earthquakes be?" asked Steve letting out a deep breath. He knew from what President Kateland had told him that they were expecting some extraordinarily powerful earthquakes. Earthquakes so powerful, that very few shelters were expected to survive.

"More powerful than anything ever recorded," answered Teela scanning another one of her simulations. "Possibly on the order of magnitude ten or greater."

"Magnitude ten," gasped Christy her deep blue eyes growing wide. "And you said they could be even stronger?"

"Yes," Teela answered. "The San Andreas Fault will suffer a cataclysmic earthquake with part of the coast being engulfed by the Pacific Ocean. Other major fault lines in the United States will also become active. Earthquakes across the planet and in the oceans will cause massive tidal waves which will inundate most of the Earth's coastlines."

"We expected that," replied Steve nodding his head. President Kateland and Warren Simmons had mentioned that in their briefing.

He reached over and took Christy's hand squeezing it gently. He felt numb at hearing Teela confirm in more detail what President Kateland and Warren Timmons had already told him. No wonder they felt so doubtful about many of the underground shelters surviving. "Anything else?"

"Yes," Teela replied in a lower voice.

She had hoped that the commander would not ask for the rest of what her simulations had told her would happen to the Earth. She could tell that both Commander Larson and Christy were visibly upset by what she had already said.

"It's the volcanoes isn't it Teela?" Christy spoke feeling as if a hand had just grasped her heart and squeezed. She held Steve's hand even tighter for support fearing what she knew Teela was about to say. "They're all going to erupt, aren't they? That will signal the end of life on Earth!"

"Yes," replied Teela turning her head slightly to face Christy. "Shortly after the earthquakes start, the volcanoes will begin to erupt. There will be intense volcanic activity over the entire planet, which will grow even worse as the neutron star reaches its closest approach."

"They will make the Earth uninhabitable," Steve murmured imagining all the ash and toxic gases that would be released into the atmosphere.

"Most of the active volcanoes will erupt, and many that have lain dormant for centuries will also," Teela said, but she hadn't told them the worse. Those eruptions would actually be minor compared to what was ahead.

"There's more isn't there Teela," Christy spoke in a low voice seeing Teela's hesitation.

Yes, and it's bad," Teela replied. "The Yellowstone Caldera will erupt as well as the other five known super volcanoes. Within four weeks of the eruptions of the super volcanoes, there will be no life of any type upon the surface of the planet. I estimate that sunlight will be reduced by eighty percent due to the dust and other pollutants that will be expelled into the atmosphere. The atmosphere itself will be nearly unbreathable."

"Four weeks," murmured Christy taking a deep breath and releasing Steve's hand. Thousands of years of culture and civilization would be wiped out in less then a month.

Pausing briefly, Teela continued. "There will also be some unusually intense solar flares. An intense flare, if it strikes the Earth, could raise the temperatures on the surface several hundred degrees in just a matter of a few hours. My best calculations indicate that civilization on Earth will cease to exist, as we know it, within eleven more months at the most. There may be a few isolated pockets that will continue to survive, but even those will eventually vanish in the maelstrom that will exist below."

Steve and Christy both stared at Teela aghast. "How did you figure all of this out?" blurted Christy looking around the room. She wanted to make sure no one else had heard. "Only the Super Crays on Earth have been able to predict that and that information hasn't been given out, and they were not even near this explicit."

"You forget," Teela said putting her hands on her hips and cocking her head slightly to one side staring at the two. "I am an AI with a tremendous core system that has most of the combined knowledge of the planet below stored in my files. It's not that hard to access it and set up a program to correlate the data on what the affects of the neutron star will be."

"Teela," Steve said firmly glancing over at Christy. "I don't want you broadcasting this information about. At least not yet. The people on this station and the Space Platform may suspect, but they need more time to get used to the idea of what's going to happen."

Closing her eyes, Teela accessed one of her core programs and ran a quick study on the results of revealing the information to the crew. She also had crew dossiers in her files on everyone on board. As of late, Jennifer and she had changed the virtual reality program to allow her to access the rest of her system just by briefly closing the eyes of her holographic figure. It happened so quickly, that to most people it would seem like nothing more than an eye blink.

"I think you would be surprised by their reaction commander," Teela said after a moment. "The crew trusts you implicitly to protect them and bring them through any emergency. But I will follow your command and not tell anyone."

"We probably can't keep this from the crew much longer anyway," commented Christy, her blue eyes staring into Steve's brown ones.

"I suspect your right," replied Steve nodding his head in agreement.

He had told the crew most of what was going to happen. They knew the neutron star would seriously impact the Earth. However, they didn't know that the Earth was destined to become uninhabitable.

"Many of the scientists and others already suspect," Christy added. "Dryson and Stoler surely do. You can't keep anything a secret for long from those two."

"Just in the conversations I have had with them, it's pretty obvious they have figured it all out," Steve said confirming Christy's words.

"Since we have restored communications, there has been a constant flood of messages to Earth," Christy spoke recalling how communications between the crew and their friends and families down on Earth had substantially increased. "Our crew has been talking to their families and friends down on the surface. There is a growing unease about what's going on down below."

"I suspected that would happen,'" Steve replied with a frown and taking a deep breath. "It's all going to come out soon enough as it is. We have been talking to the crew about bringing some of their closest family members up. They know we wouldn't be doing that unless this was very serious."

"From what I have over heard, everyone has accepted that the Earth is going to go through some serious changes," interjected Teela looking at the two. "Only a few of the scientists have guessed what the end result will be, and they are not saying anything. I believe they are waiting for you to make the announcement to the crew about the end of the world."

"Thank you Teela," replied Steve thinking about what she had just said. He knew that he couldn't put off that announcement much longer. The crew deserved to know what was in their future.

"I think we need to do it soon," Christy spoke quietly knowing what Steve was thinking. "Our people need to begin making arrangements for their families."

Nodding, Steve watched as Teela walked away to visit with other crewmembers currently on duty. Teela never missed an opportunity to visit with the crew when her hologram was on. Steve smiled inwardly to himself as he saw her stop at Margaret's communications console. Steve knew that Teela had made friends with Margaret and the two spent a lot of time talking when Teela was in Main Control.

"It's still hard to believe that's Teela," Christy said watching the AI. Margaret was laughing about something Teela had said. "It's amazing how much she has changed in the last few weeks."

"How about going out to Jensens tonight," asked Steve listening to Christy and wanting to change the subject.

He had also noticed the change in Teela. He was glad the AI was back on line and working so well. He knew if the situation on Earth continued to deteriorate, they were certainly going to need her. Jennifer had worked a miracle with the AI.

Christy and he hadn't spent much time together since he had returned from Earth. Schedule and planning meetings and contacting crew family members on Earth to arrange for their immediate flights up to Star One had occupied both of them for several days now.

It had been difficult meeting with some of the crew. Some didn't want to believe that the danger was so serious that their families needed to be evacuated from Earth. Others had accepted what Steve said and had given him a list of close relatives they would like to see brought up to the station.

It had already been decided that preference would be given to younger family members and people who could be useful on the station in the coming situation. It didn't make sense to bring older parents or grandparents up who were in their late fifties or older. This was a hard necessity, particularly if it was going to be up to Star One and Tycho City to repopulate the Earth some day. If there was any place on Earth that would still be habitable after the passing of the neutron star.

"I have a better idea," Christy said turning away from watching Teela and smiling hesitantly, with a slight blush showing on her cheeks, at Steve. "Let me prepare a meal at my place. It would give you a chance to sample my cooking, and we can relax without having to worry about any interruptions."

"Sounds great," replied Steve, the idea sounded extremely appealing to him. He also could use the down time. He had spent much of the day talking to different crewmembers. The short trip outside with John had been helpful. It made Steve realize just how much he needed to take some time off.

After working through most of Star One and the Space Platform's crew roster, almost 80 people had requested to be transferred back to Earth. He had visited briefly with each one making sure they understood the possible consequences. Already, Steve had sent down a list of 600 crew family members he was requesting to be brought up to Star One as soon as possible. He was working up another list of slightly over 400 people with different skills that could be useful on the station.

The list was comprised of people from scientists to technicians to physicians that might be needed.

A relaxing evening with Christy sounded great. However, looking into her deep blue eyes he noted the excited and expectant look on her face and wondered just how relaxing the evening would actually be.

Jennifer was down in one of the ecological habitats with Julie and Kathleen. This entire habitat was dedicated to raising food. They were walking slowly down long rows of vegetables that were staked to trellises. The trellises allowed the plants to climb high above their heads. Stopping, Jennifer reached out to touch a nearly ripe tomato almost the size of her hand.

"How do you get these to grow so perfectly," she asked bending over and inspecting several other plump red tomatoes. The vines were heavy with fruit in various stages of development. Jennifer had tried some gardening back home, but had never been able to grow anything like this.

"This is all soil from the Moon," Julie said squatting down and picking up a handful of the rich, dark soil, letting it run back to the ground slowly through her slightly spread fingers. It's rich in minerals, and we have a drip irrigation system that runs throughout all the garden plots you see here. We mix a special hydroponics mixture of fertilizers and growth hormones with the water to encourage the plants to grow quickly."

"Are the growth hormones safe?" asked Jennifer looking at Julie. She had read in the past that many were not.

"These are," replied Julie smiling reassuringly. "These growth hormones are based on the plants own chemistry which encourages rapid growth."

"That's good to know," responded Jennifer standing up straight and looking around at all the plants that were growing everywhere.

Everywhere one looked, you saw growing plants. The air seemed fresh and clean, the scent of growing things played lightly on the senses.

"We also take samples regularly and only grow varieties that put out the maximum production in the different environments we have created," Julie said standing back up and waving her hand around indicating the ecological habitat.

"It's amazing all of the work you have done here," Jennifer proclaimed gazing around at all the greenery.

"Even this habitat serves a double purpose as do all the rest," Julie continued pleased that Jennifer was impressed by what she was seeing. "The plants take much of the $CO_2$ out of the air and help to replenish the oxygen, and they give us a larger variety in our station menu. In this section alone, we have a dozen different varieties of tomatoes, an equal number of peppers, several varieties of onions, potatoes, carrots and other vegetables."

"By using intense hydroponics gardening plus the rich lunar soil we can grow six to eight crops a year of most types of vegetables," added Kathleen stooping down in front of a bed of carrots with large, bushy green tops.

Selecting one, she pulled it easily out of the soft ground and scrutinized it with a trained eye. This was one of the seed types she had personally picked out.

The carrot itself was a dark orange nearly ten inches in length and probably two inches wide at its top. After cleaning the dirt off, she placed it in a small sample bag she was carrying.

"We take occasional samples from all the plots to analyze in the lab," Kathleen explained. "We test for flavor, hardiness, and the plants ability to adapt to the environment in the habitat."

As they walked along the clean, even paths between the thick plots of vegetables, Jennifer noticed an occasional grouping of small fruit trees. "What type of trees are those?" she asked curiously stopping to look at a large plot with 6 twelve to fourteen foot tall, bushy trees growing in it.

"Those are apples," replied Julie stepping over to the trees and inspecting the buds, which were in abundance. "We have a number of different varieties of dwarf fruit trees planted in all the habitats depending on the environment most suitable for them. We don't get a lot of fruit off them considering the number of people on the station, but it does allow for an occasional variety to our meals."

"Nothing like an occasional home made apple pie," Kathleen said grinning. "It really works wonders when you're trying to impress one of the eligible bachelors in the station."

"You would think of that," Julie said shaking her head in exasperation and laughing.

Jennifer noticed other workers were present also. About half a dozen men and women were meticulously going through the plots harvesting vegetables. Others were thinning out some of the plots that were overly thick with plant growth.

The air in the habitat was fresh and slightly warm with the temperature in the lower eighties and a higher level of humidity than the rest of the station. Bright lights in the ceiling simulated artificial sunlight. Jennifer knew, from what Kathleen had told her earlier, that they imitated an artificial day and night cycle, even though the night part of the cycle was limited to only six hours. That was to encourage maximum plant growth.

"Since we got Teela back on line, the work in the habitats is going much smoother," commented Julie wiping off her hands on her work slacks and leading them down a path towards a small two-story structure set in the heart of the habitat. "She is really good at helping us maintain all the delicate balances for the different garden plots."

Reaching the small building, the three went in to find themselves in a small room filled with equipment, pumps, and small liquid filled tanks.

"These tanks contain our liquid fertilizer and hormone supplements which we put into the drip irrigation system," Julie explained gesturing toward the tanks.

Jennifer could hear a low humming from the equipment and could see that several of the pumps were currently operating, pumping nutrients out to the growing plants. They ascended a short flight of stairs to reach the upper level, and Jennifer was surprised to find a small, efficient air-conditioned control room with two operators manning the computer consoles.

View screens on the walls showed the entire habitat from different angles. There were humidity, temperature, soil condition readouts, and various other types of information being displayed. From the look of the numerous displays, each individual plot must be monitored somehow.

"This is all amazing," spoke Jennifer gazing at the banks of monitors. "Do you monitor every single plot?"

"Each habitat is set up this way," answered Kathleen walking over to a set of gauges and visually checking a couple of readings. "We can monitor everything we need to from this room, adjust the temperature, humidity, plant nutrients, and even the light intensity itself if necessary."

"No wonder you needed Teela back on line," Jennifer spoke realizing how complicated it must be to monitor so many different things in the habitat.

"We do monitor each plot with buried sensors, and we can direct the controls to water or reduce the water to a single specific plot of plants as required," Kathleen responded. "Teela lets us know immediately if anything gets out of balance."

The girls spent the next several hours walking through each habitat. Jennifer wanted to get a proper feel for what Teela was expected to do so she could talk to her about it during their daily sessions. She knew that Julie and Kathleen needed Teela in order to maximize production in the habitats, as well as replenish the station's oxygen and water supplies.

She was amazed by all the work that had been done to establish the large ecological habitats and the large variety of plants, animals, and the complexity of maintaining the entire system. She could well understand why Teela was so indispensable to Julie and Kathleen.

Christy looked at herself for probably the tenth time in the last fifteen minutes in her full-length mirror. She was wearing a white button up blouse that dipped down to just above her breasts showing only a small hint of cleavage. She also wore a dark blue skirt that fit snugly around her waist and reached to just above her knees, she had been thinking about tonight for hours, ever since she had asked Steve to come over. She hoped everything would go well. She couldn't believe how nervous she felt. She felt like a teenager getting ready for her first real date.

"You look absolutely gorgeous," Teela said from where she was sitting on Christy's bed watching her with interest. Christy had asked Jennifer to install holographic image projectors in her quarters because she wanted to be able to work closely with Teela. "Commander Larson will be impressed."

"I hope so Teela," Christy said shaking her head making her blonde hair bounce slightly. She wondered if she should allow her hair to grow out some. She normally kept it cut pretty short.

The chime at the door suddenly rang, and she felt a sudden thrill of anticipation race up and down her spine leaving behind a tingling sensation. "If you don't mind Teela, Commander Larson and I would like some privacy tonight. I'll call for you when it's okay for you to come back."

"I understand," replied Teela with a knowing smile. She had read up on the subject of human romance in her files and Doctor Blackwater

34

had done a lot of explaining. "See you in the morning." The hologram snapped off causing Teela instantly to disappear.

Turning, Christy left her bedroom and walked through the small kitchenette. Teela was learning fast she thought, very fast. Glancing at the stove, she noticed that her meal still lacked another fifteen minutes according to the timer above the oven. Reaching the front door of her quarters, she pressed the button next to it and watched it slide quietly open revealing a pleasantly smiling Steve standing before her.

"Hi," he said walking in and looking around. "Something sure smells good." Leaning forward, he kissed her gently on the lips and then stepped back.

"It's some of Julie's new catfish she has been raising on her fish farm," Christy replied pleased with the compliment. "Jensen gave them to me, and I'm baking them in the oven. My mother had a special sauce she used for catfish that I hope you will like. It's a secret family recipe." Leading Steve into the kitchen, they both sat down at the small table that she had carefully set with twin white candles burning softly in the center.

When she had gone to Jensens, she had also picked up a bottle of Steve's favorite wine. The wine was chilling in a small bucket filled with ice on the side of the table.

"What's the latest word from the FarQuest?" asked Christy handing the wine to Steve to pour. She was curious if Ty had sent any additional messages.

"The transmission time lag between us and Ty is steadily getting longer," replied Steve wishing it was easier to carry on a conversation with the FarQuest. It's next to impossible to carry on a meaningful conversation with the ship now. It has reached the point that they are sending mostly status updates and crew condition reports. Ty and I did try to carry on a conversation earlier today, but it was tough with the time lag. So far, according to Ty, everything seems to be fine. They've put the three mission scientists into deep sleep, and Lieutenant Strett is monitoring their conditions."

"Everything seems to be going very well," Christy commented, her eyes focusing on Steve. She was glad he had agreed to this evening.

Closing his eyes briefly, Steve frowned. "Right now, I'm more concerned about Senator Farley. The latest news reports indicate that he and the group of Senators and businessmen he controls are holding a secluded meeting at his vacation home up in the mountains this weekend."

"That doesn't sound good," Christy said with a worried sigh. "I wonder what he's up to?"

"They are supposedly trying to decide on how to handle their response to this emergency," Steve responded. The aromas from Christy's cooking were beginning to make him feel hungry. "There are rumors that they are working on a measure they are going to introduce in Congress. It would prevent the President from diverting any funds away from projects that are already approved. That would curtail a lot of the President's plans to deal with this emergency. If she can't divert the money needed to enact the emergency projects, they might not get done."

Getting up, Christy walked over to the stove and stirred the fresh vegetables that Kathleen had dropped by earlier. Bending over, she glanced inside of the oven. She wanted to see how the fish were coming. They were just turning brown from the simmering sauce they were cooking in, another few minutes and they would be ready.

Behind her, Steve opened the wine and began pouring it into two crystal glasses. He couldn't help admiring the generous expanse of Christy's leg that was revealed as she bent over the stove.

"Senator Farley could still cause us a lot of trouble," Steve spoke as he finished pouring the wine. "Tim McPhryson feels that there could be some problems world wide very shortly when the entire truth comes out."

Sitting back down, Christy took a small sip of the wine. "How much longer does he think the secret can be kept? If the news gets out that we expect most if not all of the world's population to die within the next year, what will happen?"

"Tim says it will probably be one or two weeks before it's out completely anyway," answered Steve worriedly, taking a sip of his wine. "There are just too many scientists in foreign countries that can extrapolate the results from the data we have released. They also have the ability to collect the data themselves with their own radio telescopes down on Earth. Remember, they still have some extremely powerful telescope arrays on the surface. There are many scientists down on Earth who are already predicting the end, but so far they are being ignored."

Christy remained silent thinking about the ramifications. Their lives were going to get terribly complicated shortly, and the responsibility of protecting the station and its crew would weigh heavily on Steve and her.

"Tim and the President believe that when the news gets out almost anything can happen," Steve said slowly sipping his wine and enjoying the smooth taste. Jensen had done a superb job picking out this particular vintage of wine. "They want us to get our people up here as quickly as possible."

"I talked to Jane earlier today," Christy said. "They are decreasing the downtime for turning the shuttles around after a launch at the cape. They are adding additional crews to conduct the safety and system checks. Jane said it was necessary so they could get all the people and supplies up to Tycho City and us."

Steve nodded not feeling surprised by this decision. "Tim said they were also preparing a couple of military shuttles with some special equipment for us. They are to be sent up in a couple of weeks. He was very evasive as to what it was they would contain other than he felt we would need it. I also understood that several other special shuttles are being prepared for Tycho City as well."

"I wonder what's up with that?" Christy asked curiously, her eyes taking on a thoughtful look. "What could be on those military shuttles?"

"I'm not sure, but I suspect it has to do with defending the station and Tycho City," Steve replied. "General Karver had hinted that he would be sending us something along that line. I just don't know what it could be."

The chime on her stove went off, and Christy jumped quickly out of her chair rushing over to the oven. Opening the door, she removed the baking pan of fish and placed it carefully on the stove top. In a few minutes, she had a steaming plate of catfish and fresh vegetables, with some of Jensens home made rolls setting on the table in front of each of them.

Steve took a small bite of the fish and was pleasantly surprised at how rich the sauce made the catfish taste. He had always loved eating fish and had experienced it cooked hundreds of different ways. This was unquestionably one of the best.

"This is great," he exclaimed taking another bite followed by a small taste of wine. He hadn't realized that Christy was such a talented cook. This might be something they would have to do more often.

"My father always liked it," Christy said pleased with Steve's response.

For the next half hour, they enjoyed their meal and made small talk about the station and the progress that was being made in the different departments. Each department was working toward doing their part to make the station entirely self-sufficient.

When they were through eating, Steve helped Christy put up the dishes and the two retired to the living room where Christy had already turned on some relaxing, romantic music.

As the evening wore on, the two relaxed and talked about their earlier lives on Earth. They even discussed why Christy had joined the space program. They both had avoided discussing the present situation since their meal, wanting to spend some quality time with each other without worrying about the neutron star threat hanging constantly over their heads now.

Steve was surprised to hear that it was the high pay that initially attracted Christy into the space program and finally once she had joined, the thrill of the job itself. He told Christy that he had always wanted to explore space and to build the space station, which he had hoped would be mankind's stepping-stone someday to the stars.

They were listening to the soft music and sitting next to each other on the couch. Steve's arm was around Christy, and her head was lying on Steve's shoulder. They were both relaxed and just enjoying the intimate closeness of the moment. Turning her head, Christy looked up at Steve, and they kissed.

The kiss quickly became passionate, and they could both feel the heat in their hidden desires. Christy leaned back as Steve kissed her on her lips and then on her neck feeling his hand slowly, hesitantly reaching for the buttons on the front of her blouse. Just for an instance, she hesitated, but she knew in her heart that there was no way she was going to ask him to stop. She had been dreaming of this moment for months.

Moments later, she felt his warm mouth on her breast and the sensation was incredible. She felt Steve's arms slide underneath her, and she found herself being lifted easily and carried off into her bedroom. They both stopped only long enough to hurriedly remove the rest of their clothes before becoming locked in a tight embrace. Falling onto the bed, they kissed passionately and were soon lost in each other's bodies. In moments, they were totally consumed by the heat of passion and in each other. Around them, station life went on and continued as another night slowly passed on Star One.

# Chapter Three

Steve and Christy watched the main view screen aghast at what it displayed. The rest of the crew in Main Control also looked to be in shock. Main Control was hauntingly silent with everyone watching the view screen spellbound. Rioters were running rampant, and entire city blocks were on fire. Numerous fires were burning, and billowing black smoke filled the sky. Police and fire fighters were helpless in the out of control situation.

Several fire trucks were burning, where rioters had overwhelmed the firefighters and then set the large trucks ablaze. As the crew looked on, military troops in heavily armored personnel carriers arrived on the scene. The mob, in a heightened state of frenzy, recklessly charged the troops as they were deploying from their vehicles.

Many of the soldiers were overrun before they could even set up a defensive perimeter. The young soldiers were ill prepared for this type of civilian violence. Some of the crazed mob, who had reached the personnel carriers, began trying to push the vehicles over onto their sides.

Shots rang out suddenly from within the crowd, and two soldiers fell lifelessly to the ground. The entire scene erupted with bloodshed as some of the soldiers panicked and began returning fire, dropping people everywhere. The mob broke and began to scatter and the soldiers stopped firing. The soldiers stood in a daze looking at the carnage around them. Medical units arrived and moved in to assist the wounded.

"This was the scene in Los Angeles earlier today after Senator Farley denounced the President and the establishment of martial law," the monotone male reporter's voice said.

"Senator Farley is calling on people across the country to denounce the government of President Kateland. He is demanding the immediate rescission of martial law and the resignation of the President," the newscaster continued. "The Senator is quoted as saying it was the President that brought about the riots today, the worst of which was in Los Angeles. The death toll is expected to rise to over 100 with nearly 1,200 injured in the rioting and fighting. Military casualties are reported at 22 dead and 37 injured. The Senate is expected to vote tomorrow on

Senator Farley's bill restricting the President's use of funds in this supposed national emergency."

"I can't believe this is happening," Christy said pulling her eyes away from the screen. "From the news reports from the last several days the entire world is going to pieces. There have been riots in nearly every country, and several governments have already been overthrown."

"The announcement from the Secretary General of the United Nations yesterday morning was the turning point," Steve retorted, angry with the man and his Third World selfishness. "If he hadn't came out and proclaimed that the economic powers of the world were responsible for this emergency and that it was only an attempt by them to reassert their control over the developing nations, we might have had a few more weeks to prepare. The man is a puppet for the other Third World nations and has been using his position to attack the larger industrial powers from day one."

"It's bad enough that Senator Farley and his group continue to claim that the entire danger is a hoax," sighed Christy as she shook her head slightly in dismay.

Christy noticed that Main Control was unusually quiet. Everyone seemed frightened and worried about what they had just witnessed on the view screen. Christy couldn't blame them, many of their close family members were still down on Earth.

"It's only adding fuel to the fire," Steve replied with growing worry in his voice.

"There will be major riots everywhere soon," Teela said stressing the soon part. She was standing next to them, watching the view screen. Teela was becoming much more comfortable around Commander Larson since she now knew she had nothing to fear from him.

"What are your latest figures?" Steve asked almost afraid to hear the answer.

In the last few days, he had come to depend on Teela more and more for her evaluations of the rapidly worsening situation down on Earth.

"Based on the events of today and yesterday we can expect to see the riots to continue to intensify," replied Teela turning her head to look at Commander Larson. "As the social order collapses, we can expect to see more governments fall, and small wars will break out in many of the smaller Third World countries," she paused before continuing accessing more information. "The major powers will

40

survive the longest because they are better prepared to deal with civil unrest. However, we can expect serious riots even in those, much worse than what we saw today."

"How long can we expect to continue to bring supplies and people up from Earth side safely?" asked Steve, his eyes watching Teela. They had just barely begun to bring up the supplies that were being stock piled at the cape and the two military launch sites.

Sometimes when he was talking to Teela, he had to remind himself that she was a hologram and not a real person standing next to him. It was impossible to tell Teela's holographic figure from a real person.

"There are a lot of variables involved," Teela replied cautiously. "We can probably expect the cape space center to continue to function normally for several more months. After that, we can expect major attacks by civilians and possibly AWOL military units when people finally realize that Star One and the Moon are the only real hope for survival. How long the cape can hold out after that it's difficult to say. Under the best circumstances, I would say no more then an additional two months."

"So we have four months to get everyone and all the supplies we need up here," commented Steve thinking hard about everything that needed to be done. Four months wasn't a lot of time.

"That's assuming that Senator Farley doesn't throw a wrench into the entire program," muttered Christy looking back at the screen, which was showing unrest in a South American country.

Fire trucks were spraying rioting crowds with high-pressure water in an attempt to force them to disperse. People in the crowd were responding by throwing rocks and bottles. Occasionally a fire would break out briefly when a Molotov cocktail was tossed toward the fire trucks. Armored police arrived on the scene and begin pushing into the crowd with their shields and using their batons on the crowd. Rioters could be seen turning and running.

"At least Ty is going to miss out on most of this," Christy added looking at a small screen on her console, which showed the current position of the FarQuest. Ty and Lieutenant Strett were scheduled to go into deep sleep later that afternoon.

"How far out are they now?" asked Steve leaning over to look at the flight path she had up on her screen.

"Almost 680 million miles," she replied punching a few keys on her console.

"In only fifteen days," Steve said thoughtfully still amazed at how fast the ship was moving away from them. "It's hard to believe that we have a manned ship out that far. It makes the Mar's missions pale by comparison."

"It's already taking nearly an hour just to get a message to the ship because of the distance," added Christy recalling her last communication with Ty. "Two hours for a response to any question we ask."

"The final data from Farside is due within the hour," Teela said checking her most recent information.

She had been waiting for this data herself for nearly a week. Perhaps once she analyzed the new information, she could determine why the neutron star was behaving as erratically as it was. She had several ideas, but was afraid to say anything. She wanted to wait until she could confirm it with hard data.

"The data will be transferred to the FarQuest's flight computer for any final course adjustments that need to be made," Christy spoke quietly. She doubted if any major adjustments to the flight plan would be necessary.

Steve moved his hands over the controls, and the view on the main screen switched to the Space Platform where several shuttles were being prepped for return flights to Earth. The shuttles were scheduled to bring up more of the crew's relatives when they returned.

In the past week, they had brought up nearly 200 additional people. They were being hard pressed to indoctrinate everyone into life aboard the station. Many of these people had never been in space before. Nevertheless, it was necessary to get as many people up from Earth as possible in the shortest amount of time.

Steve wanted everyone up and safely on Star One within the next four weeks. He was also bringing up an additional 240 scientists and technicians that he had added to the lists. The situation down below was getting too unstable. On the screen, he could see several Centaur work vessels bringing in their loads of pods from Tycho City.

Tycho City had doubled their launches from the mass driver in order to increase the amount of raw material available for Star One's facilities to process. Todd Williams was running a full three-shift operation in his raw material plants on the platform. Already in the distance, a rough structure of beams and braces was taking place where the new fuel storage facility would be.

The fuel depot would have a heavy protective coating of Luxen on it also. The work crews on Star One that were installing the Luxen shielding were nearly one-forth completed with the main wheel. John and Steve were now making daily inspection tours of the station, the platform, and the Fuel Storage facility. With so much at stake, Steve wanted to keep as close a watch on everything as possible.

Steve took a deep breath wishing things were different. Most of the crewmembers in Main Control had returned to their jobs, mulling over what they had just witnessed on the big screen. Steve couldn't blame them for their concern. He shared it also. Star One was supposed to be a center of research and future science, the neutron star had changed all of that. Looking at his watch, he noticed that it was nearly time for their daily staff meeting. They had a lot of information to go over today.

On the FarQuest, Ty had just finished drinking a flat, tasteless soupy liquid concoction that Lieutenant Strett had removed from a refrigerated storage unit. She had instructed him to drink slowly and to finish every last drop. She was drinking an identical liquid meal also.

She laughed when Ty curled up his nose at the flat taste of the liquid. "No one ever said this stuff had to taste good," she said sipping her own meal slowly, watching the commander.

"Why does everything that comes from a doctor have to taste so bad?" complained Ty frowning. "Just once I would like to be given something that tastes decent."

"That's just part of life," Lieutenant Strett replied with a slight smile.

Ty shook his head and after finishing his liquid meal made his way back up to the flight deck. He was expecting the final flight data from Star One to arrive at any moment.

An hour later, Ty was finishing up his duties on the flight deck making sure that all the controls were set on automatic and under supervision from the ship's computer. Ty wished that Teela was here. He would have felt much more comfortable with the intelligent AI in control of the ship. From what Christy and Steve had told him the last few days, Teela was a remarkable sight now.

"How's it coming?" an inquisitive voice said from behind him.

Turning around in his acceleration couch, Ty saw that Lieutenant Strett had made her way up to the flight deck. She had been busy down below making sure all the equipment was properly stored away. She had also checked the occupied sleep chambers one final time.

Ty gestured at the main view screen, which held a dim dot in its center.

"We should be getting the final Farside data in about three to four hours to feed into the flight computer," Ty said looking at the large view screen filled with stars. "Once the data has been checked and we confirm our flight path, then you and I will join the rest of the crew in deep sleep. Our next stop will be our friend there on the screen."

Lieutenant Strett was silent for a few moments staring at the dim dot, which was their destination. "Do you think we really have a chance to make it back?" she asked with a trace of anxiety in her normally calm voice. "No one knows what we may find out there."

"I hope so," responded Ty thinking about Jennifer. "We have a good ship and a well trained crew. I think we will make it back all right. We can only wait and see what awaits us. Starting to feel nervous about our mission?"

"Some I guess," Lieutenant Strett admitted with a weak smile "So much depends on this mission that it almost scares me to death just to think about it."

"We can only do our jobs and wait and see how the dice fall," replied Ty nodding.

"I know," Lieutenant Strett spoke with a heavy sigh. "It's just not knowing what things will be like when we return scares me. The whole world could be changed when we get back."

From the latest messages Ty had received from Steve, changes were already taking place on Earth and not for the best. He also wondered just what the Earth would be like when they returned. "With a little luck, one of these days we will find ourselves safely back on Star One."

Lieutenant Strett only nodded and turned to sit down at her console. Activating it, she began checking the ship's environmental systems one final time.

Ty adjusted his controls to use the view screens to show different views of the outside of the ship. The SRBs looked unblemished attached to the powerful delta wings with the much smaller probes looking like ants in comparison. Ty spent several minutes checking over the outside of the ship satisfying himself that everything was as it should be.

They were already far above the plane of the ecliptic and had not encountered a single asteroid. Ty just hoped their luck would continue while they slept. He knew that once Lieutenant Strett and he went into deep sleep, they would be entirely dependent on the ship's computers. The ship had enough back up systems so that if something did go wrong the crew would have sufficient time to be reawakened and make the necessary repairs.

From what Lieutenant Strett had told him, if it were necessary for them to be awakened, it would take nearly twenty minutes for Lieutenant Strett to be brought awake and then another twenty for her to awaken any other member of the crew. If their luck would continue to hold, perhaps they would all be able to sleep until they reached the neutron star.

Steve was in Main Control when the final information from the Farside array arrived. It contained the latest orbital estimates on the neutron star and any course changes that might be needed by the FarQuest. As soon as the information was verified, Steve had Margaret transmit the information to the FarQuest. Steve knew that it would take over two hours before they received confirmation from the ship that they had received the data. As Steve waited, he reviewed the staff meeting that he had just come from.

All departments had reported progress in making their areas self-sufficient. Julie Gray, Dryson and Stoler, Doctor Wruggi, Lieutenant Commanders Williams, Anderson, Hernandez, and Hastings had submitted long detailed lists of parts and supplies that they felt they would need. These parts and supplies were necessary in order to maintain the station over a long period of time without continuous supply runs from Earth. Todd's list had contained a list of specialized tools he felt needed to be brought up from Earth to allow them to construct or build crucial parts and equipment the station might someday need.

The other department heads had furnished additional lists as well as requests for additional technicians and scientists that they thought might be useful. Even Doctor Wruggi had suggested the names of several young, prominent surgeons and doctors he would like to see invited up from Earth. They had all expressed concerns about the current situation.

"Senator Farley is fast forming a coalition that could seriously derail the President's plans," Lieutenant Commander Williams announced looking at Steve and the others. "From the news reports, the President's position is tenuous at best. What do we do if President

Kateland is removed or made powerless by Senator Farley's efforts?"

"It's something we are watching closely," Steve replied with a grave look on his face. "We are all extremely concerned about what is happening down below. Senator Farley is causing a lot of problems. President Kateland and Tim McPhryson have both expressed their determination that we will receive the supplies we need regardless of the circumstances."

"Is there any possibility that President Kateland's government might be forced to step down?" Blackwater asked with a frown on his face. "What would that mean for us?"

"President Kateland will ride it through to the end," Steve replied. "Right now they still have enough support in Congress to defeat any bill that Farley introduces. If necessary, the President can fall back on her establishment of martial law to get around any financial strangle holds they might try to introduce."

"The bad part is that it seems as if Senator Farley is steadily gaining support, particularly from the civilian population," commented Julie Gray shaking her head in worry. "I think a lot of what he is doing is trying to manipulate public opinion. It could only be a matter of time before he has the power to do what he wants."

"That's one reason why we must prepare ourselves as quickly as possible," replied Steve looking around the group. He had doubts himself as to how long the President would be able to continue to hold Farley at bay. The situation down on Earth was tenuous at best.

"Every day the riots are getting worse," Doctor Blackwater spoke. He had been particularly concerned about what was being shown on the news from Earth. How would those images affect the crew?

"What if they manage to damage one of the launch centers?" Lieutenant Commander Hastings spoke with worry in her voice. "We need all three launch centers functioning uninterrupted if we want to get all the supplies and people up here that we have requested."

"General Karver has moved enough military forces around the three launch centers to ensure their safety for the time being," replied Steve thinking about all the troops that were being emplaced by the general.

"General Karver will hold the launch centers," Christy added with a confident nod. "We just need to make sure every shuttle launched contains what we need. We are bringing up priority supplies first and then our wish lists later."

"I hope you're right," Ted Dryson commented dryly. "This situation could get out of hand very quickly. I don't know how our troops would respond if one of the launch centers was rushed by a civilian mob."

"It could happen," Jarl Stoler added with a frown. "Senator Farley could arrange that just to test our militaries determination to protect the launch centers."

"There are two full marine divisions assigned to protect the cape," Steve replied in a serious tone. "These are the best troops our military has. In addition, both of the military launch centers are also very strongly defended."

"There is also a carrier battle group just off the coast to provide air support," Christy added. "The cape is secure, at least for now."

Dryson and Stoler nodded, but neither was satisfied with Steve's answer. They both still had serious doubts if American troops could fire on civilians if it meant inflicting hundreds if not thousands of casualties.

The meeting finally broke up with each person going back to their workstations to look further into essential crew requirements. Each department head could request additional support crew from Earth if needed, as some already had.

Steve noticed that Doctor Wruggi had stayed behind. The doctor, for the most part, had been unusually quiet during the meeting as if he had something weighing on his mind.

"Do you have something else you want to bring up doctor," Steve asked curiously.

"With the new deep sleep drug, we could save more people from Earth," Doctor Wruggi began, his eyes taking on a serious glint.

"What do you mean doctor?" asked Steve wondering what Doctor Wruggi was alluding to.

"If we built additional deep sleep chambers in Star One, we could put a large number of people into deep sleep. They wouldn't use any of the consumables we have on board. I suspect we are going to be leaving a lot of valuable people down on Earth we would like to have up here on the station. In each meeting we have, there are more requests for additional personnel from Earth."

Christy and Steve looked at each other. They had already discussed this concern. The current lists for people to come up to the station were already much larger than they could accommodate, and the lists were only growing larger. Some people were going to have to be told that there was no room for their families.

"What did you have in mind doctor?" Christy asked intrigued.

"We have several large storage areas next to the medical section," commented Doctor Wruggi looking at the two commanders. "I would like to have those emptied and equipped with deep sleep chambers. We can bring a lot of people up from Earth and put them into deep sleep until it's time to awaken them."

"We considered that possibility ourselves," replied Steve gazing at the doctor. "We didn't feel that it would be viable in our situation." People would have to be put into deep sleep possibly for years before they could be awakened."

Steve and Christy had discussed if there was any way they could accommodate more people on the station. Deep sleep had been one option they had briefly considered then set aside as not being practical for long-term survival.

"We could be talking about years," Christy spoke shaking her head. "That's why we didn't seriously consider deep sleep as an option. How long would it be safe to keep someone in deep sleep without having to awaken them? Doesn't it become more dangerous the longer they are under?"

"I think eight months to a year would be reasonably safe," Doctor Wruggi replied. "But we could rotate people! Let one group sleep for eight months and then replace them with a second group."

Steve and Christy looked at each other surprised; this was something they hadn't considered. They hadn't considered rotating the people in and out of deep sleep.

"How many additional people could we accommodate if we did this?" asked Steve with growing hope that Doctor Wruggi might have found a solution to their being able to accommodate all the people on the lists.

There were a number of people down at the cape as well as Houston Steve would like to bring up. Even a few from the two military launch centers, as well as additional family members. If deep sleep was feasible, it could solve a number of problems.

"I have talked to my staff. The biggest problem would be building the sleep chambers along with the monitoring equipment," Doctor Wruggi stated. "We can produce sufficient quantities of the drug as well as the necessary nutrients to survive eight months of deep sleep."

"Assume you have four months and whatever materials and help you need to construct the chambers," Christy spoke animated by Doctor Wruggi's idea. "How many additional people could we save?"

Doctor Wruggi was silent for a moment deep in thought. "I would have to do some figuring, but I would estimate we could save an additional 800 to 1,200 people. The deep sleep chambers will not take up a lot of room. They can be stacked two or three high if necessary."

"Talk to your staff and give me a list of what you will need to do this," replied Steve reaching a quick decision. That might allow them to put nearly 4,000 people on the station. "I will see that you get whatever you need. I want to do this. Every person we can save only increases our own chance of survival."

Ty had just finished his last systems check when the ship's main computer began flashing signaling incoming data from Star One. This is it he thought as numbers began to flash across the screen. The last data from Farside was being transmitted. Several minutes passed as the data was received and correlated in the computer. Ty knew that the data was being sent repeatedly to ensure that the ship's computer received all of it. The computer would compare the data to ensure it had received a complete set.

"Is that the Farside data?" asked Lieutenant Strett walking up and sitting down in the pilot's seat next to Ty. She had finished her system check and didn't have anything more to do until it was time for Ty and her to go into deep sleep.

"It looks like it," replied Ty waiting for the computer to finish. He had no sooner spoke then the data transmission stopped, and the computer signaled that it had finished the upload into its memory.

Reaching forward, Ty projected the new orbital path on the main screen overlaid with the original trajectory. The two were almost identical with only a slight deviation of a few million miles at the end.

"Do we need to make a trajectory change?" asked Lieutenant Strett seeing that the two flight paths were not quite identical.

"Looks like it," responded Ty doing some quick calculations on the computer. "However, it looks as if it can wait until we are decelerating for rendezvous. I don't want to fire up the drive without the entire crew awake. I'm surprised though that we need to make such a large course change. From our previous data, we should have been a lot closer than that."

Ty spent several minutes working with the computer and then leaned back away from his console satisfied. "Everything's set," he said scanning the controls one last time and unbuckling his acceleration harness. "I'm going to make a quick tour of the rest of the ship, and then it will be time for us to join the rest of the crew."

"I'll activate the deep sleep environmental control program," replied Lieutenant Strett getting up and moving back to her console. "That will give us time to finish up and take the drug before the ship begins to cool down."

An hour later, Ty felt the injection distantly in his arm as Lieutenant Strett administered the deep sleep drug. They had both changed into the white deep sleep clothing. In minutes, his last conscious thought slowly fled to the back of his mind as he drifted off into a deep, dreamless slumber.

Moments later, Lieutenant Strett gave herself an injection and after attaching the special monitoring unit to her arm shut the lid on her cubicle. In moments she too had fallen silently and quietly to sleep.

On the flight deck of the FarQuest, the computers continued to hum and monitor the ship's systems and its sleeping occupants as the ship sped deeper and deeper into the lonely depths of empty, desolate space. The lights faded, and the temperature was allowed to drop down to 50 degrees. The ship was now utterly silent.

On board Star One, Christy had rejoined Steve and watched as the computer showed that enough time had elapsed for the entire crew of the FarQuest to be in deep sleep. For minutes, the two sat enveloped in silence as crewmembers carried on their jobs around them. With the FarQuest crew asleep, they were committed to the mission, only in case of a dire emergency would the crew be awakened before the ship arrived at the neutron star.

"Commander," an urgent voice interrupted his thoughts. Turning, he saw Margaret Sullivan the communications officer at his side. "Mase Colton in on the line. There is a problem at the Farside array he needs to talk to you about."

Nodding, Steve turned back to Christy," I wonder what that can be about." Flipping a switch on his console, he acknowledged Mase. "Mase this is Steve, what's the problem?"

"You won't believe this," an agitated Mase Colton responded after several seconds. "But I have just received a report from Farside that Teela has somehow seized control of the array's computer systems. This occurred twenty minutes ago, and she has directed them to make some type of unknown observations of the neutron star."

"Are you certain Mase?" Steve asked hardly believing that Teela would do such a thing. She had been behaving so well recently. What could have caused her to take such an erratic action?

"Yes," replied Mase sounding frantic "She has over ridden our computer controls completely, and we haven't been able to regain control of the arrays. Can you find out what is going on and have her release the arrays back to us before something is damaged? The scientists and technicians at Farside are in an uproar. We have detected a tremendous amount of data being transferred between the array's computers and Star One."

Steve and Christy looked at each other in shock. Teela had been performing flawlessly for several weeks now. Seizing control of the Farside array's computers demonstrated that she had hither-unknown abilities that they had not even suspected.

"We'll take care of it Mase," Steve responded determinedly. "I'll get hold of her now and see what the hell is going on. She will definitely have some explaining to do."

"That won't be necessary commander," Teela's feminine voice spoke unperturbed breaking in over the communication's line. "I am through with the arrays and have returned control back to the Farside computers. It is imperative that Commander Jones, you, and I talk immediately in your office. I have discovered something of immense significance that will force even Mr. Colton to agree that I did the right thing. I'm sorry Mr. Colton, but what I did was necessary."

"Very well," Steve replied confused but determined to get to the bottom of this. "But this had better be good Teela! I'll get back to you as soon as I can Mase."

Steve and Christy made the short walk over to Steve's office to see what was going on. Both were mystified over Teela's strange behavior. They found Teela pacing impatiently in front of Steve's desk. She looked as if something was really bothering her.

"What would you say if I told you I know what is causing all the discrepancies in the neutron star data," she began before Steve or Christy could get in a word.

"What," Christy exclaimed with widening eyes. "How could you discover something that has baffled our leading astronomers for several months?"

"Not only that, but the Super Crays back on Earth have gone over that data countless times and have not been able to come up with an explanation," Steve added surprised. Was this why Teela had taken over the Farside array?

"That's because they were not asking the correct questions," replied Teela coming to a stop and staring at the two of them. "Don't forget, even though I can't be classified as a scientist, all the astronomical data ever discovered is stored in my core systems."

Reaching his desk, Steve sat down and looked up questioningly at Teela. He had a foreboding feeling that he wasn't going to like what he was about to hear. Christy walked around Steve's desk and was standing behind him. Both were staring at Teela waiting for an explanation.

"The neutron star is in a tight orbit around a massive invisible body," Teela said suddenly looking at the two.

"Oh my God," Christy said with growing concern spreading across her face.

"What kind of body," Steve asked evenly with a dark suspicion beginning to form in the back of his mind. He was familiar with most stellar objects. There was only one type of object that Teela could be talking about.

"A black hole," Teela replied, her deep blue eyes looking intensely at the two. "The neutron star is orbiting a black hole that is 42 miles in diameter and twelve times the mass of the Sun."

"A black hole," muttered Steve closing his eyes and shaking his head. This situation couldn't get any worse. All their planning may have been for nothing.

"The neutron star in is orbit around the black hole at a distance of 12,000 miles," Teela added. "Please look at the main view screen behind you."

Turning around, Steve and Christy looked at a stellar panorama of space with a highly magnified view of the star field around the neutron star. The neutron star was circled in red, and another area next to it was circled in yellow.

"Watch the area in yellow closely," Teela instructed. "I have correlated the observations for the past several months to show the movement of the neutron star and the black hole."

As Steve watched, he could see the two areas gradually move across the sea of stars, twice he saw stars seem to blink out only to reappear later as stars were occluded by the object in the yellow circle. There could be no doubt something indeed was there.

"Twelve times the mass of the Sun," Steve said slowly knowing that this discovery might just have signed all of their death sentences. He felt an empty feeling in the pit of his stomach as he tried to accept the reality of what Teela was saying.

"Yes," Teela replied. "I've confirmed the size and mass."

"That would account for the change in Pluto's orbit so soon," Christy said worriedly looking at Steve as she tried to grasp what all of this might mean. She knew their situation had just gotten much worse.

"What will the effects be Teela?" asked Steve fearing the worst.

"I'm still in the process of correlating that part of the data," Teela replied with a worried look on her face. She slowly looked from Steve to Christy and then back to Steve. "But it will definitely speed everything up considerably."

"What can we do to help you?" asked Steve feeling numb at the now decidedly dim prospect of their survival.

"I need more time with the arrays at Farside," replied Teela in her very feminine voice looking at Steve. "If you could clear it with Commander Colton where I could use the arrays uninterrupted for several hours, I could give you a clearer report on how this will affect us."

"Consider it done," responded Steve feeling a growing knot in the pit of his stomach. "I'll call Mase right now. We will meet six hours from now to review the data. Will that be enough time?"

"Yes sir," replied Teela relieved that the commander was not angry with her. "That will give me time to correlate the data and extrapolate the results."

Steve spent several minutes on the com line with Mase explaining that Teela needed time with the array. Steve explained that Teela had discovered something of tremendous importance and that it couldn't be discussed over the com. Steve told Mase that he would send a complete report on the next shuttle going from Star One to Tycho City. In the end, with little arguing, Mase agreed to clear the use of the array with the Farside astronomers. He had known Steve long enough not to question his requests.

"Teela," Steve said in a more serious tone gazing at the young woman standing in front of his desk. "Next time ask permission before you do something like this. Unless it involves a serious immediate threat to the station, I want to know before you take any type of similar action in the future."

"Yes sir," Teela replied in a meek voice. "It won't happen again." With that, Teela vanished as she deactivated her hologram.

"I don't think I'll ever get used to that," Steve muttered looking at Christy. "It's not normal the way she can just vanish in the blink of an eye."

"This is bad isn't it?" Christy said with a worried look on her face. "This black hole changes everything."

"It looks like it," Steve said quietly not wanting to lie to her. "The gravitational stresses will be much worse, and the affects on our Sun could now be catastrophic. I don't know how this will affect the FarQuest mission."

"Oh my God," moaned Christy thinking about the mission. "Ty and the rest of the crew are already asleep. There's no way we can tell them the danger they're heading into."

"We could awaken the crew in an emergency," Steve reminded her. "However, Doctor Wruggi recommends that we don't because a person needs to wait at least four weeks before they can take a second dose of the deep sleep drug. We'll have to wait until Teela is ready with her report before we can make any type of rational decision."

Standing up, Steve walked over to Christy and took her in his arms holding her tightly in a warm embrace. "We can't give up hope," he said looking down into her eyes. "We'll figure someway to survive this also."

Christy said nothing, just allowing Steve to hold her. She was afraid that the black hole had just taken away their only chance to survive.

Hours later, Steve, Christy, and Todd Williams were in Steve's office waiting on Teela to give them her findings.

"A black hole is incredible," Todd said with wide eyes drumming his fingers on his knee absentmindedly. "We have never had an opportunity to study one up close. We have always believed that a large black hole exists in the center of our Galaxy drawing in the core stars. To find one this close to the Solar System implies that they are a lot more common than we originally believed."

Looking at Steve, he went on. "Did you know that Pierre LaRann has written a paper theorizing that a black hole can be used as a gateway, or a short cut through hyper space to other parts of our galaxy or even other universes?"

"I read his paper," replied Steve wishing that Teela would hurry up. "Professor LaRann is the top man in his field in Space Time Theory.

Some of his ideas are on the cutting edge."

"Commander," Teela said suddenly appearing next to Steve's desk," She was dressed in her standard Star One uniform and stood smartly looking at the three. "The news isn't good. I used the arrays to check the neutron star and the black hole. I also did some quick checks on the major planets in the outer system. If you know what to look for, we are already seeing minor deviations in the orbits of Pluto, Uranus, and possibly Saturn."

At the rate the neutron star and black hole are closing on the Solar System, we can expect substantial weather changes within four months maximum down on Earth," Teela reported in a grave voice. "Earthquakes and massive volcanic activity will follow gradually increasing over the following two months making the Earth nearly uninhabitable."

"That's really speeding everything up," Steve spoke worriedly. "That puts a deadline of four to six months max before all three launch facilities are incapable of launching shuttles."

I also estimate that there is a 40 percent chance that the Sun could go nova from the gravitational stresses it will be exposed to." Teela continued. "At the very least, we will be exposed to massive solar flares and tremendous amounts of radiation."

Pausing, she looked upset as she continued. "At the nearest approach of the neutron star-black hole binary, the Earth and the Moon could be pulled apart by the conflicting gravitational stresses, the earthquake activity, and the volcanic eruptions. Both may be cracked open like an egg. Even if they're not, the orbit of Earth will be changed so dramatically that life on its surface will be impossible outside of totally enclosed habitats." She stopped and as she did Steve's computer came to life. "I'm loading a detailed analysis of the data for you to review."

"Will we be safe here on the station?" Christy asked almost afraid to hear the answer.

"I estimate that the station will be safe for another 300 days, but with the gravitational stresses affecting the Earth and the Moon we will not be able to maintain our current position in the Lagrange point," replied Teela looking over at Christy.

"We could be pulled down to the Moon's surface!" Todd Williams said sharply. "We are only 37,000 miles away from the Moon."

"If possible, I would strongly recommend we find some way to move the station as far away from the Earth and the Moon as possible," Teela suggested her deep blue eyes looking at Steve. "If they do break up, the debris could seriously endanger the station. I have computed that the extra Luxen coating will protect the station from the radiation and solar flares, but it will not protect it if the Sun becomes a nova."

"What can we do?" asked Todd frowning. "We can't move Star One or the Space Platform."

"I would suggest equipping the station with ion thrusters, which could be used to move the station over a long distance if necessary," Teel recommended. "Our fusion reactor can furnish the necessary power."

"Ion thrusters," Lieutenant Commander Williams repeated surprised. "Can the station take that type of stress?"

"Yes, if we make some slight modifications," Teela responded. She had already run the simulations on what needed to be done.

"Let's not go overboard with this yet," Steve cautioned. "I want to go over this data with Dryson and Stoler and some others. We have some time to formulate a plan."

"We have some time commander," Teela agreed with caution, but not a lot. "If we are to make the changes necessary for the station to survive, we need to begin within the next two weeks."

"This changes everything doesn't it," Christy stated feeling as if the room had gotten much colder. She shivered and looked over at Steve.

"Yes it does," relied Steve wondering just what they needed to do.

Steve wanted to review with Dryson and Stoler, Teela's suggestion about equipping the station with ion thrusters. The station had some small station-keeping thrusters, but nothing like what Teela was talking about. He also wondered if something could be done about the Space Platform. He hated the idea of abandoning it.

The three sat in stunned silence for several minutes lost in their own private thoughts. Each one wondering about what they should do.

"Do we dare inform the President?" Lieutenant Commander Williams finally whispered. "If this gets out down below, it's hard telling what will occur. This news might ignite a powder keg down on Earth."

"We have to tell her," responded Christy looking at Steve and Lieutenant Commander Williams. "After everything she has done for us, she has a right to know."

"I agree," said Steve pulling at his chin thinking. "However, with the situation as it is now down on Earth it might be a good idea for us to wait a few days or even several weeks. We have a shuttle leaving for Tycho City tomorrow; we can send Mase a complete report on our findings and our recommendations. He can also run it past his people and see what they think. I don't know how this will affect his preparations at Tycho City."

"I'll speed up our flight operations in order to get all the supplies and people we need up here as quickly as possible," Christy added. She would have a talk with Jane and impress upon her the importance of speeding up the shuttle launches even more.

She knew it might mean less time to inspect shuttles before they were loaded and launched back to Star One. It could significantly increase the likelihood of an accident.

"Once Commander Colton has received the black hole information, I'll see if we can further increase the mass driver launches of raw material from the Moon." Lieutenant Commander Williams said. "We have some excess capacity, and with the use of a little overtime, we can increase our processing of raw material considerably."

"Also see if you can think of some way to increase the maneuverability of the Space Platform," Steve replied. "I'll look at the same thing with Star One. I just don't know if the ion thruster idea is feasible for the station."

"It is commander," Teela replied confidently.

"What about installing a fusion reactor on the Space Platform?" asked Lieutenant Commander Williams weighing several different options in his mind. "That might allow us to install ion thrusters on it as well."

"We may need to," answered Steve nodding his head slightly. "I'll meet with Dryson and Stoler about the possibility. I don't know if we have enough time left though before the situation down below makes the shipment of equipment needed for such a project impossible."

"Teela," Steve said turning to where she still stood quietly in front of his desk.

"Yes sir," she responded.

"I want you to work with Christy on the essential supply lists. You know what we are trying to do as far as making the station self-sufficient. Correlate the lists and make certain we are not leaving anything off. Keep in mind that we do have a limited manufacturing base here on the station and the Space Platform. We need to pay particular attention to items that we can't produce, or we would find extremely difficult to replace."

Looking around Steve leaned back in his chair rubbing his forehead slightly. "We know what needs to be done, let's get started."

# Chapter Four

Christy, Steve, Julie, and John Gray were eating a quiet lunch in Jensens taking some time off from the frantic pace of the last few days. Steve had been so busy that he had found it next to impossible to spend any private time with Christy. Other than that one evening when their passion had over come both of them. They had both been too busy with their station duties to be able to spend any real time together.

"What are on those two military shuttles due today?" asked John drinking a fruit juice mixture that Julie had recently recommended to Jensen. Much to his surprise, this one didn't taste bad at all.

"I don't know," Steve replied. He was curious himself as to what was being sent up on the two military shuttles. "Tim McPhryson seemed pretty adamant about the importance of these two shuttles. I just learned today that when they return to Earth, they will be reloaded and launched again almost immediately to the Moon."

"Curious," John spoke with an intense look in his eyes. "I wonder if General Karver had anything to do with what's on those two shuttles?"

"I strongly suspect that he did," Steve replied. "I guess we will find out later today when they arrive."

"Since they are coming from the two military launch sites they could contain almost anything," Christy added. She wondered if the general was sending weapons up to Star One. She knew they might be needed, but she still felt uncomfortable with the idea.

"So have Steve and you been able to spend any time together recently aside from work," Julie asked Christy with a twinkle in her eyes.

Christy blushed and looked guiltily at Steve before replying. "We've been so busy the last few days. It has been difficult just to find the time to eat, let alone spend time together. There's so much that needs to be done, and so little time to do it in."

John looked at Christy's blush and smiled winking at Julie. "Looks to me like the two of you have been getting along just fine. Is there something we don't know about?"

"How is your work going Julie?" asked Christy trying to change the subject feeling uncomfortable with where this conversation was going. Was there nothing that was a secret on this station anymore? As well as the Grays knew them, a secret would be impossible to keep for long anyway.

"Great, with Teela's help," responded Julie smiling knowingly at the two. "All the habitats are finished and functioning almost perfectly. We are still finding it necessary to fine tune here and there, and some plants are not doing as well as we had hoped, but over all, I'm very satisfied."

"What about the food situation?" Christy asked. "Are we going to be able to feed 3,000 people over a long term?" This was something she had been worried about.

"We should be able to produce enough food to feed the entire station's crew with a small reserve left over," replied Julie recalling the latest computer figures that Teela had run. "We are keeping two of the park areas, but we are putting in more of the dwarf fruit trees in both of them to augment our food production. We are already building up a reserve food supply of dehydrated fruits and vegetable in case of an emergency."

"I was hoping we could keep the park areas," Christy spoke relieved. "They will be a big boon to morale if we have to stay on board Star One for an extended period of time. The reserve food supply is a good idea."

"We will have to control usage of the parks though," Steve commented thoughtfully. "We can work out some type of schedule that will be fair. I agree that the parks will be a tremendous help with station morale."

"You both should come down and check the habitats out," Julie suggested pleased that both Christy and Steve agreed with her keeping the two park areas. "I think you will be surprised at the progress we've made."

"We may do that," responded Steve feeling extremely tempted by the idea.

From what some of the station's crew had said, Julie and Kathleen had worked miracles in the habitats. Steve had routinely checked them out on the station's view screens, but had not had a chance for a formal inspection for several weeks. Maybe it was time that he did so.

They continued to enjoy small talk and eat the tasty meal that Jensen himself had oversaw the preparation of. The four of them enjoyed times like this, which had been occurring very seldom recently. Looking at Christy, Steve knew that he needed to work in some free time for both of them as well. They still had a lot to talk about. He sighed deeply, there was just so much that needed to be done. He was worried they might not have the time to finish it all.

Several hours later, Steve and Christy rode the main elevator up to Alpha to receive the two military shuttles. Both were curious as to what McPhryson was sending up. Reaching Alpha, they walked carefully in the lower gravity to the unloading area where one of the shuttles had already docked.

They watched curiously, as the shuttle hatch opened. To their surprise, a young marine captain appeared at the hatch and walked hesitantly towards them taking one careful step at a time. It was oblivious that low gravity was new to him. Stopping before them, the young officer saluted and handed Steve a packet.

"Captain Allen Gerald at your service sir," he spoke smartly, pausing he smiled at the two before continuing. "The station is very impressive. Is there somewhere we can go privately to discuss my orders, preferably with more gravity if that is possible. The packet I gave you contains a private message from the President and General Karver."

"Follow us please," replied Steve feeling confused. What was a marine captain doing on the shuttle?

"I think we can help you with the gravity captain," Christy commented with a slight smile. It was obvious the young captain was extremely uncomfortable in the light gravity of the unloading area.

Steve led Captain Gerald to a small conference room on the outer rim of the wheel where there was normal gravity. Steve could tell from the relieved look on the Captain's face that he was glad to be able to feel his normal weight again.

"There is a message disk inside the packet," Captain Gerald said taking off his cap and laying it on the conference table. "If you will play the message disk, I believe it will explain everything."

"Teela, will you please make your presence known," ordered Steve as he opened the packet and took out the small shiny disk.

Instantly the AI appeared, standing just to the right of Captain Gerald.

Captain Gerald jumped and stared wide eyed at the gorgeous young woman who had just appeared out of nowhere. She was dressed in a regulation Star One uniform with shoulder length black hair and captivating deep blue eyes. "I don't understand," he stammered gazing at Teela in confusion.

"This is Teela, our AI," Christy explained to Captain Gerald who was staring open mouthed at Teela. Steve and she had both forgotten what a surprise Teela was to people who were not familiar with her. It made Christy realize just how much they were taking the amazing AI for granted.

"Teela," Captain Gerald spoke slowly gazing inquisitively at the AI. "General Karver mentioned that you had an AI on the station, but I didn't expect anything like this. Can she talk?"

Teela walked over until she stood directly in front of the now extremely nervous young captain. She looked the young man up and down. "So you're a captain in the United States Marines," she stated calmly.

"Yes," Captain Gerald replied not sure how to address the AI. He hadn't been prepared for this.

"Teela is completely sentient and is an active member of this crew," Steve explained curious to see Captain Gerald's reaction to the AI. "She is completely capable of running this entire station on her own. I asked her to make her appearance known because I want her evaluation of the President's message."

"That's your decision sir," Captain Gerald replied with his voice returning to normal and shifting his gaze from Teela to Commander Larson.

Steve took the small disk and placed it in the room's computer terminal for playback. The message would be displayed on the large view screen on the wall. The screen flickered on instantly with a view of the President and General Karver sitting in her office looking grim.

"I'm sorry to have to keep this mission so secret Commander Larson," President Kateland began amiably. "But if the word was to get out, it would create a serious uproar and possibly even an international incident. Who knows what Senator Farley would do with this information?"

Pausing she looked at General Karver before continuing. "We presume from the activity with Teela and the Farside array that you now know about the black hole that is with the neutron star."

Steve and Christy looked at each other in confusion. How had the President found out about Teela and the Farside array? Steve and Mase had agreed to keep the information about the black hole a secret for now to ensure it didn't get out Earth side. Someone on the Moon or perhaps even on Star One had managed to get the President a message about Teela and the arrays. But more confusing was the fact that President Kateland sounded as if she had already known about the black hole.

"The Super Crays located the black hole weeks ago, and we have kept it a secret," President Kateland continued evenly. "If the word were to get out, we believe the entire world would go off the deep end in just a matter of a few days. Yes, we know that the Earth probably cannot survive the passing of both. We also know that when people and nations down here on Earth realize that Star One and perhaps Tycho City are the only hopes of survival there could be attempts made to seize or even destroy one or the other or even both. That's what these military shuttles are there to prevent. The two shuttles contain 120 highly trained men and women in equal numbers whose job it will be to protect the station and the Space Platform. I will let General Karver explain the particulars," she stopped looking over at the general.

"These men and women are highly trained in various fields and can be used to help wherever needed as well as in their military capacity," General Karver began. "In the packet Captain Gerald has given you, is a complete dossier on each member of his team. You have final say so in all matters, and Captain Gerald understands that you, Commander Jones, and then Lieutenant Commander Williams are the direct line of command."

Steve looked over at the young marine captain and then back at the screen.

"He and his men have been instructed to obey your orders without question," General Karver continued. "In the cargo holds of these two shuttles are 80 Black Knight interceptor missiles, similar to the ancient Patriot missiles of the late twentieth century, but these are highly upgraded versions. The missiles are fourteen feet in length, contain conventional explosives, and are capable of intercepting any threat that may come within 1,000 miles of Star One."

"Missiles," Christy said worriedly glancing over at Steve. "Do we really want weapons on Star One?"

"I don't think we have a choice," replied Steve pausing the message. "If Senator Farley has his way, he could very well try to destroy the station. It might be a good idea to have something we can defend ourselves with."

"The Black Knight missiles are very advanced," commented Captain Gerald looking at Steve. "I can assure you that they are perfectly safe.

They won't be armed unless we are forced to use them."

"It's going to take a little getting used to," Steve replied. "I never considered arming the station."

Steve pressed the play button and looked back up at the screen.

"On a second flight, we will be sending you a small group of special Black Knight missiles with tactical nuclear warheads as well as ten rail guns," General Karver continued with a grim look upon his face. "These missiles can be used for the station's protection or may be needed to divert debris if the Earth or the Moon breaks up from the coming stresses."

Nuclear missiles Steve thought, he didn't like the idea at all of having those on the station. Nevertheless, he could also see the need if the station became trapped in a cloud of debris. The rail guns though were different. He knew a little about them. Some of the new rail guns on navy ships had a range of nearly 120 miles. He knew that mounted on Star One, a rail gun would have a much greater range than down on Earth. They were also extremely accurate.

"There is an awful lot of behind the scenes maneuvering currently being done by Senator Farley," President Kateland began after General Karver had finished. "He has been contacting people in the military and other power groups around the country. Some of my people have even suggested that we arrest the Senator, but the general and I feel that would only ignite the powder keg that is coming even sooner."

The President paused looking over at General Karver before continuing. "We are sitting on a time bomb that could go off at any moment. I have instructed Jane Kinsey to increase shuttle launches to the maximum possible without violating too many safety protocols. We can have the rest of Star One's crew up within two weeks and devote the rest of the launches to supplies. Tycho City launches will take longer, and I fear that we will not be given the time to get as many people up to the Moon as we had originally hoped," she paused and took a deep breath.

"Steve, Star One could be humanities only real hope for survival. The Super Crays recommend that you move the station away from the Earth-Moon system. Put as much distance between Star One and the Sun as possible in case there is a nova. I wish there was more that I could do. Tycho City has a remote chance of surviving. If the underground caverns can survive the stress, then Commander Colton and his people may survive. We have nearly completed the two secret underground complexes that we have been constructing. They might have a slim chance to survive if the Earth doesn't break up due to the stresses we will be subjected to from the neutron star and the black hole. Several other countries are also building underground shelters that might have a slim chance of survival. You need to prepare for the worst. We will be in touch," she finished as the screen went dark.

The four stood silently as the President's final words echoed in their ears.

"What's your assessment of President Kateland's message," Steve asked Teela.

Teela paused for a moment. "The President does not believe she can stay in power much longer," Teela replied as she quickly analyzed the President's words. "That's why Captain Gerald and the weapons are here. There is also some doubt as to how long they can hold the launch centers. That is why they are speeding up the launches even more. She also doesn't believe that the Earth will survive the passing of the neutron star and the black hole."

Turning, Steve looked closely at Captain Gerald. His face had turned pale after hearing Teela's words. The young captain looked to be in his early thirties, powerfully built, brown hair, and used to command. But Steve knew that this would be a totally new situation for him.

"What type of quarters will your people require?" Steve asked. "I assume it would be best if we put your people all in the same area together."

"If that would be possible sir," Captain Gerald replied courteously. "The men can be doubled up, and I know the women would prefer that."

"Very well Captain," Steve replied turning to Christy. "Commander Jones will take care of your quarter assignments," Steve said formally. "For the time being, you can store your equipment on Alpha in one of the special cargo holds. The holds can be locked, and Teela will ensure that no one enters. I will need you to direct the cargo handlers on the storage and handling of these missiles the shuttles are carrying."

For the next several hours, Steve, Christy, and Captain Gerald worked non-stop supervising the unloading of the two shuttles, billeting the marines, and storing their supplies. Teela was everywhere, explaining things to the young marines and making sure the missiles were stowed properly.

It had taken several minutes for Captain Gerald to explain to the marines who Teela was. It had been necessary for her to perform her vanishing act several times in order to make the marines understand that she wasn't real.

The dockworkers had been surprised when the large crates containing the interceptor missiles were unloaded. Captain Gerald had opened up one of the crates under the watchful eyes of Steve and Christy. He wanted to show Steve and Christy the sleek black missiles contained in the crates. Steve had taken the precaution of restricting the dock crew personnel to senior members only who knew how to keep their mouths shut.

"These missiles have a special stealth coating of material that will make them undetectable to radar," explained Captain Gerald replacing the lid carefully back on the crate.

"You are sure they are safe to store on the station?" asked Christy eyeing the crate, which contained four missiles.

"They are perfectly safe until they are armed with the correct arming codes," Captain Gerald assured them. "You could drop or crush one of these and nothing would happen. We would like to mount several interceptor missile launching platforms on Star One and perhaps one on the Space Platform also."

"I would suggest you familiarize yourself with Star One and the Space Platform over the next several days, and then we can meet and decide the best place for your missile platforms," Steve said evenly eyeing the large crates. He knew that he would sleep a little better knowing they had a way to defend the station and the Space Platform.

"I can have one of the lieutenant commanders show you around the station," Christy informed the young captain.

"After that's been done, talk to Teela and tell her what you will need," Steve added. "She can help determine the best places to set up the missile platforms. When the two of you have made a decision, then Commander Jones and I will review what you have come up with."

"Very well sir," replied Captain Gerald nodding his head.

Steve hoped the missiles didn't become necessary, if they did, then the situation on Earth would have taken a decidedly turn for the worse. It would also mean that President Kateland was no longer in control.

A few minutes later, all the supplies were strapped down in the storage compartment. The missiles and other weapons the marines had brought were stowed away securely. The three made a final complete check of the missile storage area to ensure that everything was firmly fastened down. Steve didn't want those missiles shifting. Teela confirmed that everything was as it should be and that she would keep a special round the clock watch on the weapons.

"With your permission when we finish getting settled in, I would like to place two guards on permanent duty in this storage area as a safety precaution," Captain Gerald suggested.

"I agree," said Steve nodding his approval. This was something his own security people were not qualified to handle. "Once you get settled in, I would like you to join Commander Jones, Lieutenant Commander Williams, and myself for a meeting in my office, so we can determine how best to make use of your people. Let's set up a meeting for tonight about 20:00 hours. That will give my staff and I time to review the information in the packet you furnished us and determine how best to proceed. Teela will show you how to get there."

"Very well sir," Captain Gerald replied. "I'll get my people situated and see you then." Turning smartly around, he followed Christy to the elevators to go down to the main wheel where his troops had been taken earlier by station personnel.

Steve made his way over to Alpha's launching bay where John was waiting in one of the Centaur work vessels. John had met the troops earlier as he was coming up to Alpha. Steve wanted to take a quick trip out to the Fuel Storage Facility to check on progress.

"How do the new troops look," John asked as Steve closed and sealed the hatch before taking his seat. John hadn't been too surprised to see them.

"Very disciplined," replied Steve fastening his safety harness. "Captain Gerald seems to be a highly efficient and his troops are supposed to be handpicked. We'll just have to wait and see how this works out."

"Centaur C3 ready for launch," John reported over his com to Alpha's flight control. "Troops on the station are bound to raise a lot of questions."

"I've already thought about that," Steve replied. "I'll announce that they are a specially trained unit to help with security on the station and with on going construction projects."

"That might work," replied John nodding as his hands flew over the controls. "We do have a lot of construction projects going on."

On the view screen, the hatch directly above them opened, and John expertly maneuvered the Centaur out of the narrow opening to hover above Alpha. John fired the RCS thrusters moving the Centaur slowly up and away from the station and above the extended solar panels.

Looking down, Steve could see that one of the two military shuttles was still docked, and the other was already over at the Space Platform being prepped for its return flight. A sudden slight burst of acceleration sent the small craft soaring off on a jet of flame into the darkness towards the coordinates of the Fuel Storage Facility.

The Fuel Storage Facility was nearly sixteen miles away from Star One. Looking at the rear view screen, Steve and John watched as the station slowly shrank in size. The station quickly became a brilliant sparkling jewel in the velvet dark sea of stars surrounding it. Out the front view port, the Earth floated looking pristine and tranquil with its deep blue seas and covering of fleecy white clouds. Sometimes, Steve felt the Earth looked close enough to reach out and touch.

"Hard to believe what's in store for our planet," John mumbled with a sad look on his face.

"I know," replied Steve gazing at the teeming life bearing planet. "Our job now is to survive this catastrophe and perhaps someday resettle the Earth."

"If it's still there," John reminded Steve cryptically.

On the main view screen, the Fuel Storage Facility rapidly grew into a jumble of girders, pipes, and plates covering its incomplete structure. When completed, it would be a globe 400 feet in diameter with flat poles to allow ships to dock. The internal structure was nearly complete, with some of the protective outer layer all ready being installed.

Steve knew that crews had been working on the facility around the clock for several weeks now. The problem was that with the advent of the black hole, would the facility be worth completing. Steve knew that somehow or another it almost needed to be maneuverable.

"We have an emergency message coming in," John said suddenly becoming more attentive.

Steve reached forward and thumbed on his own com. He wanted to hear what John was receiving.

"This is Centaur C10; we have a power failure in scooter S2. It is drifting away from the Fuel Storage Facility. Rate of drift is 2.4 feet per second and current coordinates are green 4 sector 2. The scooter is already too far out for us to attempt a rescue due to low fuel reserves. Please send another Centaur out to effect the rescue. The worker is not in any immediate danger, and she is in radio contact with us currently."

"This is Centaur C3 John Gray piloting, we are on an inspection tour on the far side of the Fuel Storage Facility, we will handle the rescue," John spoke quickly into his com.

"Confirm C3," the other Centaur responded. "We would appreciate it."

"I can't believe someone screwed up and didn't have a Centaur on station with sufficient fuel reserves to handle a rescue," said Steve perturbed. "I will definitely have to look into this screw up. We can't afford to get too lax with the safety of our people."

John fired the ship's small engine and the Centaur flew smoothly up and around the structure homing in on the distress beacon showing in green 4 sector 2. Each section of the Lagrange point had been marked off into cubes with spatial coordinates just so they could handle this type of emergency, which did happen on rare occasions.

Steve watched the ship's small radar screen, which showed them rapidly nearing the small white dot that designated the stricken one-man scooter. Looking out the front view port, he could see the small scooter rapidly increase in size until it and its bulky space suited occupant were visible. The worker waved at the Centaur as John used the ship's small thrusters to maneuver up next to the scooter.

"Hi," a young woman's voice came clearly over the com system sounding slightly relieved. "It sure was getting lonely out here."

"We'll have you aboard shortly," John replied. "I'm gong to use one of the robot arms to latch onto your scooter and bring you in."

Using one of the ship's robot arms, John reached out and latched onto the scooter pulling it up firmly next to the Centaur.

The worker released herself from the scooter, and using her jet pack worked her way quickly to the ship's small airlock. In seconds, the worker was safely inside. Once inside, she took off her helmet.

"Are you okay?" asked Steve looking back at the young woman. "Why didn't you use your jet pack to get back to the Fuel Storage Facility?"

"I was near the end of my shift sir," she responded seeing that Steve was in the Centaur and feeling extremely nervous about facing the commander in this situation. "My jet pack was nearly exhausted, and I didn't want to risk using the emergency reserve. I knew that if I stayed with the scooter, I would be safer and easier to pick up with its emergency homing beacon and emergency oxygen supply."

"Good thinking Ms. Harris," replied Steve approvingly seeing her nametag on her suit. "The best thing to remember out here is not to panic and not to take any unnecessary risks. We know that from time to time equipment may fail no matter how hard we work to try to prevent it. Have a seat and enjoy the ride back."

Steve watched as the young woman, with a relieved look on her face, took one of the two seats behind Steve and John. "Back to the station John," Steve said looking back out the front port. The young woman would then be able to catch a crew shuttle back to the Space Platform.

Minutes later, the Centaur was back home aboard Star One and Steve was soon back in his office. A quick call to Lieutenant Commander Williams, on board the Space Platform, and Steve found out that the Centaur that was supposed to be on station for emergencies had been delayed in launching by a fuel problem. The officer in charge had not thought the delay was worth launching another replacement vehicle since the delay would be less then twenty minutes. He had also failed to notify anyone of his decision. Todd said that he would make sure the young man would never make that mistake again.

Sitting at his desk, Steve began the process of going through the packet that Captain Gerald had delivered. He reviewed General Karver's orders, looked at the long list of supplies he had sent with the marines, and read the brief dossiers on the individual marines. It didn't take long to see that these people had been very carefully chosen.

There were specialists in computers, electronics, maintenance, construction, and several other useful fields. For the most part, they were in their middle to late twenties. Yes, these men and women could indeed be extremely useful to Star One. Matter of fact, they might be particularly useful helping Doctor Wruggi install his deep sleep chambers. It might also be a good idea to switch a few of the storage areas in Alpha over to barracks for the troops and make Alpha their main headquarters area.

Jennifer was in her office speaking to Teela. The two had become extremely close and sometimes Jennifer had to remind herself that Teela was an AI and holographic projection. At times, she seemed so real. The two had taken to confiding in each other on a regular basis. Teela had progressed to the point now where she talked and acted like a young women instead of a teenager.

"What are your plans for tonight?" asked Teela walking over and sitting in the chair, in front of Jennifer's desk. "Could we go to Jensens and try out the new holographic projectors that Andre installed."

Jennifer could detect the pleading in Teela's voice. She was constantly talking Andre into installing more projectors in different areas of the station. She doubted that even Commander Larson knew just how many projectors had been installed.

"Do you realize the amount of pleading Andre had to do just to talk Jensen into allowing the projectors to be installed?" Jennifer reminded her. "Don't forget that a lot of the pranks you used to play took place in Jensens, and he still hasn't quite forgiven you for some of those."

"I know," Teela replied in a regretful voice. "But so many of my new friends eat there, and I would really like to be able to spend time with them away from work. I also want to try out some new programs I've designed to help me to fit in better."

"I'm glad you are making friends Teela, I really am," Jennifer responded. She knew that a number of the crew were becoming friendly with Teela since the new holographic imagers had been installed in their work areas.

"It's nice to have so many people to talk to," Teela replied smiling. "Can we please go to Jensens?"

Jennifer looked at Teela noticing that Teela's hands were fidgeting nervously. She was clearly getting quite adept at using the hologram to show her feelings.

"All right," Jennifer agreed after a few seconds of silence and careful thought. "Let me check with Kathleen and see if she wants to come, maybe between the two of us, we can survive this."

"I promise you won't regret it," Teela said excitedly, her eyes glowing. "Now I just need to decide what to wear." With that, the hologram blinked out, and Teela was gone.

I wonder what I've gotten myself into now Jennifer thought. With Teela, you could never tell.

A few hours later, Jennifer and Kathleen were sitting in Jensens, with Teela looking around excitedly between them. Jennifer appraised Teela's outfit critically wondering if she had been talking to Kathleen. Teela was dressed in a short skirt with a tight fitting blouse that fit snugly around her breasts accenting every curve and making them stand out even more. Jennifer was glad that she had designed the program for a smaller sized bust and not anything larger. She sighed deeply shaking her head knowing that Teela's clothes obviously were a result of Kathleen's suggestions.

Looking around the restaurant, she spotted Daryl Jensen making his way towards them with a happy smile on his face. This could be extremely entertaining she thought, as Daryl reached their table. Yes, very entertaining indeed.

"Good evening ladies," he said in his stylish French accent with a broad smile. "I would like to recommend our new chicken breast filet cooked with a special sauce that will make it truly a dining experience."

Looking at each of the three, he paused when his eyes took in Teela. "And who do we have here?" he asked curiously. "I don't believe we have met before."

Teela looked uncomfortably at Jennifer as if wanting her to answer.

Jennifer just folded her arms across her chest and looked at Teela. This was Teela's idea, and she would have to learn how to handle these situations.

"Hello Mr. Jensen," Teela replied trying to sound as cordial as possible. "Your restaurant here is beautiful! I've always wanted to experience its atmosphere and your legendary hospitality."

Jensen beamed at Teela. "I'm glad you like it so well, I only hope we live up to your expectations. What did you say your name is?"

"I'm Teela," she said a little uneasily watching Jensen for a reaction.

"Teela!" exclaimed Jensen turning slightly pale and taking a step back. "It can't be." He looked closely at the lovely young woman and walked slowly over to stand beside her. Hesitantly, he put his hand out to touch her, jumping back slightly when his hand found no resistance, and passed easily through the young woman's shoulder.

"I promise to behave," Teela said worriedly with that pleading look in her dark blue eyes. "I won't cause any problems."

Jensen hesitated, looking slightly unhappy. "Very well," he said forcing a smile. "I agreed to allow your holographic projectors to be installed, and you are with two trusted patrons, so we will see how it works this one time. But I'm warning you young lady; you had better be on your best behavior."

"Oh I will," Teela replied with a serious look on her face.

After Jensen left with Jennifer and Kathleen's orders, the three sat talking about what was going on in the station and how their jobs were going. Jennifer was extremely impressed by Teela's ability to make small talk and sound just like a normal young woman in her early twenties. Looking around the room, she noticed Todd Williams come in. Spotting them, he made a beeline for their table.

"Good evening ladies," he said politely. "Mind if I join you?"

"Not at all," the three said in unison and then broke into laughter.

Sitting down across from Teela, Todd eyed her critically before commenting. "You look gorgeous tonight Teela. I'm glad you don't dress like that when you are on duty!"

Teela blushed slightly not sure how to respond. "Thank you Lieutenant Commander Williams."

"Just call me Todd when I'm off duty," he replied with a relaxing smile.

Jennifer was surprised to see Teela blush. It was obvious that Teela had been tinkering with the holographic image program quite a bit. She would have to talk to her about that later to see just what she had done. The program was doing a number of things that Jennifer had not designed into it.

The four talked easily for several minutes about Todd's work on the Space Platform, only being interrupted long enough for Jensen to take Todd's order and to check on Teela.

Jennifer noticed bemusedly that Jensen was poking his head out of his kitchen on an almost regular basis to glance over in Teela's direction. Jensen was obviously making sure that Teel behaved as she had promised.

A few minutes later, he returned with a waiter and served them their meals. The two girls were having the chicken breasts and Todd had ordered a large medium rare steak with French fries.

"Can't cook these too much," explained Todd using his knife to cut off a tender piece. "My dad always said a good steak cooked medium rare was hard to beat, and he was definitely right about that."

Teela eyed the food in front of Jennifer for a moment before closing her eyes and accessing several programs she had designed for just this occasion. In a blink of an eye, a complete holographic setting duplicating the food that Jennifer and Kathleen had as well as the wine appeared magically on the table in front of her.

"This should be interesting," Todd said slicing up his steak and taking a bite of the savory red meat. He had become used to Teela's little tricks with the holographic projectors. He paused for a moment, watching her as he applied butter to the large bread roll on his plate.

"I designed a program to allow me to fit in better at meals," Teela said nervously looking at the three. "It should even simulate the tastes and smells of the food and wine." Taking her fork and knife, she cautiously cut off a piece of the chicken, as she had watched Jennifer do, and took a hesitant bite. "This is delicious," she said wondrously.

"No wonder people like to eat so often."

Her three companions laughed and dug into their food as well. The meal was quickly polished off, and Jennifer noticed as time went on that conversation between Teela and Todd was becoming much easier.

When Jensen reappeared, he said nothing about the almost empty plate in front of Teela or the empty glass of wine. He only stared at the other three perplexed.

"Don't worry Daryl," Kathleen said grinning at his obvious confusion. "It's a hologram also."

"This meal was great!" Teela said excitedly. "I used one of my programs to simulate the food you had prepared for Jennifer and Kathleen and it tasted fantastic. I've never experienced anything like this before."

Jensen looked at Teela with a smile finally breaking through. Perhaps this young woman wasn't so terrible after all.

Later, Kathleen and Jennifer left Jensens leaving Todd and Teela still sitting at the table. They were engrossed in deep conversation about Todd's experiences on the Space Platform and the early days of life on Star One. Jennifer had a feeling that Teela had made a new and very special friend. With an uneasy feeling, Jennifer wondered where this might lead. It was something she would have to watch closely. Teela had made so much progress, and she didn't want the AI to get hurt.

# Chapter Five

Steve, Christy, Lieutenant Commander Williams, and Captain Gerald were in Steve's office listening to the frantic message they had just received from President Kateland. Disaster had struck! It had been sudden and unexpected. The message had been sent on a fast military drone rocket, from a military base just outside of Washington D.C. It had taken less then eight hours for it to reach Star One. Steve had been surprised at the small rocket's capability and even more surprised at where it had been launched from. Rockets were never launched near heavily populated areas.

It had been eight frantically short weeks since Captain Gerald and his marines had arrived on Star One. A lot had been accomplished in those weeks. Captain Gerald's men had set up quarters in the Alpha Wheel. They had built three missile defense platforms. Two had been installed on Star One and another one on the Space Platform. They had also set up ten rail guns on Star One for added security.

During all of this, Steve had questioned whether Star One actually needed such powerful defenses. It was almost as if the space station had become a military base. The marines could be seen in nearly all sections of the station as well as over on the Space Platform as they carried out their work assignments. Now it looked as if they might indeed need those weapons to protect themselves.

Teela, Lieutenant Commander Williams, and Christy had worked closely with Captain Gerald assigning work details for the marines. A number of Captain Gerald's people had been assigned to work with Doctor Wruggi on constructing the deep sleep chambers. Doctor Wruggi had been pleased to get the extra help, and rapid progress was now being made on the chambers. One of the storage areas had been completely converted and chambers installed. The first 220 sleepers were already resting in deep sleep with another 200 scheduled to join them shortly.

Steve had hoped that things Earth side would continue to stay calm for at least a few more weeks. The shuttle supply flights were on schedule, and a lot of needed supplies and people had already made it up to Star One. Senator Farley had been quiet, and things seemed to have calmed down on the political front. There was still so much that needed to be done to get ready for the coming of the neutron star-black hole binary.

There was still some unrest across the country as well as the rest of the world due to the threat of the neutron star. The media stations, as well as the internet, were full of frightful predications of what might happen to the Earth.

Doomsday prophets were turning up on every street corner with their cries of Armageddon. Churches were booming with increased attendance and offerings. Riots had stopped due to the heavy presence of U.S. military troops in every community larger than 10,000 inhabitants. There was an uneasy peace in the American cities as people waited nervously for more news.

The first hint Steve had that something was wrong, was early that morning when communications with Earth based stations in the United States started to fail. From orbiting satellites, it was obvious that widespread fighting had erupted in the United States and other countries. There were also massive riots breaking out in nearly every major American city. Margaret had tried repeatedly to reestablish contact with various communication centers but to no avail. They retained communication with the three launch centers on encrypted radio bands, but very little else.

From the cape launch center, Jane Kinsey had worriedly informed Steve that many of the communication lines into the cape were also down. From the scattered news reports she had managed to receive, she had pieced together the startling news that a military coup was ongoing in the United States. The military forces guarding the cape had not been attacked, but had been placed on a higher level of alert as a precaution. She had some limited communication with President Kateland earlier, but that had ended and only silence was now coming out of Washington D. C.

It was just a few minutes after talking to Jane that Teela had detected the military drone launch from outside Washington. Once the drone broke the outer atmosphere, it began broadcasting a message that it contained important documents and a message from the President for Steve on Star One. They had tracked the drone keeping two of the stations rail guns targeted on it the entire time in case it was a trick of some kind. The drone had stopped twenty miles from Star one and the Space Platform. A Centaur had been sent to retrieve the message disk and other documents contained in the drones small cargo compartment. They were now viewing the message in Steve's office.

On the view screen, the President appeared.

"Senator Farley and a group of military personnel are trying to overthrow the government," began President Kateland looking haggard and stressed on the screen.

Steve thought she looked as if it had been quite some time since she had managed a decent night's sleep. There were dark spots under her eyes and lines on her face he hadn't noticed before.

"They have the support of a surprisingly large number of military units and have succeeded in seizing most of Washington and a number of other vital areas around the country. They also have widespread support of the general population, not only that but similar coups were also made simultaneously in several of the countries allied with us. From the latest reports, Canada, Britain, and several other governments have already fallen. I believe this was a coordinated attack set up by Senator Farley and those he represents."

Steve could see the shock on the faces of the other three as they listened and watched the video message. Even though Teela had warned of the possibility of something like this happening, Steve had not wanted to believe that it could occur in the United States. The ramifications of what was happening could be disastrous.

"There is widespread fighting in many countries and across the U.S.," President Kateland continued in a subdued voice. "Many of our communications are being jammed and we are having a hard time getting messages out. That's why I sent you this drone. There are documents and orders in it authorizing you to take certain actions. General Karver believes we can continue to hold the cape and our military launch facilities for the time being with our loyal units, but he can't give me any idea of how long. I have ordered another carrier battle group to the coast next to the cape. We may need their firepower. We are trying to consolidate our positions and hold as much of the country as possible, but General Karver is not sure if we can maintain control. If Senator Farley manages to gain control of the country, you can expect immediate attempts to take control of Star One or to destroy it!"

The President paused evidently listening to someone else in the room with her. "We have just received word from General Karver, he's out in the field with his troops, and it's much worse than we had feared. Military units that we were counting on to help control some sections of the country and possibly retake Washington have gone over to Senator Farley's insurgents."

Steve glanced at Captain Gerald who was shaking his head in disbelief. It was hard for the captain to imagine military units turning against the President.

"General Karver reports that all he can hope for now is to mount a successful defense of our launch facilities. General Karver is trying to strengthen the protective zones around all three launch facilities with all the loyal troops he can muster. Fortunately, the troops at the facilities were handpicked and remain loyal. All three facilities are still under our control. I'm trying to get word to Jane Kinsey to launch ever shuttle they have loaded or that can be loaded as quickly as possible. We will be going to round the clock launches. We are also shipping up additional military hardware for Captain Gerald from our military launch facilities. Tim McPhryson is at the cape, and I've ordered General Karver to proceed there and take command. We are evacuating all of our key people at Houston to the cape."

The screen seemed to shake, and the lights in the room President Kateland was sitting in seemed to dim. "We are under attack here now, and I don't believe we can hold out much longer. We were not expecting the Senator and his group to try something like this. It was the last thing we expected," the President paused, letting her tired eyes rest for a second. "I have no intention of surrendering to Senator Farley. We are going to try to escape from Washington shortly if we have enough loyal troops left to break through the insurgent lines. Good luck Commander Larson, I know deep in my heart that you will succeed in saving that part of humanity that I've entrusted to you." The screen went dark, and the room was silent.

-

"Oh my god," cried Christy looking panic stricken at Steve. "If she won't surrender what will happen to her? What if she can't get out of Washington?"

"Especially with Senator Farley who has always hated her in charge," Todd muttered angrily. "You know he will do everything in his power to capture her."

Steve looked at the dark screen for several seconds before replying. "I think the President knows she can't escape, I could almost hear the despair in her voice. She has made sure that General Karver and Tim McPhryson are safe at the cape. We don't know about the Vice President."

Pausing he looked around at the small group. "Captain Gerald have your troops go to red alert for possible attack from Earth," Steve ordered firmly seeing the trapped President in his mind. She wanted Star One to survive, and it was up to Steve and his people to make sure it happened.

"Do you think the threat is that real?" Christy asked not wanting to believe that anyone would dare attack the station. They were so far from Earth that an attack seemed impractical.

"There is a chance Senator Farley and his group could gain control of a missile launch facility," Steve replied worriedly. "From what President Kateland said, too many military units have gone over to his side. There could be an attack launched against us at any time, if they have the missile arming codes. What do you think captain?" Steve looked over at Captain Gerald wanting his opinion.

"It depends on which facilities they take," replied the captain thinking about the capabilities of the different missile launch sites. "If it's one of the command facilities and the generals in charge go over to his side, they may acquire the launch codes very quickly. Fortunately, very few missiles have the necessary range to reach us. The missiles will have to be modified first. I don't believe we are in any immediate danger, but that could change in a few weeks."

"Very well captain," replied Steve relieved to hear that. "However, if any missile or space vehicle is launched from anywhere other than one of the protected launch facilities, it is to be shot down," Steve said coldly. He would not risk the station.

"Yes sir," Captain Gerald replied evenly. "We will activate our missile defense platforms immediately, as well as the rail guns. We should be able to shoot down anything they send toward us."

"Christy, I want you in Main Control checking each shuttle launch and verifying with ground control that it's a legitimate launch," continued Steve looking over at her. "You know the people on the ground; also implement Code Omega signals immediately from each shuttle at midpoint. If they don't respond with the correct response, they are to be shot down."

Steve, Christy, and Jane Kinsey had worked out weeks before specific codes to be used in case of a situation like this. Each shuttle commander knew the correct responses. Anyone else would be at a loss as to how to respond.

"Todd, I want you to get with Captain Gerald and begin arming two of our shuttles with Black Knight missiles. We don't know what we may have to deal with, but I want the ability to meet it as far away from the station as possible. We can surely adapt the Black Knight interceptor missiles to work from a shuttle."

"Shouldn't be a problem," Captain Gerald responded going over in his mind rapidly what would need to be done. "I have several people that have been working with Lieutenant Commander William's crews that can help with the installation. We can modify several of the older cargo shuttles. We need the passenger shuttles to continue bringing up people from the cape. Teela can help us with the design specs."

"How did all this happen?" asked Christy not believing how quickly everything was falling apart down on Earth. She let out a deep breath not wanting to believe that they could be cut off from Earth at any time.

"Senator Farley must have been working with some key members of the military for weeks," answered Captain Gerald recalling some of his intelligence briefings from General Karver prior to being sent to Star One. "Senator Farley could not have planned something of this magnitude without help from key military officers."

"Our own military," Christy said shaking her head. "I wouldn't have believed it to be possible."

"The business consortium that is behind Senator Farley could have helped with setting up the coups in other countries," Lieutenant Commander Williams added. "With their business contacts in the governments, it could have given Senator Farley the connections he needed to orchestrate this."

"This was well planned," Captain Gerald said with a frown on his forehead. "The President's popularity has been steadily decreasing for weeks. Senator Farley just waited for the exact moment and then he struck."

Teela suddenly materialized in front of Steve's desk with a look of fear and desperation on her normally pristine face, "Look at the screen. We just picked this up from one of the surveillance satellites."

Everyone looked at the large view screen, which Teela had switched to a view as seen from a satellite high above the Earth. Brilliant white flashes were appearing across parts of Europe and the Middle East.

"It started two minutes ago," Teela said quietly. "From the few reports I've managed to intercept from Earth, a radical religious group seized two nuclear launch facilities in the Middle East and launched against Europe and Israel." Teela paused cocking her head slightly to one side as if listening to someone.

80

"Those are low yield nuclear explosions, probably in the ten to twenty kiloton range," Captain Gerald spoke in a subdued voice. He felt sickened, not since Hiroshima and Nagasaki had nuclear weapons been used on a human target.

"Why would they do this now?" asked Christy staring wide eyed at the screen not wanting to believe what it was showing.

"With the coup attempt going on in the U.S., it has left a power vacuum," replied Captain Gerald. "They know the U.S. at the moment, is powerless to intervene. They are taking advantage of the situation."

"But Israel has nuclear weapons too!" Lieutenant Commander Williams said worriedly. "Don't they know that Israel will retaliate?"

"The launch facilities are in two different Middle East countries. Both governments claim they did not authorize these launches. They are asking for time to retake the launch facilities from the terrorists," Teela reported as she continued to monitor the events occurring on Earth.

"The terrorist groups must have infiltrated the launch facilities," Captain Gerald stated shaking his head in disbelief. "They had to have had inside help to get the arming codes and to launch the missiles. Israel will not give them time for explanations! They will retaliate shortly, and it will be devastating."

Steve could see that at least one, maybe two nuclear weapons had gone off over Israel, perhaps more. Steve knew without any doubt that Israel would retaliate in kind. He felt a knot grow in the pit of his stomach. He wondered if they were watching the beginning of the end of the world.

"This could break out into a full fledged nuclear war," warned Todd gazing at the view screen. "You can't throw nuclear weapons around like that and not expect to be struck back."

"I doubt whether the radicals care, they are fanatics," Captain Gerald replied watching the screen, knowing that Israel would strike back shortly.

"When Iran developed a nuclear bomb back in 2012 and 2013, it resulted in a nuclear arms race in the Middle East," Teela spoke informatively. "As a result, a number of Middle East countries now have nuclear weapons. There are a dozen nuclear missile launch sites scattered across the Middle East plus those in Israel."

"I am picking up a broadcast from the radicals," Teela reported as she translated the demands instantly into English. "Their leader is demanding the immediate release of all political prisoners, as well as a number of convicted terrorists that are currently incarcerated. If not there will be a second, more widespread attack against other western targets. They claim the first attack was in revenge for past attacks against their organization and its leaders."

On the screen, Steve could count at least ten brilliant flashes that designated nuclear detonations across the western and central parts of Europe as well as at least four now over Israel. He knew that underneath those nuclear fireballs thousands if not millions of people were dying.

"They're mad!" exclaimed Christy with horror in her voice realizing the extent of the death and destruction that must be occurring down below. She gazed in shock at the screen. "What are they doing, don't they realize what they are destroying!"

"They don't care," Captain Gerald repeated with hard, angry eyes. "We have been briefed on several of these militant organizations. The taking of innocent lives means nothing to them, as long as they can accomplish their goals."

"With the U.S. out of it, the radicals must have felt this was their best opportunity to attack," commented Steve trying to keep his voice calm.

"Nuclear launches detected," Teela broke in suddenly, her gaze turning to the view screen. "Israel is launching their retaliatory strike."

Over the next several minutes, they watched as a series of brilliant nuclear detonations began to spread across other Middle East countries. Twelve nuclear fireballs appeared above the known launch facilities in the Middle East.

"Those are larger detonations," Captain Gerald spoke as he watched the screen intently. "Probably in the forty to fifty kiloton range. Those will be extremely destructive. Nothing will survive underneath those blasts."

For several minutes, everyone was quiet. No new flashes of nuclear death appeared on the view screen. Steve hoped that it was over and calmer heads would now reign. Enough people had just died.

"No new launches are being detected sir," Teela spoke feeling shocked by the violence and loss of life that the nuclear signatures testified to. "The terrorists were not able to get off a second strike."

"Then it's over for now," Christy said in a subdued voice.

"We need to find out what's going on in the United States," Steve spoke determinedly. "Teela, see if you can use the satellites to find out what's going on in Washington."

Teela became quiet as if listening to another voice and then looking petrified; she looked back up at the screen as it changed to a view of Southeastern China and Taiwan.

"The Chinese have launched an invasion fleet across the channel separating them and Taiwan," Teela stated. She magnified the view on the screen showing a fleet of military ships and troop transports in the Taiwan Strait.

"What now?" Christy asked her blue eyes watching as the world seemed to be falling apart. When was this going to stop?

"The power vacuum created by the coup in the United States," replied Captain Gerald. "We were Taiwan's biggest supporter, without us to back them China is seizing this moment to retake the island."

"The Taiwanese President has threatened to use nuclear weapons if the ships are not turned back immediately," reported Teela listening to the high priority messages between the two countries. "The Chinese Premier has refused and is demanding Taiwan's immediate surrender and the rejoining of the two nations."

On the screen, low yield nuclear explosions began to appear over the narrow stretch of water separating the two countries. Bright flashes of light blocked out the view of the Chinese invasion fleet.

"Taiwan has launched a preemptive strike against the Chinese naval force approaching their shore," Teela continued to report." Six low yield weapons glowed on the screen boiling the ocean and ships beneath them.

"I've tapped into the military satellites above the area," Teela said using her powerful memory core to create new programs almost instantly and override the security codes on the satellites. "The invading Chinese fleet has largely been destroyed, only a few vessels survived, loss of life is very high. I'm detecting missile launches from mainland China."

Scant minutes later, much larger nuclear detonations began to roll over the Taiwan countryside vaporizing everything below as China's vengeful response struck. Taiwan launched a feeble counter strike with its remaining launch platforms, with only four small yield nuclear devices managing to reach China's shore and erupt briefly over the countryside. Then all was quiet. From start to finish, the entire exchange between China and Taiwan had lasted less then twenty minutes.

Everyone in the room sat quietly, too stunned by these new developments to move. Everyone wondered what was next. It was as if the entire world had suddenly gone mad.

"It seems to be over," Teela reported as she used the satellites to scan the surface. "The fighting in Washington has also died down. It looks like the insurgents have control of most of the Capitol. There is still some fighting going on around the White House, but it looks like just isolated pockets of resistance to the insurgents."

"All right everyone," Steve said finally breaking the eerie silence. "Let's get going, we have work to do. Teela let me know if anything else happens Earth side. For the time being, I want hourly status reports. Especially if you hear anything else about President Kateland. Captain Gerald, please tell your people at Main Control to keep a close watch for any missiles that may be hurled our way. It seems like all hell is breaking loose down below."

"Yes sir," Teela and Captain Gerald replied together.

Down on Earth, President Susan Kateland sat quietly in her office, in the underground bunker, deep beneath the White House. A member of her secret service team had just told her that they didn't have the forces needed to break out of the under ground command complex. The remaining military forces up above had surrendered to the insurgents. It would only be a short matter of time before the insurgent forces forced their way down into the bunker.

She looked sadly around the small well-furnished room that served as her office in case of a National Emergency. The flag of the United States and the seal of the President hung behind her. In her entire stint as President, she had never had to come down here other than to familiarize herself with the bunker's function. She had always thought that if she did, it would be to protect her country from a foreign aggressor. Not from her own countrymen. President Kateland let out a long, heavy sigh not wanting to believe what was happening to her country.

She had turned off the screens that showed the disaster rolling across many parts of the globe. The underground bunker had been able to receive communications, but had not been able to transmit anything for several hours. She had managed to contact General Karver earlier several times before their last line of communication had been discovered and cut off. She had given him specific orders to follow if she didn't make it out of Washington.

She was grateful that North America had so far been spared the horror of the nuclear carnage that had consumed other parts of the world. She bowed her head, praying briefly for her country and its people who she had failed so miserably.

Several large deafening explosions shook the underground bunker, causing the American flag behind President Kateland to crumble to the floor. The room became filled with dust. She could smell smoke as if something was burning. She continued to pray knowing that deliverance would not be forth coming. The insurgents were obviously using explosives to blast their way into the bunker.

Her prayer was interrupted by a series of yells and shots out in the hallway where several marines and secret service agents had been guarding the entrance to her office. Moments later, the door was kicked violently open and solders wearing blue armbands stormed in, one was clutching a bleeding arm from a wound received in the fighting outside in the hall.

They stopped when they saw the President sitting at her desk staring at them with disdain. Glancing around the room nervously, not able to look President Kateland in the face, they satisfied themselves that no one else was present. They stepped back out closing the splintered door behind them.

Several minutes later, President Kateland heard voices out in the hallway, one she recognized. Standing up and holding her head defiantly, she waited grimly as the door opened and Senator Farley flanked by several military officers triumphantly entered the room.

"Hello President Kateland," Senator Farley said with a smirk striding over to stand in front of her desk. "You are my prisoner, and I command you to tell your remaining military forces to stand down or they will be destroyed. There will be no reprisals for those who surrender."

Looking Farley squarely in the eyes, President Susan Kateland replied defiantly. "You can go to hell before I bow down to the likes of you!"

Senator Farley's face turned livid with anger, and he raised his hand up as if to strike her, before pausing and regaining his composure.

"Do you want to die?" he snarled with madness dancing in his eyes. "You are my prisoner, it's over, there's nothing else you can do!"

"Perhaps not," replied President Kateland standing straight and looking disdainfully at the officers with him, several turned away not willing to meet her glance. "But I will never surrender this country to you, or cooperate with the likes of you in any way what so ever!"

"That's the same thing the Vice President said just before he was placed in front of a firing squad," replied Senator Farley smiling cruelly. "Oh well, we will just tell the people you were killed accidentally in the fighting." Turning, Farley left the room followed uneasily by the military officers.

A minute later, two hard faced soldiers entered and drawing their pistols shot the defenseless President where she stood. Hired thugs she thought as she fell and life left her shattered body. Her last fading thoughts were of General Karver, knowing that he would do everything in his power to finish what they had started. Star One would survive! So died the last American President.

In Main Control, Christy was monitoring the six shuttles that the cape had frantically launched in the past four hours. The shuttles had been loaded with the last scheduled crew members that had made it to the cape and some vital equipment Star One and Tycho City still needed. If there were time, more people would be sent up. However, at the moment, no one knew how many shuttle launches would be made in the future, and each one needed to count.

Satellites around the globe had not detected any more nuclear detonations, even though it was obvious that widespread fighting had erupted across many areas. Heavy fighting raged in numerous countries, and rioting had spread unchecked through many of the world's major cities.

Checking the main view screen, which was focused on the Space Platform, she could see a lot of activity around the two cargo shuttles that were setting there. Several Centaur work vessels and one-man scooters were hovering near the two shuttles. A number of white spacesuited workers were also visible.

Todd and Captain Gerald were in the process of converting both shuttles into delivery vehicles for the interceptor missiles. Christy knew that most of the spacesuited figures she could see were Captain Gerald's military personnel. She had never thought she would feel this way, but she was glad Captain Gerald and his marines were on the station.

Looking around Main Control, she was pleased with how efficiently the crew was handling this emergency. Even the new weapon's control station was calm. Lieutenant Sandy Emerson and two other marines controlled the station's new interceptor missile platforms as well as the recently installed rail guns.

Hearing the door to Main Control slide open, she saw Steve come in with a worn look on his face. Christy knew that he had been on a secure com line with Mase Colton for quite some time. She knew he was under a lot of pressure with the responsibility that he was now saddled with.

"What's the latest from down below?" asked Steve taking his command chair next to Christy and rubbing his forehead.

"General Karver is massing his loyal troops around the cape and the two military launch centers," reported Christy. "Jane spoke with him a short while ago, and he is still in the process of positioning his forces."

"I just hope he can continue to hold them," Steve said shaking his head worriedly. "We still have a lot of supplies and people I would like to get up here." With the on going construction of the deep sleep chambers, Steve had added a number of additional people to the list of who needed to be brought up to the station.

"General Karver is fairly certain he can hold the launch centers," Christy replied. "He is moving more loyal military units into position. He still controls enough naval and air power to hold off any attacks from the insurgents for the time being."

"Any word from Senator Farley?" Steve asked his eyes moving to the screen, which was still showing the work going on over at the Space Platform.

"Senator Farley is demanding that the general surrender immediately or nuclear weapons will be used to take out the launch centers," Christy replied. She couldn't imagine the Senator actually carrying out the threat. There was no way he would actually set off a nuclear weapon on American soil!

"The man is totally insane, I can't believe that so many intelligent people have fallen for his lies," retorted Steve drumming his fingers on the console in front of him. "The neutron star is now common knowledge worldwide, but Senator Farley still refuses to believe it."

"We have also picked up scattered news reports that President Kateland and the Vice President were accidentally killed during the fighting in Washington," Christy reported deeply saddened by the news. "Supposedly, the President was killed by friendly fire while trying to leave the Capitol. The Vice President was reportedly killed in a car wreck trying to reach the President."

"If they're dead, I would bet Senator Farley is responsible in both instances," muttered Steve hoping that the reports of President Kateland's death were incorrect. She had been an outstanding

President and at one time extremely popular with the people. She didn't deserve to die like this.

"General Karver has also sent word that there will be shuttle launches from both secured military sites tomorrow morning," reported Christy recalling the latest message from the general that Jane had relayed.

"How's our communications?" asked Steve looking over at Christy and noticing the tension on her face. He could see the worry and concern in her eyes.

"We have good communications with all three launch facilities. A computer virus disabled communications earlier with the other military command centers. With the special firewalls in the launch center's computers, all three were immune."

Looking at Steve, Christy continued in a more subdued voice. "The shuttles from the military launch centers will contain the nuclear interceptor missiles that General Karver promised us earlier, plus a small group of specialists to handle them."

There had been a delay in sending up the missiles as originally planed. It had been necessary to modify them significantly, so they could be deployed from Star One.

"We may damn well need them now," Steve said shaking his head still trying to grasp in his mind everything that was occurring down on Earth.

"The group is to be placed under Captain Gerald's command," continued Christy repeating what General Karver had told Jane. "There will be twenty specialists on the shuttles bound for us. Four shuttles will be launched in all, two for Tycho City and Two for Star One. He also requests that all four military shuttles be returned to their launch points as soon as possible."

"We can do that," replied Steve knowing that if necessary they could turn the shuttles around in just a few short hours.

"He wants to try to get the final parts for the Space Platform's fusion reactor loaded on them and back up to us while the launch sites are still secure," Christy spoke wondering how much longer all three launch facilities would stay under General Karver's control.

"We need those parts for the Space Platform," replied Steve gazing back at the main view screen and the work being done on the two shuttles. "Todd needs that fusion reactor, so we can install the ion thrusters."

"The general also says he still controls enough of the countries nuclear arsenal to prevent the rebels from using the nuclear weapons they have seized against his positions," Christy said.

A sudden shimmering began next to Steve and Teela appeared in her uniform looking unhappy. Her rich blue eyes looked almost dark. "I've analyzed the data from the nuclear exchanges down on Earth. Most of the Middle East and some areas of Europe will have to watch out for radiation. The loss of life will be in the tens of millions."

"So many," Christy said repressing a shudder and drawing in a deep breath.

"The exchange between Taiwan and China did little harm to China itself, but Taiwan was nearly wiped out," Teela continued. "Very little of Taiwan's population will survive the radiation. The death toll will be over 25 million. The soil will be poisoned for years. The only good news is that because most of the nuclear weapons used were small, the radiation levels outside the affected areas will only increase slightly."

"Can you tell how the fighting in the U.S. has been going?" asked Steve knowing that Teela could access nearly any satellite she wanted to now.

"I've taken over all the military spy satellites to monitor the situation," confessed Teela knowing that Commander Larson would not have a problem with that in this current situation. "Controllers on the ground have tried to retake control of the satellites, but they can't succeed. I imagine they are highly aggravated at the situation."

"You are to keep control of those satellites," Steve ordered. "I want them used to keep an eye on what is going on down on Earth."

Looking at Steve and Christy with a very serious look, Teela continued. "I can tell you that Senator Farley was at the White House when the President was supposedly killed. His forces have taken the White House, and he was seen going into it and coming back out.

"Senator Farley was at the White House," Christy repeated. "Are you sure Teela?"

"I have video taken by a satellite that shows his presence there," reported Teela knowing that according to her simulations the Senator had probably been responsible for the President's death.

"That doesn't surprise me," replied Steve with anger showing in his voice. He wished there was some way the man could be brought to justice for his crimes.

"Senator Farley's forces do control some of the countries nuclear arsenal and almost the entire country now," Teela continued.

"That's not good news," commented Steve taking a deep breath. He wondered how many people that were supposed to come up to Star One and Tycho City were now unable to reach the launch centers.

"Many of the loyal units were cut off by the insurgents and forced to surrender," Teela continued to report. "Many refused to fire on fellow Americans."

"That's not too surprising," said Christy knowing how difficult it would be for American soldiers to fire upon one another. "It's hard to blame them."

"General Karver is rushing all of his remaining loyal military forces to the launch sites," Teela added. "He still controls several major nuclear launch sites that should hold the insurgents at bay, or at least prevent them from using nuclear weapons. My own estimates indicate that the insurgents will need several days to a week to consolidate their positions before they dare move against the general's fortified positions."

"Will they be able to take the launch sites?" Steve asked deeply concerned since they still had a lot of supplies stock piled at the cape waiting for shuttles to bring them up. There were also quite a few people, who worked at the cape, he would like to bring up to Star One if possible.

"Eventually," Teela replied calmly hiding her fear. "If the insurgents are willing to accept the heavy casualties involved, General Karver will not be able to hold for long. They will need to move in a lot of heavy armor and reduce General Karver's air cover considerably. Fortunately for General Karver, he has a large force of attack helicopters at his disposal that should give the insurgents fits. The two carrier groups off the cape are loyal and will provide the air support he needs for now."

Steve and Christy were both silent staring worriedly at one another. They both knew that their lifeline to Earth would soon be cut permanently. There was also no doubt in Steve's mind that Senator Farley would not care about the casualty count, as long as he could take and destroy the launch centers.

Farley would be utterly uncaring about the casualties; nothing would keep him away from his fixation on wiping out the nation's space launch facilities. They both knew that they had a long night still ahead of them; the situation on Earth would have to be monitored extremely close.

"Keep us informed Teela," Steve ordered. "I want to know instantly if anything changes."

Later that evening, Teela was sitting in Jennifer's quarters feeling extremely worried. She knew that all of her friends were in immediate danger, and that there was very little she could do. Even worse, the neutron star and black hole threat were still months away.

"Commander Larson and Commander Jones are very worried about what's going on down below," Teela said watching Jennifer change out of her uniform and into more comfortable clothes. "We may even be attacked here on the station by the insurgents."

"It might very well happen Teela," replied Jennifer pulling a loose fitting light sweater down over her head. "But the commander has taken steps to protect the station. We knew that eventually we would be more or less on our own. It's just going to happen a little sooner than we had originally thought."

"I just wish there was something I could do!" Teela said sounding upset. "I have all this information in my core memory, and it can't seem to help us any at all."

"Sometimes all the knowledge in the world is of no use," responded Jennifer sitting down in a chair across from Teela. "People have to use their experience and instinct to survive. New challenges have to be met by strong, dedicated people willing to sacrifice to overcome them."

"Experience is what I'm short of," Teela admitted quietly. "Even when Todd and I are talking, sometimes I don't know how to respond to what he is saying, I feel so unsure of myself around the Lieutenant Commander."

"I've noticed that you and Todd have become very close friends," Jennifer said cautiously not sure how to proceed with her questions. "How do you feel about him?"

"I enjoy every moment we spend together. He's even asked me to go to Jensens several times. He treats me like a real person, not a hologram," Teela said excitedly with a smile on her face. "We even sat in one of the observation lounges last night looking at the stars and talking about the FarQuest mission late into the evening. He has even installed hologram projectors on the Space Platform so I can appear over there."

"Teela," Jennifer ventured carefully not sure how to put the delicate question. "Are you in love with Todd?"

"In love!" Teela exclaimed surprised, with a scarlet flush appearing on her face as she considered the unexpected question. "How can a hologram fall in love with a real human, or the other way around? It isn't possible is it?"

"What to you think?" Jennifer asked her eyes focused on Teela.

Teela became silent as a sudden dawning realization came over her. Reviewing Todd and her actions for the last several weeks, she knew that Jennifer was right. "It can't be true Jennifer, can it? I mean, I can't really fall in love can I?"

"Teela you are so very much like a real woman. Beautiful, intelligent, pleasant to be with, yes it could be true. You have demonstrated many of the other human emotions. Your program is so advanced why couldn't you fall in love?" replied Jennifer soothingly waiting for Teela's reaction.

"What am I to do?" asked Teela quietly, looking into Jennifer's eyes. "I didn't mean for this to happen. I thought Todd and I were just good friends, but now I realize it's much more than that. I think I do love him. How can he ever love me? I'm not real!"

"Teela, this is an important phase of your development. For the time being, I don't see any harm in it. You and Todd should have all the fun you can, but it's important that both of you remember that your body is a hologram and not real. The physical part of love can never occur between the two of you. You need to remind him of that occasionally," answered Jennifer hoping that Teela wouldn't be too disappointed and that Teela understood what she was saying.

Teela was silent for a moment, thinking about how Todd had been treating her and remembering that he had said several times that he knew she was a hologram, but a very beautiful one. "I don't think that will be a problem Jennifer," she replied calmly. "But I will be very careful where Todd is concerned. I don't want to hurt him. But I do want our relationship to continue."

Jennifer nodded satisfied. She was amazed at this development. She would keep a watchful eye on it. Teela didn't need to be upset or severely disappointed at this stage of her development. She was a valuable member of Star One's crew.

In Main Control, Steve and Christy were preparing to go to their quarters for some well-deserved rest. They had been monitoring various Earth communication networks trying to keep abreast of the fighting raging around the globe. Many governments had fallen, and the work of the peacemakers for decades had fallen along the wayside. Ethnic unrest, ages old enemies, tyrants waiting for an opportunity to attack their weaker neighbors had all taken advantage of the situation. Chaos was sweeping across the globe.

Todd had reported finally that he and Captain Gerald would have two shuttles armed with six Black Knight interceptor missiles each prepped and ready to launch in 72 hours. Crews would be on permanent standby, and the shuttles could be launched with a 30-minute warning. Captain Gerald's people would be working around the clock with Todd's to complete the work on the shuttles.

Down on Earth, the fighting had died down in the United States. Senator Farley's people now controlled everything except the three heavily defended launch facilities, two strongly held nuclear launch sites, and several deep underground bunkers in the mountains that had been constructed to survive the neutron star threat. The two bunkers he knew nothing about.

The bunkers had been completed and staffed before this latest round of fighting broke out. They had been built in secrecy to prevent the general public from learning of their locations. For the time being at least, they were safe. Steve also knew that now with Senator Farley in charge no more would be built.

On the main screen, a display was presently being projected showing Star One and the six shuttles currently in transit. All six had gotten off safely and responded properly with code Omega responses. The four military shuttles were scheduled for launch at 0:800 hours in the morning and two more cargo shuttles would be launched from the cape around 10:00. The two cargo shuttles were bound for Tycho City.

Jane Kinsey was in control at the cape and wanted every shuttle currently there to be prepped and launched within 72 hours. Steve knew that six more shuttles were available to launch if time permitted. Knowing Jane, if there was any way possible, she would get them up. Two of the shuttles would be coming up to Star One, and the other four would go on to the Moon.

If they still controlled the cape after the shuttles were unloaded, they would be returned for a second cargo trip. In all, they had, counting the military shuttles, 26 shuttles available for use.

"We need to get some rest Steve," Christy said putting her hand over his and squeezing gently. "We need to be rested for tomorrow. It could be a long day. Things seem to have quieted down for awhile down below."

Nodding, Steve stood up, and the two left Main Control as Lieutenant Commander Miguel Hernandez took over Steve's command chair. Minutes later, they were both in their own quarters sound asleep from exhaustion.

# Chapter Six

John Gray fought the shuttle controls as the interceptor destroyed the inbound missile exploding it less than a hundred yards from the thundering boosters. The explosion threatened to topple the shuttle and push it off its course. Already in the past four weeks, five shuttles had been shot down during launch and two more attempting landings. Shuttle debris littered the landscape around the cape and the ocean floor. The cape's defenses were being hard pressed to protect the defenseless shuttles as they continued their neck-breaking launch pace.

"John are you all right?" a worried Jane Kinsey's voice came over the com.

"We're okay," replied John scanning his instrument console for any amber or red lights. He glanced over at his shaken copilot who was also checking her instruments for any sign of damage to the shuttle or the boosters. "The interceptor caught the inbound about a hundred yards away; it rocked us, but we are stable and still climbing."

"We still have two more shuttles left to launch," Jane said worriedly. "General Karver says he can't hold his defensive lines too much longer. There have already been two human wave attacks this morning. The last one nearly broke through."

"Jane, just make sure you're on that last shuttle. You and Tim both, if Senator Farley gets a hold of either one of you, he won't hesitate to kill you, just like he did the President and Vice President," John warned.

"We'll see," Jane replied calmly. "We have a lot more people that deserve those last 80 seats than we do."

In the distance on the shuttle's main screens, John could see defensive interceptors knocking down more incoming missiles in brilliant fireballs as they exploded. At their current rate of climb, the shuttle would be out of range in another minute.

Julie and Steve had both objected stringently when he had volunteered to fly the shuttles back and forth between Earth and Star One these past few weeks. However, John was the best pilot they had, and it was hard to argue with his logic.

They desperately needed the stockpiled supplies from the cape. John and the handful of shuttle pilots he led had volunteered to fly even though it meant dodging missiles as they landed and as they took off. This was John's seventh flight in the last four weeks. The sky above gradually darkened and John felt relieved as they slid into the black safety of space. The rest of the trip should now be uneventful.

On the ground, twenty miles north of the cape, General Karver and his remaining command staff poured over the maps of their hard-pressed defensive lines. They had formed a ragged defensive line 32 miles out from the cape. General Karver and his forces had fought for every piece of ground as the insurgents had slowly pushed them back. Thousands of dead lay upon the battlefield. Tanks and armored personnel carriers littered the landscape, some still burning. The fighting had been vicious and unrelenting.

"Forward observers report a massive build up of insurgent armor here," Colonel Wilmington reported pointing to a spot on the map northwest of their current position.

"They're getting ready for their final push," General Karver spoke eyeing the map. "If they can break our lines, they can move their heavy artillery up and take out all the cape's launch facilities."

"We don't have enough heavy armor or artillery left to stop them without suffering heavy casualties," commented General Mann wiping the sweat off his forehead.

"They have been holding their armor back in reserve, sacrificing foot solders to wear us down," General Karver continued nodding his head in agreement. "We have managed to knock down most of their missile attacks with our defensive interceptors, but we're starting to run low."

"The latest reports indicate they have begun to move troops toward our advance positions here," General Mann said pointing to an area on the map that two massive human wave attacks that morning had hammered severely.

"If it's a major attack, we won't be able to hold them," Colonel Wilmington said looking at the map and thinking about the terrain in that area. "We've been to hard hit in that area. We don't have the manpower or the armor to hold them back."

"Can we reinforce that area?" asked General Karver looking over at General Mann.

"I don't see how," replied General Mann replied letting out a deep breath. He had watched a lot of brave and dedicated young men and women die over the last few weeks. "I don't know where we can get the troops."

General Karver gazed at the map with a trained eye. If he moved troops from any of the other critical areas, those areas would be vulnerable to attack. The insurgents had worn down his defensive lines to the point where they could finally launch a successful attack, and there was very little he could do to stop it.

Over the past two weeks, he had lost nearly 12,000 soldiers in the fighting and another 4,000 to desertions. He hadn't expected so many former army units to side with the insurgents in this battle for the cape.

"The second army division and fourth marines are currently entrenched in that area," added General Mann tapping the map with his index finger. "After the heavy casualties they have taken the last several days; they are way under strength. They won't be able to hold back another assault particularly if insurgent armor is involved."

"General Strong still has some armor available," Colonel Wilmington spoke, his eyes focusing on General Karver. He had just left that area earlier that morning to attend this meeting. General Strong was the commander of the second army division. "He still has six battle tanks and some artillery. However, ammunition is running low for his artillery."

"It looks like this is it then," General Karver stated with a heavy sigh staring at the map and the dedicated men around him. "They took out both of our military launch sites with tactical nukes last night!"

General Karver knew that Senator Farley must have been desperate to risk using nukes. No doubt due to the constant shuttle launches from both sites, which he had been powerless to stop. The on going launches had evidently infuriated the Senator to the point where he had risked using the nukes.

"What about the shuttles?" asked General Mann looking at General Karver in surprise. Neither General Karver nor he had expected the insurgents to use nukes.

"The last two were launched yesterday afternoon," General Karver replied relieved that the shuttles had gotten safely away. "They carried the last of the supplies we were sending up to Tycho City from the military sites."

"We have tactical nukes ourselves," General Mann spoke looking at General Karver. They had warned Senator Farley what would happen if the Senator used nukes first.

"I won't use nukes against our own people," General Karver replied in a firm voice. "We won't stoop to Senator Farley's level!"

97

"I thought the military launch sites were protected by interceptors?" spoke Colonel Wilmington. "How did they get through?"

"Whoever is helping Senator Farley with the military side of this operation is no fool," General Karver replied with a scowl. He wished he knew who the traitor was.

"How did they get past our defenses?" General Mann asked. He knew that the air defenses around the two military launch centers should have been able to stop this type of attack.

"They used stealth attack fighters flying extremely low to sneak in past our radar and dropped the nukes on the launch centers before we could respond. Casualties at the bases were heavy, and I have directed the survivors to surrender. We have made it extremely clear that if nukes are used against the cape that we will retaliate in kind."

"That's only a threat," General Mann replied. "You and I both know that we won't use the nukes."

"We know that, but Senator Farley doesn't," General Karver replied evenly.

"It's becoming more evident all the time that they want to capture part of the cape intact," Colonel Wilmington commented. "Without the cape and its launch facilities, they can't launch a successful attack against Star One or Tycho City."

"You're probably right," General Karver said nodding his head wishing he could do more to delay the insurgents.

With the round the clock launches of the last four weeks, they had managed to get almost all the supplies and people originally scheduled up to Star One and Tycho City. It had been a tremendous job, but it had been done. General Karver knew that President Kateland would have been proud of what her people had accomplished. Some of the people on the priority lists hadn't been able to make it to the cape, but others just as qualified had been substituted. Many of them had worked at the cape in some capacity.

"What about the cape complex?" General Mann asked. He knew that they could not allow it to fall into the insurgent's hands.

"We need to make sure that the cape complex is useless to them after we launch the last two shuttles in a couple of hours," General Karver replied in a grim voice. "That's why I've ordered demolition crews to place explosive charges through out the complex. Nothing useful will be left standing for the insurgents."

"It's hard to believe the cape will be gone," Colonel Wilmington spoke in a more subdued voice. "That's going to seriously upset Senator Farley."

"It's necessary," General Mann said in agreement. "Without the cape and its launch facilities, it will be weeks or possibly months before Senator Farley can launch an attack against Star One or Tycho City."

"By then, both will be ready for an attack," General Karver spoke.

The general knew that both facilities were already heavily armed, but that information was classified at the highest level. Only a few people knew what he had sent up to protect Star One and Tycho City. Senator Farley would be in for a rude awakening if he ever attacked either of the two.

General Karver had hated making the decision to destroy the launch center, but he knew there was no other choice. It drove home even more just how serious the situation was with the insurgents. The cape had been a symbol for nearly a generation now of America's power and resurgence as the world leader in space exploration.

"Colonel Wilmington," General Karver said looking over at the young colonel. "I want you to return to the cape and make sure all the demolition charges are set. Once we launch the last two shuttles, we will evacuate the cape and set off the explosives."

After making their final defensive plans for the coming assault, the group broke up going back to their respective commands. General Karver knew that this would be the last time he would see many of them. They had served him and their country faithfully.

Several hours later, General Karver was in the air in a fast attack helicopter flying high above the fighting, which had erupted once again down below. The clear early afternoon sky allowed for an unobstructed view of the terrain and the opposing forces. He knew that the last two shuttles were scheduled to be launched within the hour. He needed to hold just long enough for them to get away safely.

He wished that one of the two aircraft carrier battle groups had survived. Somehow, Senator Farley's forces had managed to gain control of several nuclear attack submarines. Senator Farley's forces had launched a major air attack against the two aircraft carriers the week before. Under cover of the air attack, the two submarines had managed to move in and take out both carriers with torpedoes and cruise missiles. Both of the submarines had been destroyed by depth charges from several navy frigates.

The remaining navy ships had moved in closer to shore to add their defensive firepower to the capes against incoming missile fire. The Destroyer Cleveland had been the last to be destroyed. She had been sunk only two days ago by the last of Senator Farley's cruise missiles.

In the distance, General Karver could see insurgent armor consisting of a long column of M-4A heavy tanks interspersed with numerous armored personnel carriers probing his defenses. His fast attack helicopter and the fourteen others following close behind were the last of his air arm that remained. He had held these back in reserve for just this moment. They would make the insurgents pay a heavy price in the upcoming battle. Dozens of other attack helicopters littered the landscape below and around the cape with their burnt out blasted remains.

General Karver held on as the helicopter banked tightly to the right and hurled itself at high speed at the armor juggernaut assailing his now meager defensive line. Several attacking tanks had already been taken out by scattered artillery fire and shoulder launched anti tank weapons. He cold see General Strong's last six heavy battle tanks moving up to engage the approaching insurgent armor.

Anti armor rockets belched out of the helicopter's launch tubes impacting on two of the approaching tanks. The rockets depleted uranium tips penetrated the tanks heavy armor exploding inside. Two large, fiery explosions marked the positions of the tanks as their magazines and fuel exploded showering debris on the other armored vehicles around them.

The other attack helicopters following close behind poured their fire into the helpless armor column wrecking havoc with the speed and ferocity of their sudden attack. General Strong's advancing tanks added their deadly fire to that of the attack helicopters decimating the insurgent's heavy armor.

For a moment, it looked as if the insurgents advance was going to stall. Smoke filled the air and burning tanks and armored personnel carriers littered the landscape. Insurgent troops could be seen running for cover, and even a few were headed back away from the fighting. Massive explosions began tearing huge holes in the ground, as General Strong's remaining artillery pieces opened up.

Suddenly General Karver heard the helicopter's threat warning go off as interceptor missiles from shoulder held launchers locked onto the helicopter. General Karver felt the pilot push the craft over and dart toward the ground as counter measures shot out from the tail in an attempt to confuse the inbound interceptors. The helicopter pilot pulled up seemingly scant feet from the ground skimming the surface then darting back up and to the left.

Behind them, several powerful explosions in the air and on the ground bore mute testimony to their successful evasion of the interceptors. However, looking back General Karver saw that four of his accompanying attack helicopters hadn't been so successful. Their burning wreckage littered the ground between the defenders and the attackers.

The enemy armor started to advance once more firing round after round into General Strong's outnumbered tanks. In less then two minutes, the massed fire of the enemy had destroyed all six defending tanks. The insurgents heavy armor then turned their fire upon the defenders heavily fortified and battered positions. Insurgent artillery also began to join in, rolling in waves of towering explosions that marched across the defensive lines. General Karver felt ill knowing that hundreds of loyal troops were dying below.

The attack helicopter made a second run taking out another tank and a personnel carrier, once again having to dodge and juke through rebel interceptor missile fire. One missile exploded in the air so close to the helicopter that it was actually knocked over briefly on its side from the concussion.

As the helicopter righted itself and banked once again, General Karver saw the first rebel tanks begin to breach his defensive lines pouring withering fire into the defending troops. In just a few minutes, a major break thorough was occurring over a wide front. The defenders didn't have the firepower to stop the rebel armor and most of the attack helicopters had been knocked down by rebel missiles. Only three others besides General Karver's still survived. Looking out the cockpit window for a moment, he made a quick decisive decision.

"General Mann," Karver spoke over the radio.

"Yes sir," General Mann's voice came back instantly. General Mann was second in command and was monitoring the insurgent attack from the field headquarters.

"I'm going to the cape to oversee the launching of the last two shuttles and to make sure the demolition charges are set. I need you to hold for another hour at which time I am directing you to surrender to the officer in charge of the insurgent troops." General Karver heard only silence at the other end. "General Mann, many of these men and women will die if we don't surrender. We can't hold the cape much longer anyway. We need to think about saving lives."

"Yes sir, we will do as you ask. Good luck sir," General Mann finally replied, then after a moment his voice returned over the radio. "Sir, it's been an honor to serve with you."

Several minutes later, General Karver's helicopter landed in front of the cape's main administration building where Jane Kinsey and Tim McPhryson stood waiting for him. In the distance, he could hear the din of fighting, the explosions from the tank and artillery fire, and heavy weapons.

"Come with us general," Jane Kinsey pleaded not wanting to see General Karver's life wasted needlessly. "We're going up on the shuttles. We don't dare let Senator Farley capture us with the information we have about Star One and Tycho City."

"My duty is here," began General Karver preparing to turn and walk away to check on the demolition charges. Too many troops had died the last four weeks. He would make his final stand here at the cape. He had already decided that he would not be captured.

"No general." Raising his hand firmly McPhryson stopped him. "We need you on Star One. You know that eventually Farley will attack it and Tycho City. We need your expertise to stop those attacks. You know he won't rest until Star One and Tycho City have been destroyed. We can't allow that to happen!"

Not knowing what to say, General Karver allowed himself to be led to a waiting vehicle and whisked off to the two waiting shuttles. He knew that Tim was right. Once the cape was gone, Senator Farley would try to destroy Star One and Tycho City. By destroying the cape, he was only delaying that attempt.

"We will be taking two separate shuttles," McPhryson said as the vehicle neared the two towering shuttles. "Jane and I will be on one and you will be on the other. With all the interceptor missiles being launched at our shuttles, at least one of the shuttles should get through. If we don't see each other again general, it's been a privilege to serve our country with you. President Kateland would have been proud!"

General Karver was escorted quickly to the nearest shuttle and taken to the top. As the elevator climbed, he had a good view of the cape. Everywhere the remaining cape personnel were in the process of evacuating the area. Numerous vehicles were leaving the cape and proceeding south way from the fighting.

General Karver knew that, within minutes, the only people left would be in launch control and the security people still guarding the immediate perimeter. In moments, he was being buckled into an acceleration couch directly behind the shuttle's commander and pilot.

"Welcome aboard general," the shuttle's commander said turning around slightly in her seat to smile at General Karver. "We will be taking off shortly, hang on because with all the missile fire, this could be a bumpy ride."

General Karver watched the main view screen in silence as it showed the other shuttle preparing to launch first. He saw the main engines ignite followed seconds later by the two SRBs, as Karver watched the other shuttle slowly rose above the tower on a pillar of flame.

"Our turn is next," the pilot said flipping several switches.

Thirty seconds later, General Karver felt the engines of the shuttle ignite and the increased pressure pushed him back into his acceleration couch. A low rumble filled the cabin as the engines gulped fuel and pushed the shuttle skyward. As the shuttle rose toward safety, on the ground specially placed demolition charges began to explode destroying years of work and billions of dollars worth of irreplaceable equipment.

The massive shuttle launch platforms collapsed as carefully placed charges brought them down in piles of useless twisted rubble. Huge explosions rolled across the cape as fuel, and unused SRBS exploded in clouds of fury scattering debris for miles. In a few seconds, the work of decades had been reduced to burning rubble and fiery ashes. An enormous pall of dark gray smoke rose from the cape covering the countryside causing a brief lull in the fighting as everyone realized its significance.

From launch control, Colonel Wilmington looked out across the cape. He had pressed the detonator buttons that had caused the destruction. With satisfaction, he knew that he had carried out the general's last order. Everywhere there were fires and twisted wreckage. Looking up into the sky, he gazed at the two shuttles that were climbing away to safety on pillars of fire.

High in the sky, two blinding arrows climbed slowly towards space fighting their way towards safety. On the ground, fighting came to a sudden stop as insurgents and defenders alike turned to watch the two ascending shuttles trying to escape. Defenders felt immense relief that this was the end and the shuttles had safely gotten away. Insurgents felt angry that they had failed to stop the final launches.

A squadron of insurgent aircraft patrolling out over the ocean, kicked in their after burners and climbed high in pursuit of the accelerating defenseless shuttles. They had been waiting for this moment. Since these were the last shuttles, they would have high priority targets on them trying to escape. Senator Farley had saved these fighters for just this moment. He didn't want Jane Kinsey, Tim McPhryson, and General Karver to escape.

Defensive missile fire arrowed up from the remaining launchers on the outer perimeter of the cape trying to knock the planes out of the sky before they could launch their deadly cargos. Several of the planes were hit and vanished in exploding fireballs, but the survivors launched their deadly interceptor missiles at the distantly climbing shuttles.

From the ground, the remaining air defenses launched all their available missile interceptors trying desperately to defend the rising shuttles from their impending doom. High-speed interceptor missiles arrowed up into the smoke filled sky targeting the inbound missiles. Seven fiery explosions high in the air marked their limited success, but two of the insurgent interceptors darted through the defensive missile fire to strike one of the rising shuttles.

Both missiles penetrated the main fuel tank and then detonated. A colossal explosion and fireball blew the attached shuttle into a thousand pieces. An expanding fireball seconds later was all that marked the shuttle's quick demise. Tim McPhryson and Jane Kinsey never knew what killed them. It had been sudden and decisive.

General Karver stared at the main view screen, which showed the bright fireball, which only moments before had been a United States space shuttle. He felt shock knowing that he had lost two more close friends. There had been so much death since the advent of the neutron star. General Karver closed his eyes and said a quick prayer for his fallen comrades.

The two pilots were shaken by the destruction of the other shuttle, but their radar was clear of any more of the dangerous missiles. They would get away free, but both knew that it could have been their shuttle that had been destroyed just as easily.

General Karver opened his eyes. He felt remorse and anger at the deaths of his friends. However, their deaths would not be in vain, both had died for something they had believed in. Someday, Senator Farley would be made to pay, and General Karver would see to it that Star One survived to extract that revenge.

On the ground, Colonel Wilmington watched as the wreckage of the destroyed shuttle rained down upon the cape and the nearby ocean. The operations officer in mission control had already told him which shuttle had been hit.

Over the radio, he could hear General Mann ordering a cessation of all fighting and an immediate surrender of his troops. The fighting here and around the cape was over, but Colonel Wilmington couldn't help wondering what was next. He looked up at the now distant shuttle barely visible through the smoke that lay over the cape. General Karver had survived, and Colonel Wilmington strongly suspected that Senator Farley hadn't heard the last from the general.

On board Star One, Steve and Christy stared aghast at the fireball, which marked a shuttle explosion low in Earth's atmosphere. They had been using the spy satellites to monitor the fighting around the cape. They had both intently watched the shuttle launches and the destruction of the cape.

"Tim and Jane both," breathed Christy fighting back tears. She had known both quite well, and Jane Kinsey and she had been friends for years. "They didn't deserve to die like this. Not after everything they have been through."

"The other shuttle is up safely and out of immediate range of their missiles. General Karver at least survived," replied Steve feeling the deep loss.

Steve was glad the general had survived. He could use the general's guidance as well as his help in defending Star One. The world they now lived in had gotten even more dangerous today.

Steve had known Jane for a long time. She had supported his efforts for years to get Star One built. Tim had always been someone that Steve could count on whenever he needed a favor. Now both had died in that fiery fireball above the cape.

"The cape launch facilities are destroyed," confirmed Teela checking the spy satellites, which she now controlled. "Fighting around the cape has stopped except for a few isolated pockets. General Mann has surrendered his forces to the rebels as General Karver ordered. All incoming shuttles are currently on safe flight trajectories."

"I'm glad the general escaped," Captain Gerald said walking over from the weapons station. "If we are attacked up here, he could be very useful. His knowledge of the weapons that could be used against us and his experience could be invaluable."

"Rest assured Captain Gerald," Steve replied ominously. "Senator Farley will do everything in his power to destroy us. It will take everything the general, you, and all the rest of us can do to survive the next few months."

"Christy, I want to have a department head meeting in two hours in the main conference room. Teela, continue to monitor the situation down below. Captain Gerald, I want you at the meeting to report on our defensive preparations," ordered Steve standing up.

Moments later, Steve left Main Control and retired to his office. Sitting down, he poured himself a glass of ice water. Leaning back with eyes closed, he thought about the many times that Jane and Tim had helped to bail out Star One and keep it safe from Senator Farley. It was a tragedy that neither would ever have the opportunity to see what they had helped to build up close.

Opening his eyes, he let out a deep breath and took a long drink of the cold water. Taking out a note pad, he began going over what he needed to cover in the staff meeting. They had a lot of planning that needed to be done, especially if the station was to survive.

Christy was still feeling numb from the sudden destruction of the shuttle and the demolition of the cape. She understood why the cape facilities had to be destroyed, but it still didn't make her feel any better. They were now completely and totally cut off from Earth. Standing up, she walked over to Margaret's station to speak with her. She just needed someone to talk to for a few minutes while she tried to make sense of everything that had happened.

The conference room filled rapidly as the department heads and senior officers filed in and took their places expectantly. Everyone was familiar with what had been occurring on Earth, and some already knew about the tragedy that had occurred earlier that afternoon. In a few quick minutes, the room was full and unusually quiet. The normal banter between the department heads was missing. Everyone looked nervous and unsure of themselves.

Steve stood up and looked at the concerned and unsure faces of his friends and fellow crewmembers of Star One. This was a good group of people. However, could they deal with their new situation? They were now totally cut off from Earth and on their own.

"As all of you have probably heard, the cape fell a few hours ago. As of right now, we have no support on Earth at all," Steve said looking around at the expectant group of faces.

The group was silent listening intently. "Also, I am sad to inform you that Jane Kinsey and Tim McPhryson were both killed when their shuttle was struck by several insurgent missiles which broke through our air defense," continued Steve trying to keep his voice steady.

"God, Jane and Tim both!" one of the department heads uttered in shock. "How could that happen?"

"The insurgents had a squadron of jet fighters just off shore waiting for us to launch," Steve spoke with a poignant look on his face. "Our defensive missile fire was overwhelmed, and two missiles broke through. The shuttle was destroyed instantly."

"Their deaths were instantaneous," Christy added with a pained look upon her face. "I doubt if they even knew the shuttle had been hit. The second shuttle, with General Karver on board, escaped and is presently in route to Star One. We currently have six shuttles in transit to us with supplies and people on board. There will be no more."

"We are on our own," Steve said looking around the group. There will be no more help from Earth."

"We still have Tycho City," Ted Dryson commented. "We can still get raw material from their mass driver."

"It's just us and Tycho City now," Julie spoke nodding her head. She had felt vastly relieved knowing that John's shuttle had made it, and he was on his way safely back to Star One. "At least we're not completely alone."

"We knew this would happen eventually," Steve spoke trying to sound as calm as possible. "At our latest count and including the people on the inbound shuttles, we will have 3,824 people here on Star One and another 8,200 or so safely on the Moon at Tycho City."

"Can we handle that many people?" Julie asked with concern in her voice. "We have made a lot of improvements in the ecological habitats, but I'm not sure they can handle that many people. It will be stretching our food and oxygen supplies."

"Shouldn't be a problem Julie," spoke up Doctor Wruggi. "We still need another couple of weeks, but we will have around 1,200 of those people in deep sleep. With the help of Captain Gerald's marines, the last of the deep sleep chambers are nearly ready."

"We already have 620 people in deep sleep," Steve reminded everyone. "We will be a little crowded for the next few weeks until the rest of the chambers are ready, but we will manage."

"What about Tycho City," Jarl Stoler asked. "We need that mass driver operating."

"I have spoken to Mase Colton in the past hour, and they are busy shoring up the defenses around Tycho and digging themselves in deep below the surface," added Steve wanting everyone to understand the seriousness of their current situation. "The mass driver will be well protected."

"The only problem is, we are between the Earth and the Moon," Ted Dryson commented worriedly. "Any attack on the Moon can't be made until we are eliminated."

"Mase and I agree with that," replied Steve nodding his head. "We feel that the main danger of attack will be against us here on Star One. We can't see them moving against the Moon unless we are eliminated first. At the moment, Senator Farley has no major launch platforms or shuttles left that can be used to mount a serious attack against us. We are safe for the time being."

"What about missile attacks?" Martain Blackwater asked worriedly. "They may not be able to mount a manned attack, but there are still a lot of unused missiles down below, thousands of them."

"That is the immediate danger," admitted Steve nodding his head in agreement. "While it is true that they can't launch a shuttle against us. There are some rockets, which could be modified for an attack. However, it will take a lot of effort on the insurgent's part to make a successful attack feasible. I'll have Captain Gerald explain the steps we have taken to protect the station from missile attack." Nodding towards Captain Gerald, Steve sat back down.

Captain Gerald stood up and looked around the room at the attentive faces. In the past few months, he had made a point of meeting and introducing himself to as many of the people on Star One as he could, particularly the different department heads. He knew that, in an emergency, it was essential for these people to be able to trust him, and not question his decisions.

"As most of you know, we have installed ten rail guns on the outer rim of Star One's main wheel. These rail guns are powered by the station's nuclear fusion reactor and are capable of destroying an incoming missile as far as 25,000 miles away. The rail guns are made of Luxen and are capable of firing a projectile round once a minute if necessary."

"Are these rounds explosive?" asked one of the other department heads with concern in his voice.

"No, a rail gun uses the velocity of the round to destroy its target," Captain Gerald explained. "It uses magnetic fields to accelerate the

108

round to very high speeds, which allows the round to penetrate and destroy its target."

"A range of 25,000 miles should give us plenty of time to take out inbound targets," Lieutenant Commander Todd Williams said. "They are not our only weapon of defense either."

"This gives us the ability to destroy ten inbound targets per minute if needed," continued Captain Gerald nodding his head. "On the upper wheel, we have installed two interceptor missile launching platforms for Black Knight missiles. We have also installed one missile launching platform on the Space Platform."

"Missiles!" exclaimed one of the women department heads. This was something she hadn't heard about. "What kind of missiles?"

These are smart missiles fourteen feet long with an effective range of slightly over 1,000 miles. Once these missiles have acquired a target, they will home in on that target and destroy it regardless of any defensive maneuvering the target may do. Each launching platform is capable of firing six missiles each. We have a large supply of Black Knight missiles, and we feel that our defensive missiles can take out anything that gets through our rail gun defenses. The defensive weapons console in Main Control is manned around the clock, and we feel certain that we can intercept any threat aimed at us."

Captain Gerald sat back down, and Steve stood back up. "I know we didn't get all the supplies up we had hoped for. Even so, we did manage to get the last parts for the new fusion reactor for the Space Platform. Also, everything on our essential lists, plus a lot on our reserve lists. Dryson and Stoler, along with a number of marine specialists and our own people are working around the clock to complete installation of the new fusion reactor on the platform."

"We should have it completed in less then two more weeks," Lieutenant Commander Williams added from his spot to Steve's left. "Once it's installed, we will have artificial gravity and can begin installing the ion boosters we have planned for the Space Platform."

"That will give us plenty of power for the Space Platform and the material processing plants," Steve added. "We will be receiving a lot of raw material from the mass driver on the Moon. We still have a lot of Luxen we need to produce."

"Installation of the reactor has been proceeding smoothly, and many of the parts were already assembled when we received them. General Karver's people on the ground really helped us out a lot there," reported Todd.

"Excellent," replied Steve. He would feel a lot better when that fusion reactor was installed and operating.

"Teela will you give us a quick run down on the situation Earth side," Steve said looking over at the AI.

Teela stood up and calmly looked around the room. Everyone was used to seeing her dressed in her regulation Star One uniform. Todd smiled warmly at her, and Teela could feel her cheeks flushing slightly. Sometimes she wondered if she shouldn't tone down the programs that helped show her emotions. They could be embarrassing at the most awkward moments.

"Currently Senator Farley controls the entire United States, plus parts of Northern Mexico and all of Canada," she reported. "Only two nuclear weapons were used in the U.S. and those were low yield tactical weapons against the military launch centers."

"I still can't believe Senator Farley used nukes," Ted Dryson said shaking his head in disbelief. "The man must be mad."

"We estimate that over two million Americans have been killed in the fighting and rioting that spread across the country," Teela continued quickly checking the latest casualty figures.

"Two million," Andre said shaking his head sadly. "So many wasted lives."

"Senator Farley has a firm grip on everything his forces control and has established a military government with him at its head to control the United States as well as the territory in Mexico and Canada the insurgents have taken over," Teela continued. "No one dares to challenge him, if they do they disappear."

"Megalomania," Doctor Blackwater commented. "He has all the classic symptoms. Commander don't underestimate this man. He is capable of almost anything!"

"We won't doctor," Steve replied with a glint in his eyes "We know what type of man we are dealing with. Go ahead with your report Teela."

"For the last several days, he has been broadcasting constant reports that the threat from the neutron star was totally fabricated by the previous administration. He also says that they have found collaborating proof in secret files in Washington that he will be releasing shortly. The public seems to be buying it. Every time someone, who used to have authority, questions it, they disappear rather quickly."

110

Everyone in the room looked shocked at what they knew must be happening back down on Earth. Under Senator Farley, Freedom of Speech and many of the other basic freedoms everyone had taken for granted for generations would be gone. Senator Farley would strictly control what news and information the public would receive.

"But surely with all the information his people found, he has to know the truth about the neutron star," interrupted Julie Gray looking around the room. "I mean how much more evidence does he need? There are countless scientists on Earth that understand what's happening."

"I don't believe the man will ever accept the reality of the neutron star, even when he can see it plainly in the sky above him, and the Earth begins to die," Martain Blackwater stated sadly. "It's part of his paranoia."

"Why's that?" asked Steve curious. He wanted to know everything he could about Senator Farley.

Steve had found it hard to believe that Senator Farley could continue to refute all the hard evidence they had. Steve had always thought that, at some point, even Senator Farley would have to admit that the neutron star was real and a serious threat.

"The man is suffering from a prosecution psychosis," began Martain Blackwater looking at Steve. "He has been so fervently against the space program, Star One, and everything that it has stood for that he saw the neutron star as a personal threat to his career. He has blinded himself in the belief that it's a fraud and nothing anyone can say will ever convince him otherwise, until possibly at the very end, and I do mean the very end. Even mad men at times become sane when they are faced with imminent death."

"What about the rest of the world," Jennifer asked. "Is there no one that we can turn to for help?"

"All of Europe is currently involved in what the twentieth century would call ethnic cleansing," replied Teela trying to keep the disgust out of her voice. "After the nuclear attack, many governments, which were already weak, fell. The infrastructure of Europe has largely been destroyed. Many of the great cities have been looted, and rioters have burned down large areas. Africa is currently engaged in a series of border wars that show no signs of stopping."

"What about China and Russia?" Stoler asked. "With the size of their armies, particularly China I can't see civil unrest taking them down."

111

"China and Russia are largely intact," Teela responded. "News reports and spy satellite data indicates large troop movements around their adjoining borders. Both have been making threats for weeks toward each other. The threat of the neutron star and the wars spreading close to their borders has brought back the communist party in Russia with a vengeance. War will probably break out there at any time."

"Are there any safe areas?" asked Julie shaking her head at everything that was going on down on Earth.

"The only safe areas currently seem to be Japan, Australia, and perhaps South Africa, but they dare not offer us any help," Teela replied. "Senator Farley has been contacting all the surviving world governments and making it very clear that Star One and Tycho City are off limits." Teela stopped sitting back down. She knew that her report had not contained any good news.

"We are on our own then," Steve said flatly. He had expected this. "I have all the confidence in the world in each and every one of you. We will continue to receive raw material from Tycho City for our processing plants. The Fuel Storage Facility is nearly complete, and we have the FarQuest mission that must be monitored."

Steve opened up a large folder in front of him. "I want to spend some time going over each department and where we currently stand. Julie lets begin with yours."

For the next several hours, the group discussed Star One's current condition and made plans to cover future operations. Much of the conversation was extremely detailed with Teela helping to furnish each department head with needed information.

Later that evening, Christy paused hesitantly outside Steve's door to his quarters. Then straightening her shoulders, she placed her hand on the touch pad. Almost instantly, Steve was standing before her with a surprised look on his face. "I gave up on you coming to my place," she said demurely "Aren't you going to ask me in?"

Taking Christy's hand, he pulled her into his apartment and they were soon locked in a hot, passionate embrace. It would be a quite a while before she returned to her quarters that night. However, they would both feel extremely rested the next morning. For a little while, they would be able to forget about the new, harsh reality that Star One was now in.

# Chapter Seven

Senator Farley gazed in unbridled anticipation at the large view screen in the underground command center. The screen showed a powerful missile rising into the air on a pillar of fire. On top of the missile was a warhead containing multiple nuclear weapons. "Go damn it," he muttered watching the rising missile. "So you thought you could escape me General Karver, well this is my answer to you and Steve Larson."

"The missile is on course," the general in charge reported after checking a data screen.

"What about the other missiles?" Farley demanded his dark eyes finding the general.

"All twelve are launched and are on target," the general replied carefully. "Star One and the Space Platform will both be history by this time tomorrow."

Senator Farley sat back down in his cushioned chair lighting up a cigar. "They better be," he warned his dark eyes glaring at the general.

The general almost reminded the Senator that smoking was not allowed in the underground command center. However, thinking better of it, he decided it might be best to let this particular infraction slide. He drew a deep breath gazing at several small screens that showed some of the other missiles. The general was markedly relieved that all twelve missiles had launched successfully. If even one had failed, there was no doubt in the general's mind that Senator Farley would have gone mad with anger.

Senator Farley took a deep draw on the cigar and then blew the smoke out watching it slowly rise toward the ceiling. "You guaranteed me that these missiles would do the job general," Senator Farley reminded the general in a sharp voice. "Don't disappoint me."

The general in command listened quietly. He was use to the Senator's tirades. For weeks, military technicians had been working on the missiles modifying them for this attack on Star One and the Space Platform. Senator Farley had made it abundantly clear to the general that he wanted Star One and the Space Platform annihilated. But more importantly than that, he wanted General Karver and Steve Larson dead!

General Karver, Steve, Christy, and Captain Gerald were all in Main Control. Lieutenant Commander Kevin Anderson had hastily summoned them when Teela had detected missile launches from the surface of the Earth. They were waiting tensely for the final confirmation reports from the Earth spy satellites, which Teela still controlled. Numerous attempts had been made to retake command of the spy satellites, but Teela had easily blocked them all. No computer on Earth could come close to matching Teela's current abilities.

"It's confirmed sir," Teela said materializing in her normal spot at Steve's side. Her rich blue eyes gazed at the commander, and her dark black hair lay against her shoulders. Not a strand was out of place.

"So they have finally launched against us," Steve spoke sharply his eyes focusing on Teela. He heard Christy take a deep breath behind him.

"I was hoping they wouldn't actually do this," Christy sighed. "Why couldn't they just leave us alone?"

"Senator Farley wants us all dead," General Karver said looking over at Christy. "We represent the only resistance to his rule, and my being here doesn't help matters either."

"From the spy satellites and our own detection instruments we have confirmed twelve launches from the United States within the last twenty minutes," Teela spoke with a slight nod. "From the scans, the missiles are all modified long range missiles, and they are all on trajectories to intercept us here at Star One!"

"Can you show us one of the missiles up close?" General Karver asked with concern evident in his normally deep voice. He had been expecting this attack for some time now. He was curious to see which missiles Farley was using for this attack.

"Yes sir," Teela replied respectfully. Over the past several weeks, she had discovered that General Karver was highly professional and business like, and even treated her courteously. "Several of the spy satellites picked up some excellent close up shots of the missiles on their way up. I'll project their images on the main view screen."

A large two-stage missile was depicted rising up into the sky. A plume of fire and smoke trailed for miles behind the rapidly rising missile tying it to the ground far below. It continued to rise as both boosters burned out and fell behind until only the warhead and a small course correction booster remained. Teela magnified the deadly warhead until it swelled to fill the entire screen.

"A Hammer Head 2 warhead," Captain Gerald stated, sharply drawing in his breath and his eyes widening as he recognized the warhead on top of the missile. "It contains six 150 kiloton nuclear warheads which can be independently targeted. They're the most advanced weapon in the U.S. arsenal. Test results from trial launches showed 100 percent accuracy in the independent targeting systems."

"One single warhead has enough firepower to incinerate this station completely," added General Karver taking his eyes off the screen and addressing Steve. We can't risk any of those warheads coming anywhere near the station or the Space Platform. Who ever is in charge down there certainly picked the right weapon for the job."

"That's 72 warheads coming at us," spoke Steve frowning. Senator Farley must really want them dead. In normal circumstances, this would be over kill. "General what would you recommend?"

"These missiles were designed to take out hardened defensive installations and enemy military targets," replied General Karver gazing back at the large view screen and the deadly missile warhead being displayed."

"Each warhead has ten times the destructive power of the Hiroshima bomb," commented Captain Gerald looking over at General Karver. "If the controllers back down on Earth are smart, they will MIRV the warheads early. That would give them a better possibility of over loading our defensive envelope."

"What are the chances that they don't know how well Star One is defended? They may not know about the new missile platforms or the rail guns," Christy said looking at the lethal warhead still up on the screen. She felt a cold shiver run across her back. Those missiles were aimed at destroying Star One and the Space Platform.

"They can't know much about what we have done," Captain Gerald replied his eyes turning to Christy. "The Black Knight missiles and even the new Luxen rail guns were top secret."

Christy knew that Senator Farley must have pushed his military extremely hard to launch a strike against Star One so quickly after destroying the two military launch facilities and capturing the cape. Fortunately, General Karver had ensured that the cape was useless to Senator Farley. The demolition charges he had set had taken care of that. Spy satellites had confirmed the devastating destruction wrought by the demolition charges. It looked as if a war had been fought across the cape.

115

"The size of this attack indicates that they must feel the station isn't totally defenseless," Steve said indicating the screens, which were currently tracking the twelve inbound missiles. "General Karver, Captain Gerald what are your recommendations?"

"They may suspect that we have been able to put together some type of defense," General Karver said crossing his arms. "If anyone with any real intelligence is still in charge down there, he won't take any chances. That's probably why they launched twelve missiles. They can't know about the Black Knight interceptors. They were one of our most closely kept defense secrets. The few people that did know are dead. They were killed when the military launch sites were taken out with the nukes."

"They may suspect that we have put together some type of defense, but nothing that could stop this type of attack," suggested Steve. "That may be an advantage for us."

"That would be my assessment," General Karver replied. "That's why the over kill with the missiles they launched. They probably believe we can take out one or two, but not all of them."

"They can't know about the rail guns either," added Captain Gerald as he listened to General Karver. "Everyone still thought they were in the design stage waiting for the correct power source."

Pausing, the general looked around Main Control. The crew was all at their posts and doing their jobs. They were all very professional. Even in this situation with a dozen nuclear armed missiles coming toward them. General Karver was genuinely impressed by the quality of people that Steve had on the station.

"We have an advantage in the fact that they probably don't know how well we can defend ourselves," Steve commented. "They can't know that we have armed two of our shuttles either."

"Of course if Senator Farley is commanding this operation, he may just be trying for over kill," General Karver spoke his eyes returning to look at Steve. "He may not be listening to his military people. He may be wanting to make an example out of us for the rest of the world."

"Senator Farley has moved into the White House," commented Teela putting a picture of it up on the main screen. "Over the last several days, there has been a lot of encrypted communication between the White House and the missile launch facilities."

"I just don't understand how anyone can feel the type of hate that Senator Farley does," Christy said shaking her head with an angry glint in her eyes. "Why is he so bent on destroying us?"

"We are a symbol," replied Steve staring at the White House on the screen. He noticed that all signs of the recent fighting had been cleaned up. "We are a constant reminder that he does not rule and control everything."

"He has shown a definite lack of faith in anything the military or other people have tried to tell him in recent weeks," General Karver continued. "Even in the attack on the cape, he wasted a lot of lives trying to break through our lines."

The general had spent a lot of time with Teela and Captain Gerald using the orbiting spy satellites to keep an eye on what was going on down on Earth. There was very little that had escaped their notice over the past two weeks as they watched developments on the ground.

The civilians, who had expected things to change once the old government was overthrown, still found martial law in effect. The excuse being used now was to protect the population from terrorist attacks from renegade military units still loyal to the old government. What the people were not being told was that there were no renegade military units.

"So you think he is running this show, and not his military people?" Steve asked surprised. He felt Christy's hand touch his shoulder. She was listening intently to what General Karver was saying.

"That could give us a distinct advantage," General Karver said looking over at Captain Gerald. "I recommend that we launch the two shuttles that we have armed with Black Knight interceptors immediately. We can intercept and destroy most if not all of these missiles before they become a threat to us."

"Captain Gerald, are the shuttles ready for this type of action?" Steve asked. He knew that Lieutenant Commander Williams and Captain Gerald had been working extremely hard on the two shuttles trying to get them ready for this.

"Yes sir," replied Captain Gerald nodding his head in affirmation. "We can be ready to launch within two hours. I just need to let Lieutenant Commander Williams know to get the two shuttles prepped."

"If these missiles have a chance to MIRV, we will be dealing with 72 separate targets that will need to be destroyed," General Karver warned. "By launching the shuttles back toward Earth, if Senator Farley is controlling this attack, he may believe that it's only refugees trying to escape the station's destruction. He may believe that Star One is defenseless. It may get him to hold off MIRVing the missiles until it's too late."

"We've also modified the shuttles over the past several weeks where they can now carry eight Black Knight interceptors," Captain Gerald informed them. Teela had worked closely with them in the design modification. "Each missile can be targeted separately from the fire control computers we have installed in the two shuttles."

"Let's do it then," ordered Steve knowing it was their best option. "I want to destroy as many of those missiles as far away from the station as possible. Perhaps in all the confusion the shuttles can make their return safely."

"We will hold the rail guns back in reserve," General Karver said. "We will use them if needed, but I think it would be wise not to reveal all the cards we are holding too quickly."

Two hours later, on the Space Platform, John Gray was running quickly through his prelaunch check along with his co-pilot Alvin Strong. Both of the defensive shuttles had been recently equipped with new long burning boosters similar to those that had been used on the FarQuest. Both shuttles were currently equipped with two of the new boosters. With liberal use of the boosters, it would give them the ability to get to their targets as quickly as possible. Much faster than what the Earth military expected.

"Twelve nuclear missiles," Strong said frowning. "I guess the people down on Earth genuinely don't like us anymore."

"Senator Farley has made us into the enemy," replied John reaching up and turning on two computer screens.

John watched as data began to appear. He had told Julie what was happening and that he would be flying one of the two shuttles. She hadn't liked hearing that; she didn't care to see John putting himself in danger.

"I'm glad we armed these shuttles,' Strong said looking back at the two marines sitting at the missile interceptor console behind them.

Turning, John looked at Corporal Cathy Cooper who operated the targeting missile fire control console that had been added to the shuttle. The lithe red head, in her marine uniform, was finishing her preflight check confirming the status of the ship's armaments. Another marine sat next to her assisting with the computers.

"Black Knights check out okay sir," she reported smartly, tossing her head back and gazing at John. "Let's knock some of those bastards out of space!"

Smiling, John nodded then speaking into his com unit. "This is Lexington; we are ready for immediate launch."

"Confirmed Lexington," Lieutenant Commander William's voice came back over the com system. "Good luck and good hunting, you are cleared for launch."

John diligently activated the shuttle's maneuvering RCS thrusters and moved the shuttle up and away from the Space Platform. From all the added weight the Lexington now carried, it maneuvered more sluggishly than what he was used to. John made several adjustments increasing power to the lateral thrusters bringing the ship smoothly around. On the shuttle's main screen, the platform gradually grew smaller as John moved the Lexington to a safe distance.

"Maneuvers like a damn whale," John mumbled as he brought the shuttle around to her launch position.

"It's all the extra weight," Strong replied as he checked the boosters.

"Course entered on the flight computer," reported Strong flipping a row of switches. "Ready for booster firing."

"Confirmed," replied John making sure the straps across his chest were secure. "Stand by for booster ignition."

John's thumb pressed the large red booster firing button. The flight computer took over lighting the two powerful rocket boosters. John felt himself pressed back into his acceleration couch as two gravities of acceleration built up quickly and the shuttle rapidly accelerated away from the Space Platform.

The twin boosters burned brilliantly leaving a dim gaseous trail behind them. A gentle vibration could be felt in the shuttle as the shuttle's speed rapidly increased. For six minutes, the boosters burned until half their fuel was expended and then they shut down. The shuttle was suddenly quiet, as it rushed down toward Earth and the deadly flock of missiles waiting in the darkness.

"We are in the groove," Strong said checking out their trajectory on the flight computer. "Speed is at 16,000 miles per hour. Estimate contact with targets in eight hours, forty-two minutes."

"Very good," replied John loosening his safety harness and looking back to check on Corporal Cooper. She was looking slightly pale and shaken from the acceleration. "You'll get used to it," John said giving her the thumbs up sign and an encouraging smile. The other marine seemed to be okay.

Cooper nodded forcing a wane smile on her face as she checked her console for any problems caused by the launch. All eight Black Knight missiles showed in the green.

Behind them, the second shuttle launched, accelerating rapidly to take up a position slightly behind and to port of the Lexington. The Pericles and the Lexington would attack simultaneously trying to eliminate as many incoming missiles as possible. John hoped that their controllers on Earth wouldn't realize what was happening until too late. With any luck, the shuttles would eliminate the threat to Star One before the people back on Earth knew what had happened.

Down on Earth, Senator Harlen Farley leaned back in his large deeply cushioned chair. He was in a heavily shielded underground bunker far beneath the Pentagon. He stared wolfishly at the missiles being tracked on the big screen, which covered an entire wall. Technicians were busy monitoring the missile's progress and communicating with the missile tracking stations.

In the past several weeks, he had used his control of the military to gain a firm hold on the country along with the Northern part of Mexico and all of Canada. No one dared resist him, especially with the threat of nuclear destruction hanging over their heads. Farley had made it abundantly plain to the other nations of the world that he would not hesitate to use nuclear weapons against anyone that might oppose him. As long as they left him alone, he would leave them alone. He now had more power than any other President did in history.

Using new evidence from some of the scientists that he controlled, they had presented enough data in the past several weeks to discredit the neutron star rumor. Senator Farley still found it laughable how intelligent people could have fallen for such a ruse. A neutron star, you would have thought that Steve Larson and the former space happy government could have come up with something more believable.

His people had presented enough evidence to the United Nations to disprove that ridiculous story. The object detected by the Farside array was nothing more than a large distant comet. The Third World President of that body had confirmed that the evidence presented by Senator Farley's people was true. The President of the U.N. had stated that other scientists in other countries had confirmed that the neutron star story was a farce. Senator Farley had thoroughly discredited the former President and the scientists and astronomers on Star One and at the Farside array.

There were still rumors being spread on the internet that the neutron star was real. Several reputable astronomers even claimed that a black hole had been detected approaching with the neutron star. Anytime these stories popped up they were quickly downplayed or discredited by Senator Farley's people.

Now with these powerful missiles, his military leaders promised him, they would obliterate Star One. Then a few weeks from now, when the rest of the missiles had been modified, they would take out Tycho City as well.

In a little over sixteen hours, Steve Larson and General Karver would be dead. Feeling confident that everything was going his way, Farley took a long draw on the expensive Cuban cigar he held in his right hand. Glancing at the cigar, Senator Farley reminded himself to have one of his aides order several more boxes. These were the best damn cigars he had ever smoked!

The Senator had been extremely disappointed several weeks earlier when General Karver had escaped the cape in the last shuttle. He had wanted to see the general die. He could still picture, with barely controlled glee, the shuttle explosion and the resulting fireball that had taken out Jane Kinsey and Tim McPhryson. The fighter pilot that had launched the missiles had been personally awarded in a special ceremony held at the White House by Senator Farley.

"Senator Farley," a stern faced general said walking up to him. "We have detected two shuttle launches that may be aimed to intercept our missiles. We would like to MIRV the warheads before interception to decrease any chance that they might be able to knock out some of our birds."

"What can those shuttles possibly do?" huffed Farley blowing smoke up into the air, and watching it drift upwards to be caught and drawn out by the room's ventilators. "Star One isn't armed, it never was. The only thing they can hope to do is ram our missiles with their priceless shuttles. I can't see them doing that."

"We don't know what type of weapons they might have shipped up there, especially from the two military launch centers," the general objected concerned knowing that his future rested on the success of this attack. "We have to assume that Star One is not totally defenseless."

121

"We questioned a lot of the cape survivors general," replied Farley becoming aggravated. He hated it when anyone questioned his decisions and authority. Why couldn't these people in the military just do as they were told?

"There were no weapons shipped from the cape, and we took out the two military launch centers with nukes. They didn't have time to get anything useful up to Star One," Farley said with a trace of arrogance in his voice. "They were concentrating on people and supplies."

"So we've been told," the general responded not convinced. "But we don't know for sure what General Karver might have sent them. I don't believe we should take the risk."

"With the suddenness of our original attack, they didn't have time to gather anything that could be made into a useful defensive weapon," insisted Farley turning angry eyes toward the general.

"But it still took us four weeks to take the cape," the general reminded the Senator. "A lot could have been done in those four weeks!"

The general knew with General Karver's outstanding military reputation that he should not be underestimated. If something could have been done, General Karver would have done it. By now, some type of defense had to be in place. He just wondered what it was and if these two shuttles might be part of it.

"I personally saw to it, while in Congress, that nothing that could be used as a weapon was ever sent up to that damn station!" Senator Farley replied in a louder voice beginning to express his anger at the general. "No general, they are defenseless, in a few more hours they will all be dead. Those shuttles probably contain refugees trying to escape to Earth before the station is vaporized by our missiles."

"Perhaps," the general replied still not sounding convinced. "I would still like to go ahead and MIRV the warheads."

"Not only that," Farley went on gazing sternly at the general. "You said earlier the later we waited to MIRV the missiles the more warheads would arrive dead center on target. I want Star One and their precious Space Platform annihilated!"

Pausing, Senator Farley drew in a deep breath. "Have people ready to seize whoever is in those shuttles when they land, I don't care where they come down at. I want everyone on board brought to me."

The general nodded not wanting to bring down Senator Farley's wrath. He had already watched too many good men and women die for

122

questioning the Senator's actions. Turning, he went back to his station ordering his people to track the two shuttles and let him know as soon as possible, where they might be landing. He still had a bad feeling about those two shuttles. He wished General Karver wasn't on Star One.

On Star One, the main subjects of Farley's anger watched hours later, as the shuttles and the missiles rapidly closed their range. So far, the missiles were still intact, and none had MIRVed releasing their deadly cargoes of nuclear warheads. They had maintained radio silence with the two shuttles so as not to give anyone listening on Earth any hint as to what was planned. Total surprise was essential.

"The two shuttles will be in weapon's range for only two minutes," commented Teela checking her calculations once again. "The missiles and the shuttles are closing on each other at over 25,000 miles per hour."

"Can the Black Knight missiles handle intercepts at that speed?" Steve asked with concern looking over at General Karver who had been pacing back and forth between the weapons console and Steve's command console. He had stopped several times to talk to Lieutenant Sandy Emerson at her weapons control station. This was a different type of warfare than what he was used to.

Every once in a while, General Karver would stop and talk with Captain Gerald who was standing watchfully behind Lieutenant Emerson. The minutes before a battle had always weighed heavily on the general's mind, especially when so much was at stake. He knew that Captain Gerald's people were the best that could be found. He had personally hand picked many of the men and women that were in Captain Gerald's unit.

"No problem," Karver replied confidently. "The Black Knights were our countries biggest military secret. With them, we felt we could knock down any incoming missile launched against us with impunity. In case of a nuclear war, they were to be our main defense. It was estimated that they could knock down nearly 90 percent of a saturated missile attack against the U.S. once they were deployed."

"Contact in three minutes," reported Teela looking over at Christy noting that her face was almost white.

Teela also felt tense. She had turned several of the Earth spy satellites outwards toward space to show the interception.

"It will be all right commander," Teela spoke quietly to Christy. "We will destroy the missiles."

"I know Teela," replied Christy trying to smile.

Christy knew Teela was trying to reassure her, and she appreciated it. But so much was at stake, they couldn't afford to miss a single missile. Christy also knew that Teela was keeping Julie informed as to what was happening. Christy could just imagine how worried Julie was about John.

Teela nodded and turned her attention back to the missiles. She was constantly running simulations on the intercept of the missiles by the shuttles.

-

John watched intently on the Lexington's radar screen, as the nuclear missiles came ever so much closer. In order to all arrive and strike Star One together, they were fairly well bunched up. Even in space that meant a distance of a mile or more between most of the on rushing missiles and their deadly cargos.

As the two shuttles drew within firing range, John felt tension and adrenaline flood his body. "Stand by for weapon's launch," John said firing the RCS thrusters to line the shuttle up with the on coming missiles.

Next to him, Alvin Strong used the ship's radar to paint each individual missile, transmitting the data back to Corporal Cooper's console. "Tracking looks good," he reported as he had solid contacts on all twelve of the missiles. "Let's hope this works."

John looked back at Corporal Cooper who was busy at her console assigning targets to the interceptors. John hoped that they would all still be alive in a few more minutes. There was a chance, a very remote chance that they could collide with one of the on coming missiles. If any of the warheads went off too close to the ship, the shuttle could be destroyed. They would launch first followed by Pericles two minutes later. Under his orders, everyone had donned their in-flight spacesuits as a safety precaution.

-

Down on Earth, Senator Farley watched with nervous excitement as the missiles and the shuttles neared one another. At any moment, he expected the shuttles to activate their thrusters and avoid the on coming missiles. He didn't think the pilots would risk colliding with one of them. Why hadn't they turned away from the on coming missiles already?

The general in charge watched the screens with a growing feeling of dread. He knew if the shuttles were going to evade the missiles, they should have already done so. There was no longer any doubt in his mind that General Karver had sent the shuttles to destroy the missiles. There was something definitely amiss here.

The general was tempted to go ahead and MIRV the warheads on his own authority. But if he did and he was wrong, Senator Farley would have him shot. Maybe it would be better if he could find some excuse to leave the underground command center briefly. Once outside, he could requisition a vehicle and flee. He glanced over at the exit wondering if he could step out without Senator Farley noticing.

-

"Launch at your discretion corporal," John spoke tightening his chest harness and looking up at the main view screen that showed the empty space between them and the distant Earth. Star One and Julie were waiting and watching far behind them.

Corporal Cooper watched as the nuclear missiles reached the Black Knight's extreme interception range. The Black Knights were smart missiles, fire and forget. They would seek out and destroy any target assigned to their tracking computers. Corporal Cooper waited a few seconds until she was satisfied that all the interceptors were targeted properly. She was confident the missiles would easily find their targets. Reaching up on her console, she flipped eight switches rapidly one after another.

From the outer wings of the shuttle, sleek black interceptor missiles blasted away on their powerful boosters. Small targeting computers made minor course corrections as the Black Knight interceptor missiles closed with their doomed targets. As each missile launched, the Lexington rocked slightly as the interceptors dropped away and dwindled rapidly from sight.

-

Down on Earth, Senator Farley sat up straighter in his chair when the tracking screen suddenly blossomed with eight new blips that appeared at the location of one of the shuttles and then raced off toward his missiles. "What the hell are those!" he demanded looking over at the general who had a horror-stricken look upon his face.

"Interceptors," the general groaned aloud knowing he was done for. "They're damn interceptors, and they have targeted our missiles. They are nearly invisible to radar; we are tracking their rocket flares."

-

The interceptors sped toward the nuclear missiles closing with their targets then exploding on contact in a bright fireball. Missile after missile was annihilated in fiery explosions as the interceptors met them head on.

On the main view screen, John watched as small bright explosions lit up space in front and to the side of the shuttle. He could picture the Black Knight warheads vaporizing the nuclear missiles spreading their debris across their path. He was already firing the RCS thrusters trying to move the shuttle away from the expanding debris field.

"We got some hits!" exclaimed Strong excitedly seeing the bursts of light on the screen. He turned his attention back to the radar trying to see how many missiles they had destroyed.

John knew he would have to watch the radar closely, even though the shuttle had a light coating of Luxen on its outer hull, a large piece of debris encountered at high speeds could still spell disaster.

"Six confirmed kills and one probable," reported Corporal Cooper checking her data sounding slightly disappointed. She had hoped for a kill from each interceptor. "One of the Black Knights suffered booster shut down too soon and did not reach its target."

"Good shooting corporal," John replied as he used a quick burst from the shuttle's main engine to steer them around several large pieces of debris. The RCS thrusters were not moving them into the clear fast enough. "If the Pericles does as well we should get them all."

Moments later, John watched as the Pericles launched her interceptors. More explosions littered space. Interceptors and nuclear missiles merged turning into brief, bright fireballs, which faded rapidly in the cold silent blackness of space. Unfortunately, there was too much debris from the earlier strike and not all the interceptors found their targets. Several hit large pieces of missile debris.

Down on Earth, Senator Farley's face was livid. He had already given the order for the general in charge to be taken outside and shot. The general had been dragged out protesting by Senator Farley's personal guards. He had left screaming curses at the Senator.

"How many missiles did we lose?" he demanded of the general who had replaced his former commander.

"Ten sir," the general replied tight lipped. He knew that he would have to walk a tight rope if he was to survive the next few hours. He didn't plan to repeat his predecessor's mistakes.

"How did they manage to destroy our missiles?" demanded Farley calming down some as he saw the last two missiles continue safely on past the shuttles that had attacked so viscously only minutes before. Most of his missiles had been destroyed, but two remained. Enough to finish off Star One and the Space Platform.

"It was rumored that General Karver had been involved in a special high tech project to design and build some high speed interceptor missiles, code named Black Knight," replied the general recalling the rumors he had heard about the program. "These missiles were to be used only in case of a massive missile attack against our country. No one could ever confirm that rumor. Other than for a few prototypes, the missiles were never supposed to have been built. They would have violated several missile treaties and the repercussions from building them would have been disastrous for our country."

"Evidently that didn't bother our dear general," Farley spat with anger in his eyes. "It's obvious that he had a few of them built and managed somehow to sneak them up to Star One."

"It won't matter sir. Once our missiles MIRV, they will have twelve separate warheads to track and destroy. With the reported range on the prototype Black Knights, they will never be able to destroy all the warheads in time. Some will get through," the general replied confidently.

The general knew that it would take only one warhead to obliterate Star One. He doubted if General Karver had any more of the Black Knight missiles. If he had, surely he would have used them. The general was certain that the missiles on the shuttles had been General Karver's big defensive play. Yes, the station would certainly be destroyed, that would ensure him a favorable position in Senator Farley's inner circle. If he played his cards just right, this could work out extremely well for him.

"They better general, let's just hope we don't have any more unpleasant surprises," warned Farley leaning back in his chair, closing his eyes, and rubbing his forehead.

The military had been such a disappointment to him. First at the cape and now here. He couldn't believe the total incompetence he was surrounded by. He had thought the American military was better trained.

Hours later on Star One, Steve watched as the missiles quickly closed the range. At 20,000 miles distance, the missiles MIRVed, and instead of two targets, there were now twelve.

"Missiles have MIRVed as expected," Teela reported. She looked at the screen depicting the twelve targets knowing that it would only take one to end her very short life.

"Coming up on extreme missile range," Lieutenant Emerson reported from her console, as the warheads began to cross the 10,000-mile marker. The Black Knights were good at 1,000 miles. They could launch now, but the Black Knights would run out of fuel before reaching their targets.

Lieutenant Emerson and two other marines currently controlled the station's defenses. General Karver and Captain Gerald stood directly behind the Lieutenant watching over everything.

"Projected impact time is T-minus forty minutes," Teela reported as she scanned the missiles with the station's radar and other scanning equipment. She felt nervous and frightened. These were feelings she didn't care for. She wished Todd were here in Main Control.

On the outer hull of the main rim, the two missile platforms swiveled and locked onto targets. Everything was done by computers. On the Space Platform, an additional missile platform turned to face the on coming missiles. Computers fed the targeting data to the missile targeting systems. At a signal from Lieutenant Emerson, the two weapons officers activated the platforms. Instantly twelve Black Knight missiles blasted from their protective missile tubes and hurtled away from the station.

"Black Knights launched," she reported as she attentively watched her screens. She was already feeding updated targeting data to the missile platform on the Space Platform.

General Karver watched the lieutenant closely. General Karver knew she was one hell of a marine to be able to handle herself so well in this situation.

"Interceptors on target and closing," Teela reported. "The warheads are not attempting to evade."

"They're only equipped with special fins, which can be used to adjust their trajectory in atmosphere," Captain Gerald reported. "In space they can't change course. That gives our missiles a chance to hit from this range."

Twenty minutes later, on the main screen, small brilliant fiery explosions lit up the space between the Earth and Star One signaling the destruction of some of the in coming warheads.

"Nine down," Lieutenant Emerson replied with a little disappointment in her voice. She had hoped to get all twelve, but the distance had been too great. "Range is closing, Space Platform interceptors ready to launch. Powering up rail guns in case one gets through."

They waited tensely as the inbound warheads closed. General Karver wanted to intercept these at the Black Knights optimum interception range of 1,000 miles. Finally the warheads came into range and General Karver nodded at Lieutenant Emerson. "Take them out Sandy."

On the outer rim of the main wheel, ten large rail guns powered up, and their targeting systems became active. The targeting systems located the inbound warheads and the rail guns swiveled until they were pointed at the approaching targets. Due to their location on the outer rim of Star One, only six of the rail guns were able to lock on their assigned targets.

"We have target lock with the rail guns," Lieutenant Emerson reported as data flowed across one of the screens on her console.

From the Space Platform, three more missiles blasted away, then twenty seconds later two more launched. This time Lieutenant Emerson planned to use the two follow up missiles to take out any stragglers that the first three might miss.

"Interceptors launched," Teela reported as she followed the interceptors with the station's radars and scanners.

Everyone in Main Control watched the view screen as the missiles closed on each other.

"Stand by with the rain guns," General Karver ordered with a grim face. "If any warheads get through fire at will."

"Two minutes to station impact," Teela voiced quietly. "My scanners show interceptors on target and closing."

Steve reached out and took Christy's hand squeezing it gently, his eyes glued to the main screen.

"Missile intercept," Teela reported as all eyes focused on the main view screen, which suddenly lit up with several small explosions.

"All targets destroyed," reported Lieutenant Emerson jubilantly allowing her emotions to surface. She felt physically and emotionally drained and let out a heavy sigh of relief.

"Good job lieutenant." General Karver said then nodding to Captain Gerald. "Your people preformed flawlessly, they are to be commended."

"Teela can you detect anything else that might be a threat to us?" asked Steve feeling relieved now that the missiles were destroyed.

"No commander," replied Teela checking the station's radars, scanning equipment, and the spy satellites. "All incoming targets have been destroyed, and the two shuttles are beginning to go around the Earth."

In another few hours, they too would be safe. Teela was keeping a special eye on the Lexington; Jennifer was close friends with Julie and John Gray. "We may have some small debris to worry about from the destroyed missiles, but there is nothing remaining that is large enough to harm the station."

"Power down the rain guns," General Karver ordered. "The danger is over for now."

Lieutenant Emerson reached forward and switched the rain guns back to standby.

"Great job everyone," Steve spoke aloud to the crew in Main Control. He also made a quick announcement over the station's com system letting everyone know that the threat was over.

Down on Earth, Senator Farley watched satisfyingly as the firing squad shot the latest general to fail him. At this rate, he would soon run out of generals, at least others could be promoted if necessary. Surely, somewhere there was someone in the military that could do the job he demanded.

He had raved and thrown chairs when the interceptor missiles had wiped out his last warheads. The cowardly general had tried to sneak out, but Farley had spotted him before he could escape. The imbeciles, it was unbelievable how inefficient the military was. They couldn't even complete one simple assignment.

General Karver and Steve Larson might have won this round, but he wasn't through with Star One. He would destroy the station if it was the last thing he did. Turning, he walked over to where his car awaited, behind him the members of the firing squad dragged the general's body off to be disposed of.

Later that evening, Steve and Christy were at Jensens waiting on Todd Williams. Steve had some ideas he wanted to go over, particularly after today's attack, with Todd. He also wanted to spend a little quality time with Christy. He felt relieved, especially since Teela had reported that the shuttles had made it safely around the Earth and were on their way back to Star One. Steve and Christy had just been seated when Todd came in and spotting them hurried over.

"Good evening everyone," Jensen said as he arrived at the table to check on his favorite customers. Will there be a fourth person joining you?" he asked looking at Todd expectantly.

"Ah," Todd began not sure what to say.

"It's all right Todd," Christy said smiling. "Teela you can make an appearance."

Steve looked at Christy slightly confused.

Christy knew of Todd and Teela's relationship and even approved of it. Teela and she had even discussed it some. Teela had been good for Todd. Christy suspected Teela was probably watching them right now anyway.

Teela materialized in the empty chair next to Todd and smiled nervously at the commander, confirming Christy's suspicions that she had been watching. Jensen nodded at Teela, he had gotten used to her sudden appearances. She was always complimentary about his restaurant and was now extremely well behaved.

"I think I'm missing something here," Steve muttered quietly where no one but Christy could hear him.

Christy kicked Steve lightly under the table saying quietly in return. "Don't worry about it, I'll explain later."

Jensen took their orders and returned to his kitchen leaving the four by themselves.

They sat quietly for a few minutes sipping some of the special wine that Jensen liked to serve his special customers. It was a comforting change just to be able to enjoy the relaxing atmosphere of the restaurant. Steve was surprised that Teela also had a glass of wine and seemed to be drinking from it. I'm obviously missing something here he thought, glancing over at Christy who had a restful smile on her face.

"Todd," Steve said noticing that Todd's eyes spent a lot of time looking at Teela, and he could swear that they were holding hands, but that was impossible, you couldn't touch Teela. However, her hand was clearly lying on top of his. Todd seemed to take it for granted as if it was not a big deal.

"I've been thinking about the maneuverability of Star One and the Space Platform," Steve continued his eyes focusing on Todd. "We have added a number of small ion thrusters to both to allow us to maintain station as the neutron star and black hole approach. We can even use them to move us farther away from the Earth if necessary. After today's attack, I feel it may be prudent for us to move both Star One and the Space Platform away from the Lagrange point as soon as possible. Does anybody have any suggestions or ideas?"

"Perhaps," Todd said taking his eyes off Teela for a moment. She was extremely sexy looking tonight with the black dress she had on, which dipped dangerously low in the front.

"Teela and I have run some simulations that might solve our problem. It would involve a lot of work, but it would give us the maneuverability we need," replied Todd looking first at Steve and then at Christy.

"What did you two have in mind?" asked Christy feeling curious. With Teela involved, they could have come up with almost anything.

"We both feel that Star One and the Space Platform are not maneuverable enough especially with the gravity forces that will soon be affecting us," Todd replied. "Even with the fuel in the Storage Facility augmenting our other station keeping thrusters we can not maintain our position indefinitely."

"The gravity stresses from the neutron star and the black hole will not allow us to maintain our position at the Lagrange point," affirmed Teela glancing at Todd in agreement.

"But what if we go ahead and move the station and the platform now?" Steve asked. "With the new ion thrusters we could do that."

"It would take awhile," replied Todd nodding. "Even with the new thrusters it would take days to put any real distance between us and Earth."

"What can we do?" asked Christy looking at Teela. They had worked hard just getting the new ion thrusters installed. Was it all for nothing?

Christy had the impression that Teela's breasts were slightly larger and fuller than they had been. She had noticed earlier in Main Control that Teela's hips seemed to flare outwards more. Christy wondered if Teela was modifying her program to make herself look more appealing. She wondered what Jennifer would have to say about that.

"Steve and I have tried to come up with a solution, but we haven't managed to come up with anything we felt comfortable with," Christy said focusing herself back on the subject at hand. "We know we need to move the station away from the Earth-Moon system and go out deeper into the Solar System. Even with the new ion thrusters that will take a lot of time, time we don't have."

"What Teela and I have come up with is this," Todd began leaning forwards. "What if we take the Space Platform and join it to the bottom of the Power Wheel on Star One."

"Do what!" interrupted Steve looking at the two as if they were crazy. "The station keeping thrusters on the platform are not any stronger than those Star One is equipped with? How will that help us?"

"That's one we never thought of," Christy admitted intrigued by the idea wondering what else the two had in mind. She also didn't see what good it would do.

"I realize that commander," Todd replied. "But if we join the Space Platform to the Power Wheel, we can use the fusion reactors from Star One and the Space Platform to power four full size ion drives that can be built into the Space Platform. We can store a tremendous amount of fuel in the Space Platform itself for our shuttles and support craft from the Fuel Storage Facility."

"Full size ion drives," said Christy taken aback at the suggestion. "Won't that tear the station apart if we were to use them at full power?"

"No," replied Teela shaking her head. "If the thrust is kept under one-fifth gravity and applied very slowly there will be no harm to the station's actual structure. Also, by adding more Luxen cables between Star One's three wheels, we can tremendously increase the station's stability."

"If we double the current number of cables, the station would be able to handle a lot more stress if it becomes necessary to use the ion drives at higher levels," Teela stated. "I've run the simulations, and it will work."

Christy and Steve looked at each other deep in thought. If Todd and Teela thought it could work, then it probably would. Teela had mentioned smaller ion drives before to Steve, but nothing like this.

They were interrupted as Jensen returned with their meals. Jensen waited as Teela concentrated and another plate of food materialized in front of her. Steve noticed with surprise that it was baked shrimp in one of the special sauces that Jensen was always bragging about. For Steve, this was the first time he had witnessed this little trick of Teela's. He clearly needed to meet with Jennifer. The station's AI had obviously grown into something much more than what he had expected.

"An excellent choice my dear," Jensen said smiling approvingly. "Let me know what you think of it. I think you will find it exquisite."

133

"I'm sure it will be," Teela replied politely. "All your food is absolutely wonderful!"

Steve could scarcely believe his eyes and ears. Jensen was actually asking Teela for her approval. He obviously needed to talk to Jennifer. Teela's program was much further advanced than he had possibly imagined. No wonder she and Todd were becoming so close.

The four continued to talk as the meal progressed. Steve found himself being drawn into conversation with Teela and forgetting at times that she was only a hologram. Teela and Todd described in detail what would be necessary to join the Space Platform to the Power Wheel. They were right when they said it would be a big project. However, Steve liked the maneuverability they would get from it.

They could actually move the station anywhere in the Solar System if they wanted to. They might be able to move Star One far enough out in the Solar System where it could survive a small nova. As they continued their meal and talked, he watched Teela more closely. Watching her eat and drink her wine was like watching any other attractive, intelligent young woman out on a dinner date.

The evening finally ended, and Steve and Christy watched as Todd and Teela left arm in arm and walked out of the restaurant totally caught up in one another. They had decided to hold a staff meeting the next day to discuss linking up the Space Platform with Star One. Steve wanted to hear some opinions from some of the other department heads.

"That's totally unbelievable," said Steve watching the two leave. "How long has this been going on, and why didn't I notice it before?"

Christy smiled reaching over and taking Steve's hand in her own. "Teela has become a very important member of this crew. Not as an AI, but as a person," she replied. "Teela and I talk a lot, and her feelings for Todd are very real. I suspect his are for her also."

"I thought I noticed a change in Todd recently. He has seemed to be more energetic, and carefree," responded Steve drinking the last sip of wine. "I think I will talk to Jennifer, maybe Teela needs to be recognized more as a member of this crew. She certainly deserves it."

After leaving the restaurant, they walked slowly along the concourse staring into the store windows and laughing at some of the items they saw. Finally, arriving at his quarters, Steve felt contented when Christy followed him in and fell into his arms in a passionate, warm embrace followed by a kiss. Within moments, the two were lost in passionate lovemaking.

Afterwards, Christy couldn't help feeling sorry for Teela in some ways. Even though she had all the feelings and desires of a young woman, they could never be full filled. Teela could never experience some things. Turning over, Christy put her arm across Steve's chest and was soon sound asleep.

# Chapter Eight

In Main Control, Steve watched the large view screen apprehensively, as the Space Platform slowly grew larger. Thrusters were firing sending white jets of flame off into space as they fired continuously moving the massive structure steadily closer.

"Everything looks good," commented Lieutenant Commander Anderson from his position next to Steve.

They were both sitting at the center command console. Lieutenant Commander Anderson was in constant communication with the other stations in Main Control over the mini com attached to his right ear. Each Main Control station involved in the operation was monitoring the Space Platform's approach very closely.

"Lieutenant Gray is piloting the Space Platform," Steve replied his eyes still glued to the view screen. "He's the best we have. If anyone can handle this maneuver, it's him."

"He has been practicing this maneuver using some holographic displays that Teela set up," Anderson replied as he listened to a report from the radar operator. The Space Platform was right on course. "I watched him several times, and the simulations were very realistic."

"Yes, I heard about that," Steve replied with a forced smile. "I understand he only crashed into Star One twice."

"Only at the beginning sir," Anderson replied with a grin. "It never happened again once he got a feel for how to use the platform's thrusters."

"Let's hope everything goes well this time," commented Steve knowing that John had put in a lot of hours with Teela perfecting this intricate maneuver.

For several weeks, the station's crew had labored around the clock. New thick Luxen cables had been stretched taunt between all three wheels on Star One. From a distance, it looked as if a giant spider had spun a web between the three. It was difficult not to look for the spider as you approached the station.

The four ion drive chambers were nearly complete on the Space Platform. Using newly installed heavy thrusters, the Space Platform itself was being moved into position beneath the Power Wheel. Once there, it would be attached permanently to Star One.

Lieutenant Commander Williams and Captain Gerald had worked their people to the limit on installing the new thrusters and working on the new ion drives. They wanted to get the job done as quickly as possible. Captain Gerald was becoming quite versatile, having learned how to operate the station's space scooters and maneuver in the bulky spacesuits used for space construction.

Lieutenant Commander Williams was on the Space Platform along with John Gray. John was controlling the movement of the platform as its continually firing thrusters brought it ever nearer to Star One. John was sitting at the Space Platform's main thruster control console along with two flight technicians controlling the platform's slow movement.

"So far so good," commented Todd looking over John's shoulder at the navigation screens.

One of the screens was three-dimensional and showed the exact course the Space Platform needed to follow. It was like looking down a tunnel with a blinking green line running down its center. All John had to do was stay in the center and follow the blinking line. This whole operation had been Teela's and his idea. Todd crossed his arms across his chest watching everything intently. He was watching for any hint of a potential problem.

John was watching his instruments closely as well as the computer screens. Teela had set up a program, which showed the exact path and speed the platform needed to move at in order to dock successfully with Star One. This path was represented by the blinking green line on the three dimensional screen.

In addition, Teela was standing next to Todd and slightly behind John monitoring the entire operation. She was using Star One's radars and sensors to track the slow movement of the Space Platform. The main screen above them showed Star One steadily growing larger as the Space Platform approached the Power Wheel.

In open space around Star One, numerous Centaur work vessels waited and watched. If there was an accident and the Space Platform or Star One was damaged, the Centaurs were prepared to move in quickly to repair the damage. Several of the Centaurs carried sheets of Luxen in their mechanical arms in case a hole was knocked in the Power Wheel. Everyone watched anxiously as the Space Platform moved ever closer to the massive space station.

"Looking good John," Todd said once more as the platform moved smoothly down the center of its planned course for docking. The only other pilot Todd would trust doing something like this was Captain Simpson who was on the FarQuest.

"This thing handles like a truck with four flats," mumbled John concentrating on the controls. He deftly fired two of the thrusters in a quick three second burst to guide the platform along its projected path.

"Just don't scratch up my Space Platform," Todd reminded John with a forced smile. The tension in the small control room was unusually high.

"I'm more worried about scratching up Star One," John replied as he double-checked their current approach speed. "Steve would never forgive me if I scratched or dented up his space station."

"You are doing fine John," Teela assured him, as she checked the docking simulation she was continuously running in her core system.

She knew to within a fraction of an inch just how far off course they were. John was doing surprisingly well in maneuvering the sluggish platform to a position underneath the Power Wheel. Evidently, the holographic simulations she had set up were paying off.

They had run this simulation probably a hundred times in the last few weeks, and John felt he could do it in his sleep now. John fired two short bursts from two of the aft thrusters bringing the platform into position directly beneath the Power Wheel. Then firing the port thrusters, he brought the platform to a stop. He let out a long breath, not realizing he had been holding his breath for the last few seconds. The computer screen in front of John now changed to show the Power Wheel and the Space Platform.

"Almost there," Todd spoke trying to sound calm.

"Now comes the hard part," replied John taking in a deep breath.

It was doing this next maneuver that he had crashed the Space Platform into Star One during the simulations. Once he had knocked Star One completely out of the Lagrange point heavily damaging the Power Wheel. The second time, he had managed to avert damaging the space station, but had badly damaged the Space Platform instead. After Teela and he had worked out what the problem was, the simulations after that had steadily improved as he became more adept at using the thrusters to control the Space Platform's movement.

A set of coordinates appeared on the screen showing the current alignment of each. The Space Platform still needed to be rotated slightly to line it up for docking. John carefully fired several small lateral thrusters slowly rotating the platform until the two sets of coordinates matched perfectly. John watched the computer screen intently, but much of what he was doing was nothing more than old fashion seat of the pants flying.

"Alignment is good," Teela commented as she quickly checked her docking program. "Couldn't have done it better myself."

"I almost wish you were doing this," John muttered as he shook his hands trying to relax.

"We needed a human pilot," Todd reminded John. "Teela has never flown anything."

"Ready to implement final docking maneuver," John spoke into his com. Now would come the hard part. He placed his hands back on the controls.

"We're ready here," Christy replied from her position in the control room of the Power Wheel where she was monitoring the operation.

Dryson and Stoler were both with her watching the docking with interest and some concern. The Power Wheel had been evacuated in case of an accident. A minimal crew in space suits was in the two reactor rooms ready to shut the reactors down if necessary.

"Proceed," Steve spoke over the com. "We have plenty of time John, back off if it doesn't look good or feel right."

"Can't have my piloting skills blemished," John retorted lightly trying not to sound nervous.

"No one's ever tried something like this before," Steve reminded his friend. "I'm sure everyone down on Earth is really confused about now. They must be trying to figure out just what we're doing."

"They will never figure this one out," Todd replied over the com.

Firing the thrusters again, John eased the platform ever so gently upward so as not to jar the station when the two actually joined. The thrusters had been adjusted to allow John to fire small, short bursts. Six massive Luxen docking joints had been constructed on both the top of the platform and the main hub of the Power Wheel, so the two could be melded together into one stable structure. These docking joints were what John was now attempting to join together.

"Thirty feet," reported Teela using her station sensors as well as the platforms to monitor the docking as the two structures slowly neared one another. "Twenty feet," she said as John fired more thrusters slowing the rate of ascent. "Ten feet, five feet, two feet, locking joints are starting to engage."

More thrusters fired slowing the platform's rise to just inches per minute. Teela was watching everything through her remote cameras ensuring that nothing went wrong. This had been Todd's and her idea, and she felt responsible if anything were to go wrong. She felt nervous and apprehensive as the two structures slowly joined. Sometimes her program triggered emotions at the oddest times.

"Almost there," Todd said anxiously watching the computer screen and the view screen at the same time. "Just another few inches."

"Zero feet and we have a firm dock on all locking joints," Teela announced with relief as she activated the locking joints engaging them and joining the two structures.

"Perfect John," Todd said approvingly finally allowing himself to relax. "I knew you could do this." Others in the control room broke out in cheers and applause; they knew that an extremely difficult maneuver had just been completed.

In space, the Centaur work vessels moved in closer to visually inspect the joints. The crews of all the Centaurs had been holding their breaths as the two structures were joined together. Now the next phase of the project would commence.

On board Star One, Teela appeared in her customary position next to Steve in Main Control. Her dark blue eyes looked over at the commander.

"Locking joints have been engaged sir," Teela reported with a contented smile. Teela wore her regulation uniform, which fit her well-rounded form extremely well. Her dark black hair lay on her shoulders without a single strand out of place.

"Confirm engagement of locking joints," Lieutenant Commander Anderson affirmed as he listened to reports from the different duty stations coming in over his mini com.

"All stations report," Steve ordered into his com allowing himself to take a deep breath.

The docking had gone much smoother than he had imagined. John had demonstrated once more, why he was one of the top shuttle pilots. Steve felt a vast sense of relief now that the complicated maneuver had been completed.

"Power Wheel docking joints engaged and locked." Christy reported from her position in the control room of the Power Wheel. "We didn't feel anything during the joining. It was very smooth."

Dryson and Stoler were watching a board with now steady green docking indicator lights. This had been a risky maneuver, particularly since the hub of the Power Wheel contained the fusion reactors. They were also checking for any undue stress on the Power Wheel. So far, everything looked acceptable.

"Space Platform docking joints engaged and locked," reported Lieutenant Commander Todd Williams, relieved that the docking maneuver was finally over. "Everything is in the green and no problems are showing up what so ever. It was a beautiful maneuver. John didn't even scratch the paint up!"

"Good job John, Christy, Todd," Steve replied with a smile. "I had a bucket of paint ready if he did scratch the station. Let's get the work crews out and begin the outer construction jobs."

Steve knew from their plans that additional Luxen joints would be attached to the Space Platform and the Power Wheel to ensure that the melded together structure would be stable under acceleration. Most of this would be done using the Centaur work vessels and the space scooters. A number of workers in spacesuits would also be required to inspect everything.

Large Luxen bracing joints had to be attached to the rim of the Power Wheel in forty different places to ensure a stable structure capable of handling the thrust from the four ion drives. Steve had insisted that an extra safety margin be built into the plans.

On the main screen, eight Centaur work vessels and twelve space scooters came into view as the waiting crews moved towards the Space Platform to begin their part of the job. The Centaurs were carrying large Luxen beams and cables to complete the installation.

"I'm glad that's over," General Karver stated from behind Steve where he had been watching the entire maneuver. "Senator Farley will be scratching his head trying to figure out why we did this."

"The telescopes down on Earth as well as in orbit will leave no doubt that we have attached the Space Platform to Star One," Teela added in agreement. "There will be a lot of guesswork as to why we did this. I have already picked up increased encoded radio traffic between a number of defense installations."

"They will only be able to speculate as to why we did it," answered Steve hoping Senator Farley would get a headache trying to figure out what they were up to. There was no way Senator Farley would guess that they were contemplating moving the station.

Tension in Main Control was almost gone now since the docking maneuver had been completed. Steve watched as Lieutenant Emerson walked over from her weapons console where she had been using the spy satellites to keep track of events down on Earth. The attractive young woman, over the last few weeks, had become an integral part of Main Control's crew. She was also becoming highly popular with the single young men on the station.

"The weather down below has really broken loose," she said worriedly stopping in front of the command console looking at Steve and General Karver. "Severe storm activity has increased by nearly 70 percent over the past two weeks, and we are tracking more hurricanes than ever recorded before. It's becoming extremely difficult to monitor what's going on in the U.S."

"The first effects from the neutron star," replied Steve knowing full well the significance of the increasing storms. Teela had been keeping him informed of the weather developments down on Earth. Steve knew that they were only going to get worse.

"We are no longer monitoring just small hurricanes," Lieutenant Emerson went on showing concern. "But huge category five storms, several of which are more severe than any ever recorded before. There is one storm, even now in the Gulf of Mexico, with sustained winds reported of nearly 260 miles per hour."

"A category six," Teela responded not feeling surprised. She had predicted this. She had been monitoring the hurricane and had noted its rapid increase in wind velocity over the last several days.

"That's one hell of a hurricane," General Karver said realizing what it implied. He knew that a storm of that magnitude would be devastating, sweeping everything away in its path.

"I've been monitoring some of the news stations in the U.S., and Senator Farley is blaming Star One for the increase in severe weather," added Teela shaking her head sadly. "He claims we are manipulating the weather patterns around the globe."

"Controlling the weather," uttered Steve in disbelief his eyes growing wide at the accusation. "It seems that Farley is going to blame us for everything. What about other countries? What are they saying?"

"No one is disagreeing with him," replied Teela turning her dark blue eyes toward Steve. She routinely monitored the radio and media transmissions of nearly every nation on Earth.

"They won't," General Karver commented in a grave voice. "If they did, it's hard telling what his response might be."

"Of course, the President of the United Nations issued a statement earlier today supporting Senator Farley's claim that Star One was the source of the bad weather the Earth is now experiencing," Teela added.

She still had a hard time understanding why people acted the way they did.

Teela projected an Earth newscast up on the main view screen, which showed heavy rain and wind striking a city on the coast of Texas. Teela turned up the sound, so everyone could hear.

"Gale force winds are already striking the Texas coast from Corpus Christi to Galveston," the newscaster was saying. "Local weather bureaus have clocked wind gusts in the last hour of over 120 miles per hour with torrential rains now moving into many coastal areas. Hurricane Rachael is still over 240 miles from landfall, moving to the west northwest at twelve miles per hour. Widespread coastal flooding and destruction from the tornadic strength winds is expected to continue to get worse as this killer storm approaches. Already hundreds of thousands of people have been evacuated and moved inland from low-lying areas. Land fall of the eye of the storm is expected to be slightly south of Freeport."

The screen shifted to show tornadoes in Kansas and Oklahoma. The enormous twisters were shown tearing through the heart of several Midwest cities leveling structures, tearing roofs off, and ripping power line poles out of the ground causing horrific explosions of sparks.

"Much of the Midwest continues to suffer under the onslaught of a record number of tornadoes," the newscaster continued. "In the last week, over 100 tornadic storms have ravaged much of the center of the country spawning nearly 300 tornadoes."

The screen changed once more showing a view of the Earth almost entirely wrapped in heavy clouds, as seen from Star One. General Karver, Lieutenant Emerson, and Steve all turned to look at Teela.

"That's typical of the newscasts from around the entire world. The weather situation will only continue to get worse as the weeks go by," Teela concluded.

"How much worse will it get?" Lieutenant Emerson asked with a slight quiver in her voice.

She knew that a lot of people down on Earth had to be suffering due to the inclement weather. She still had close family members that were trapped down below. They hadn't been able to get them safely to the cape in time to be brought up to Star One. The fighting had gotten too bad too quickly. A number of personnel had seen their families become trapped.

"The amount of severe weather will continue to increase steadily," replied Teela looking at Steve and then turning to face Lieutenant

Emerson and General Karver. "There will be widespread flooding, heavy snowfalls in mountainous areas, and almost total crop failure world wide."

Lieutenant Emerson was quiet thinking about her parents who lived just outside of Boston. She had accepted that there was nothing she could do for them, but it still hurt just to think about what they were going to go through. She wished that her sister had made it to the cape. Turning she walked slowly back to her console.

"This is going to be difficult for a lot of our people," commented General Karver watching the lieutenant go back to her station. "Watching the destruction on Earth will not be easy."

"I've already talked to Doctor Blackwater," replied Steve agreeing with the general. "He is setting up counseling sessions for those that will be hit the hardest. Those with close family members still down on Earth."

"This is a good crew," General Karver stated knowing how difficult this must be for some. He knew that Lieutenant Emerson's sister had been trapped down on Earth and hadn't been able to make it to the cape. "They will cope with the situation, we all will."

"Everyone on the station has family or friends still down on Earth," Steve said with a heavy sigh. "This is going to be rough on all of us."

"It's one hell of a situation," General Karver replied with a nod.

"What's the current status of the FarQuest Teela?" asked Steve looking up at a small screen, which showed the FarQuest's current position in relation to the neutron star. The two were rapidly nearing one another.

"Latest telemetry shows all systems functioning normally and the crew still in deep sleep," Teela replied evenly. "The flight computer has only had to activate the ship's thrusters one time to move the ship out of the path of a possible asteroid."

"That's good," spoke Steve glad that the mission was going so smoothly. He had been concerned about the entire crew being in deep sleep and not able to respond quickly to an emergency.

Teela kept a very close track of the FarQuest because Jennifer asked about it quite often. "The crew should be coming out of deep sleep in eighteen days, which will put them within 233,660,960 miles of the neutron star-black hole binary. Interception will occur at a range of nearly eight billion miles from Earth."

Steve leaned back thinking hard about what still needed to be done. So much depended on the information the FarQuest would be sending back. Already the Farside array had firmed up the trajectory of the neutron star-black hole binary. If it held true, which it should, every planet in the Solar System would be seriously affected. Several might end up being pulled into the neutron star-black hole binary. Mercury would probably fall into the Sun, and it was doubtful the Earth would survive the stresses the planet would be put through. Even if Earth did survive, its orbit would make life untenable on its surface.

"Lieutenant Commander Williams is on the line sir," Teela said.

"Yes Todd," Steve spoke into his com.

"Everything went smoothly with the docking," Todd reported. The work crews have begun placing the extra support beams and the Luxen cables in place. The job will take about two shifts to complete."

"Very well," replied Steve. "Todd, have John meet me in the Alpha launch bay. I want to take a Centaur out to inspect the work being done on the Power Wheel and Space Platform."

"John is already on his way," Todd responded smoothly. "He thought you might want to do that."

Twenty minutes later, Steve watched through the Centaur's main front view port as the Centaur swung around the rim of the main wheel and down towards the Power Wheel and Space Platform. Centaur work vessels and numerous scooters were visible. Workers were busy attaching beams and stretching the Luxen cables in place.

"That's a lot of work going on," commented John gazing at all the activity. Flying the Centaur was a thousand times easier than maneuvering the Space Platform.

"I had Todd remind everyone about safety," replied Steve watching the work with a critical eye. He didn't want anyone hurt doing this.

As they neared where the two structures were being joined, Steve thought about how unsightly the melding of the two space structures was. He had always felt that Star One had an aesthetic beauty all of its own, and now part of that was marred. It almost seemed, looking out the view port that the entire station was resting on the Space Platform.

Welding arcs flashed and thrusters fired as the Centaurs hovered and worked around the joining points. Workers in spacesuits swarmed over the structure firing small jets packs mounted to their backs. The structure was being strengthened to withstand the acceleration from the four ion drives that were soon to be finished inside the Space Platform.

As the Centaur continued its downwards arc, it passed beneath the platform to the platform's wheel, which was slowly rotating beneath it. Even this would be evacuated when the main ion drives were activated. The four drives were on the corners of the Space Platform.

"We can always undock the Space Platform later," John said looking at the structure now attached to Star One. "If we have to move the station, we can always separate the two when this is all over with."

"I just wonder if it will ever be over," Steve said thinking about their future. "There is still so much we don't know still ahead of us John."

"Teela thinks we will survive," John said recalling some of the conversations they had while he was running the docking simulations.

"I hope she's right," responded Steve letting out a deep sigh. Would they be moving Star One from place to place in the Solar System just to survive? Would they be mining the asteroids and small moons to get needed resources? What would the Solar System be like after the neutron star and black hole left? Would there be any other survivors?

As the Centaur turned and began climbing slowly back up the other side of the station, Steve had an unobstructed view of the Earth hanging serenely in space between the unwinking stars. Earth lay there as if nothing was different, except for the fact that much of it was covered in a dense layer of clouds. Only in a few isolated areas were there vistas of deep blue visible, where small areas of the ocean still managed to peek through the shielding cloud layer.

Looking to the side of the station, he could see the pock marked crescent of the moon. He knew that Mase was busy blasting and tunneling deep under the surface. Mase was trying to get deep enough so that they could survive a minor nova if the sun did flare up. Steve talked to Mase every day.

Steve knew from their daily communications that Mase felt that if he could complete his deep installations soon enough, with the thick Luxen walls they were putting in place, that the Tycho City installation might survive. For the last several weeks, Star One had been making daily shipments of Luxen to Tycho City as they raced against time to prepare for the coming earthquakes that would soon shake both the Earth and the Moon. Tycho City was now also producing Luxen in its own reactor. However, the Luxen from Star One produced in zero gravity was slightly stronger than that produced in Tycho City's reactor.

Fortunately, Tycho City was in a relatively earthquake free area. Mase had been using some of the nuclear weapons furnished by General Karver to relieve the pressure on as many fault lines as possible that might pose as a menace. The Moon had trembled as the many kiloton explosions had rumbled through its depths blasting the fault lines and creating huge caverns deep beneath its shattered crust, throwing up clouds of moon dust far above its surface. The clouds of dust had even been visible in Star One's telescopes, which had been observing the areas being subjected to underground blasts.

"Mase has a good crew," John said seeing where Steve's eyes were focused as he fired the Centaur's thrusters to pass around the main wheel. "If there is any way for them to survive, Mase will find it."

"I know," Steve replied somberly looking at the Moon. "It's just hard to believe that, within months, the only members of the human race left alive may be on Star One, Tycho city, and those two deep Earth installations that Senator Farley knows nothing about."

"It's amazing that they have remained hidden so long. I really believed that Farley would have found them by know," replied John slowing down the Centaur as it neared Alpha.

"He probably would have if he knew they existed. The few people that do know are not talking," replied Steve thinking about the thousands of men and women locked away in the deep underground bunkers.

The structures were designed so they could be expanded, and many of the underground rooms had still been under construction when they had been forced to seal up. Fortunately, all the material to finish construction was already inside, as well as plentiful stocks of food and water. If the Earth survived, the two bunkers would form the foundation of two new underground colonies deep beneath the Earth's surface.

"What about other countries?" asked John looking over at Steve. "Surely other shelters are being built abroad. Everyone can't have their heads stuck in the ground."

"Not really," Steve replied dejectedly "Senator Farley and the President of the United Nations have made it plain to everybody that they believe the entire neutron star affair to be a hoax. No one dares question that, for fear of retaliation, numerous scientists and others have been reportedly put to death for even bringing the subject up. Also, many of the people in other countries, that seized power when Senator Farley did, believe as he does. They are following his lead."

"How can everybody be so blind?" asked John shaking his head disgustedly.

"If any more underground shelters are being built, they are being done in utmost secrecy and in nearly inaccessible areas," Steve replied. "Teela has not seen any signs of that, and we have been using the military spy satellites, when the weather has permitted, to scan the globe for any type of preparation. Of course, with the heavy cloud cover the last several weeks anything could be happening down below. Most of the Earth has been hidden from us as well as from Senator Farley."

"What about Russia and China, they both have scientists that must know the truth, both are capable of building shelters?" questioned John finding it hard to fathom that no one was taking precautions.

"China and Russia are in a state of near war," answered Steve. "If either does anything suspicious the other would probably launch an all out nuclear attack. They are constantly threatening each other and deploying massive amounts of ground troops. They are so paranoid about the other that the neutron star threat has taken a back seat. Any attempt to build underground shelters that might stand a chance to survive might be looked on as an attempt to survive a nuclear exchange. Neither side dares build shelters for fear of the others instant retaliation."

"Talk about sticking their heads in the ground," John muttered. "Don't they realize that if they do nothing the neutron star will finish them off?"

"Some of their leading scientists know," answered Steve recalling some of the radio messages they had intercepted. "We have had some communications with their astronomers on the Mir 4 stations. They have told us secretly that they have confirmed our neutron star observations and other scientists on the ground also know the true situation."

"But they are powerless to do anything," replied John wondering what the astronauts on those low Earth stations thought about this situation.

With the weather currently sweeping the globe, he didn't see how any of the people on the low Earth stations could get back to Earth. They were trapped in orbit.

"With the current communists in control, they are being very careful about what they report back to Earth," Steve continued. "They think some scientists and their families may be trying to set up a survival cell in one of the deeper caves in Russia unknown to the military. Because of the secrecy involved and their lack of government support, the people on the Mir's don't believe they will stand much of a chance of survival."

John fired several more bursts from his thrusters, guiding the Centaur back into Alpha's brilliantly lighted docking bay. With practiced ease, he sat the small craft back down gently on its circular landing pad. The bay was quickly pressurized, and several crewmen rushed over to secure the Centaur.

John knew that Steve still had a long day ahead of him. John was scheduled to meet with Julie and Kathleen down in one of the ecological habitats. Julie had promised him, if he behaved, he could actually try fishing in one of the catfish ponds that was ready to be harvested. The thought of fried catfish for supper was almost enough to drive the worries, for a while at least, from John's mind.

Steve returned to his office and was surprised to find Christy there waiting for him. "Hi gorgeous," he said taking her in his arms and smothering her in a long drawn out kiss. She felt so soft and vulnerable in his arms. Drawing back, he looked into her deep blue eyes and released her stepping back smiling.

"Hi yourself," she responded with a pleased look upon her face.

"Todd and you did a great job with the docking today," Steve said walking around and sitting down behind his desk.

Christy took a seat in front and leaned back brushing her blonde hair off her shoulders relaxing and crossing her legs. She had let her hair grow out over the last several months.

"Todd's people are so easy to work with," Christy said. "Also, some of Captain Gerald's people have really turned into an asset. I don't know what we would have done without their help at times these past few months."

"Captain Gerald and his people have really worked out well," Steve agreed. "That group of marines is really talented."

"General Karver did a great job picking them out," added Christy agreeing with Steve.

Steve leaned forward with his arms on his desk changing the subject. "Ty will be awake in another eighteen days. We have already loaded all the black hole information into their on board computers. I'm sure it will be a shock when they realize what we are sending them into."

"Ty has a good crew," Christy said reading the concern in Steve's voice. After all, Ty was his closest friend. "The FarQuest has preformed flawlessly so far, Ty will get the job done and be back with us in another six months."

"Perhaps," Steve said with a far a way look in his eyes. "But that's a damned black hole out there Christy. We never expected something like that when we sent Ty on this mission."

"Ty has never failed in a mission Steve," responded Christy. "He won't fail in this one. Don't forget that Pierre LaRann is on board, and he is an expert on black holes."

"LaRann is an expert in many astronomical fields," Steve replied. "That's why he is on this mission."

"When they wake up, we will have plenty of time to decide how to proceed," Christy said reading the concern in Steve's eyes. "LaRann will know how to safely continue the mission."

"By the time they return, we may have already moved the station far away from Earth," Steve said with a heavy sigh. "The black hole will be within four billion miles of Earth and getting closer. We may have no choice other than to begin moving the station to keep it out of harms way. We are only six months away from its closest approach."

Both sat silently for a few minutes. "If we move the station, where will we take it?" Christy asked finally.

"That depends on what Ty finds," Steve answered. "Once we know for sure what the effects are going to be, we can begin our preparations."

"What about Senator Farley?" Christy asked. "We haven't received any threats from him at all the past several weeks. It makes me nervous. I just wish I knew what he was up to."

"So do I," Steve replied with a worried frown. "Underneath the cloud cover he could be doing anything. One thing for sure, he definitely hasn't given up on knocking off Star One. That's one reason why as soon as we can move the station away from Earth, we might be wise to do so. The more distance we put between Senator Farley and us the better I will feel."

Steve recalled some of the stuff Teela had observed just before the heavy cloud cover had moved in over the military bases. "We know that he was working on more missiles before the storms moved in. This weather has probably put a damper on that at least."

Jennifer was in her quarters brushing out her hair after a long, luxurious shower. The months aboard Star One had been extremely exciting, her job, the new people she had met, and of course Teela.

Every day was full of new challenges and new experiences.

"Only eighteen more days," Teela said quietly from where she was sitting on Jennifer's bed watching.

"It's hard to believe that it has already been over five months since they left," replied Jennifer pulling the brush smoothly through her hair. "The time has flown by so quickly."

"Would you like me to insert a personal message into the FarQuest's computer from you to Commander Erin?" inquired Teela knowing that she could do it rather easily if she wanted.

"No Teela," replied Jennifer remembering the last meal that she had shared with Ty. "Commander Erin will have enough to worry about when he awakes."

Teela was quiet as she watched Jennifer brush her hair. It was times like these that she sometimes wished she were human. Of course, the holographic imaging program and its virtual reality interface allowed her to experience many of the feelings, smells, and tastes of the real world. Even so, she often wondered what other little things she might be missing out on.

"How are you and Todd getting along?" Jennifer asked. She tried to keep well abreast of Teela's relationship with the Lieutenant Commander.

Her development since she had fallen for Todd had been truly remarkable. Jennifer had taken particular note of Teela's modification of her original program giving herself slightly larger breasts and more flaring hips. Teela had taken on the appearance of a more mature attractive young woman, and Jennifer had approved. It showed an interest in looking attractive and appealing to the opposite sex, but not to the point of going over board. She had also cautioned Teela about taking the modifications too far.

"Todd and I spend a lot of time talking," Teela responded leaning back on her arms on the bed.

Jennifer could see her in the mirror and couldn't help noticing that the bed didn't react at all to Teela's presence since her holographic figure had no weight.

"He is so smart and kind. Last night we spent hours in one of the observation lounges looking at the stars and talking about what might be out there."

"I'm glad that you and Todd are getting along so well." Other than Commander Erin, Jennifer hadn't tried to go out with other men.

Kathleen had taken her out several times dancing and to eat, but other men didn't attract her as Ty did.

"He treats me like a real person," Teela responded with her eyes wide. "When we're talking it's so strange. I listen to his every word, and for some reason, it seems very important for me to do so."

"I've been meaning to ask you, how are you picking out your clothes to wear when you and Todd go out? Christy has mentioned that you are dressing a little revealingly. Are you sure you want to stimulate Todd that way?" Jennifer asked, carefully watching Teela's reaction in the mirror.

Teela hesitated a moment before replying. "Todd doesn't mind my dressing a little revealingly, he seems to enjoy it," she replied with a slight blush showing on her cheeks. "We know that we can't enjoy any type of physical relationship, even though I did offer to work something out using virtual reality if he really felt the need to. But Todd says that, for now, our relationship is very satisfying and stimulating enough. As for dressing up, I got Kathleen to give me some pointers."

"I should have known," said Jennifer shaking her head amusedly. Kathleen and Teela together sounded like an extremely dangerous combination. With a sigh, she finished brushing her hair while Teela watched.

# Chapter Nine

Far out in the depths of space, a timer reached zero. It triggered a computer command and an antidote to the deep sleep drug was automatically administered to Lieutenant Strett. Her nonmoving form was resting peacefully in her cubicle. On the flight deck of the FarQuest, the environmental computer activated another program that began bringing the ship's environment back up to human norm.

Time passed as the drug gradually took effect until Evelyn Strett painfully opened her eyes to the sudden brightness. The cubicle lid opened, and Lieutenant Strett took a long, deep breath. She lay there for quite some time as she regulated her breathing and waited for her strength to return. She felt so weak, she wasn't sure she could stand up.

Sliding her legs out of the cubicle, she nearly fell as the room spun before her. This isn't right she thought as she grabbed the edge of the deep sleep cubicle to stop herself from falling. "Why do I feel so weak?" she mumbled feeling a dryness in her throat. From the symptoms she was experiencing, she wondered if she was dehydrated.

As the room steadied, she walked slowly over to a small cabinet and opened one of the doors. She took a container off one of the crowded shelves and popped the lid open. Placing it against her lips, she slowly drank the refreshing contents. It was a combination nutrient and protein drink, which should quickly restore her strength.

After several more minutes, she began to feel closer to normal, but still terribly weak. Walking over to the other deep sleep cubicles, she quickly checked the occupants noting with relief that they all seemed to be okay. She went over to one of the medical supply cabinets and took out a syringe. She would wake Commander Erin up next.

Ty struggled weakly against the darkness, as he slowly opened his eyes to see Lieutenant Strett bending worriedly over him. Instinctively he put his hand over his eyes blocking out the bright light. Finally, his eyes adjusted to the light and he removed his hand seeing an anxious Lieutenant Strett standing by his cubicle. She held an empty syringe in her right hand.

"Take it easy commander," she said gently, laying down the syringe. "The deep sleep drug has left you exhausted and very weak. Sit up slowly and drink this," she said helping Ty into a sitting position and handing him a steaming cup of soup broth. "Sip this slowly. It has

153

some vitamins in it and some other things that will help to restore your strength. You are also dehydrated from the deep sleep."

Ty took the cup and took a cautious sip realizing that his mouth felt exceedingly parched. Looking around, he saw that only Lieutenant Strett and he were awake.

"What about the others?" he managed to croak out between sips.

"They appear to be fine," she reported watching Ty closely. "The drug depleted our body's energy reserves more than Doctor Wruggi predicted. It took me nearly an hour just to get the strength to crawl out of my cubicle and give myself a stimulate. I injected you with a powerful stimulate first and then with the antidote to the deep sleep drug."

"I feel terrible," Ty mumbled as he continued slowly to drink the soup in the cup.

"The broth you're drinking should help you to recover more quickly than I did," Lieutenant Strett added. "We will all have to watch ourselves for the next several days until we get our strength back."

"How's the ship?" asked Ty starting to feel better as the broth began to take effect.

"I checked the flight deck briefly, and everything seems to be functioning normally," she replied taking Ty's pulse. She nodded to herself satisfied that it was near normal. "I want you to finish the broth and then lie back down for a few minutes. I'm going to wake up Captain Simpson next."

"You should be strong enough to make it up to the flight deck in about thirty minutes, not before," she added sternly. "It will take about an hour for Captain Simpson to regain consciousness."

Thirty minutes later, Ty made his way carefully onto the flight deck, and a quick scan of the consoles showed everything still in the green with no amber or red warning lights showing. On the main screen, the neutron star was brighter but still over 200 million miles away. Strapping himself loosely into his command chair, he began playing the messages that were waiting from Star One. He was anxious to find out what the latest status was on their mission, as well as the current political situation back on Earth.

Ty was still there an hour later when Captain Simpson struggled weakly onto the flight deck and with a sick grin took his place in his pilot's chair.

"I feel as if I've been run over by a herd of elephants," he groaned activating the flight computer and checking their current position and trajectory. "I thought we were supposed to feel rested after a long sleep like that."

"I know," replied Ty recalling Steve's ominous words recorded earlier that morning on the FarQuest's computer. "I don't think any of us expected to feel this weak when we woke up."

Captain Simpson began checking his console wanting to make sure all the ship's primary systems were still functioning normally. He was surprised at how weak he still felt. Just moving his arms seemed to take a lot of effort.

Ty became silent thinking over what he had just heard from Steve. He knew that the black hole, which Steve had spoken at length about, made their mission much more dangerous to complete. A damn black hole Ty thought, how had they missed that at Farside?

Reaching forward, Ty adjusted the main view screen to the coordinates Steve had mentioned just to the left of the neutron star and boosted the screen magnification up to the maximum. Looking at the center of the screen, Ty could barely make out a small area of blackness that seemed to have outer edges tinged in dark violet and purple.

"What in God's name is that?" asked Simpson seeing the small dark area on the screen. He felt a chill go down his back. It seemed as if it was alien and out of place. It was something that should not be there.

"It's a black hole," replied Ty quietly gazing at the screen in fascination. "That damned neutron star is in orbit around it. That's what has caused all the problems with the data. Teela discovered it using the Farside array just after we went into deep sleep."

"We are heading right into it," Simpson said concerned his eyes focusing on the flight computer and their projected course. "If I read all of this correctly, our speed is already beginning to increase from the combined gravity of the neutron star and the black hole. I wonder if our speed is high enough so that a course correction can take us safely around it."

"Let's check the ship's systems out first," replied Ty wanting to give the black hole a wide berth. "We may want to make that course correction very shortly." He also wanted to talk to Pierre LaRann about the black hole. If Ty remembered correctly, LaRann was an expert in that field.

With that, both men got busy going over long checklists to ensure that the FarQuest was still in prime operating condition. They both knew that shortly the ship would be subjected to a lot of stress. Perhaps more than she had been designed for!

Over the next several hours, the rest of the crew filed slowly in until everyone was awake and at their duty stations. Ty made sure the scientists were aware of the black hole data and wasn't too surprised when Pierre LaRann requested that the cargo bay doors be opened. A few moments later, one of the FarQuest's telescopes was activated and focused on the distant, dark object.

The highly magnified image was projected on the flight deck's main view screen, and a dark maw with darker colors around its edges filled the screen. The whole mass seemed to be swirling around like a hurricane with calm at its center. The exact center was black, or lacking words to describe it, totally void of color, just a vast emptiness that swallowed light itself. The outer areas of the black hole were tinged in dark violets and purple as it swirled and turned around its massive center.

"We need to make a course change within twelve hours," Captain Simpson stated looking up from the data scrolling across his computer screen.

"So soon," said Ty surprised. He had thought they would have more time than that.

"We are several million miles off our projected course and will be drawn into the black hole if we maintain our current heading," Commander Simpson replied as he ran more figures on his computer. "We could delay the course change by nearly 24 hours if we want to use the SRBs, but I prefer to save them for later."

"How long will we need to fire the ion drive?" asked Ty wanting to conserve as much fuel as possible.

"The ion drive will need to be fired for eight hours to allow us to pass both the neutron star and the black hole safely and not be torn apart by the gravitational stress," answered Captain Simpson as the data came up on his screen. The course change had already been calculated back on Star One and transmitted to the FarQuest's flight computer.

"That really looks scary," Lieutenant Strett said from just behind Ty where she had been standing looking spellbound at the screen. She had just finished putting everything up in the deep sleep compartment. "What is it?"

"A damn black hole," Winston muttered from his console where he had been checking the ship's fusion reactor. "What's going to turn up next?"

"Lieutenant Strett go down to the science section and check on our three scientists," Ty ordered not wanting to leave the flight deck at the moment. "We need to start transmitting data back to Star One as soon as possible. I don't know what kind of problems the black hole may cause with our transmitting equipment as we draw nearer to it."

"Yes sir," Lieutenant Strett replied. "I need to check on them anyway to see if they have fully recovered from their deep sleep experience."

Ty watched as she vanished down the central hatch heading towards the science levels.

"We will give the scientists four hours to take observations and readings," Ty said to Captain Simpson. "Set up our course change maneuver to begin exactly four hours from now."

Looking at the screen, Ty felt an ominous feeling at the back of his mind as he stared into the swirling depths of the black hole. He knew that they would have to fire the drive to increase their speed and angle their trajectory just enough to take them past it. Then they would spend another six days decelerating and then accelerate back around to study the neutron star-black hole binary in more detail. If everything proceeded as planned, in another eighteen days they would be back in deep sleep and safely on their way back to Star One.

Several hours later, Ty and Lieutenant Strett were down on level eight watching the scientists complete their readings.

"Absolutely amazing," Pierre LaRann mumbled from the view screen where he had been using one of the ship's telescopes to photograph the black hole in detail.

"What type of particle emissions are you finding?" LaRann asked LeAnn Kelly who was using several of the ship's more sensitive instruments to probe the spectra in and around the black hole.

"I can't believe some of this stuff," she replied, her eyes glowing with excitement. "At the exact center of the black hole, I show nothing, just emptiness. However, from its outskirts I have gathered a lot of data that could be extremely useful. This stuff is really amazing."

"I've almost completed my initial study on the neutron star," added Juan Raol stepping back and rubbing his eyes from where he had been using a stellar spectrograph to record data. "It's 18.24 miles in diameter and 2.26 times the mass of our Sun. It's rotating on its axis 1.95 times per second. Its mass is sufficient to form a gravitational lens, which is bending the radiation emitted by the star."

Ty listened to the scientists as they talked excitedly about what they were finding. All three seemed to be highly thrilled with the information they were gathering.

"We will have our initial reports ready to transmit in about 30 more minutes commander," Pierre stated taking off his glasses and polishing the lenses with some lens cleaning paper, which he always carried. "Our readings will give the scientific community years of study and conjecture. This black hole may even contain a corridor to another time or another section of space if we just had the technology to take advantage of it. The ramifications are truly astounding."

"You believe it's actually possible?" asked LeAnn Kelly looking speculatively over at Professor LaRann. "Could this black hole contain a traversable wormhole?"

"It's large enough and the center does not seem to be rotating from what we can observe of the event horizon and the outer environs of the black hole," Pierre replied thoughtfully. "The problem is keeping the wormhole open while an object passes through. Most theories demand the use of some type of exotic matter, but I'm not so certain that is actually necessary. Other forms of matter might suffice if contained in the proper type of field in suspension."

"You are saying it would be possible to travel from one section of our universe to another in an instant using this traversable wormhole?" Ty asked intrigued by the idea. It sounded like science fiction, but someday with the right technology who knew what might be possible.

"Theoretically it's possible," Pierre replied with a nod, putting his glasses back on. "This is the first time we have been able to examine a black hole up close. Perhaps with this information, we will know if a wormhole such as I described is possible."

Nodding, Ty looked around at the animated faces of the three scientists. "Let me know as soon as you're ready to transmit the data. We need to fire the ion drive soon, or we could end up getting a very close and personal look at that black hole ahead of us," Ty warned.

Two hours later, Ty watched as the last of the data was transmitted back to Star One and the Farside array. The data had been transmitted four times to ensure that a complete copy was received back at the receiving stations. Ty knew the information they were transmitting would create quite a stir back home.

"Thirty seconds to drive ignition," reported Captain Simpson as he watched the countdown timer wind down.

"Ion drive chambers on line and ready to fire," Winston reported from his station as he watched the temperature rise inside the chambers.

"Everything is green on my board," Karl Velm reported from engineering where he was strapped into his acceleration couch in front of the master engineering console.

"Ship systems are good," reported Lieutenant Strett tightening her safety harness making sure it fit comfortably.

"Stand by for ion drive ignition," Captain Simpson said pressing the ion drive activation button on his crowded console.

In the ion chambers, the temperature suddenly went up as the drive activated feeding argon to the hungry drive. The twin rocket tubes lit up brilliantly as the FarQuest was accelerated to one-fifth gravity. Under the power of the ion drive, the ship began its slow course change.

Ty felt the drive come on, and the force of acceleration press him back slightly in his acceleration couch.

A sudden alarm began sounding hauntingly on Winston's board drawing his attention. "We have a power surge in the fusion reactor," Winston reported his hands flying over his board looking for the problem. Several amber lights were flashing and then two of them turned a threatening red. "One of the containment fields is becoming unstable!"

"I have red warning lights here also," reported Karl worriedly from engineering where his board was suddenly showing a series of red blinking lights demanding attention. "I'm not sure what is causing the power surge."

"Do we need to shut the drive down?" Ty asked alarmed by all the red lights that were now appearing on the consoles. He looked back at Winston who was intently watching a computer screen.

"Damn energy in the reactor is surging again," Winston said sharply. "It shouldn't be doing that. Karl do you see anything on your console that might explain this?"

"Nothing definite," Karl replied quickly. "I am running a diagnostic to try to trace the problem. It will take several minutes."

"I don't think we have several minutes," Winston warned as another light turned red. "We need to shut the drive down now!"

Ty felt himself suddenly pressed farther back in his acceleration couch. "Deactivate the reactor!" Ty ordered as the ship began to vibrate. On his console, he saw that the ship was accelerating rapidly, and they were already moving at double the planned rate of acceleration.

It was at that moment that a powerful explosion rocked the ship and the acceleration from the ion drive suddenly increased even more. Ty felt himself pressed firmly back into his acceleration couch as a force of nearly one gravity tried to hold him down. Lieutenant Strett screamed in fear, and Winston cursed as all the lights on his board went out.

"The fusion reactor is over heating! We have had a failure in one of the magnetic containment fields," Winston warned as he tried to get his console to power back up. "We have to shut the drive down first before we can shut down the reactor, or we risk an explosion in the argon tanks from a possible flare back."

Ty watched as Captain Simpson worked the controls on his board and then turned to Ty with a strained look on his normally calm face. "I can't shut it down, the systems not responding! Too much argon is being fed into the drive. The extra argon and the power surge are increasing our acceleration. The drive is not designed for this high of acceleration. It could be seriously damaged if we don't shut it down quickly."

"Karl," Ty said into the ship's com trying to sound calm. "You need to get down to level twenty and manually shut down the drive from the emergency control station. Do it quick, we are running out of time!"

"On my way commander," replied Karl unstrapping himself from his acceleration couch and running over to the central hatch, which led down into the lowest levels of the ship.

Tense minutes passed on the flight deck as more red and amber lights flared up on the control boards. "Reactor will reach critical temperature in five minutes," Simpson reported calmly watching a computer screen that was now set to show the reactor core readings. "The magnetic containment fields will not be able to control the reaction. We will have a containment breach."

"What will happen if we have a breach?" asked Ty fearing the worst.

"The high temperatures contained in the magnetic fields will be released, and the ship will melt," Simpson replied in an anxious voice. "It will be over in an instant."

Lieutenant Strett closed her eyes with her hand going to her throat. She hadn't expected to die this way, not due to an accident on the ship. Her breathing quickened, and she slowly opened her eyes looking at the main screen, which was still focused on the black hole.

"I have power back on my console," Winston yelled as he began quickly typing in commands. "Karl, where are you," he asked as he tried to find the problem with the drive and the fusion reactor.

"I've reached the emergency control console," responded Karl breathing hard over the com. "Implementing emergency shut down of the drive now."

Seconds later, the ship was rocked by another larger explosion, which caused the FarQuest to shudder and shake noisily. The lights flickered and went out to come back on seconds later glowing dimly. From one of the twin ion tubes, a huge ball of flame seemed to appear and die out. Then both tubes faded into darkness as the drive shut itself off.

"Shutting down the reactor," Winston breathed heavily activating the shutdown program. He saw that the reactor was less then a minute away from a full containment breach. "We're going to vent a hell of a lot of plasma."

Seconds later, the ship was in darkness except for the softly glowing emergency lights, which had come on automatically when the ship's power was cut.

"Activate the fuel cell banks Lieutenant Strett," ordered Ty looking at the powerless control consoles on the flight deck. He wondered worriedly what the last explosion had been. Just how badly damaged was the FarQuest?

"Powering up," Lieutenant Strett said as she flipped several switches and keyed in commands from her touch pad.

The lights gradually brightened and then came back on full. Moments later, the consoles came back on one by one as more power was generated. Numerous red lights still covered the consoles. With a sinking feeling, Ty knew that the FarQuest had to have been badly damaged.

"Karl, what was that last explosion?" Ty asked when the ship's com system came back on line." Only silence came back as Ty waited for a response.

"He's not going to respond commander," Lieutenant Strett spoke in a stricken voice. She was looking at a diagnostic of the ship's environmental system. It showed a vacuum in level twenty.

"What do you mean he is not going to respond," demanded Ty looking over at Lieutenant Strett.

"I'm showing a hull breach on level twenty," answered Lieutenant Strett trying her best to sound calm. "My console is reporting the entire level is in a vacuum, and the pressure hatches have automatically sealed off that section of the ship. Karl never had a chance to get out before that last explosion."

The four members of the flight deck crew stared at one another in shock feeling numb by the appalling reality of what had just occurred. Karl was dead! Everything had happened so quickly. Ty was finding it hard to grasp that he had just lost a valuable member of his crew.

"Commander," Simpson said quietly with a pained look on his face. "The ship is tumbling from that last explosion. We need to use the RCS thrusters to reestablish control."

"Do it," Ty ordered moving his gaze back to his console. This was the first time he had ever lost a crewmember. He had watched people die in the Antarctic Police Action, but not like this. "We need to get the ship back under control and see what the damage is and if it can be repaired."

Thrusters fired on the FarQuest's hull and soon the tumbling was slowed then stopped as the ship resumed a normal state of flight. On the main screen, the black hole loomed ominously dead ahead of the now helpless spacecraft.

Six hours later, Ty had the entire crew assembled in the galley sitting at the main table with the screen focused on the black hole.

"The damage report is not good," began Ty looking around at each crewmember. "It will take us nearly half a day to repair the damage to the fusion reactor's magnetic containment field. There is a small hull breach on level twenty and major damage to ion drive chamber number two. Repairs to the drive chamber, as near as we can determine without actually inspecting it, may take up to a week."

"Can we fire the SRBs to make our course change?" Pierre LaRann asked, calmly cleaning his glasses. He knew that the FarQuest was already deep into the gravity well of the neutron star-black hole binary. It was not a good place to be in their current situation.

Ty looked at Captain Simpson before replying. "The explosion in the ion drive damaged the control connections for the boosters. We believe that we can have those repaired in about eighteen hours. However, we dare not fire them until the hull breach has been repaired. That will require us to do an EVA to weld a patch of Luxen over the hole in our hull."

"So how long before we can fire the boosters?" Lieutenant Strett asked afraid of the answer.

"At least 30 hours," Ty replied simply. "It will be 30 hours before we dare risk firing the boosters."

"That's not soon enough is it?" asked Winston softly looking at the screen and the waiting black hole.

"No," Ty replied with a long sigh. "The explosion and the brief acceleration from the ion drive pushed us more in line with the black hole. We don't have enough power to avoid it. If the ion drive was still fully functional, we could still pull away. Without it, we will be pulled into it. The closer we get to the black hole, the faster we are being pulled in by its gravity."

"Then we are going to die," said Lieutenant Strett with fear in her eyes. She had known this mission was dangerous, but she had expected to make it back home.

"Not necessarily," Pierre LaRann uttered thoughtfully, his face lined in deep thought, looking at LeAnn Kelly.

"The wormhole at the center of the black hole," said LeAnn Kelly looking at the older astronomer. "You want to try to go through it don't you!"

"That's crazy," objected Winston raising an eyebrow. "We don't even know if there is a wormhole at the center. That's all theory. It's never been proven."

"Won't we be crushed by the intense gravity?" Captain Simpson asked not pleased with the thought. It sounded as if the scientists had given up all hope of being able to make it back to Star One.

"No," replied Pierre shaking his head. "The black hole will draw us faster and faster toward the wormhole at its center. I will have to do some calculations to determine our exact trajectory. Can we still use the other ion drive chamber at all?"

Winston Archer looked up from where he had been staring dejectedly at the table. "The other drive chamber is undamaged, and I can rewire the system and change the programs where the remaining chamber could be used. We would have to cut off the flow of argon to the other chamber, but there is a bypass valve, which can be used to do that easily enough. It will take awhile."

"There's no way we could use the SRBs and the ion drive together to slingshot us around the black hole is there?" asked Lieutenant Strett realizing that if they did survived the passage through the black hole they would never see home again. They would be hopelessly lost in space.

"We might be able into get a slingshot orbit, but the gravity stresses would tear the ship apart, even with its Luxen coating," responded Ty trying to think of some other way out of this situation. Professor LaRann's solution was radical, but Ty could think of nothing else that might allow them to survive.

He remembered the creaking of the ship when they had done the slingshot maneuver around the Moon. This would be a hundred times worse. The ship would be torn apart. Ty seriously doubted that they would find out what lay on the other side of the wormhole even if they managed to reach it. The gravity inside the black hole would crush the ship.

"Has anyone calculated how much time we have before the black hole pulls us in?" asked Captain Simpson leaning forwards.

"Our speed will continue to increase every second now," Pierre replied. We are well into the gravitational field of the black hole. I estimate we have no more then 36 hours before we reach its center."

The room was silent as each individual thought about the ramifications. Any chance of returning home was gone. Even if there was a wormhole at the center of the black hole, the ship would probably be torn apart by the gravitational stresses. If they did manage to transit the wormhole, they could end up anywhere in time and space. Eventually their supplies would run out. They would most likely starve to death in the ship somewhere in deep, unexplored space.

"Then let's get busy," ordered Ty reaching a decision. A small chance was better than none. "We will do the EVA first and patch the hole in our hull. We have extra plates of Luxen for that purpose.

An hour later, Ty floated at the end of a tether secured inside the FarQuest's main airlock. He was using his small jet pack to maneuver a three-foot wide piece of Luxen over the hole he had found in the hull. The hole itself was on the upper section of the hull above the ion drive chamber. It measured nearly two and a half feet across. Ty had already used a special cutting torch to smooth out the jagged edges a few minutes earlier so the patch could be placed over it. Later he would add a second patch from the inside to cover the interior section of the hole.

As Ty worked, he glanced up occasionally to gaze at the stars around him. From this distance, the neutron star and the black hole were indistinguishable from the other stars that littered the void. Ty spent long minutes welding the Luxen patch securely to the hull watching as the bright arc from the special welder glared in his visor covered eyes.

Finally, Ty was finished and moved back to look at the job he had just completed. He felt extremely lonely floating by himself in his cumbersome spacesuit outside the FarQuest. The clean, cool air from his suit was continuously recycled for breathing and helped to keep him calm. Using his jet pack, he moved back into the airlock pulling the tether line inside before shutting the outer hatch.

Early the next morning, after a few hours of drug induced sleep, Ty waited for Winston to report from main engineering. Winston and Captain Simpson were finishing the final adjustments to the magnetic containment field for the fusion reactor. Without power from the fusion plant, they could not send a clear message home through the interference from the neutron star and the now very near black hole.

Back on Star One, no one would be able to guess what had happened. Their original data should have arrived after twelve hours of transit time, and now for nearly eight additional hours there had been no communication from the FarQuest, Ty could imagine the confusion and concern back on Star One. Ty knew that Steve would have realized by now, that something was terribly wrong.

"Ready to go on line commander," Captain Simpson reported from engineering. "We will run everything from the main engineering console, that way if there is a problem we can handle it from here."

"Let's do it," Ty responded. Looking back over his shoulder, he saw that Lieutenant Strett was at her console monitoring the ship's systems.

"Magnetic containment field established," stated Simpson over the com as the reactor was brought slowly back to life.

Ty watched closely on the flight deck as fusion power was gradually restored and Lieutenant Strett shut down the fuel cells.

"Everything looks normal," she commented checking her systems carefully. Power levels are in the green and ship systems are functioning normally."

"Commander," Pierre LaRann's voice came over the com. "I would like to launch two of the ion probes into the black hole as soon as possible."

Glancing at Lieutenant Strett, who was busily checking her console, Ty replied. "Why launch the probes, what can they tell us that we don't know already?"

"By launching the probes, one at a time, they will be pulled into the black hole and possibly the wormhole before we are," LaRann replied.

"What good will that do? Ty asked confused.

Ty knew that once the probes got close to the black hole communication would become impossible. The black hole itself would prevent any transmission because of its mass. Once the probe reached the event horizon, all telemetry would cease instantly. Nothing could pass through the event horizon; it would capture everything, including light and radio waves.

"The probes can report back on conditions they encounter before we get there. Also at some point, the gravity from the black hole is going to make communication with the probes and our transmissions back to Star One impossible. We want to transmit data back until the very last possible minute. Also, by monitoring the probes, we can better adjust our course for the wormhole."

"Can you give me the times you need the probes launched and what course trajectory you need them on?" Ty asked. He still didn't see how this would help any.

"We'll have it to you within ten minutes," Pierre responded.

Twenty minutes later, Captain Simpson was back at his flight control console readying the two ion probes for launch. Ty had run a computer study trying to estimate what their current speed was. The numbers didn't make any sense. Their speed was now increasing dramatically as the intense gravity from the neutron start and the black hole drew them in. At their current rate of increase, they would enter the black hole itself in another 24 hours.

Ty wondered how Steve would take this news. Ever since they had restored fusion power, they had been transmitting non-stop back to Star One relaying what had occurred and what their plan of action was. Ty didn't believe that Star One could get a message back to them before the interference from the neutron star-black hole binary ended communications.

"Probes ready for launch," Captain Simpson reported as he powered up the first of the ion probes attached to the FarQuest's delta wings.

"Launch probe one," Ty ordered.

The FarQuest shuddered slightly as the first probe was released and its ion drive flashed on driving the small probe ahead of the FarQuest. On the screen, Ty watched the brilliant glow from the probe as it angled its trajectory to take it close to the outer edges of the black hole.

Professor LaRann wanted to see how close the probe could come to the edge and not be lost in the black hole's event horizon.

Twenty minutes later, the second probe was launched on a different course that Professor LaRann thought would take it safely into the wormhole. If LaRann's calculations were correct, the probe would reach the wormhole an hour before the FarQuest.

On the main screen, Ty watched as the two probes vanished from sight flying into the maw of the black hole, which now dominated the screen.

Time passed as the crew hurriedly worked on repairs and prepared the ship for the hazardous passage through the wormhole. Data was being sent back to Star One continuously from the ship's high gain antennas as it was received from the ship's instruments, which were constantly recording data, as the ship came ever so much closer to the black hole.

The exhausted crew finally finished the repairs in the ion chamber. Ty and Captain Simpson had hoped to recover Karl's body from the emergency control station, but it was not there. Captain Simpson thought that Karl might have been pulled out into space when the hull had been breached.

From all of their checks, the remaining undamaged ion chamber checked out fine. The problem with the magnetic containment field, which had caused the first explosion in the other chamber, had been found. A relay between two CPUs had blown, and the backup had not activated automatically. Another programming problem, which hadn't been found in all the simulations they had run back on the Space Platform.

They had found the damage in the second ion chamber to be a far less severe than earlier believed. Several hours of welding new Luxen plates in the chamber and rerouting control circuits to the main engineering console would allow even that chamber to be used for a short time. Closing the access hatch behind them Ty, Captain Simpson, and Winston headed back exhaustingly to their control stations.

In the science section, Ty was stopped by Pierre LaRann and LeAnn Kelly where they were working on a strange looking apparatus. Ty recognized it as a modified magnetic containment field generator.

"What's that," he asked seeing that the generator had been hard wired into the ship's main power system.

"In order to safely transit the wormhole, we must make sure it stays open long enough to allow us safe passage," Pierre explained.

"The wormhole by its very nature is unstable, anything trying to pass through unprotected would in all likelihood be destroyed," LeAnn Kelly added. "That's why a lot of theories require exotic matter to be used in the passage."

"Fortunately for us, the ship is coated heavily in Luxen which is nearly impervious to radiation and heat. Much of the radiation from the wormhole will be reflected by the Luxen coating helping to hold the wormhole open," Pierre stated making a small adjustment on the generator.

"We will use the magnetic field containment generator to create a revolving magnetic field around the FarQuest when we begin to enter the wormhole," LeAnn went on standing up and stretching the kinks out of her back. "The hyper excited electrons from the ion drive will be captured by the revolving magnetic field and will act as a barrier between us and the wormhole helping to keep it open. From the calculations we have done; this should allow us to make the transit safely."

"That's a lot of ifs," commented Ty shaking his head worriedly. He knew the odds of this working were extremely low.

"The math says it will work," stated LeAnn looking at Ty. "If we can get to the wormhole, I feel sure we can safely transit it."

"I hope so," Ty responded looking at the two.

"We will make it commander," Pierre stated patting the generator. "This will work."

Nearly four hours later, everyone was strapped into their acceleration couches. Ty tried not to think about how fast they were now moving. Speeds like this had only been talked about in science fiction movies and books. This was real life.

Already the first probe was entering the outer fringes of the black hole. The scientists, with the exception of Pierre LaRann who was strapped securely to his acceleration couch in front of his recording instruments in the science level, were strapped down in the level just below the flight deck. That particular level was protected by a thicker layer of Luxen shielding for the safety of the crew in case of an emergency.

"Stand by to fire up the ion drive," Ty commanded as Captain Simpson laid in the course the FarQuest needed to take according to professor LaRann.

"Flight computer is ready. Drive firing in 30 seconds," Simpson responded. "Are you ready for this?" Simpson asked looking briefly over at Ty.

"Yes," Ty responded simply. "What other choice do we have?"

Ty knew that if this worked they would be leaving everything they knew behind. There would be no returning. They could end up thousands of light years from the Solar System. There was a slight chance they could even end up in another time. Letting out a deep breath, Ty thought briefly of Jennifer. He wished he had sent her a message, now it was too late. He wondered if he could have had a future with the brilliant AI programmer. Now, he would never know.

The seconds counted down, and the computer lit the ion drive at the count of zero. The ship trembled as the hyper excited electrons were stripped from the argon fuel and expelled out the twin exhaust tubes. Two brilliant drive flares glowed brilliantly as the FarQuest dove even faster towards the heart of the ever-consuming black hole.

"Data from the first probe has stopped transmitting," Pierre reported. "From the readings I got back, I believe it has passed the event horizon. Some of the readings I received just before it stopped transmitting are unbelievable. It was almost as if time itself was coming to a stop. The second probe is still on course and should be entering the wormhole in another 30 minutes."

Ty and Captain Simpson watched as the FarQuest's acceleration built up rapidly to one-half gravity. This allowed them to adjust their trajectory into the black hole ever so slightly to follow what Pierre believed to be a safe path. Minutes slowly stretched on as the swirling black hole loomed ever nearer and nearer.

"I've lost contact with the second probe," Pierre reported. "I don't think it was destroyed, I believe the black hole's gravity field at its core is preventing the data from escaping. However, I did get a picture of what must be the wormhole. I will put it up on the main screen."

A new still picture appeared on the screen. It showed what looked like a bright tunnel of light with darkness at its center rotating slowly in the center of the black hole.

"I want you to look at the exact center of the wormhole when I magnify this picture," Pierre said excitedly.

The picture swelled on the screen and the dark area swelled until small pinpoints of light were revealed.

"What are those?" Lieutenant Strett asked confused. I thought the center of the wormhole would be empty."

"It is," Pierre replied smugly. "What you are seeing is the space on the other side of the wormhole. Those are distant stars you are seeing, our destination."

Everyone was quiet looking with renewed hope at the screen.

"I thought it was impossible to see anything once the probe passed the event horizon," Captain Simpson stated. "How is this picture possible?"

"I don't know," Pierre replied with a frown. "Perhaps it has something to do with the wormhole itself. It is something I will need to study."

"Have you transmitted this back to Star One?" Ty asked.

"Yes, along with everything we have done to allow us to transit the wormhole," LaRann replied. "I also added all the theories we have come up with to cover the phenomenon we have witnessed. It is being transmitted repeatedly even though I don't know how much they will actually receive. The interference from the black hole and neutron star will be affecting our transmissions the closer we come to the wormhole. Once we pass the event horizon all communication will cease."

Ty watched the screen intently, as the FarQuest entered the outer layers of the black hole. For two minutes now the SRBs had been firing, adding their two gravities of acceleration to the ion drive to allow for more course corrections as Pierre modified their trajectory to line them up with the waiting wormhole. Ty just hoped it was enough.

"I'm activating the magnetic field generator," Pierre warned as a loud humming flowed through the ship.

"This is it," Lieutenant Strett spoke nervously staring at the view screen. She closed her eyes not wanting to see what was about to happen. She knew there was a very good chance they were all about to die.

"Almost there," Captain Simpson spoke.

On the main screen, Ty and Simpson watched as their destination became slightly cloudy from the captured electrons in the revolving magnetic field that surrounded the ship. In seconds, the FarQuest reached daringly for the speed of light and then vanished into the wormhole.

Ty felt as if his brain was about to explode. He thought he could hear someone screaming on the flight deck. For what seemed like microseconds or an eternity he could almost grasp the secrets of the universe, and then his thoughts faded as he lost consciousness in a sudden explosion of white light.

# Chapter Ten

Steve sat quietly in Main Control staring unseeingly at the main view screen. The last recordings from the FarQuest had just been played back showing the wormhole growing on the screen and then nothing. All contact with the ship had been lost. The rest of Main Control was quiet except for the low hum of equipment. Everyone sat spell bound held captive by the drama they had just witnessed being played out on the screen in front of them.

"The event horizon of the black hole is blocking anymore transmissions," Jar Stoler commented staring in rapt astonishment at the screen. "I still don't understand how some of those transmissions passed through the event horizon. We shouldn't have been able to receive them."

Steve looked over at the physicist nodding his head in understanding. He knew what Stoler was saying, but Steve's mind was still numb from shock over what had happened to the FarQuest. Steve had asked the scientist to come up to Main Control once he realized the dilemma the FarQuest had gotten into.

"Perhaps it was the way they had the probes staggered," Lieutenant Commander Anderson suggested running a hand through his red hair and looking at Stoler. "Some of those photos of the wormhole may have been taken just as the probe or FarQuest entered the event horizon."

"Perhaps," Stoler replied with a frown still deep in thought. "I will need to study the data in more detail. Perhaps the conditions between the event horizon and the wormhole aren't quite what we believed. It's possible the wormhole may be influencing space time between its aperture and the event horizon allowing for the transmissions."

"He's gone," said Steve quietly not wanting to believe what he had just witnessed. "The entire crew is gone, and there's nothing we can do to bring them back."

"They may have survived the passage through the wormhole," Christy said feeling Steve's grief. "Professor LaRann felt that the FarQuest could safely make the transit."

"Not only that," Teela said from Steve's side where she had stood quietly watching the entire drama unfold on the screen. "Look at this last data we received from the FarQuest's instruments. I am enhancing it considerably because of the disturbances in the wormhole."

On the screen, a dozen stars shone brilliantly.

"Stars," Stoler said in surprise gazing at the screen. "That's the other end of the wormhole we are seeing. This is amazing!"

"These stars were visible briefly through the wormhole during one of its brief stable periods," Teela reported. "I am in the process of comparing it with star charts currently in my files to find a match. Unfortunately, there is nothing particularly outstanding about the stars in view. None of the stars are red giants, or other giant types. Several seem to be doubles, but the instability of the wormhole makes judging their actual luminosity and spectral type very difficult."

"So the FarQuest may have made it to where those stars are?" General Karver spoke from where he stood next to Lieutenant Emerson at her console. "Why did we lose contact with the ship so abruptly?"

"The intense gravity in a black hole is so intense that it does not allow light or any other electromagnetic radiation to escape from it," Teela responded. "The event horizon is the area near the black hole where its gravity is so powerful that nothing can escape. Not radio waves, or even light."

"So we lost contact when they got too close," General Karver replied in understanding.

"The FarQuest passed the threshold where their communications could not escape the effect of the black hole as they neared the wormhole at its center," Teela replied. "Only the relay from the probe allowed this one picture and some other data to get through. I don't understand how they even managed that. It should have been impossible from what we know of the gravity affects a black hole has on light and other radiation. Perhaps Jarl is correct in that the wormhole had something to do with it."

"What are their chances of surviving the transit of the wormhole?" Steve asked still finding it hard to accept that he would never see Ty or the rest of the FarQuest's crew again.

"I've been evaluating the data that they sent back along with Professor LaRann's theories about black holes and wormholes," Teela continued in her soft voice, her deep blue eyes looking at Steve. "From the data I've analyzed so far, it looks as if the FarQuest stood a very good chance of making it safely out of the other side of the wormhole."

"How good a chance?" asked Steve hoping the ship had survived.

"At least 50-50 if the data is correct and Professor LaRann's theories are plausible," answered Teela looking at Steve.

"The first interstellar flight," Christy said looking at Steve in wonder, her eyes wide in disbelief at what she was hearing. "That was always one of Ty's dreams."

"How long before all the data is correlated?" asked Steve turning from Christy to face Teela and Jarl Stoler who was now standing next to her.

"The data is currently being down loaded into the computers of the scientists who need to process the information we received from the FarQuest," Teela responded. "There is a lot of data on the neutron star and a tremendous quantity on the black hole. A preliminary report could be ready in about six hours."

"There was a lot of data being transmitted from the FarQuest," Stoler spoke. He had glanced briefly at some of it already. "There's a lot of information to sift through."

Standing up, Steve spoke to Christy. "Set up a staff meeting six hours from now. I want to go over the preliminary results as soon as possible." With that, Steve left Main Control and walked over to his office. He needed some time alone. He had just lost his best friend.

Christy followed him there a few minutes later and found Steve sitting in the dark. She turned on the lights and took a seat in front of his desk.

"What do we do now?" she asked knowing Steve was feeling a lot of anguish over losing the FarQuest and its crew. "The loss of the FarQuest will be a terrible blow to morale."

"I don't know," Steve replied in a low voice. "I do know that Ty and his crew are probably still alive, but what are their chances of survival on the other side of the wormhole. Even if they can find a planet with a breathable atmosphere, they would have to land the FarQuest without aid from the ground. The ship would need a flat area miles in length in order to survive a crash landing intact."

Christy stood up and walked around Steve's desk. She reached out and put her hands gently on his shoulders. She knew Steve felt horrible over Ty's loss. It was difficult for her to find the right words to ease Steve's suffering.

"Ty is very resourceful," said Christy massaging Steve's shoulders gently. "Just think, they may be establishing the first human colony outside our Solar System. Ty would want us to use the information

174

they transmitted back to us. He would want us to use that information to survive. And who knows, perhaps someday our descendants and his will meet up again out in space somewhere."

The two stayed together in Steve's office talking about the FarQuest. They spoke of how Ty had always wanted to explore space. They remembered the long conversations they had together, with Ty always pushing for deep space exploration. Whenever Steve needed someone to remind him of why Star One and the Space Platform had been built, or when Steve felt any doubts, Ty had always been there to strengthen Steve's resolve.

Hours later, the station's staff was gathered in the main conference room seated around the large table with Steve at its head. Everyone was talking in subdued tones, not sure what was in store for the station now. They knew that the information the FarQuest had sent back could well determine what their fate would be.

"As everyone knows," began Steve standing up and looking at the expectant faces. "The FarQuest has been lost in the wormhole at the center of the black hole. There is a good possibility that the ship was able to transit the wormhole safely to exit out into another section of space."

"Do we know where?" asked Julie still finding it hard to accept the fact that they would never see Ty again.

"Teela has been searching known stars to find any that might match the ones we saw in the photo we received from the FarQuest," replied Steve looking over at Teela.

Teela shook her head with a disappointed look on her face. "So far, there has been no match," she responded. "I am expanding the search, but it could be days before the search program is done. Even then, we might not find a positive match. The FarQuest could be anywhere."

"So Ty and the FarQuest are lost somewhere in deep space," Jennifer spoke quietly, the shock still evident on her face.

"We are assuming they made it through the wormhole," Jarl Stoler commented. Dryson and he had been studying the FarQuest data on the black hole for several hours. They were particularly interested in LaRann's theories on black holes and traversable wormholes.

"Do you think they did?" asked Steve hoping the FarQuest had managed to survive the transit of the wormhole.

"Possibly," Ted Dryson spoke up. "From what Jarl and I have been able to understand of LaRann's theories on traversable wormholes, it's definitely possible. Particularly with the use of the rotating magnetic field they established. From what we have studied of the math involved, it may just have worked."

"We can only pray that it did," Christy said simply looking around the group.

"How long can they survive with the supplies they have on board," Jennifer asked. She knew it couldn't be indefinitely.

"Their water and oxygen is recirculated and can last almost indefinitely," Todd Williams replied. He was extremely familiar with the specs of the FarQuest. "However, their food supply is another matter. Possibly six to seven months if they ration it."

"Could be much longer than that," Doctor Wruggi interjected. "If they make use of the deep sleep drug, they could considerably extend that. Perhaps by several years."

"I have asked Teela to give us a brief summary of what we have managed to learn from the preliminary study of the FarQuest data," Steve said.

Standing up, Teela moved to the head of the table to stand next to Steve. "The neutron star-black hole binary is now only eight billion miles away from our sun," she stated in a calm, soft voice. Her deep blue eyes moved across the staff members capturing everyone's undivided attention.

On the main view screen, a colored schematic depicting the Solar System and the planets in their orbits appeared. The trajectory of the neutron star-black hole binary was marked in dark red.

"As you can see the neutron star-black hole binary will intersect the Solar System disk at 1.46 billion miles from the sun," Teela spoke in a calm lecturing voice.

"Close enough to screw up the Solar System," commented Dryson shaking his head.

Walking over to the large view screen, Teela used a laser pointer to show the intersection point. "Fortunately, Jupiter and Saturn will both be on the far side of the Sun at this point and will not be drawn into the black hole. However, because of the strong gravitational stresses from the neutron star-black hole binary, almost all the orbits of the planets in our Solar System will be markedly changed." Another schematic showing a much different Solar System flashed up on the screen.

Many of the asteroids were gone, swept up by the changed orbits of Jupiter and Saturn, which now rode in an orbit much closer to each

176

other than before. Pluto was gone, cast off into the depths of interstellar space. The orbits of Mars and Earth now nearly intersected just inside the orbit of the few remaining asteroids and Earth came dangerously close to the orbit of Venus at its closest approach. Mercury's orbit was largely unchanged, and the orbit of Venus was more elongated than it had been.

"Those are some really drastic changes," Todd Williams spoke up eyeing the schematic. "Life on Earth will be impossible with that orbit."

"No more Goldilocks zone," Stoler spoke with his eyes focusing on the screen. "At the fartherest distance from the Sun on that diagram even the Earth's oceans will freeze. As the Earth nears Venus, the oceans will melt and begin to boil as the water temperature rises. After a few years, there will be very little liquid water left on the surface, and the atmosphere will be unbreathable."

"Assuming the Earth stays together from the gravity stresses it will be put through," added Andre gazing at the screen. He had run some simulations, and in several of them, the Earth had been broken apart.

"What about the Moon?" asked Julie seeing that the Moon was not depicted in orbit around the Earth. For that matter, many of the moons of the outer planets were missing.

"We don't know yet how many of the satellites of the different planets will be affected," answered Teela stepping back over to her position beside Steve. "Some may survive intact to continue to orbit the planets they do now. Others may be pulled out of their orbits. Some may be cast off into space escaping the Solar System altogether."

"What about the Moon?" General Karver asked wanting an answer to Julie's question. He wanted to know what would happen to Tycho City.

"As for Earth's Moon, we don't know yet," replied Teela switching her gaze to the general. "Several of the simulations show the Moon remaining in a much closer orbit to the Earth. Others show the Moon breaking apart and becoming an asteroid field encircling the globe."

"What will the effect be on our Sun?" asked Dryson staring intently at Teela. "Will it go nova?"

Teela hesitated before answering. "The latest information indicates an 84 percent chance that the Sun will undergo a major transformation."

"What kind of transformation?" Julie Gray asked afraid of the answer. She still hadn't recovered from the news about Ty. John had taken it extremely hard. He was still back in their quarters with their kids.

"It will experience a nova transformation, how large a nova is speculative," Teela replied in a lower voice.

"Then we are trapped," said Christy letting out a heavy sigh. "We can't move the station to safety in the time we have left. A nova will affect the entire Solar System; we couldn't possibly get clear in time."

The room was quiet as everyone weighed their options. Any type of nova would incinerate Star One, no matter where it was in the Solar System. They couldn't move it far enough away from the Sun for the station to be safe.

"There is a solution," Teela ventured cautiously. She had run a number of simulations and hadn't talked to anyone about what she was going to suggest. She hadn't even had time to mention it to Todd. She looked over at the commander with a strange pensive look appearing on her face.

"The wormhole," Steve responded his eyes widening in sudden understanding. That was what the strange look on Teela's face meant. "You think we should attempt to take Star One through."

"The wormhole!" Dryson repeated sharply looking stunned. His eyes narrowed as he considered the possibility. He glanced over at Stoler who had an equally stunned look on his face. "Is it possible?"

"Yes," Teela replied relieved that the commander had realized what she was going to propose. "We know from Professor LaRann's data what conditions are like and what they did to attempt passage through. With the ion drives on the Space Platform and the addition of some SRBs plus strengthening the station's structure, it is feasible. It would be possible for us to reach the black hole and navigate through the wormhole before the nova occurred."

"Ridiculous," Stoler said shaking his head in denial after thinking about the ramifications. "To move the station that far and attempt to go through the wormhole will be next to impossible. The station's structure would not survive the gravitational stress of the black hole long enough!"

"Not necessarily," retorted Todd thinking about the station specs and the thrust the four recently completed ion drives were capable of putting out. "We can get the station there. I am sure of that."

"Can the station survive the stress?" asked Christy looking over at Todd. She knew he had studied the stress levels the station was capable of. It had been necessary when calculating the maximum thrust for the ion drives. "That would be a long boost to get us there in time."

"The ion drive chambers installed in the Space Platform are capable of nearly one-fourth gravity of thrust if needed," replied Todd looking over at Teela who nodded back in affirmation. "Our artificial gravity could be adjusted to compensate for the thrust making it unnoticeable to the crew. The station is currently capable of handling the thrust from the ion drives without any additional modifications."

"Could the ion drives handle that amount of thrust over a long period?" Stoler asked. He knew the ion drives had been designed to move the station over relatively short distances before needing to be recalibrated. The station was just too massive.

"I would recommend only boosting at one-tenth gravity," answered Todd thinking about all the specs. "We could boost the station for eight hours and then coast for eight and then boost for another eight. That will give us time to check the systems between boosts for any potential problems. We have almost unlimited fuel supplies in the Space Platform for the drives, and we could do this for weeks."

Turning to Teela, Todd asked her a question. "If we boosted the station that way how long would it take us to reach the black hole?"

"From the time we begin boosting the station, it would take us 132 days to reach the black hole." Teela responded doing the calculations effortlessly.

Turning to Dryson and Stoler, Steve asked. "The FarQuest used a modified magnetic containment field generator to surround the ship with a revolving magnetic field. The field trapped electrons from the ion drive to form some kind of barrier to stabilize the wormhole and keep it open to allow their passage. Star One is a lot bigger than the FarQuest. Can you design a big enough generator to surround the station with a revolving magnetic field like the FarQuest?"

Dryson and Stoler looked at each other and then after talking quietly for several moments responded. "It can be done," Stoler replied with a nod. "But we're still not certain this plan is feasible."

"I don't think we have any other choice," Christy spoke looking at the two physicists. "If anyone has any other ideas that might allow us to survive a nova, now is the time to speak up."

The room was quiet with everyone looking at one another.

"Can you build the field generator in time?" Steve asked the two scientists once more. It looked like Teela's plan was going to be adopted. There just was no other option.

"We have plenty of time to build the equipment we would need," replied Dryson his eyes narrowing in thought.

"We can build a generator that will be much more stable and powerful than the one the FarQuest used," Stoler commented after a moment. "We would have to study the data to see why LaRann felt the revolving magnetic field with the trapped electrons would stabilize the wormhole for their passage through it. With the time we have, we might be able to come up with something better and more dependable."

"It will have to be much stronger in order to keep the wormhole open and stable during our passage," Dryson continued thinking deeply. "The station is much larger than the FarQuest."

"We will have to look at LaRann's theories on wormholes very carefully," Stoler said. "We need to understand exactly why he needed the magnetic field."

"Since Star One is much larger the stresses inflicted from the wormhole will be tremendous," Dryson stated. "From the very nature of the wormhole Professor LaRann describes in his theories, it will be inherently unstable. If I understand his theory correctly, it is the trapped electrons in combination with the revolving magnetic field that holds the wormhole open as we pass through. Not only that, but we can't activate the magnetic field until just seconds before entering the wormhole itself."

"Very well," Steve said letting out a deep breath. "I don't think we have a choice in this. I want everyone to prepare their departments to boost the station ten days from now. That will give us time to prepare the station, and completely review all the data we received from the FarQuest. Julie, you and Kathleen need to see how the boosting will affect the ecological habitats."

"So we are going to attempt to go through the wormhole to where Ty and the FarQuest are?" asked Jennifer as she realized just what was being proposed.

"That's what it looks like," Steve replied. "Unless anyone can come up with another solution between now and the time we begin boosting the station."

Jennifer was silent as she thought about this. She would ask Teela some detailed questions later. There was a lot of this she didn't understand.

"Teela, what are the latest reports from Earth side, any chance that Senator Farley can do anything to prevent us from leaving the

Lagrange point?" asked Steve looking over at Teela. Senator Farley had been quiet for several weeks now due to the increasing severe weather down below. Steve had been expecting another attack, but so far, none had been launched since that first missile attack.

"I don't see how," she said thoughtfully. "Look at these newscasts from down below that I have been monitoring for the last few hours."

On the main screen, a scene of destruction was being displayed. The view was of the South Carolina shore just north of Myrtle Beach. It showed massive waves being driven onto the defenseless shore by powerful storms at sea. The waves could be seen smashing buildings, tearing down power lines, and flooding miles and miles of helpless coastline. News crews flying high above the flooding were broadcasting the destruction.

Other scenes showed rivers overflowing their banks. Massive levees were being desperately thrown up to hold back the torrents of rising water. Enormous efforts were being made to prevent the raging floods from bursting through and sweeping entire towns and villages away. Military forces along with frightened townspeople were emplacing sandbags trying to control the flooding. Teela played the scenes for nearly five minutes.

"The storms on Earth are out of control," Teela reported. "Most of the Earth is being exposed to monsoon like rains. Hurricanes and typhoons are almost too numerous to count. Already millions of people in the low-lying areas of China, India, Japan, the Philippines, Indonesia, Europe, and even the United States have been made homeless. Many others have lost their lives due to the increasing severe weather."

"What about the food situation?" asked Julie staring awe struck at the view screen. "With the weather this terrible, it's bound to have had a catastrophic effect on the world's crops."

"A state of emergency has been declared in every nation," replied Teela trying to sound calm. "Much of the year's harvests have been inundated with floods. Some countries will be facing widespread starvation in just a matter of weeks. The U.S. has curtailed all exports of grains and other food stuffs until the emergency is over."

"It won't be over," Andre commented sadly. "It is only beginning."

His words weighed heavily on everyone. They all knew that shortly the earthquakes would begin, followed by the volcanoes. Conditions down on Earth would only continue to deteriorate.

"Civil unrest will spread very soon," Martain Blackwater stated, looking around the group. "Anarchy will begin to spread across the globe as hunger spreads. Fortunately, the weather will prevent the wholesale slaughter of people fighting for what food remains, many will just die in their homes."

"What about the earthquakes?" asked Steve watching Teela. He had come to depend on her a lot recently. "What are the latest estimates on when those might occur?"

"We could see some major earth movements within the next 30 to 60 days." Teela replied as she quickly accessed a simulation. "The heavy rains are not helping the situation. From the models we have put together, I don't believe that we will see a widespread increase in volcanic activity for another 60 to 90 days. However, there is a possibility that some of the earthquakes could trigger a few major eruptions."

"Very well," replied Steve nodding at Teela. "Let's get to work then."

Down on Earth, Senator Farley sat in one of the deep underground retreats built to protect the President and his staff in case of a nuclear war. He had gathered together many of his closest friends and business associates to sit out the terrible weather raging up above.

Martial law still reigned in the country. The severe weather pounding the countryside held the country in a death grip. Many bridges were out, thousands of square miles of coastland and river bottom were flooded. The nation's crops were almost a complete loss. The continuous rain was preventing farmers from getting into their fields, which had turned into swamps. They couldn't even harvest the pitiful remains of their decimated crops. Many people were already wondering where their next meal would come from.

Clutching a smoking cigar in his right hand, Farley looked around the conference table where his advisors had gathered. Many had a look of fear and desperation on their haggard faces. Already, several who had fallen into disfavor with Senator Farley had been cast out of the shelter into the raging storms above.

"What's the latest reports?" he demanded taking a heavy puff on the cigar with a scowl on his face.

A two star general at the far end of the table stood up. Scant weeks before he had been a young colonel in the marines.

"We can hardly move anything," General Young reported in a steady voice. "Whenever there has been a break in the clouds or a lessening of the rain, we have moved some supplies with helicopters. So many bridges are out and roads flooded that moving anything for long distances is next to impossible. Many communities are isolated, and their only contact is by radio. Much of the nation is out of power with power lines down and electrical generating stations flooded or damaged."

With a livid red look across his face, Farley took another long puff on his cigar sending rings of smoke upwards.

"What about food supplies, how are they holding out?" he demanded looking over at another individual.

An older, frail looking man stood and slowly looked around the group, the aging Senator from the agricultural sector, who had always been one of Farley's staunchest supporters, replied. "The harvest for the year is almost a total loss. What few crops we did manage to get in are of very poor quality. With the carry over from last year's harvest, we can get by for another 90 to 120 days, after that we will be forced to slaughter livestock and anything else that can be used for food. We are already starting to ration food wherever possible. Before we can get the next crop in and harvested, we will be facing wide spread famine. There are already shortages in most of the major cities."

"What about our project at White Sands?" Farley grumbled. Surely someone had some good news.

Another man stood up; he occupied the position of Science Advisor to Senator Farley. With a despairing look in his eyes, he began his report. He knew that the Senator would not like what he was about to say.

"We have made some progress on the new laser battery at White Sands New Mexico. Unfortunately, even that area has been suffering heavy rainfall. We are weeks behind schedule, and it will be at least 30 more days before it will be ready to test."

Senator Farley staggered to his feet. In the last few months, he had put on a lot of weight, since he insisted on throwing lavish meals for his guests. He had made sure that this shelter was well stocked with food and other luxurious comforts he didn't want to do without.

"Will the laser battery have the power to destroy Star One?" he demanded loudly, his eyes glaring.

"Yes sir," the Science Advisor replied. "But only by over loading it will it have the range. My people report it will only fire for about 30 seconds before it melts."

"But it will destroy Star One," Senator Farley spoke breathing heavily. He wanted General Karver, Steve Larson, and Star One annihilated.

"The laser is made out of Luxen, but even that material will not be able to resist the power we will be using for long," the man replied. "We plan on doing a short test shot taking out one of the orbiting satellites. If the test is successful, we will set up the main firing sequence to take out the station. However, keep in mind this will be a one shot affair."

"Then make sure you don't miss!" Senator Farley ordered sharply.

"Our computers should be able to lock on to the target," the Science Advisor replied, his eyes looking away from Senator Farley. "We won't miss."

Sitting back down, Senator Farley let a satisfied smile flit across his face. "So Star One only has only 30 more days to exist. I would like to see the look on those bastard's faces when we hit them with the laser."

Farley looking up saw that the Science Advisor was still standing looking extremely anxious "What else is there?" Farley growled he had already heard enough bad news for today.

"We have a report from the Mauna Kea observatory in Hawaii. They had some clear skies for a few hours last night and took some sightings on a strange object." Hesitatingly, the Science Advisor looked around the group for support, but no one would meet his eyes.

"Go on," Farley spoke in a low, threatening voice, his eyes narrowing.

"The astronomers report that the object has all the characteristics of a neutron star and it is within eight billion miles of our Solar System. They claim it is the cause of our weather problems, not Star One."

"Shut up fool," screamed Farley jumping up and leaning forward his hands shaking on the table, his face livid with uncontrolled rage. "Star One is responsible for our weather, there is no neutron star, those astronomers probably looked at a comet, and I don't want to hear this nonsense ever again!"

Nodding, the Science Advisor sat back down trembling. There was no doubt in his mind what the astronomers had seen. However, he knew that if he pressed the issue, his life could be shortened considerably. He had no desire to be sent to the surface.

Farley still stood fuming at his Science Advisor. What is wrong with all of these fools? Star One was the cause of this weather everyone knew that. Turning, he stalked off in anger. He needed to get away from his advisors.

Up on Star One, Steve and Christy entered Jensens after taking a relaxing stroll down the concourse spending a little time going into some of the small shops and looking around. They needed to get away from all the pressure of their jobs. A few hours of uninterrupted leisure time were a necessity. Steve was still feeling badly about the FarQuest and this would help to take his mind off it, at least for a few hours.

The shops were still well stocked. Steve had seen to it that a lot of additional supplies for the shops had been shipped up while the shuttles were still flying. As long as people could do some shopping and get lost in trying on clothes, buying articles for their quarters, and gifts for special occasions, the shops served a positive purpose as a morale booster. Steve had sat patiently for a few minutes in one of the smaller clothing stores as Christy modeled several dresses she liked. After getting Steve's reaction, she had put one back to pick up later.

Entering Jensens, they were shown to a large table that was already partly filled with the others they had invited to dine with them that night. Julie and John Gray were there, Todd Williams and Teela, as well as Kathleen and Jennifer.

Taking their seats, Steve saw with a smile that Jensen was already on his way with several waiters carrying trays. One tray was full of glasses, and the other tray had several bottles of Jensen's special wine. Steve wondered just how much of the wine Jensen had put back. He knew that Jensen had managed to get several unusually large crates shipped up to Star One at the last minute. It had been called to Steve's attention since they were not on the manifests, but owing to the fact that Jensen was one of the station's biggest morale boosters Steve had let it slide.

"Good evening everyone," Jensen beamed speaking in his best French accent. "What would you like tonight?" Jensen nodded and the two waiters began pouring generous portions of wine into their glasses.

In moments, everyone had placed their orders and were becoming engaged in quiet dinner conversation. Steve relaxed leaning back in his chair, enjoying the restaurant's atmosphere, listening to the soft music playing in the background, the subdued lighting, and the company of friends. This was just what he needed to unwind from the days events.

He just wished that Ty were here with them. He tried not to let his mind dwell on that thought.

Jennifer and Kathleen were busy talking in quiet voices about Teela. They were both curious about how Teela and Todd were getting along.

"She has become so relaxed and confident in herself. I can hardly believe it," Kathleen said looking across the table at Teela who wore a low cut dress that dipped suggestively down into the swell of her now ample breasts. Kathleen thought the dress looked perfect on her; it was something she would pick out to wear.

"I'm so happy for her," responded Jennifer taking a small sip of the rich red wine that was in her glass. "Teela and I talk for hours it seems like every day. She is still full of questions, but sometimes I get the feeling that she wishes that she and Todd could have more of a real relationship."

Teela glanced at Jennifer and smiled. Sometimes Jennifer forgot that Teela's sensors could pick up everything she said.

Changing the conversation, Jennifer asked Kathleen how work in the ecological habitats was going. Jennifer knew that Kathleen loved her work almost as much as she enjoyed dressing up. Even tonight, Kathleen's dark blue dress was very revealing. Looking around, Jennifer almost laughed at John Gray's panicked expression when he realized which dress Kathleen was wearing. From Julie's look of mirthful satisfaction at John's discomfort, it was abundantly clear that she had already noticed and was enjoying watching her husband squirm.

Steve was holding Christy's hand and talking about how once everything was settled, they would get a larger apartment and move in together. Christy had suggested several weeks back that they should go ahead and move in together. They were already spending a lot of nights in either his small apartment or hers as it was now. Their love affair was no longer a secret on the station.

"I know you think it's silly to go ahead and wait," Steve said in a quiet voice. "But I want us to be married when we finally do move in together, and right now with everything that is going on, we have to wait. I promise that if we make it through the wormhole, we will get married immediately afterwards."

Christy took a long sip of her wine listening patiently to Steve. She understood his reasons and even respected them, but it would still be nice to wake up each morning with Steve at her side. Looking down the table, she eyed Kathleen and Teela, briefly marveling at their daring in the dresses they wore. She could never get the nerve up to dress that revealingly in public. But then again she thought turning back to Steve, if she did, it might give Steve the added encouragement to speed things up a little.

The evening wore on as the little group talked and laughed letting the days stresses die completely out. After a filling meal specially prepared by Jensen himself, the little group broke up and went their separate ways. Christy ended up in Steve's apartment.

-

Julie dragged John back to their quarters. Once Julie finished checking on the kids, she took a nice hot shower knowing what kind of mood John would be in after staring at Kathleen out of the corner of his eyes all evening. Julie would have to remember to thank her tomorrow.

-

Todd and Teela sat up into the late hours of the evening talking and listening to music in Todd's quarters on the Space Platform. Teela watched as Todd finally feel asleep on the couch and then, with a pleased smile, she disappeared as she switched the holographic imager off. Teela felt a touch of deep sadness wash over her. She wished that she could actually touch Todd, to feel his tender hands holding hers, to experience a kiss and more. The holographic imager and virtual reality software did a good job at imitation, but Teela knew it wasn't real. Trying to put the sadness out of her mind, Teela accessed the computer core and began reviewing the data gathered that day from the FarQuest and other projects going on aboard Star One. Teela didn't need any sleep. Another reminder for her that she wasn't real.

# Chapter Eleven

Steve and Christy were seated at their master control console in Main Control. Their eyes were focused tensely on the main view screen that currently held everyone's attention. A small hastily put together space probe with several long-range cameras was hanging out in space several miles away from Star One. One of its cameras was currently focused on the station. Its small solar panels were extended soaking up power to operate the small computer, cameras, and tracking devices that it had been equipped with. Its job was simple, to monitor Star One's impending exit from the Earth-Moon system.

"I can't believe we are doing this," Christy breathed feeling the excitement in the air. "We are finally going to put ourselves out of Senator Farley's reach." It would be a relief not to have to worry about the Senator anymore. Every day when she was on duty, she felt like she was on pins and needles waiting for the Senator to make his next move. She didn't know how many times she had asked Teela if there was any danger coming from Earth.

"It will make everyone feel more secure," replied Steve glancing down and looking at the small screens on the side of his console, which showed other sections inside the station. Everyone seemed to be ready for the big event. He then looked back up at the larger screens, which were displaying views of the outside of Star One.

Steve could feel the tension in the air, as everyone waited anxiously for the newly installed ion drives to be fired. They would be launching Star One toward its crucial meeting with the black hole. Looking around the room, Steve saw that Lieutenant Emerson and her two people were busy. They had been assigned to use their detecting instruments to sweep ahead of Star One and search for any asteroid or other pieces of space debris that they might encounter. The weapons station would be manned 24 hours a day. General Karver was currently standing behind Lieutenant Emerson observing everything.

If such an object were found, the rail guns would be used to blast it out of their path. At the speed they would be traveling, any collision could be disastrous, and they would be traveling closer to the ecliptic than the FarQuest had. There wouldn't be a danger during the first part of their flight since all the near Earth asteroids and debris were well charted, but the farther out they went the more dangerous it would become. Especially with a structure as large as Star One, which wasn't highly maneuverable.

Lieutenant Commander Anderson and Lieutenant Commander Hastings were also present, calmly making their rounds of Main Control and talking to the different crewmembers. They wanted to make sure each person knew what their responsibilities were when the ion drives were fired. Everything in the station as well as on the Space Platform could be monitored from Main Control.

Steve looked over at Margaret Sullivan who was in communication with Mase Colton's people on the Moon. They would be observing with their instruments, from the surface of the Moon, the orbital departure of Star One. Andre Matheson was operating the main computer station to Steve's right on the far wall.

"Five minutes to firing," reported Teela standing smartly in her customary spot next to the commander. Her hands were behind her back, and her deep blue eyes were focused on the main view screen. "All systems are in the green and all crewmembers are in their prelaunch positions."

Around the room, every crewmember was busy checking instruments, communicating with other sections of the station, and preparing for what was to come. They had already gone through several dress rehearsals. Steve knew that his people were ready.

"Todd reports that everything looks good on the Space Platform. The fusion reactor is on line, and he is ready to ignite the ion drives," reported Christy.

"I hope John is ready for this," Steve commented with a nervous smile. "Teela will be controlling most of this, but John will be assisting with the RCS thrusters to keep the station stable."

"I am sure John is ready," Christy replied with a twinkle in her eyes. "Star One will be the largest space craft ever flown; John wouldn't miss this for anything."

"He seems to be quite excited about it," commented Teela looking over at the two. "He feels very confident that everything will go smoothly. He says that after flying the Space Platform, Star One will be a breeze."

They had moved the Space Platform's control room to the center of the platform since it now possessed Earth normal gravity due to the power from the new fusion reactor. They had also added an extra layer of Luxen around the control center to protect it in case of an accident.

Around the station, all non-essential personnel were in their quarters lying down waiting for the drives to be lit. Damage control teams were on standby. If everything functioned as planned, the crew should not notice any perceptible change. Teela would be controlling the artificial gravity and compensating for the gradual thrust of the ion drives.

Water had been drained from the streams and ponds in the ecological habitats as a safety precaution. Even the station's swimming pools had been emptied, and the water safely stored away. The station had been made as secure as possible.

"All departments report ready," commented Teela scanning the entire station and the Space Platform with her computer interface. "We are as ready as we are ever going to be." Teela looked expectantly at the commander.

"I would like to see the look on Senator Farley's face when we leave orbit," Lieutenant Emerson commented from her station, glancing back at General Karver. "When he realizes we're leaving, he will probably go ballistic."

"I hope so," General Karver replied in a steady voice. "It's a shame we can't bring Senator Farley to justice to account for his crimes, but leaving him stranded down on Earth will be justice enough."

"I imagine so," Steve added listening to the conversation between the two. He was glad that they would no longer have to worry about what the deranged Senator was planning. "I would hate to be around him when he finds out what we're doing."

"With the weather conditions down on Earth, it might be awhile before they realize we are leaving the Lagrange point," Christy said reaching out and squeezing Steve's hand before turning back to check her console.

"The orbital stations will see our departure," commented General Karver looking over at Christy. "I suspect at least one of them will report what's happening to Senator Farley."

"Ignition in one minute," interrupted Teela using all of her abilities to monitor the station closely. "We have magnetic containment buildup in the ion drives, temperatures are rising towards preset ignition parameters."

"All crewmembers, standby for ion drive activation," Steve spoke over the station wide com system. "All systems are green, and this should be a smooth transition. Standby for future updates."

"Thirty seconds to ignition," Teela said evenly continuing to monitor the station. If anything went wrong, she would know instantly. She was monitoring every square inch of the station, as well as the Space Platform.

Teela had run thousands of simulations and possible scenarios of what could go wrong. If something did, she had instructions from the commander to correct it instantly. It made Teela feel good to know that he trusted her that much. She stood a little taller gazing at the main screen, which showed Star One.

"It's time," Christy spoke quietly. She could feel the increased adrenalin in her body from the excitement.

Steve turned and looked expectantly toward the main view screen. He could feel the tension and the growing anticipation. They were about to embark on a historic journey that could determine the survival of humankind.

On the screen, Star One seemed to float majestically in the star filled void waiting. Its aesthetic beauty was missing. The Space Platform attached to the Power Wheel and the numerous Luxen cables, which connected the three wheels, made for a strange sight. It was as if a giant space spider had enclosed the three wheels in its metallic web. It made you want to look for a giant spider that wasn't there.

"Ignition," Teela reported suddenly watching data stream in from every section of the station and particularly from the computers monitoring the ion drives.

On the screen, four small flares lit up on the bottom of the Space Platform. The flares brightened rapidly and would have been nearly blinding to an unprotected observer. Four visible streams of fire could be seen spreading out beneath the station. Steve felt the station vibrate and quiver as stresses the station had never been designed for encompassed Star One.

"I never heard the station groan before," Christy commented uneasily hoping everything was okay. A quick glance at her console showed everything in the green.

"It's nothing," Teela assured them. "It's mostly the Luxen cables tightening up under the acceleration. It was expected."

Steve could hear the station groaning in feeble protest as the stress from the four ion drives pushed at Star One's enormous mass. Gradually the four ion drives began pushing the station out of its orbit. In minutes, the station was accelerating outward away from the Earth at a constant speed of one-tenth gravity. The groaning noise from the station had also stopped.

"Stand by for initial SRB firing," Teela spoke as she brought the internal temperatures of the SRBs up for ignition. She checked the SRBs one final time to ensure everything was ready.

The SRB firing was necessary to allow the station to develop enough acceleration to break out of the gravitational hold of the Earth and the Moon. The ion drives had been ignited first to allow the station to handle the SRB firing better. By firing the ion drives, tension had been placed on the new Luxen cables and joints, which had been used to strengthen the station. Teela analyzed the stress being put on the station's structure and found that it was minimal. All the Luxen cables were holding.

On the main screen, Star One almost seemed to glow as the long filaments from the ion drives stretched out behind. Steve's hands clenched the edge of his chair tightly as he waited for the SRBs to light. This would be the crucial test. If the station could handle the stress from the added acceleration, they would be all right. They would be able to escape the Earth's gravity field and make a try for the wormhole at the center of the black hole.

"We have SRB ignition," stated Teela watching the computers as the temperatures rose high enough in the SRBs to ignite the slow burning fuel.

Eight more brilliant drive flares blossomed around the edge of the platform where the powerful SRBs had been mounted. They were held in place by massive Luxen brackets welded to the side of the platform.

The station shuddered, and Steve could hear the metal of the station protesting loudly to the added acceleration. Just hold together he thought, as he tensed up. This acceleration was necessary if they were to escape. Glancing around Main Control, he saw that each person was watching their consoles closely, looking for any signs of trouble.

"The stations really protesting," Christy commented with a weak smile. She could feel the vibration from the SRBs as it was transmitted through the hull. It was very faint, but it was there.

"Star One is holding up within the acceptable parameters to the additional acceleration," reported Teela checking the station's stress monitors as they began to register considerably more stress than they had with just the ion drives.

"Keep us informed Teela," ordered Steve glancing down at his console seeing everything was still in the green. No sections were reporting any problems.

Several stress monitors were nearly reading in the red but were still within acceptable limits. Teela made a note of these, as they would have to be strengthened before they neared the neutron star-black hole binary. She sent the information to Christy's console as this was one of the things Christy was monitoring closely.

The SRBs added another one-third gravity of acceleration to the station giving it the speed necessary to escape the Earth-Moon system. On the main screen, the station could be seen visibly moving against the background of stars, which surrounded it.

Everyone in Main Control felt the added strain as the station creaked and groaned. Crewmembers looked around nervously, as this was a sound they were not used to.

Teela's holographic image stood calmly as she monitored the station and the Space Platform. She stood next to Steve, completely oblivious to the slight strain that he was showing as his station made protesting noises he had never expected to hear.

Christy reached over and gently squeezed Steve's hand. "The station's doing fine."

Christy was listening to Todd's constant reports over her mini com. She knew that John was also in the Space Platform's control room using the station's RCS thrusters to keep the station stable. She was also monitoring the stress areas that Teela had pointed out to her. She would have Lieutenant Commander Hastings organize some work crews to strengthen those areas once the initial boost was over.

Steve watched the view screen nervously, glancing down occasionally to scan the instruments and computer readouts on his console watching for any signs of trouble. He was tapping the top of the console with his index finger as he listened to the station. It almost sounded as if it was talking to him. He could hear loud creaking and groaning noises from the station as it bent and shifted slightly to the stresses from the acceleration. A noise he had never heard in the station before. It gave him an eerie feeling knowing that the station was protesting so loudly. It was almost as if it had a life of its own. From everything that he could see, the added Luxen coating, the new cables, and support beams were handling the stress as well as could be expected.

"How are we doing Teela?" asked Steve looking over at the AI.

"No problems," she replied with a slight smile. "Our trajectory looks good, and the SRBs and the ion drives are functioning normally."

"We're on our way," General Karver spoke in a pleased voice. He wished he could see Senator Farley's reaction when he realized that Star One was no longer within his reach. A slight smirk covered his face as he imagined the anger Senator Farley would feel when he realized that Star One had escaped him.

For nearly ten minutes, the SRBs continued to burn accelerating Star One by brute force to the speed necessary to escape the gravitational hold of the Earth-Moon system. General Karver paced slightly between the weapons console and Steve and Christy's command console. Deep in his heart, he knew that President Kateland would have been proud of what they were attempting. If it worked, humankind might just survive after all.

Steve watched the view screen as the SRBs continued to fire and then finally shut off. For hundreds of miles behind Star One, space was full of the glowing expended gases from the now quiet SRBs. Only the light acceleration from the ion drives continued pushing the station farther and farther into space.

"The SRBs have shut down," Steve announced over the station wide com system. "Everything is proceeding according to plan. There have been no reported problems so far."

In her quarters, Jennifer was lying on her bed with a safety harness holding her firmly in place. It was a precaution in case there had been an accident with one of the SRBs or one of the ion drive containment fields.

"How are you doing Jennifer?" Teela's voice asked with concern. She had been keeping a close eye on the crew. However, Jennifer was still her best friend. She always kept an extra careful eye on her.

"I'm fine," Jennifer replied, visibly relaxing now that the SRBs were shut off. "Did everything go as planned?"

"So far everything looks good," Teela replied. "Todd says it couldn't have worked better. He is very satisfied with the way the ion drives are performing. He does not expect any problems. Everyone is supposed to stay in their quarters until we turn the ion drives off. You can get up, but no one is supposed to be wondering around."

"Do you think the FarQuest really made it?" Jennifer asked in a more quiet tone. She had been thinking about Ty a lot recently.

Especially since they lost contact with the ship after the FarQuest entered the wormhole.

"I think there is a good chance," responded Teela understanding why Jennifer was so concerned. "From what I have learned of Professor LaRann's theories about black holes and wormholes, the ship stood an excellent chance of making it through. If we are successful in our transit of the wormhole, we should find them waiting on the other side."

"I hope so," Jennifer replied wistfully, her eyes looking over at Teela's monitor. "I would really like to see Ty again!"

Down in the main control room for the ecological habitats, Julie and Kathleen were watching all their monitors closely. Each habitat had its own set of screens and controls in the control room with dedicated technicians closely monitoring the stress each habitat was being subjected to.

"It's a good thing we drained the streams and ponds," stated Kathleen looking at the different screens around the large room. "If we hadn't we would have water everywhere from the vibration of the SRBs."

"The habitats seem to be holding up well," Julie replied looking at some readings on the computer screen in front of her.

"Of course, we won't know for sure until after the twelve days of acceleration are over with," Kathleen commented looking at a view screen, which showed one of the park habitats. "We don't know what the lasting effects of this type of acceleration against the pull of gravity will have on our habitats."

"Hopefully none," Teela's voice spoke as she quickly scanned the habitats for any problems. "The soil is mostly held firmly in place by vegetation in the habitats. There may be some minor shifting where the soil is loose from the slight vibration of the ion drives. But all the simulations I've ran indicates it should be minimal. Our actual boost is quite small compared to a shuttle launch."

"At the low acceleration of the ion drives, we should not see any adverse effects to the plant life," Julie continued thoughtfully. "However, the higher thrust from the SRBs worry me some. Especially in areas where the soil hasn't had time to settle properly. We need to watch those areas particularly close Teela."

"I will, but since we normally operate the station under normal Earth gravity, I don't believe there will be any problems," Teela replied.

"I am compensating for the thrust and keeping our gravity at Earth normal. This should reduce or alleviate any potential problems being caused by the slight vibration being transmitted by the ion drives."

Down in the Space Platform control room, Lieutenant Commander Todd Williams watched his instruments closely, pacing back and forth from one control station to the next. Dryson and Stoler were both present carefully monitoring the fusion reactor's power level as it fed energy to the four ion drive chambers. Todd also had a mini com in his right ear so he could speak to Christy as needed.

"Reactor looks to be holding up well," Ted Dryson commented as he studied some readings on his computer screen. "Containment fields are holding within two percent of optimal."

"Sounds good," replied Jarl Stoler with a nod of his graying head. "Power is holding steady, and we should be able to continue the boost."

"Very well," Todd replied with a nod. He felt better with these two experts monitoring the fusion reactor and the ion drives. He quickly reported Stoler's comments to Christy.

"Everything is in the green," John Gray stated from his pilot control station that controlled the SRBs, the four ion drives, and the RCS thrusters.

John was currently watching the RCS thruster firings. They were set on automatic to keep the station stable, but he could take over in an instant if necessary. The control station was extremely complicated covered with instruments, screens, and controls. Two other pilots sat next to John ready to assist him if needed. Teela was controlling the ion drives and the SRBs with John watching closely for any signs of potential problems.

"Fuel consumption is right on the line, and we are dead center on our plotted trajectory," one of the copilots reported as he studied the data flowing across one of the computer screens.

"We are experiencing a little bit of a wobble due to the weight balance of the station, but we are countering that with occasional short bursts of the station's RCS thrusters," John added watching the RCS thruster firings intently. "It will cost us a lot in fuel for the twelve days of thrust we have planned, but fortunately we have plenty of fuel for the thrusters thanks to what we had stored in the Storage Facility."

"It's a shame we had to leave so much of that fuel behind," commented Todd standing behind John. "At least we did manage to top off the fuel storage tanks in the platform."

"How does everything look?" asked Teela materializing next to Todd. She already knew from her own analysis. However, she knew it made people feel better when she asked for their opinions.

"Almost perfect," answered Todd smiling. "Could you run a thruster fuel analysis of how much fuel we will be using to maintain the station's stability during the ion boost? We have a slight wobble that keeps showing up. We are correcting for it periodically. The wobble was one thing we hadn't planned on in our simulations. It shouldn't be a cause for concern, but I would like to confirm what our fuel use will be just in case."

"No problem," replied Teela nodding. "I just need to monitor it for a few minutes. I will get back with you shortly." With that, she vanished.

"She's quite a girl Todd," spoke John smiling and watching as he had the computer fire the port RCS thrusters for an extra four seconds to maintain the station's equilibrium. "She has really come a long ways."

"Don't I know it," Todd replied with a grin. "She has one of the most inquisitive minds you can imagine. She can talk for hours, and her voice is one you never get tired of listening to. She's so innocent and honest about everything. I know some people think our relationship is a little strange, but Teela means a lot to me."

"I don't think it's strange at all," John replied.

In Main Control, Steve and Christy watched the view screen as Star One slowly built up acceleration and left the camera satellite far behind at the Lagrange point. A steady rumbling could be dimly heard from the bowels of the station, and a slight almost undetectable vibration was constantly present.

"Commander Colton says we have really lit up the night sky," Margaret Sullivan reported from her communications console. "He says most of the inhabitants of Tycho City are watching on their screens or from the surface. He wishes us the best of luck sir."

"Tell Mase I'll contact him later, and thanks for the support," Steve replied with a nod."

"I hate leaving Mase and his people behind like this." Christy said quietly where only Steve could hear. "What will happen to them if the Sun does go nova? Do they stand a chance of survival?"

"If they can complete their deep shelters soon enough Mase feels they stand a chance," replied Steve. The two had discussed it when Steve had made the decision to move Star One. "They will have nearly five miles of lunar soil over their heads, and six inches of Luxen walls as protection. If he has to, he can put many of those people into deep sleep possibly for years if need be. Mase isn't too worried; he thinks he has a decent chance of surviving."

"I guess that depends on how big the nova is," Christy replied with a deep sigh. She knew from what Teela had said that it could be anything from a minor flare up to a full-fledged nova. If it was a full fledged nova, nothing in the Solar System would survive.

Steve punched up a command on one of the computer screens on his console and looked at the stress indicators for the station. All were well within the green. Glancing up at the main view screen, the fiery electron trail behind Star One stretched out for hundreds of miles. If people on Earth could see, it would be a highly visible spectacle.

-

Unfortunately, down on Earth it was visible and had caused quite a stir. Senator Farley was hastily summoned to the massive under ground facility's war room when the officer in charge realized the significance of what he was seeing. He knew that Senator Farley would blow a gasket when he realized that Star One was escaping.

"What is it now?" rumbled Farley angry at being disturbed from his sleep.

Farley didn't normally get up until late morning and here it was not even 7:00 a.m. yet! He wasn't used to someone having the gall to demand his immediate presence. He definitely didn't care for it. He had been forced to leave two gorgeous secretaries that routinely shared his bed with him. Maybe it was time he made an example out of somebody else again. Nothing kept order like the fear of death, especially where these military people were concerned.

"Senator," the young general in charge said hurrying up to Senator Farley as he entered the large room. "As you know, we have a spy plane that we launch periodically above the cloud layer, when conditions permit. We have been using it to monitor the storm situation around the U.S."

"This had better be more important than the weather," Farley warned still seething with anger at being summoned out of his warm, luxurious bed.

He didn't have time for a damn weather report. He had plans for the secretaries as soon as he got back to bed. Just what was this young general thinking? Perhaps he should have put an older man in charge.

"It is sir," General Young said hastily. "As you know, whenever possible we have the plane take routine sightings of Star One, as you previously ordered, with the long range instruments on board. Look at the screen. This is what the plane is picking up at this moment."

Farley turned to look impatiently at the big screen on the wall to see a long, fiery trail in space. Due to the distance involved, he couldn't make out what it was.

"It looks like a comet, have your people never saw one before, maybe we will get lucky and it will collide with Star One," puffed Farley finding it hard to believe that this young idiot had interrupted his sleep to look at a comet on a TV screen. A firing squad might very well be in order.

"It's not a comet Senator," General Young replied with a frown. It was obvious the Senator didn't understand what he was seeing on the screen. "Twenty minutes ago, Star One left its orbit at the Lagrange point. Those fiery trails you see are what's left of the drive flares from four ion drives that we have detected operating on Star One. From the instruments on the spy plane, we have measured Star One's current acceleration at one-tenth gravity of acceleration. They have also used some SRBs that were evidently attached to the station to give them escape velocity. Now we know why they attached the Space Platform to the bottom of the station."

"Escape velocity?" asked Farley looking confused, his eyes widening. "What the hell do you mean by escape velocity? Are they going to the Moon?"

"It doesn't look like it," General Young replied with a shake of his head. "From their present trajectory and acceleration they are going farther out into the Solar System."

"But where?" demanded Senator Farley realizing that Steve Larson and General Karver might be putting themselves beyond his reach. "They can't get away, our laser isn't ready yet! They must not escape! They have to be destroyed!"

"We don't know yet where they're going," General Young replied, his eyes shifting nervously about. "We will need to monitor their course for a number of hours and then extrapolate it out to see what it intersects with if anything."

Fuming, Farley stared with obvious hate at the view screen on the wall. Two more weeks and his laser would have been completed, and Star One would have been doomed. He would have sat in this very room and watched that infernal station being incinerated by his super laser.

"Damn them," Farley said aloud in frustration. "Someday I'll destroy you Steve Larson, someday we'll meet again, and then you and your precious station will die!"

-

On Star One, the object of that rage watched as the station continued to accelerate away from the Lagrange point. Christy reached over and took Steve's hand smiling.

"Well we are on our way; I just hope that our luck continues to hold. I can just imagine what Senator Farley must be thinking right now," she said.

"So can I," Steve replied in agreement giving her hand a gentle squeeze. "At least that is one threat we won't have to worry about anymore."

"Do you think he will bother Mase on the Moon?" asked Christy wondering if Tycho City would be safe.

"I don't think so," General Karver answered walking over to stand in front of their console. "He was after Star One, not Tycho City. Besides, he has too much to worry about down on Earth. Mase also has some Black Knight missiles if he needs them."

"He knows about our escape," Teela spoke reappearing next to the general. "I've picked up some transmissions from a high altitude reconnaissance plane that detected our departure."

-

Hours later, Steve and Christy watched as the ion drives shut down on schedule. Current plans called for eight hours of boosting, and then eight hours of rest giving the scientists and technicians an opportunity to check all the systems. After the systems were checked, there would be another eight hours of boosting.

Steve knew that, at the end of the second boost period, they would be traveling at a speed of nearly 35 miles per second and twelve days from now their final speed would be an incredible 422 miles per second. If they stayed on their planned schedule, they would meet the neutron star-black hole binary at four and one half billion miles from the Sun.

-

An hour later, Steve was down in the platform's control room checking with one of the crews that would operate it during the off boosting hours. Christy had gone to her quarters to get some much needed rest since she would be in charge of the next boost sequence. Steve and Christy had decided to rotate to allow them time to rest and stay sharp. Most of the boost personnel had already left except for Dryson who was busy at a computer terminal checking some type of readouts.

"What's up Ted," asked Steve strolling over to stand above the scientist looking over his shoulder at the computer screen. It was covered with a lot of complex mathematical formulas.

"I'm just reviewing the performance of the reactor during the boost," Dryson replied not taking his eyes off the screen. He was plugging in numbers and watching as the computer recalculated the formulas.

Looking around the room, Steve watched for a moment as the busy crew prepared for the next boost in a little less then seven hours. This crew would be rechecking and calibrating everything to ensure that all the systems were ready for the next boost period.

"Have you and Stoler had a chance to work on our revolving magnetic field generator?" asked Steve returning his attention to Dryson.

"We have made up a preliminary design," Dryson responded as he put in another series of numbers into the computer. "We should have it ready to test in about two weeks. From what we can understand from Professor LaRann's papers on black holes and wormholes, it should stabilize the wormhole long enough for us to make the transit."

Turning, Dryson looked Steve directly in the eyes. "You realize though that taking a structure as large as Star One through the wormhole will be extremely dangerous. From the few readings we managed to get from the FarQuest, the station will be subjected to a lot of stress."

"I know," replied Steve recalling what he had read about black holes. "But it's the best chance we have of surviving the nova. Teela has said that there is a good chance the station will receive some damage as we transit the wormhole, but the station should be able to make the transit relatively intact."

"I'm just not to sure how intact that's going to be," commented Stoler frowning.

The two talked for several more minutes and then Steve made his way back up to the Power Wheel to stand and stare at the reactor. Looking around the large room, Steve nodded satisfied at the technicians on duty, noticing the slower more relaxed pace now that Luxen was no longer being produced. They had abundant supplies of the alloy for emergency use if needed. The steady hum from the fusion reactor, which was funneling its power throughout Star One, was audible in Steve's ears as he turned and made his way to the main elevator.

Several minutes later, Steve stepped out into one of the ecological habitats, breathing in the fresh air, and nearly bumping into Kathleen who was carrying several sample bags in her hands.

"Commander," she stammered embarrassed from nearly knocking Steve over. "I didn't see you!"

"Kathleen," replied Steve smiling. At least she was dressed in her regulation uniform. "What's the hurry?"

"We're taking a few samples to check on how some of our more delicate plants are handling the vibration from the ion drives. Julie wants to take a few samples after each boost to monitor for any stress the plants may exhibit."

Steve looked around at the trees, which nearly touched the tall ceiling and the now empty stream and small pond, which the day before had held water and trout.

"How did the animals in the other habitats hold out during the acceleration?" asked Steve noticing a few butterflies floating in the air amongst the trees and flowers.

"Just fine from what we can tell," answered Kathleen adjusting her sample bags, making sure they were marked correctly. "We sedated most of the larger animals through the acceleration, but the birds, squirrels, and insects were left to fend for themselves. Other than a few confused squirrels everything seems to be fine."

"How is everyone else holding up?" Steve asked. "We haven't been able to talk much recently, and I know you get to see a lot of the station's crew."

Kathleen smiled at Steve's obvious reference to her partying and socializing when off duty. "A lot of people are scared, particularly the new arrivals. Some don't understand fully why we have to move the station. The old timers have been filling them in and doing a lot of explaining. For the most part, everyone trusts your judgment."

"What about you?" asked Steve curiously. While he had never been close to Kathleen, he knew that she was brilliant in her work or she would never have landed the job as Julie's assistant.

Kathleen hesitated a moment. The commander had always made her a little nervous. "I believe we will survive. I believe that we will find Ty and the FarQuest on the other side of the wormhole waiting for us. I have to believe commander, what other choice is there?"

Steve caught a glimpse of a squirrel in a nearby tree gingerly walking out on a limb. He almost smiled at the squirrel's nervousness as it took one cautious step at a time.

"We all have to believe Kathleen," Steve replied. "What is life without hope, and who knows what we may find on the other side of the wormhole."

Later, Steve returned to Main Control and took his command seat to stare thoughtfully at the main screen, which now showed Star One as a bright dot surrounded by stars. These people believe in me. He looked around at the crewmembers in the room knowing that he couldn't let them down. I just hope I'm leading them to a better place.

Changing the view on the screen, he stared at the cloud shrouded Earth. He knew from their latest reports that the people living on that globe were suffering horribly from the ceaseless weather and now widespread shortages of food. What other choice do we have he thought, thinking about what the living conditions on the ground must be like.

From their latest reports, tens of millions of people had already lost their lives in the flooding that was raging everywhere. Changing the screen again, it showed a view of distant space with a dim dot at its center, the neutron star with its companion black hole that was invisible on the screen. Our destiny he thought, staring at the screen. For several long minutes he gazed at the screen, wondering what awaited them at the black hole.

# Chapter Twelve

Day twelve arrived uneventfully as the final eight-hour boost of Star One ended. Steve breathed a tired sigh of relief as the ion drives shut off leaving the station hurtling through the void of space at an appalling speed of 422 miles per second. The station was quiet, and the steady vibration from the ion drives was finally absent. Already in the twelve days the station had been boosting, they had traveled nearly 200 million miles. Looking around Main Control, Steve could see a look of tired relief on everyone's faces.

"Todd reports everything normal on the Space Platform," a worn out Christy reported from her console next to him. "They will be doing a complete recalibration of the entire ion drive system since the drive is going to be down for awhile."

"It should take 72 hours to complete the entire job," Teela commented from where she was standing next to Steve's console. "They will also be checking the ion drive chambers for any wear to the Luxen lining after such a long boost period."

Looking over at Christy, Steve reached out, took her hand, and squeezed it. Her eyes were blood shot and Steve knew that she had spent a lot of hours walking around the station talking to the crew and being at her station during boost. For that matter, Steve also was nearly to the point of physical and mental exhaustion. A good meal tonight and then a decent night's uninterrupted sleep would definitely be a cure all for himself as well as the rest of the crew.

"We're committed now," Steve spoke to Christy knowing she needed some rest. "I just hope we made the right decision."

"It's the only decision that has a reasonable chance of Star One surviving," Teela commented watching the two. At least being an AI, she didn't feel tired.

Steve nodded his head knowing Teela was right, but it had still been a hard decision to make. He was still feeling nervous about the course they were being forced to take in order to intercept the neutron star-black hole binary. They were following a course closer to the plane of the ecliptic than what the FarQuest had, much closer. Already, the station's rail guns, under the command of Captain Gerald and Lieutenant Emerson, had been used six times to blast small asteroids into harmless pieces that had ventured too close to their intended path.

Lieutenant Emerson along with Captain Gerald and the station engineers had redesigned and reprogrammed the stations long-range sensors and radars. This allowed them to extend their detection range out to slightly over 200,000 miles. Still that only gave them barely eight minutes of early warning from the time an object was detected to the time it could potentially collide with Star One.

The effective range of the rail guns required that an object be within one minute of impacting Star One before it could be destroyed. Captain Gerald and Lieutenant Emerson had full control of the rail guns from the weapons station in Main Control. At least one of them had been at the weapons console since Star One had left the Lagrange point.

To be on the safe side, General Karver had ordered that they maintain crews at two of the actual rail gun stations on the outer rim. In case of an emergency, these could be fired by manual control. Each rail gun contained its own targeting computer, which could be used if the main system in Main Control went down.

Lieutenant Damon Carter had been undergoing additional training to share the burden of commanding the rail guns. Now that the boost was over, he would command the rail gun station one shift per day, which would allow the three to rotate to just one eight-hour shift in a twenty-four hour period. It would help to relieve the pressure and strain that Captain Gerald and Lieutenant Emerson had been under. General Karver had suggested training several others just in case they were needed.

Steve also planned on using Todd to help share the command load in Main Control. The three duty officers were qualified, but none had the command experience that Todd did.

"Commander," Teela said interrupting his thoughts with a grave look on her face. "I have picked up reports of a massive earthquake in the Los Angeles area along the San Andreas fault line."

"Oh no!" Christy moaned in anguish knowing what this might signify. She looked over at Steve seeing the same look of anguish on his face.

"Contact General Karver and ask him to report to Main Control," Steve ordered crisply. He knew that the general would want to know about this earthquake. Steve wondered if this was the beginning of the next disastrous phase for the Earth.

Teela was still able to monitor Earth through the orbiting satellites even though communication one way now took nearly eighteen minutes due to the lengthening distance. They were still maintaining daily contact with Tycho City, even though it was becoming more difficult to carry on a conversation as the distance between the two steadily increased.

"General Karver is on his way," Teela reported after finding the general in one of the cafeterias eating a light meal.

"How serious is the earthquake Teela?" asked Steve feeling disturbed at realizing what the Earth would soon be going through. This could be the advent of the serious and dangerous earthquakes they had been expecting. He suspected this earthquake was probably the result of the influence of the neutron star-black hole binary.

The heavy rains had been causing numerous mudslides and sinkholes to appear all along the densely inhabited California coast from Santa Rosa to San Diego. There had been several minor earthquakes already, and Steve had been afraid that a major Earth movement was inevitable. Particularly the closer the deadly binary came to Earth.

The Earth was still inundated with storms, and the situation was steadily getting worse day by day with no end in sight. Each day they could hear repeated pleas for help on the radio waves as beleaguered communities and people became steadily more desperate.

"I have several TV stations that are reporting from the California area," stated Teela scanning all the reports she was receiving. I can put them up on the main screen."

Over the past few months, many of the broadcasting stations had gone completely off the air. Most due to a lack of available power as the power grid became too damaged to operate. Power companies just couldn't keep up with all the damage being done to their transmission facilities and power lines by the storms.

The main screen flickered and then a clear picture of the Greater Los Angeles area came into view. Main Control became deathly quiet as everyone stared in shock at the screen. It was obviously being filmed from a slowly circling helicopter high above the disaster. Light rain was falling in a cloud covered gray sky, but the devastation was overwhelming.

Los Angeles was gone! The Pacific Ocean had moved in and reclaimed the city. Only a few of the cities tallest buildings were still visible above the dark blue ocean water. Even those building showed a tremendous amount of earthquake damage. Most of the windows in the buildings were broken, and several buildings were leaning over at

206

odd angles as if they were about to teeter and fall into the encroaching water.

Debris and countless bodies were plainly visible in the swirling water around the surviving structures. Even as they watched, one of the remaining buildings seemed to tremble and then disappear as it collapsed on its foundation allowing the ocean waters to swallow it with little effort.

"The area is still experiencing severe aftershocks," Teela commented as she scanned the available media stations.

Steve heard the door to Main Control open and looking over saw General Karver enter. The general walked over to Steve and Christy glancing up at the main view screen.

"Teela said there's been an earthquake in Los Angeles," General Karver said looking at the devastation being displayed on the screen.

"It's bad," Christy said in a low voice. She knew that millions of people had just died in the earthquake and the water pouring in from the Pacific.

The view switched to another helicopter camera showing survivors clinging to floating debris and waving frantically at the helicopter for help. The view swelled as the camera zoomed in to show a mother holding desperately onto her young child as the waves slowly pushed them out towards the deeper ocean waters.

The scene was replayed hundreds of times in the next hour. Scene after scene of helpless survivors adrift in the debris, or waving from the tops of shattered buildings trying to attract attention so they could be rescued. What made it even worse was the total absence of any type of organized rescue. Desperate survivors trying to get out of the water more often than not capsized the few small boats that did appear.

"How large an area has the ocean covered?" General Karver asked his eyes riveted to the screen. They had known this was going to happen, but seeing it was still shocking.

"From orbital satellites approximately 4,200 square miles are now underwater," replied Teela doing some quick calculations and checking the latest reports from the satellites. "The death toll will be in the millions. Due to the increment weather the country has been suffering under for several months now, there is no longer any type of organized federal government capable of launching the type of rescue and relief effort that is needed."

"It will only get worse won't it Teela," commented Steve knowing what was still ahead for the Earth.

"Yes sir," Teela replied her dark blue eyes showing sadness. "Local governments still exist in some parts of the country. They have maintained some order and have even done a good job dispersing the limited quantities of food and fuel supplies at their disposal, but none of them are capable of responding to a catastrophe such as this. Many communities in California are pleading for help, both due to earthquake damage and an influx of hundreds of thousands of survivors who have fled the rising water."

"This is only the beginning," Christy mumbled shaken by the tragic loss of life. It was all she could do to watch the screen. "As the weeks go by, there will be more and more earthquakes and even volcanic eruptions. Add that to the weather situation and the people left alive on Earth will be living in hell."

"Turn the screen off Teela," Steve ordered not wanting to watch any more. "The Earth is doomed, we already knew that. We all know that there will be a lot of suffering. There is not a single member of this crew that doesn't have loved ones still down on Earth. All we can do is hope and pray for their safety and turn all of our efforts towards our own survival."

"I agree," said General Karver nodding his head. "Earth is finished, our future lies ahead of us.

Down on Earth, Senator Farley watched the Los Angeles disaster on the main screen in the military operation's room. Minor earthquakes had become a routine occurrence over much of the globe for the last several weeks. The seismograph almost never stopped recording the earth tremors, which were steadily increasing in number and strength. This was by far the most powerful one yet.

"What is causing these earthquakes?" he demanded of his frail Science Advisor who stood trembling before him. "Now that Star One has left, why is our weather not clearing up? I want the truth damn it!"

The weather situation had reduced his hold on the country to a tenuous one at best. He no longer had any way to enforce control. Local governments and National Guard units were beginning to depend more on each other rather than the Federal Government that he was the head of. What military units he still commanded were finding it next to impossible to carry out his orders to maintain a firm grip on the country. Many areas were cut off and on their own.

The Science Advisor stood in front of the Senator knowing that like so many others before him, his life could probably be counted in mere minutes. However, before he died he decided that for once Senator Farley would hear the truth, whether he liked it or not. Nodding towards one of his associates, the main screen switched to a view of space with a dim dot highlighted in a small red box.

"You have doomed us all you fool," the man stated with a surprisingly steady voice, his eyes glaring at Senator Farley. "We have confirmed beyond a shadow of a doubt that the object in the red box is indeed a neutron star bearing down on our Solar System. The neutron star will destroy us all. In a few short months, we will all be dead including you. You're nothing more than a pompous, ignorant fool that has led us all to disaster. Your stupid desire for revenge against Star One has doomed everyone. Instead of building ships and deep retreats that could possibly survive, we have wasted all of our resources on your idiotic whims. The neutron star is causing our weather problems, not Star One!" he yelled passionately his anger at Senator Farley rising. "The neutron star, not Star One has caused the increase in earthquakes, and this is only the beginning. We are all going to die, and there is not a damn thing you can do to prevent it!"

Senator Farley stood glaring at his Science Advisor with fury growing on his round face, his eyes taking on a wild almost deadly look. No one could talk to him like this. It was not to be tolerated, after all, just who did this man think he was? Reaching out, he pulled out a pistol from the holster of one of his personal guards and calmly shot the raving Science Advisor between the eyes. Everyone in the room was stunned, as the now dead science advisor fell to the floor in a slowly growing pool of blood.

"Take this garbage outside," ordered Farley gesturing with the smoking pistol.

When no one made a move to obey, he angrily looked around the room. With stunned surprise, he saw that everyone was staring at him with utter contempt and revulsion. With a sudden panicky sensation, he knew that he had pushed them too far this time.

"I don't think so Senator," General Young spoke stepping forward, flanked by two marines with their assault rifles pointed in Farley's direction. "We are all tired of living in constant fear of you and your henchmen. It's time to set things right, at least for the limited amount of time we have left."

"What your science advisor said was true, we all know that," the young general added. "Your hatred for Star One has blinded you to the truth, and for that, this nation is doomed."

The general gestured for his other men in the room to disarm the Senator's bodyguards. "We have known the truth for weeks. We should have taken action earlier."

"Because of you, a lot of people are going to die that could have possibly survived this carnage," commented General Young gazing with contempt at Senator Farley. "If you would have used our resources wisely instead of for your own personal gain, it's hard telling what we could have accomplished."

"You little piss ant," Farley snarled enraged. "I made you a general, is this how you repay me? You won't get away with this. I'll have you court martialed and shot before the day is out!"

"I don't think so," replied General Young standing in front of the Senator defiantly. "You have executed those in command who might have supported you. Now there are only those of us left that want to survive. We can't with you in charge. I have enough loyal troops in this complex to round up all your pathetic supporters. This complex is deep enough and secure enough that we might be able to save some of the human race, once the worthless ones that you brought in are disposed of. There are enough good people still left up on the surface that deserve a chance at living. We will find those we can and bring them down here. Perhaps by doing this, we may be partially forgiven for what you have done to this country."

"I won't allow it," growled Farley lunging at the general and reaching for his neck only to be grabbed and restrained by two beefy marine guards.

Several hours later, Senator Farley found himself and several dozen of his staunchest supporters on the surface surrounded by a squad of hard faced marines. The driving rain made seeing for more than a few yards almost impossible. Already, Farley was drenched through to the bone, his eyes contemptuously held straight ahead refusing to look at the marines.

The young general stopped in front of him, taking a moment to stare sadly at the now powerless Senator.

"We are giving you enough supplies for several days. If you or any of your people are spotted in this area again, they will be shot on sight. Do you understand that Senator?"

"Go to hell!" spat Farley glaring at the general. "One of these days I'll return and kill you and your feeble military force. You were all incompetent anyway. I'll find more men. When I do, I'll return and deal with you."

"I doubt that Senator," replied General Young shaking his head. "You know as well as I do that this retreat is nearly impervious to attack. Whether you want to admit it or not, my men are highly trained. We have already put the word out over our communication's equipment that you have been found guilty of crimes against humanity and banished to the surface. No one will give you any aid. You have killed and doomed too many people. There is no one that wants you anymore, no one that wants to follow you. You are through!"

Nodding to his men, the general and his marine detachment returned to the small building that concealed the elevators, which led down to the deep underground complex. The guards in the small building were doubled to ensure that no one could forcibly gain admittance.

Senator Farley looked around his group and then trudged off into the rain leaving the supplies lying on the ground. Someone else could carry them, he wasn't. After a few minutes he stopped and looked back, no one was in sight. Everything was hidden in the driving rain that fell like sheets across the desolate countryside. The dismal roll of distant thunder echoed through the trees. A few small hailstones began to fall.

The rest of the people banished with him were gone. He was alone with no supplies. The fools he thought as he turned and struggled on through the ankle deep mud. Some day he would return and get his revenge. Moments later, Senator Farley disappeared into the heavy, dark rain.

On Star One, General Karver, Christy, Todd, Teela, Julie, Dryson, Captain Gerald, and Steve were holding a meeting in the small conference room next to Steve's office. Their goal was to return Star One to a semblance of normalcy now that the boosting of the station was done. They had 120 days of flight time ahead of them before they reached the neutron star-black hole binary.

"What is the current status of the station?" asked Steve looking inquiringly at Teela.

"The station came through the boosting in excellent shape," Teela reported. "I can detect no damage to any of the station's structure."

"That's good to hear," commented General Karver.

"Anything else Teela?" Steve asked.

"We did have a number of areas that were subjected to more stress than originally estimated in our original simulations due to the constant vibration from the ion drives. While all sensors showed the stress factors stayed in the green, some were very close to the upper limit we had allowed for. Some of those areas have already been strengthened. There are still some others that need to be addressed. These areas should be strengthened before we reach the black hole."

"I have already talked to Lieutenant Hastings, and she is scheduling work details to handle it," commented Christy looking down at some notes on a pad in front of her. "We should have all the areas in question strengthened adequately within two weeks."

"What about the Space Platform?" continued Steve waiting for Todd to answer.

"We will be checking the ion drive chambers tomorrow," Todd began. "We want to go through the entire system to see how it held up during the boosting. After that, we will be checking the SRB boosters and running more simulations on structural integrity, particularly where the platform and Star One are joined."

"I have recordings of all the stress reactions from each boost," Teela reported. "We will use those to check for any additional problem areas."

"Teela and I have been looking into the stress the station will be subjected to when we near the neutron star-black hole binary," continued Todd looking over at Teela who smiled back. "We definitely still have some sections of the platform and Star One that need to be strengthened, as well as those we have already mentioned."

"What about the ecological habitats Julie?" Steve went on letting each individual report on their respective areas.

"They came through fine," Julie responded. "We had some minor damage in one of the vegetable growing sections where some loose soil shifted slightly, but nothing we can't correct with a few days of hard work. We had a few animals that were injured, but they should be fine after a few days of rest."

"We need as much food production as possible during the next few months," Steve said taking a deep breath. "We don't know what type of damage the station may suffer when we transit the wormhole. I want as large a food reserve as possible."

Pausing, Steve looked over at Ted Dryson. "What about the station's fusion reactors, how are they functioning?"

Dryson and Stoler were now in charge of all three of the station's fusion reactors. The solar panels had been taken down and stored. They would not have held up to the thrust or the passage through the wormhole. The forces exerted on them would have torn them loose from their mountings.

The two large reactors, one in the Power Wheel and the other in the Space Platform, were each capable of furnishing all the power the station could possibly need. The small research reactor had been converted to be used as an emergency power source. It could handle the power requirements for the station briefly in case of an emergency.

"We're going to be taking each reactor off line during the next several months and going through the entire system," Dryson said looking at a few notes he had brought along. "We will also be installing another fail safe system to scram the reactors in case of a catastrophic emergency. Currently all three reactors are functioning normally. The boosting seems to have had no effect on them what so ever."

"Excellent," Steve replied pleased. The fusion reactors were their key to survival. The reactors would allow them an almost unlimited long-term source of power.

"Captain Gerald, it seems like we are going to have to depend on the rail guns more than we had originally thought," Steve stated with concern in his eyes. "We have already had to use the rail guns six times to clear our flight path of small asteroids. Will the rail guns hold up for another four months?"

Captain Gerald opened up a folder lying in front of him and then answered. "I have a copy of the specs for the rail guns here," he said gesturing at the folder. "Lieutenant Emerson and I have talked in length about keeping the rail guns continuously powered up and on line. As you know, they were not designed to stay activated continuously. Lieutenant Emerson believes that by keeping four rail guns down at all times for routine maintenance that the system can be maintained. That would give us six rail guns under remote operation from Main Control. We will keep two crews on the outer rim manning two of the rail guns at all times in case there is a problem in main control. By rotating the rail gun downtime, we should be able to maintain the system almost indefinitely."

"We are also training additional personnel to operate the rail guns from Main Control," General Karver added. "Captain Gerald and Lieutenant Emerson have done a fine job over the last twelve days, but they can't continue to work at that pace and stay efficient. We have already begun training Lieutenant Damon Carter to command one of the shifts. We will be training two more additional officers to operate the weapons console in Main Control if needed."

"Good," replied Steve knowing the two had done a great job protecting the station. "Let's go over what we need to do for the next several months to prepare the station, we also need to decide for sure which additional areas of the station need to be strengthened, and how we want to go about doing that."

"Commander," Teela interrupted visibly excited and standing up. "I just picked up a general broadcast from an underground location in the Eastern United States. You won't believe what is being reported. A General Marcus Young is reporting that Senator Farley has been removed from power for crimes against humanity. Local state governments are being given full authority to deal with the current National Emergency, and the Federal Government, other than the military, is being disbanded."

"What about Senator Farley? Does it say what happened to him?" Christy asked intrigued by this new development.

"No it doesn't. The communiqué is quite vague on that point," Teela replied. "The message is being constantly repeated."

"It's a shame it couldn't have happened sooner," uttered Steve glad that Senator Farley had finally been removed from power. He wondered why it had taken so long.

"I know a Colonel Marcus Young," Captain Gerald stated thoughtfully. "I wonder if this could be the same person. If it is, he would have found it very hard to stomach Farley's actions. The man is honest and dedicated to his career. His men are also extremely loyal. If he were placed in charge at Farley's headquarters, he could have very easily overthrown him."

"I don't believe I know the man," General Karver spoke looking thoughtful. "I wonder what this General Young plans to do now?"

"He's a good officer," Captain Gerald repeated. "We might want to consider contacting him."

"I will take that under advisement," General Karver replied. "I don't see how it would benefit us to contact Earth at the moment, but it is something we need to think about."

"Keep us informed if anything else about Farley shows up," Steve ordered pleased that Senator Farley was now powerless. "I would still like to know what happened to him."

"Do you think we should contact this General Young?" asked Christy looking at Steve and General Karver. "If he has any resources at his disposal, he could get more people into some of the militaries underground shelters."

"It's something that General Karver will have to decide," Steve replied nodding at the general. "He is still the surviving senior member of President Kateland's government."

"I will discuss this with Captain Gerald," General Karver replied. "We might also want to contact Mase at Tyco City and see what he thinks."

Steve nodded understanding why General Karver was being so cautious. Mase was closer to Earth than they were, and his opinion in this matter would be highly important.

Several hours later, Steve and Christy were seated at Jensens eating their first decent meal in days. Jensens was crowded as people tried to put their lives back to normalcy.

"Teela says the earthquakes will begin to increase in strength rapidly now," Christy said taking a small sip of the rich red wine that Jensen had poured a few minutes earlier.

"Unfortunately, that is probably correct," replied Steve picturing what life on Earth for the next several months would be like. "Teela's latest reports show that most of the coastal areas are flooded around the world. The water levels of the oceans are slowly beginning to rise. There has been some melting of the arctic ice cap and food supplies are rapidly dwindling."

"I talked to Mase earlier," Christy went on reaching out and taking Steve's hand enjoying the warmth of his touch. "He has completed his deep shelters and he does plan on putting the majority of his people into deep sleep until the neutron star-black hole binary passes."

"He has no other choice," replied Steve knowing that Mase was going to be faced with some very difficult decisions.

"He plans on keeping less than 500 people awake to operate the deep shelters and maintain his surface installations," continued Christy. "He says that will tremendously reduce their drain on consumables and give them a large reserve of food stocks for when they can safely begin to awaken the sleepers."

"Did he say how long he was going to keep them in deep sleep?" Steve asked. He knew that Doctor Wruggi, in recent days, had spent a lot of time talking to Mase and some of Mase's doctors about the deep sleep drug.

"He wants to keep the sleepers under for about a year, by then he will know how the Solar System has been affected," replied Christy knowing that this was a lot longer than Doctor Wruggi had suggested was safe originally.

"A year," Steve spoke recalling his last conversation with Doctor Wruggi on the subject. The doctor had said that longer times would be possible. However, the sleepers would have to be monitored extremely closely for any signs of ill effects.

Of course, if the Sun experiences any type of nova situation and the Moon survives, he will keep them under indefinitely," Christy said. "Even though a deep sleep period over one year could result in loosing some of the sleepers. Dr. Wruggi has estimated that a two year deep sleep could result in losses of up to twenty percent of the sleepers and five years up to forty percent."

"There are so many unknowns," Steve replied gently squeezing her hand. "For Mase and us. What will we find on the other side of the wormhole? Will it be another solar system or just empty space with nothing around?"

"I think everyone is wondering about that," Christy responded with a sigh.

"Did General Karver and Mase discuss the new situation down on Earth?"

"Yes they did," responded Christy with a slight nod. "Mase is going to try to contact this General Young in a few days. He is curious as to what happened to cause them to finally revolt against Senator Farley."

Jensen made an appearance shortly with their meals. Both spent the next hour talking about their hopes for the station and the firm belief that Ty awaited them on the other side of the wormhole.

Later, Christy snuggled up to Steve's warm body in his quarters as they both slowly drifted off to sleep. Both had been too tired for love making, but just being there next to each other was comfort enough. We'll survive Christy thought sleepily, as she fell into a deep, restful slumber.

Steve rolled over and looked at Christy's quietly sleeping form under the blanket. Putting his arm around her, he closed his eyes as a long, restful sleep quickly encompassed him.

Teela turned off her monitors in the commander's quarters. She knew that she shouldn't have been watching, but Steve and Christy shared something that she badly wished she could have with Todd. Sometimes it made her want to cry realizing that she was forever bared from experiencing what it would actually be like to touch Todd. To feel his body against hers, to be able to share what two people in love normally experienced.

Using her sensors, she saw that Todd was sound asleep. Materializing in his room, she lay down on the bed next to him. He didn't even know she was there. How could he? Her body wasn't real. He couldn't actually feel her touch. With a sob, she vanished back into the system and forced herself to go to work. She had a lot of information to go through for the commander and others. She buried herself in her work putting Todd and her dreams in the back of her mind for now.

# Chapter Thirteen

Sergeant Adams looked around the empty cave feeling disappointed. His squad of men had been sent to this location to search for possible survivors. General Young had sent the squad out to check a group of small remote caves that reportedly held survivors from the carnage that was raging around them.

Sergeant Adam's eyes swept around the cave noting the obvious signs of recent human habitation. An old shirt, a couple of dusty blankets, a torn sleeping bag, and several empty food tins were all that were in the cave.

Corporal Strong squatted down and put his hand over the remains of a campfire and then frowning touched the ashes themselves. "It's cold sir, if anyone was here they have been gone for several days at least."

"But they were here at one time," commented Sergeant Adams with a frown.

If they had only heard about these survivors earlier, they could have been rescued. Now there was no telling where they had fled to. He let out a deep breath in disappointment. They were finding few surviving people in their searches.

A small group of survivors they had found in the basement of a house had reported that a large group of survivors had taken refuge in these caves. Due to the health of several members of the small group in the basement, they had decided not to go to the caves with the larger group.

The marines had walked through nearly three miles of dense dying forest to get to these caves. There were four small caves that went back deep into the small mountain. The rain and the mud had made the trip extremely difficult, and they had struggled for nearly half a day just to get here. In addition, the necessity of wearing the cumbersome masks that allowed them to breathe clean air had made the trip even more difficult. The air deep inside the cave was not too bad, and Sergeant Adams had removed his mask to allow better communication with his marines. The air even deep within smelled of sulfur. Outside it was much worse.

"They must have run out of supplies," Corporal Strong suggested coming to stand next to Sergeant Adams. "There are a lot of empty food containers in the back of the caves. They probably ran out and were forced to leave and search for more."

With a nod, Sergeant Adams turned and walked the hundred yards back to the cave's entrance. Once at the entrance, he put his breathing mask back on and gazed out at the countryside below him. A light rain was falling, and visibility was severely limited. The forest was no longer green. Due to the contamination in the atmosphere many of the trees were dying. Dead limbs and brown leaves were evident on many of the trees. Even the grasses that normally covered the ground were dead or dying. Sergeant Adams let out a deep sigh. He had been raised in woods like these, it was sad to know that soon they would be completely dead. Very soon, he knew nothing would be left alive on the surface. The only survivors would be those in the deep underground bunkers.

Turning back to Corporal Strong, he said. "Radio Captain Wells and tell him there were no survivors at this location. We are coming in."

General Marcus Young stared at the latest reports from the surface with grave concern on his face. During the last several months since he had taken control of the complex, earthquake and volcanic activity had increased substantially. The atmosphere outside the deep bunker was almost unbreathable without some type of air filter mask to remove the contaminants. He let out a deep breath wishing he could do something else to help the few survivors still struggling on the surface.

Looking around the command center, he saw that his people were all busy working hard at figuring out how they were going to survive. A mixture of military and civilians operated the consoles and computers inventorying supplies, checking on spare parts, and possible locations on the surface that could still be searched for survivors.

Most of the large screens on the wall were filled with static. Only occasionally would one clear up briefly to show a view from one of the satellites in orbit. The communications center was fully staffed as the communication officers scanned all the available frequencies for signs of life. Each day there were fewer and fewer.

From the few scattered radio stations still on the air, Young knew that conditions on the surface of the Earth were quickly becoming untenable. There was no doubt in his mind that very soon the only people surviving would be in deep bunkers. Even some of those bunkers might not be able to survive the strong earth tremors, which were constantly shaking the globe. Even here, in Young's bunker the earthquakes were noticeable.

"What are our surface units reporting on their search for additional survivors?" he asked a young female lieutenant who was operating one of the communication consoles. They were listening to every broadcast they could find, tying to ascertain what other survivors were doing.

"No luck so far," she replied shaking her head sadly. "We thought we had a lead on some survivors living in some nearby caves, but all our search team found were some old camp fires. Sergeant Adams believes they have already moved on."

"Very well, tell them to return to base," Young ordered. There was no sense in continuing to risk his people in the steadily worsening conditions outside. The marines on the surface were using breathing masks due to contaminants in the air.

In the last two months, since he had overthrown Senator Farley, they had managed to rescue nearly 800 civilians who had managed to pass the screening process to qualify for admittance to the bunker. Most of these had been from nearby farms and small towns. In almost every case, the survivors had taken refuge in storm shelters and basements.

The screening process was not particularly difficult. If a person was healthy, willing to work hard, and had no past criminal record, or affiliation with Senator Farley, they were allowed admittance. In addition, there were nearly 400 military personnel in the underground bunker. Senator Farley had not utilized the bunker's resources to allow it to maintain the total complement of people it had originally been designed for. The bunker was capable of sustaining 2,000 people for two years, with the original supplies it had on hand. Senator Farley had substantially increased the food supply, most of it in high-end foodstuffs for his lavish meals and parties.

"The last food stores have been brought in from the evacuated military bases," Captain Wells reported as he came up to General Young.

"Think we can find anything else useful up there captain?" asked General Young turning his gaze toward Captain Wells. He knew they had searched the surrounding area over the past month pretty thoroughly.

"Not much," admitted Captain Wells knowing that anything that might be useful had already been brought into the shelter.

Captain Wells was a young marine with seal training. He was highly talented and a deadly marksman. He had been made responsible for locating any additional supplies that the underground bunker could use. He had been sending out scouting missions to nearby towns scavenging for anything they could find. One squad had located a herd of cattle that had been pinned up on a nearby farm. The cattle had plenty of hay and a large ventilated barn to take shelter in. The cattle had been butchered, and their meat brought back and stored in the bunker's large freezers.

General Young had ordered all the remaining military bases that he could contact to be closed down. The few remaining soldiers were told to go home to their families. The soldiers were allowed to take all the supplies they could carry with them, and transportation was made available to get everyone as close to their homes as possible. Even so, many found they had to walk a long ways due to impassable roads and swollen rivers. Air transportation was extremely limited.

Most of the military food rations that were left at the bases had been transferred to the deep underground command bunker and several other underground facilities. General Young was in contact with two other facilities that might stand a slim chance of long-term survival. Like the command bunker, the other two facilities were scrounging for supplies in the countryside. No one knew how long they would have to stay underground. The world outside the bunker was almost unrecognizable.

The heavy rains had devastated much of the countryside, and then the earthquakes had followed adding their fury. Cities were torn apart as buildings never designed to stand up to such powerful earthquakes collapsed, and roads buckled leaving gaping chasms that cut deep into the Earth. Death and destruction ravaged the continent as millions died in the on going carnage. Then the volcanoes began to erupt. General Young doubted if there were more than a million survivors still alive in all of North America.

On several occasions, they had been able to launch a few high altitude surveillance craft. One of the things that had surprised him was the revelation that Star One was on an intercept course for the neutron star. They had tried several times to contact both Star One and Tycho City, but interference from increased solar activity had made communication impossible. Of course, after everything that Senator Farley had tried to do to them, General Young couldn't blame them if they were receiving his messages, but were afraid to reply for fear of treachery.

Captain Wells was talking to one of the communication officers who seemed to be excited about something. Nodding the captain turned and walked quickly over to General Young.

"We just picked up an SOS from a small town about 120 miles to the northeast," he reported. "They claim to be a group of 420 survivors taking shelter in the basement of their high school."

"One hundred and twenty miles," repeated General Young frowning. In the conditions outside, that was a long ways to go. "Can we get to them?"

"I believe so," Captain Wells replied with a confident nod. "The main highway is relatively intact. I can send Sergeant Adams with some heavy trucks to get them. They also claim to have a lot of food supplies."

General Young thought for a moment. He still had plenty of room in the bunker for survivors. This might be their last chance at finding any.

"Do it, make sure you send enough marines to keep the survivors and their supplies secure," General Young warned. "Other scavengers could have heard their broadcast over the radio."

"I'll send the trucks plus two full squads of marines," Captain Wells replied. "I'll lead the detachment."

"Very well," General Young replied. He watched as Captain Wells went back to communications and sent Sergeant Adams a message. Then the captain left going to gather up his men.

Looking around the main operations center of the complex, General Young hoped that someday he could tell Commander Larson and Commander Colton how he wished he could have stopped Senator Farley sooner. At least Captain Gerald would survive. He knew that Captain Gerald had been secretly transferred to Star One. This was something he had never revealed to anyone.

Taking a deep breath, General Young leaned back in his chair and closed his eyes. He soon became lost in thought trying to think of what else they might need to survive the approach of the neutron star.

On Star One, Captain Gerald and Lieutenant Emerson sat in front of the main sensor and radar equipment monitoring their flight. Another recently promoted lieutenant was at the weapons console ready to fire the rail guns if an asteroid was spotted. General Karver stood behind the new lieutenant talking to him in a low voice.

General Karver knew that, for the last several weeks, Captain Gerald and Lieutenant Emerson had begun seeing each other occasionally on a personal basis. Because of their situation, General Karver didn't have a problem with it as long as it didn't interfere with their jobs. He had made it a point to tell both of them that just so they would understand.

Already they had blasted twenty-two small asteroids apart that had strayed too close to Star One. Many of them would not have collided with the station, but even those that passed within close proximity of the station were being eliminated. It allowed the crew to stay in practice and to be able to react if a real threat to the station should appear.

"Good morning Steve," Christy said with a smile taking her place next to the commander.

"Have a good night's rest?" Steve asked with a slight grin on his face.

Christy turned a little red since she and Steve had spent the night together, and their lovemaking had lasted for quite some time. "Very good," she said glancing demurely at her console. "How is everything this morning?"

"Everything's nominal," Steve replied with a slight smile. "The latest reports indicate that we are nearly two and one half billion miles from Earth. That puts the neutron star-black hole binary still four billion miles away."

"About another two months flight time," whispered Christy looking up at the screen, which showed the neutron star and black hole, which awaited them at the end of their flight.

At high magnification, the neutron star was a brilliant white dot and the black hole was just barely a dark blur next to it. Their conversation was interrupted by an alarm going off on the sensor array board.

"What is it?" asked Steve getting up and striding over to the weapons console where General Karver and Captain Gerald were rapidly checking the data.

Lieutenant Emerson had relieved the newly assigned weapons lieutenant and taken his seat at the console. "Another asteroid," Lieutenant Emerson replied with worry on her face. "A very large asteroid, the biggest we have encountered."

"How large?" asked Captain Gerald watching as the information appeared on the screen above the weapons console.

"It's coming across now," replied Lieutenant Emerson watching the screen intently.

"Holy shit!" exclaimed Captain Gerald seeing the answer. "The damn thing is nearly as large as the station. It's nearly 1,000 feet in diameter."

"Our rail guns won't put a dent in something with that much mass," Lieutenant Emerson stated her hands running quickly over the weapons console."

"We will have to use a Black Night with a nuclear warhead. We have four of those ready and in the missile launching platforms," General Karver said glancing over at Steve.

"Do it," ordered Steve knowing that precious time was passing. "Place the station on condition yellow, and order everyone to prepare for possible asteroid impact."

At her station, Christy spoke rapidly into her com unit as alarms started going off inside the entire station. In moments, the crew was headed towards their emergency posts. In critical areas of the station, airtight doors shut and locked.

"Station is secure," Teela reported a minute later as she appeared next to Christy. She had been watching everything and had just activated her hologram.

On the main screen, a dim dot made an appearance. At nearly 200 thousand miles, it was still distant but at their speed, only eight minutes from impact.

"Missile platform ports open," Lieutenant Emerson reported, her hands running quickly over the console in front of her. The weapons tech next to her, in the other seat, was also pressing buttons on his console readying the rail guns to take out anything that was left of the asteroid after the nuclear strike.

"Nuclear weapons launch authorized," General Karver said in a steady voice. "Just like we practiced lieutenant. It's just a rock, and it won't be shooting back."

Taking a key from around her neck, Lieutenant Emerson inserted it and turned it to the right next to a blinking green light on the console. The blinking green light signified that a nuclear tipped Black Knight missile was ready for launch. By turning the key, the missile would automatically arm itself one minute after launch.

"Missile locked on target," she continued as course data was fed to the missile's targeting computer. "Stand by to launch missile." Lieutenant Emerson double checked her board then pressed the launch button next to the blinking green light.

From the upper wheel of the station, a Black Knight missile leaped away from one of the missile platforms and accelerated on an intercept course for the incoming asteroid. Brilliant flame spread back behind the accelerating missile as it flashed towards its target.

"Impact in six minutes," Lieutenant Emerson reported. "Commander I have set up the Black Knight to impact the far right quadrant of the asteroid. If it does not destroy the asteroid, it should deflect it enough to give us a narrow miss."

"Very good lieutenant," Steve replied his eyes on the screen, which now also showed the drive, flare from the missile.

"That's a large asteroid," Christy said watching the screen worriedly. She knew it was big enough to take the station out completely.

"Activate a second missile in case the first fails," ordered General.

This was a scenario they had discussed and planned for. If they encountered a large asteroid, it might be better to deflect it than to attempt to destroy it.

"Second missile on standby," Emerson reported a moment later after taking the key out of its current slot and inserting it into another but not turning it. "If the first missile doesn't destroy or deflect the asteroid the second missile will be fired to detonate in its center," she paused doing some quick calculations. "The second missile would impact the asteroid approximately 2,000 miles from the station."

"Be ready lieutenant," General Karver ordered, his eyes focused on the sensor and radar screens. "We don't want to take any unnecessary risks."

On the screen, the asteroid gradually grew in size as Star One and the tumbling rock quickly drew closer together. It now looked like a small, jagged marble tumbling slowly around its axis.

"Impact in 30 seconds," Teela reported.

"Impact in 15 seconds."

"Impact in 5 seconds."

"Impact and we have detonation."

On the screen, a brilliant white glow covered the asteroid as the force from the nuclear explosion melted thousands of tons of rock and gave the asteroid a hefty kick in the side. For a brief moment, the asteroid was invisible behind the spreading fireball and brilliant light from the explosion.

Steve watched spellbound as the asteroid cleared the inferno and continued toward Star One. A large section of its surface was glowing white from the impact.

"How big a deflection did we get?" Steve asked concerned since the missile looked to have done little actual damage to the asteroid.

"It's enough," Teela said suddenly from Christy's side where she had been monitoring the entire crisis. "The asteroid will miss the station by about 18 miles. However, I am tracking numerous small fragments that have broken away as a result of the nuclear explosion. Some of those are on a collision course with the station."

"Confirmed sir," spoke Lieutenant Emerson as her fingers flew over her console. "We are placing all rail guns on line and preparing to fire. We are tracking over 82 separate inbound pieces of debris."

"Eighty-two," Christy said worriedly looking over at Steve, her eyes growing wide with concern. "How many are on a course to intercept the station?"

"Most of them," replied Teela with a look of worry showing in her deep blue eyes. She was hurriedly checking the station's sensors and correlating the data. "I'm giving the weapon's tracking computers the coordinates for the largest fragments that are on a collision course."

"Firing rail guns on targets," Lieutenant Emerson commented. The six rail guns kept continuously on line were all put on automatic control.

The rail guns began firing at the incoming asteroids. The other four were being hurriedly powered up. General Karver watched knowing they were not going to be able to get them all. The station was going to take some hits.

"One minute and thirty seconds until impact," intoned Teela tracking the inbound cloud of debris.

"All rail guns now on line," the weapons tech next to Lieutenant Emerson reported.

"Firing rail guns automatically on targets as they recycle," added Lieutenant Emerson keeping her eyes on the sensor and radar screens as her hands flew deftly over the controls of her weapons console. "I am overriding the safeties and setting the rail guns to fire every twenty seconds."

Steve watched as asteroids began vanishing from the screens as the largest asteroid fragments were shattered by the powerful rail gun rounds. He knew that by overriding the safeties the rail guns could over heat and their barrels could melt.

"Impact in sixty seconds," Teela reported then looking over at Steve with worry in her voice. "We're not going to get them all!"

"The rail guns will not be able recycle quick enough," Captain Gerald reported grimly keeping his eye on the sensor and radar screens.

"Impact in thirty seconds," Teela reported, her eyes growing wide.

A look of fear crossed Christy's face as she unconsciously gripped the armrests on her chair tighter.

"Impact in ten seconds." Teela continued using her interior sensors to scan the entire station and the platform."

"Impact!"

Steve felt the station shudder as a large piece of debris hit and then almost immediately several more smaller vibrations rattled the station. Alarms started going off on consoles all throughout Main Control. The alarms were quickly silenced as the Main Control crew tried to determine the damage to the station.

"We have six impact points that have penetrated the station," Teela reported with a pained and shocked look upon her face. "Our Luxen shielding stopped the others from penetrating.

"Where at?" demanded Steve knowing that the station had been damaged. "Where did they hit us?"

Three in storage areas, one in ecological habitat four," Teela paused before continuing looking shocked and visibly upset. "Two penetrated to the crew's quarters. Impact locations are Blue one outer level, no casualties. The hull sealed itself up since it was a small breach. However, the largest fragment penetrated to green level three. Airtight doors have sealed automatically cutting off that section and those in between. I have confirmation of eight fatalities."

Looking at Steve and Christy, Teela felt almost like she needed to cry. "Kathleen Preen is one of the casualties. The asteroid debris tore completely through her quarters!" Teela had watched the entire terrifying scene on her monitors. There had been nothing she could do.

Steve and Christy sat absolutely still hardly breathing.

Not Kathleen, Christy thought, how could something like this happen? Oh God, why Kathleen? Why did anyone have to die?

"It could have been worse," commented General Karver walking over and standing in front of Christy. "The station survived, and now we must go on."

"They are the first people we have lost since all of this began," replied Steve feeling numb. It had all been so sudden and unexpected.

"We need to tell Julie," Christy spoke quietly still finding it hard to accept what had just happened.

"We need to get rescue teams into those damaged areas," General Karver reminded Steve. He knew that Steve was in shock. The general knew what it was like to lose people under his command.

On the main screen, Teela changed the view to show the impact points on the station's hull. Cameras strategically placed offered views of the entire station. Most of the ruptured holes had sealed automatically due to a special sealing compound that was layered into the station's outer and inner hulls. Only one hole remained that cold not be sealed.

On the outer rim of the main wheel, a jagged hole nearly three feet across marked the impact point of a piece of asteroid debris. The small asteroid had torn completely through the station exiting on the other side of the rim. It had tumbled through several small storage compartments laying them to waste and then three sets of crew quarters, killing everyone inside, before exiting the station to continue on its desolate course.

"Get a repair crew out there as quick as possible," Steve ordered Lieutenant Commander Kevin Anderson, the first shift duty officer. The shock was wearing off, and he knew that some people were trapped in their living quarters. "Then I want all the interior sections repressurized."

"Yes sir," the lieutenant commander replied stepping over to the communications panel to contact the repair crews.

Around Main Control, the room became quiet as word of the tragedy quickly spread. They were stunned by the disaster that had just struck.

"I'm sorry commander," Lieutenant Emerson said with tears in her eyes. She felt as if she had let the station down. "There were just too many of them."

"It's not your fault lieutenant," Steve replied still feeling dazed by the disaster. "You did the best you could, everyone did. The station is still intact, and we all knew that there were dangers in what we're trying to do."

"You did fine lieutenant," General Karver said motioning for the other lieutenant to take Emerson's place. "You saved the station, you did your duty, and that's what counts."

Captain Gerald put his arm around Lieutenant Emerson. "It's all right Sandy," he spoke in a gentle voice.

"Why don't you take her to her quarters," General Karver suggested. "I can watch things here for awhile."

With a nod, Captain Gerald led Sandy Emerson to the doors of Main Control and exited.

"Are you all right Teela?" Christy asked quietly noticing that Teela had a strange extremely sad look on her face. Christy knew that Teela and Kathleen had become good friends and had been seen together often throughout the station.

"Commander, I need to speak with Jennifer," Teela mumbled still in shock.

She had never seen someone die before, and she had watched Kathleen's death on the monitors in her quarters. It had been horrible, but over in an instant. Kathleen had never known what happened.

"Go ahead," replied Steve aware that Teela was having a hard time handling what had just occurred. He hoped this wouldn't affect the AI adversely. No one had ever thought how something like this might affect Teela.

They all were having a hard time accepting what had just happened. It had happened so suddenly. Even he would miss Kathleen and her carefree, always cheerful attitude. She had been a valuable member of the crew. Steve knew that Julie and John Gray would take her loss very hard also. Steve took a deep breath and slowly let it out. He still had a station he had to look over and repairs that needed to be made. He would have to hold his grief for later.

In Jennifer's quarters, Teela materialized to find Jennifer lying on her bed staring up at the ceiling, her face slightly white. Several pictures had been knocked off the wall from the asteroid impact.

"What is it Teela?" asked Jennifer sitting up seeing the distressed look on the AI's face. She had never seen Teela looking so distraught before. Something was seriously wrong.

"Kathleen's quarters were destroyed in the asteroid impact, she's dead Jennifer," wailed Teela replaying the scene in her mind over and over again. "Kathleen's dead!"

"Oh my god," Jennifer cried tears forming in her eyes. "She couldn't believe what Teela was saying, but she knew from the look on Teela's face that it had to be true.

"Why did it have to happen? Teela cried with emotion flooding her voice. "Kathleen was so kind and generous, and she was my friend!"

Jennifer had to fight to keep her own emotions under control. Kathleen had been a good friend, but right now Teela was on the verge of collapse. Jennifer didn't know how the AI's systems would respond to this type of emotional stress.

"Teela," Jennifer said gently. "You know that things like this happen to people. All during our lives people we know, friends, family, and associates occasionally die. It's part of being human. Yes, Kathleen was your friend, she was my friend too, but we have to remember her for what she was, as long as we have those memories she will be alive inside of us."

Teela looked at Jennifer not sure what to say. She had read some on Earth's religions, but they had only confused her. There were so many different beliefs.

"Sit down," Jennifer said patting the bed beside her. "We have some time, let's talk." Jennifer reached for a tissue on the bed stand and wiped the tears from her eyes. For now, she had to focus on Teela; she would grieve for Kathleen later.

In Main Control, Steve and Christy were just recovering from the shock of losing a close friend and the other casualties. Some of whom Steve had known, not as well as Kathleen, but he had met most of them at one time or another.

Already, Lieutenant Commander Anderson was assembling repair crews to patch the outer hull. Once that was done they could repressurize the damaged areas and send crews in to begin the clean up. There would also have to be a memorial service for the dead crewmembers. In the back of Steve's mind, he remembered the last time something like this had happened, during the construction of the station when a completed section had blown out killing another of his friends. Steve felt Christy's hand take his and hold it tightly.

"We're all going to miss her Steve," Christy said, her eyes glistening from half formed tears. "But we must go on. We have a mission to complete. We knew that this was dangerous, and we could lose even more people before this is over, but we have to try or the entire human race could be lost."

"I know Christy," Steve replied with a heavy sigh. "It's just very hard to believe that she and the others are really gone. It's just like Ty, for all we know the FarQuest could have been destroyed in the wormhole. We may be attempting something that can't be done. What if we are only taking everyone to a quicker death?"

"We don't know that Steve," Christy replied. "I believe that Ty and his crew are waiting for us. I believe that we will make it safely through the wormhole. We have to!"

"I hope you're right Christy," Steve said.

He knew that he had been shaken by the disaster, so similar to the other one. Looking around the room, he saw that everyone had returned to their jobs, even though he could see tears in several of the women's eyes. He could see that Margaret Sullivan was openly crying. He couldn't blame her. This was a tragedy, one that couldn't have been prevented. He saw General Karver walk over and begin talking to Margaret. Steve knew that the general had witnessed death before on the battlefield. He was thankful for the general's presence.

We'll make it he thought, these people deserve to make it. Squeezing Christy's hand, he looked back at the main screen, which once again showed the neutron star-black hole binary. We're coming he thought, we'll be there in less then 60 days. Then we will know if this was all in vain or not.

# Chapter Fourteen

For the third time in the last hour, Steve looked anxiously at the computer monitor on his console that showed their current course and speed. They were 30 million miles from the neutron star-black hole binary and the steady pull of gravity from the two had already increased the station's speed to over 1,200 miles per second. He knew that the ever-increasing pull would continue to accelerate the station ever faster and faster as Star One approached the black hole.

"So that's a black hole," General Karver said standing in front of Steve's console staring at the main view screen, which showed a highly magnified view of the swirling black hole in front of them.

The black hole nearly filled the screen. The picture was being sent back by a remote probe that was less than two million miles from the gravity vortex of the black hole. Steve knew the probe was rapidly being pulled in and that contact with it would be lost shortly.

"It's frightening just to look at," Christy spoke feeling a chill crawl up her back. "And we are headed straight into it."

"The jaws of hell," General Karver spoke quietly still gazing at the screen. War he could handle, this was something else.

"I hope not," responded Steve looking up. "It's supposed to be our salvation."

On the screen, a swirling blackness crossed with veins of deep, dark purple swirled ominously. Somewhere inside was the wormhole, which was invisible at the black hole's massive center. The wormhole was their key to survival.

"It's pulling us toward it at an ever increasing rate," Lieutenant Emerson warned from her console where she and Captain Gerald were closely monitoring the station's far ranging sensors and radar. "Our speed is increasing rapidly."

Their search for asteroids that were also being drawn into the black hole had required extending the range of the station's sensors. A series of long-range probes had been deployed to help give them the added coverage. Sensor range currently extended out to a range of over one million miles in every direction.

Lieutenant Emerson kept her eyes warily on the sensor screens. As Star One neared the black hole, it had become necessary to keep all ten of the rail guns permanently on line. In the last twelve hours, they had destroyed over 60 small asteroids that had intersected Star One's course. The black hole was pulling in the asteroids at an ever-increasing rate. Four nuclear-tipped Black Knight missiles were being kept constantly on stand by ready to be launched if a larger target were spotted that might endanger the station.

"According to Pierre LaRann's theories, we will nearly reach the speed of light when Star One enters the wormhole. At that speed, the rail guns will be nearly useless if we encounter an asteroid," Teela stated scanning the station to ensure that all preparations for the passage were on schedule.

She was also computing the possibility of encountering an asteroid near the wormhole. The current percentage was at fifteen percent. That would likely change as Star One got closer to the wormhole and additional data was collected.

"But the asteroids should be traveling close to the same speed we are shouldn't they?" Christy asked from her place next to Steve. "After all, they will also be trapped by the intense gravity of the black hole."

"Some will be," Teela agreed as she ran a simulation of their current course and the projected location of the wormhole. "However, due to the number of asteroids being pulled toward the black hole, we may find a few that converge on our course. It may be necessary to sweep our flight path with the rail guns on continuous fire as we near the wormhole."

"How soon before we enter the black hole?" asked Steve looking at Teela. As usual, her black hair was perfect, with a slight curl where it touched her shoulders. He deep blue eyes stared back at Steve inquisitively.

"Less then four hours commander. Our acceleration will increase almost exponentially as we get closer," answered Teela doing some quick calculations. "What the conditions will be like once we pass the event horizon is only conjecture."

"We are committed now," General Karver commented with a frown across his forehead. His eyes focused back on the screen as the general wondered just what awaited them on the other side of the wormhole. He just hoped they got the opportunity to find out.

"We were committed from the time we left the Lagrange point," Steve spoke with a heavy sigh. "This may be our only hope of survival."

"Going through a wormhole in the center of a black hole," Christy whispered. "It sounds like something out of a science fiction novel, and a very bad one at that."

Steve looked around Main Control as everyone continued to do their jobs efficiently even in the presence of what could be their deaths in just a matter of a few short hours. He was extremely proud of his people. If he was meant to die today, he couldn't think of a better group of people to die with.

Over the past several months, they had worked around the clock strengthening the station, checking every system, and working on various contingency plans. If everything worked out, Star One would transit the wormhole and the crew and sleepers would build a new civilization on the other side, wherever that might be.

Todd was down in the control room of the Space Platform going over the final checks on the ion drives and the SRBs. Ted Dryson was also in the control room watching the reactor readings with a critical eye. No one knew what the affects of passing through the wormhole would have on the fusion reactors. Ted was watching the one on the Space Platform, and Jarl was watching the larger one on Star One.

John Gray sat at the pilot station with his two assistants waiting as the time neared to fire up the ion drives again. Teela had just made an appearance and was standing next to John ready to assist if needed. Already she was calculating the final course and thrust that the station would need to transit the wormhole. At the speed they would be shortly traveling, all their available thrust would only affect their course, once they were in the black hole, by a few precious degrees. Any major course correction needed to be made in the next hour or it would be too late. The black hole's gravity would be too strong.

"The calculations show we should be able to do it," Teela spoke carefully measuring her words, keeping any doubt out of her voice. She didn't want John to know just how narrow a margin of safety they had.

Todd walked over to stand next to Teela catching her eyes and smiling. "We'll make it," he said confidently. "I have faith in both of you."

Teela smiled back weakly. It was hard for her not to tell Todd that her current computer simulations were indicating that their chances of transiting the wormhole had dropped to under fifty percent. They were already committed, and there was no point in adding to the fear that was growing in the station as Star One drew closer to the black hole.

The problem was the asteroids. There were so many of them. She knew that some of them would be drawn into the wormhole with them, and that was the problem. The presence of the asteroids could destabilize the revolving magnetic field that was supposed to protect Star One.

Teela continued to update her calculations continuously as new data became available. Already two of the small probes had stopped communicating. The one nearest the black hole had gone silent as well as another. She thought an asteroid might have taken it out.

Half an hour later, John watched as numbers begin appearing on the screen in front of him. Teela was feeding in the course change needed to the flight computer and projecting their new flight path on another screen next to it. She had run the numbers herself to ensure that there was no chance for an error. At least in this instance being a sentient AI had its benefits. She could see everything the sensors were recording, she knew everything that was going on everywhere on the station, and she could send her hologram wherever she wanted. Their course would take them down the center of the black hole and straight toward the waiting wormhole.

"Looks as if we need to fire the ion drives in another ten minutes," Todd said looking at the screen over John's shoulder.

"I guess that means it's beginning. There's no turning back now," replied John taking a deep breath, stretching out his hands, and flexing his fingers.

This would be his biggest challenge as a pilot. There could be no error at all. Not if he was reading these numbers right. He looked over at Teela, and her eyes turned away. John knew she was afraid to tell him just how important the course she was projecting on the screen was. John knew enough mathematics to know there was absolutely no room for error.

They had discussed allowing Teela to fly the station through the wormhole. But her lack of piloting experience was a hindrance. They also didn't know what the radiation and other effects of the black hole might have on Teela's systems. They couldn't risk her loosing control at a critical moment.

John took another deep breath and placed his hands on the controls. "Don't worry Teela," he said softly gazing at the AI. "I understand."

Up at the main fusion reactor in the Power Wheel, Jarl Stoler and several technicians had just finished the last test on the revolving magnetic field generator. They had mounted projectors around the station that should allow them to produce a shield one mile in diameter. They had also built two back up generators in case the first one failed. They were built so that if one failed the next would kick in automatically, and if that one went the final back up would kick in. If they lost all three, they would lose the revolving magnetic shield, which was meant to keep the wormhole open while they made their passage.

"Were ready with the field generator," Jarl reported over the com to Steve.

"Very well," Steve replied. "I just hope this works."

"It will," Jarl replied confidently. "We can establish the field. I just don't know how well it will work once we enter the wormhole."

-

Up in Main Control, Steve felt Christy's hand grasp his as the two watched the main view screen.

"Do you think Ty is waiting on the other side?" Christy asked quietly, held in awe by the sinister spectacle on the screen.

General Karver walked over to stand in front of the two. "President Kateland would have been proud of what you are trying to do," he said with a nod. "She always believed in Star One. She loved the space program and what it meant to mankind. If we succeed, we could be planting a new colony on a new world."

"I hope so," replied Steve wishing this was over. "We lost voice communication with Mase and Tycho City nearly an hour ago. The interference from the neutron star-black hole binary plus the Sun's increased activity has made communication impossible. We're still trying to transmit information back on a tight beam to the Farside array, but there is no way to tell if they are receiving anything."

"I'm sure they are watching us," General Karver spoke turning to look up at the big view screen.

-

At Tycho City on the Moon, Mase Colton was watching the large view screen in his deep underground control room. It showed a large picture of the black hole as projected from the Farside array. In the center of the screen, a bright dot, which he knew was Star One, was nearing the dark maw of the black hole. The image was being transmitted from a trailing probe nearly 40 million miles behind Star One.

All voice communication with Star One had been lost over an hour ago. They were still receiving some data on a tight beam from the station, but it was intermittent. Mase knew that the interference from the neutron star and the black hole was the cause. He felt sadness in his heart knowing that he would never speak to his friends on Star One again. Where they were going, he couldn't follow.

In just a matter of a few precious hours, he knew some of his closest friends would be making a journey that people had only dimly dreamed of. He hoped and prayed that they made it. Those people on that space station so far from home might represent the last best hope for humanity to survive.

Down on Earth, General Marcus Young also watched a view screen, which showed the same scene as the one at Tycho City. The transmission was being relayed from one of the orbiting military communication satellites that had been returned to their control. General Young had finally succeeded weeks before in making contact with Tycho City and convincing Mase Colton that Senator Farley and his cronies were gone, and there was no longer anything to fear from Earth.

One of the first things General Young had done was to order the deadly laser at White Sands to be destroyed. Before doing that though, he had transmitted all the specs on the powerful laser to Tycho City. Tycho City had then transmitted the specs to Star One. If either ever needed a laser of that power and magnitude, they would be able to build it.

"Do you think they will make it," A young female lieutenant asked from her communications board next to General Young.

"We can only hope," replied Young watching the screen. The entire base had been shocked and then excited when they had learned what Star One was attempting to do. "Some of the brightest people this planet ever produced are on that station," General Young went on. "If anyone could figure out a way to survive it would be them."

Young knew that Star One could indeed be their best hope for survival. Already the surface of the globe was nearly uninhabitable with large areas flooded, earthquakes continuing to increase in intensity, and volcanoes erupting daily. The entire Pacific rim had turned into a literal ring of fire with erupting volcanoes. Millions of tons of ash and deadly gases were spewing into the planet's atmosphere.

General Young's own installation, which was supposed to be in a relatively earthquake free area, had already been rocked several times by powerful quakes in the last few days. There were also unconfirmed reports that the super volcano at Yellowstone was on the verge of erupting.

Mase Colton had confided to Young that there was a chance that the Sun could go nova due to the close approach of the neutron star-black hole binary. That was the main reason Star One was attempting the hazardous attempt at traveling through the wormhole. Currently the computer models were too close to call. If there was any type of nova, Young knew that his base and the other surviving underground bases probably would not survive. They were not buried deep enough nor protected by the wonder alloy Luxen like Tycho Cities installations.

General Young let out a deep sigh. Over the last few months, they had managed to locate a few more survivors. There were currently over 1,500 civilians and 620 military personnel in the deep underground bunker. All the checkpoints up above had been evacuated.

Only the small building above that concealed the elevators that led down to the bunker 400 feet below was still occupied. It was made out of thick concrete and the air was recirculated taking out all of the dangerous impurities. Ten marines stood guard inside, watching just in case Senator Farley made good on his threat to return. A series of cameras gave them an unobstructed view of the surrounding countryside. It had been several weeks now since they had seen anything moving. The surface above the bunker was dead, devoid of life.

Farther to the west in the Rocky Mountains, two secret underground bases were also watching the drama on their view screens. They were both tapped into the orbiting communication satellites monitoring the transmission. President Kateland had built both bases secretly when the truth about the neutron star first came out. Both bases were built deep into the Earth and were protected by thick Luxen walls.

The two bases were in secret contact with each other continuously via underground communications lines, but had stayed hidden from the rest of the world. Their orders were not to draw attention to themselves until after the catastrophe. It was firmly believed that after the neutron star passed there would be no Earthly threat to their existence. Inside the shelters, their protected humanity waited the coming of the neutron star-black hole binary to see what type of world it would leave in its wake. Warren Timmons, who had been Jane Kinsey's assistant, commanded one base. General Mann, who had made it to the mountains after the surrender in Florida, commanded the other.

Around the globe, the scattered remnants of humanity huddled in makeshift underground shelters, some no more than hastily dug caves. A few remaining government installations were nearly as well equipped as the ones in the United States. Many knew they would not survive. Starvation, disease, rising water, earthquakes, and erupting volcanoes were steadily taking their toll on the scattered underground shelters. Each day there was fewer than the day before.

In France, a husband and wife stood outside their ruined home. They had survived for months in the basement on canned food and bottled water. But now, a strong earthquake had collapsed their home driving them out into the gray, wet twilight of the late afternoon. Looking dismally about, the husband led his wife back to the feeble safety of the one wall that remained standing of their home. Sitting down, he put his arm around his ailing wife. Kissing her gently on the cheek, he smiled remembering better, happier days. Huddled together for warmth, the two watched what would be their last sunset through the low overcast sky.

Back on Star One, Steve felt the steady thrust from the ion drives. The drives were struggling to change Star One's headlong flight into the black hole by a few precious degrees. Already their speed had increased to over 3,000 miles per second. On the screen, another asteroid blew apart as it was struck by the rail guns blowing it out of their path.

Lieutenant Emerson had all ten rail guns on line. Captain Gerald and Lieutenant Emerson were keeping their eyes glued to the radar and sensor screens searching for potential targets. General Karver stood behind them watching everything carefully.

On the big screen, the black hole loomed ever more ominous as Star One rushed toward it. A slight vibration could be felt throughout the station from the ion drives. They were pushing the station slowly onto the course that would take them safely into the waiting wormhole.

"I'm scared Steve," Christy whispered with her eyes riveted on the screen. "What if we become trapped in the wormhole? We could be there forever."

"We'll be all right Christy," Steve replied gently. "We have probes out on all sides of us, and we will have advanced warning from them if there is a problem we need to deal with."

Minutes passed as Star One continued to hurtle into the black hole. Their speed continued to increase at a faster rate as the station neared the actual black hole itself.

"Speed is 20,000 miles per second and increasing rapidly," Teela reported from her position next to Steve. She had been going back and forth between Main Control and the Space Platform.

"Our speed is really increasing," Christy spoke worriedly. "It will be more difficult for John to adjust our course."

"John can handle it," Steve replied confidently. "He's the best pilot we have."

"It's time to fire the SRBs," Teela said and then vanished to reappear next to Todd in the Space Platform.

"One minute to SRB firing," Todd spoke over the com watching the computer count down. Todd glanced at Teela and smiled. "Everything is going to be just fine sweetheart, don't worry."

"I'm scared Todd, what if the station doesn't make it." Teela said plaintively. "I mean humans believe they have a soul. What about me? Will I just cease to exist? I don't think I have a soul."

"You definitely have a soul Teela," replied Todd gently. "You have too big of a heart not to."

Teela smiled warmly back at Todd. "I hope you're right."

"Ten seconds to firing Todd," spoke John Gray watching as the computer counted down the last seconds.

John wished that he could be with Julie, but he knew that he was the best pilot for this job. Julie was in their quarters with their two children. They had already said their goodbyes in case the station didn't make it through the wormhole. He knew it all depended now on his piloting skills.

"SRB ignition," Teela said as the station seemed to receive a large kick and everyone was pushed back in their acceleration couches. Then gravity returned to normal as Teela quickly adjusted the artificial gravity.

On the outer edges of the Space Platform, eight large SRBs added their power to the four ion drives, gradually accelerating the station ahead at one and one half gravities of acceleration. The Luxen cables felt the strain but did not break.

The ion drives glowed brightly leaving four glowing trails of electron fire behind the station. Already the intense gravity from the black hole was forcing the far ends of the threads of electron fire to bend and curve back toward the deadly maw of the black hole. The gaseous trails from the eight brilliant SRBs began to form behind the station; soon they too would be bent and pulled in. Nothing escaped the black hole's deadly grasp. It sucked in everything. Nothing was immune, except for the small neutron star that rotated in a tight, safe orbit around it.

Steve felt the station shudder and vibrate ominously as the SRBs continued to fire. This was much worse than the acceleration they had endured at the start of their flight. He watched worriedly as the station's stress indicators rose and then stopped way up in the green almost touching the yellow.

"Speed is up to 35,000 miles per second," Christy reported hardly daring to breathe. She knew from Einstein's Theory of Relativity that they were already experiencing a time dilation effect from their high speed of travel. It would become much more pronounced as they neared the speed of light.

"Switching rail guns to automatic computer instigated fire," Lieutenant Emerson reported. She pressed several buttons and typed in a code on her computer console.

For the next few minutes, the station's computers would tell the rail guns when and where to fire. Lieutenant Emerson would not have time to over ride them. Only the computers with their ability to process data in millionths of a second could protect the station now if an asteroid was detected. Lieutenant Emerson knew that Teela would be monitoring the rail guns closely. She was the only one with the ability and speed to over ride the firing computers if necessary. For the rest of the flight, Lieutenant Emerson and Captain Gerald would just be observers.

"45,000 miles per second," Christy said watching the speed indicator continue to rise.

It wasn't the ion drives or the SRBs that were causing the increase. It was the massive gravitational pull from the black hole itself that was pulling them swiftly in.

"One minute from magnetic field activation," Jarl Stoler reported over the com from his position in the Power Wheel.

Their speed continued to increase rapidly. Steve was aware of the station's thrusters firing almost continuously to keep the station on an even keel and properly aligned with the black hole. He knew that John must be struggling down in the Space Platform trying to stay on course and keep the station stable.

"Speed 70,000 miles per second," Christy breathed out nervously. She reached over and grasped Steve's hand, holding it tightly.

"Rail guns are on automatic sequential firing sequence," Lieutenant Emerson reported as the rail guns began firing and recycling automatically to fire again as they tried to sweep the path clear in front of them.

"Magnetic field activation," Jarl Stoler reported from the Power Wheel as he pressed a button home, which activated the first magnetic field generator. A low whine came from the equipment indicting that it had turned on.

Steve watched on the main screen as the station became surrounded by a golden halo of trapped electrons from the ion drives. They were in the center of a huge bubble.

"Two minutes to the wormhole," Lieutenant Emerson reported as another probe stopped reporting. It had been destroyed in the unstable wormhole opening.

"Probes 3, 7, 8, and 10 have all stopped transmitting," Lieutenant Commander Anderson reported from communications where he had been monitoring the probes.

"How's our course holding?" demanded Steve feeling the station beginning to vibrate even worse. He hadn't expected to lose so many probes so quickly. The station was once more making those groaning noises as its structure was put to the test.

"On course and holding," reported Christy checking her instruments. "John is keeping us dead on target."

Christy knew it must be taking a Herculean effort on John's part to keep the station on course. Just from the noise the station was making, it seemed to be protesting what was being done to it. It seemed as if the station had taken on a spectral life of its own.

Down in the Space Platform, John and the other two pilots fought to keep the station on the calculated course for the wormhole. The heavy gravitational pull was pulling on the station causing the three to have to use the station thrusters almost continuously to keep the station on course and stable. John gritted his teeth as he struggled to make all the adjustments that were necessary. He was flying mostly on instincts now.

Todd watched tensely, with Teela at his side, as Star One continued to accelerate towards the area of total emptiness at the center of the black hole. That was the location of the wormhole.

"Almost there," Teela said to Todd.

She felt apprehensive about what was soon to happen. She wondered if she would survive. She wondered if any of them would. Current simulations now only showed a 40 percent chance of success.

"Speed is 120,000 miles per second and increasing rapidly," Christy yelled as the station began to groan loudly and audible sounds of strain were heard from the station's joints. It sounded as if the station was about to come apart around them.

"Twenty seconds until wormhole entry," Teela's reported in a strained voice over the com. She had decided to stay with Todd until the transit was over.

"All personnel standby for wormhole transit," Steve barked over the station's com system. On the screen, the swirling maw of the black hole now surrounded the station. Steve felt Christy grip his hand even tighter.

"I love you Steve," she spoke not caring who heard.

"Wormhole insertion," Teela's voice announced.

"I love you to," Steve replied in a voice that seemed to last forever.

Time seemed to slow down and then stop. Steve's mind and senses seemed to explode as wave after wave of dizziness assailed him. For an instant, Steve felt as if he existed at every point in the universe. He no longer had a physical body he could sense. He could see every world, every intelligent being, he was back on Earth, on the Moon, he could feel Christy's deep love for him. He sensed with a part of his mind the first magnetic field generator do down as the edge of the field was penetrated by an asteroid. It was followed an infinity later by the second generator, and then a timeless instant later by the third!

With a resounding crash, Steve recovered finding himself back in Main Control hearing alarms pounding at his ears, amidst screams and yells of sheer panic, and then all the lights went out. Steve could hear groans and grinding sounds coming from tortured metal above the human sounds.

Steve knew that the station had been holed possibly severely. Some of the asteroids that had been pulled into the wormhole with Star One must have struck the station. The emergency lights came on dimly lighting up frightened and worried faces. Lieutenant Emerson was slumped over her console obviously unconscious, and she was not the only one.

"We need a medical team up here quick," Steve barked. "Captain Gerald, please send someone down to the infirmary to get some help. Have them take a portable hand lamp out of the emergency locker."

"What happened?" asked Christy wanting to hear Steve's voice as one of Captain Gerald's marines grabbed a hand lamp out of the emergency locker and ran out of Main Control toward the infirmary.

"I don't know," replied Steve looking about. "I think we lost the magnetic field generators," Steve had a vague memory of the generators going down and then a brilliant white light.

"Then we're trapped in the wormhole," Christy said in a defeated voice. Thinking her worst fear had come true.

"I don't know," replied Steve equally worried. "We don't have any power. I don't believe we're still in the wormhole."

"We can't be in the wormhole," General Karver spoke as he bent over Lieutenant Emerson checking her for injuries. "We must have made it out the other side."

At that instant, the main lights flickered and then dimmed to come back on at full strength. Captain Gerald was relieved to see that Lieutenant Emerson was regaining consciousness and was sitting up at her console holding her head, which had a visible bruise on it.

"She will be fine," spoke General Karver looking at Captain Gerald. He had seen enough injuries in combat to know the difference between a minor injury and a major one.

"The fusion reactor must be back on line," reported Lieutenant Commander Anderson rushing over to the damage control board, which he could see was lit up with glowing amber and red lights. "We've got some problems."

"What's our condition Teela?" asked Steve wanting a quick update on the station. With surprise, there was no answer. "Teela?" Steve asked again growing concerned and looking over at Christy.

"Matheson, what's wrong with Teela?" Steve demanded with alarm growing in his voice looking over at Andre who sat at the main computer terminal.

"I don't know sir," reported Andre punching buttons rapidly on his computer console. "I can't get her to respond either." Andre's face took on a look of grave concern; Teela was like a daughter to him.

"Todd," Steve said into his com. "What's your situation down there?

"Not good commander," Todd replied. "I believe we are operating on the emergency reactor. I haven't been able to get in touch with Stoler. We've shut down the SRBs, and the ion drives shut down automatically when we lost the main reactors. Dryson says the fusion reactor here on the Space Platform scrammed itself, and it will be a few hours before we can ascertain if it received any damage. He suspects the one in the Power Wheel probably did the same. Is Teela up there with you? I can't seem to get her to respond?"

Steve hesitated glancing worriedly at Andre. "No she isn't. Matheson is checking to see what's wrong. We should know something shortly."

"What's the damage report?" demanded Steve getting up and striding over to the damage control board.

"It's not as bad as I feared," Lieutenant Commander Anderson replied letting out a deep sigh of relief.

"A lot of the connecting Luxen support cables have snapped," he reported in amazement. "We have pressure leaks in about twenty different areas, but most of those are being sealed up from the sealant in the hull. It looks as if we took some hits from some small asteroids. Both reactors have scrammed, and we can't communicate with the Power Wheel. However, someone down there had to activate the emergency fusion reactor, that's where our power is coming from. We also have several stress indicators showing that hull structural integrity in a lot of areas is borderline. We need to get everyone out of those sections immediately!"

"How about casualties?" asked Steve hoping that there were not many.

"Unknown sir," Anderson replied. "Without Teela, we don't have any quick way to check. From this board, there will almost definitely be some, but how many is hard to say."

"Get rescue parties into those damaged areas and have the people moved to more secure locations," Steve ordered. "We can't afford to be losing people."

Steve made his way over to Matheson's console and looked at him inquiringly. Matheson had a stunned crushed look on his face.

「

What's wrong Andre?" Steve asked with foreboding. He could tell there was something terribly wrong.

"She's gone," Matheson mumbled with shock in his voice not wanting to believe what the system was telling him. "Teela's program isn't in the core anymore, it's been erased. Somehow, the passage through the wormhole or possibly the complete system power failure has destroyed her program. There's nothing we can do to restore her!"

Main Control was silent as the word was passed that Teela's program had been destroyed during the transit of the wormhole. Everyone felt the loss intensely, several of the women started crying. Teela had become a very close friend to many of the crew in Main Control. She would be deeply missed. Margaret Sullivan was crying openly at the news. Margaret and Teela had become extremely close since Jennifer had arrived on the station. Steve also wondered how Jennifer would take this. First Kathleen and now Teela. Steve wondered how many others would have to die before this was all over.

Several medical people appeared and hurried over and began assisting injured personnel including Lieutenant Emerson.

"Commander," Captain Gerald yelled excitedly.

Steve turned to see that the main view screen had come back on. It showed an outside view of nothing but stars. There was no sign of the black hole or the neutron star.

"We made it," Christy said breathing a sigh of relief and sadly feeling Teela's loss. She felt as if she had lost one of her best friends. She gazed at the beckoning stars on the main view screen and knew that if not for Teela, this would not have been possible.

"We made it," General Karver reaffirmed as a number of the crew in Main Control started cheering and clapping their hands.

Christy knew that if anyone deserved credit for their survival, it was Teela. Teela had a lot to do with all of them being alive today. It was her idea to try to traverse the wormhole.

"Commander this is Jennifer Stone," a new voice on Steve's com reported excitedly. "I need you and Todd to come to my quarters as soon as possible."

"It will be a little while Jennifer," replied Steve wondering what she needed. He also wondered how he was going to break the news to her about Teela. "We are sort of busy at the moment."

"You don't understand," Jennifer replied in a strained voice. "Teela is here, and it is imperative that you and Todd get down here as quickly as possible."

246

"Matheson," Steve said confused looking over at the station's chief programmer. "Jennifer says Teela is in her quarters. I thought you said her program was wiped."

"It is," replied Matheson looking confused. "There is no way that Teela can be in Jennifer's quarters. Whatever it is, I can assure you that it is not Teela!"

Steve got up quickly looking worriedly at Christy. "Tell Todd to get to Jennifer's quarters as quickly as he can. Captain Gerald, have a security team meet me at Jennifer Stone's quarters immediately."

"Yes sir," responded Captain Gerald passing orders quickly through his com to his people stationed throughout Star One.

Steve left Main Control and hurried down the corridor to the elevators. Fortunately, they were still working. In minutes, he was standing in front of Jennifer's quarters waiting for the security team. Captain Gerald, along with four of his marines who were well armed and Todd all showed up at the same time.

"I don't know what's going on," Steve said with concern in his eyes. "Jennifer says that Teela is in her quarters, and Matheson claims that Teela's program has been wiped from the computer core."

Todd looked visibly shaken at Steve's words. Could Teela actually be gone? If she was, who or what was in Jennifer's quarters?

"Be prepared for anything," ordered Steve looking at the marines. "We don't know what we may have picked up in our passage through the wormhole."

Pressing his hand to the door sensor, the door slid open immediately. Motioning for Captain Gerald and his men to wait outside, Steve and Todd went carefully into Jennifer's quarters.

"Steve, Todd, I'm glad you could make it so quickly," Jennifer said from the entrance to her bedroom. "Come in here." Turning, she vanished into the other room.

Steve and Todd looked questioningly at one another and then followed. The two men entered the room cautiously not knowing what to expect or what they might find. However, there sitting on the bed was Teela, with a faint enigmatic smile on her face.

"Teela," Steve said surprised with relief spreading across his face. "Matheson said your program has been wiped from the computer. How can this be, what's happened?"

"It's quite complicated commander," replied Teela standing up and walking up to him with an impish smile. Reaching out her hand, she touched his arm.

Steve froze at the touch. He could actually feel her hand! An electric shock ran through him as he realized what it implied. This couldn't be happening. Teela wasn't real!

She also reached out and ran her hand lovingly across Todd's face. Steve could tell from Todd's amazed expression that he too could feel her touch.

"I don't understand," uttered Todd in shock stepping back. "How can you touch me, what's happened?"

With an excited smile, Teela grasped Todd's hands firmly in hers. Looking at Steve and Todd both, she smiled and began speaking in her youthful exorbitant voice.

"When we entered the wormhole, there was a brief microsecond where everything became possible. Where everything that could exist did. Where the natural laws of the universe, that we are so familiar with, were not quite so definite. For just a brief micro second, my program touched this other reality. I used that reality to create a real human body and to transfer my program into it. What you see before you is real. I really do exist!"

"Teela it really is you," Todd said excitedly grabbing her and hugging her tightly. It was like a dream come true. He was ecstatic at the realization almost afraid to let her go.

"Yes Todd it is," replied Teela laughing with pleasure. She had always dreamed about what Todd's embrace would feel like. It was everything she had ever imagined and more.

Steve saw that Jennifer had a big contented smile on her face. It was as if she knew that her child had finally grown up. Teela was now an adult, a human adult.

"When Teela materialized in my quarters it was quite a shock," confessed Jennifer watching Todd and Teela together. "She explained to me what had happened, and I still find it hard to believe. But isn't it absolutely wonderful!"

Steve had to agree that it was, he could see the excitement and hope in the eyes of both Todd and Teela. Steve knew that the news that Teela had survived and was now human would excite and thrill a lot of crewmembers.

"Commander," Teela said excitedly breaking away from Todd.

"Yes Teela," Steve replied smiling.

"You might want to return to Main Control. They have located the FarQuest on the long-range sensors."

"How can you know that?" Jennifer asked with a confused look appearing on her face. "You're not connected to the computer anymore."

"That's another story," replied Teela grinning. "You didn't think that when I created this body I didn't make sure it had a few other abilities that might be beneficial?"

Steve didn't wait to hear Teela's explanation, but turned and hurried back to Main Control dismissing Captain Gerald's security team as he went. They wouldn't be needed.

Back in Main Control, Steve looked up at the view screen, which showed the FarQuest as a tiny speck in the distance.

"It's the FarQuest Steve," Christy said with a smile taking his hand. "We have contacted the ship's computer, and evidently the crew is back in deep sleep. The computer had a message for us. It's from Ty."

On the main screen, words quickly formed on it as the message was put up for Steve to see. *Hi Steve. What took you so long? Ty.* Steve turned to Christy and gently kissed her on the cheek amid the applauding and cheering in Main Control.

"I guess we made it," Christy said her eyes wide with the dawning realization that they had indeed escaped the black hole and the neutron star.

"Yes, I guess we did," responded Steve putting his arm around Christy's waist and pulling her close. They both looked up at the screen and the FarQuest and the sea of stars that now surrounded them with a new hope for a new beginning.

# Epilogue

Five years later, Star One was in orbit around a large asteroid. The Space Platform had been disconnected from the space station and was in orbit on the far side. All the damage caused by the transit of the wormhole had been repaired on both.

Nearly six years earlier, upon finding themselves in the new star system, the crew of the FarQuest had done a quick survey of the system. Much to their disappointment, the system contained no planets, but it did have a large ring of asteroids that totally encircled the system's sun at 200 million miles. The FarQuest's crew had spent nearly a month mapping many of the asteroids as they tried to determine what they should do.

Realizing that they could not survive without additional supplies, the crew had opted to put themselves back into deep sleep to wait. Their only hope was that a ship from Earth would someday find its way through the wormhole and rescue them. It was a distant hope, but the only one they had. They placed the spacecraft in a stable orbit just outside their arrival point, hoping that anyone that traversed the wormhole would spot the FarQuest. Ty also left a brief message for Steve in case it was someone from Star One that followed. They had set the deep sleep chambers to wake them in one year. At which time they would decide what their next move would be. If after one year, no one had showed up, they would know that no one was coming.

With all the data the FarQuest had sent to Star One and Tycho City on the wormhole and Ty's plan to attempt to traverse it, Ty felt there was a very remote chance someone else might attempt to come through. Others might see the wormhole as a way to escape the deadly clutches of the neutron star-black hole binary.

When Star One arrived, the survey information from the FarQuest had been transferred to the station's computers. After much consideration and evaluation of available resources, they had mounted boosters on one of the larger asteroids and moved it into an orbit closer to the sun at a range of 100 million miles. The asteroid was nearly thirty-two miles long and fourteen miles in diameter.

Steve knew they were extremely fortunate that sitting up workable space habitats using asteroids had been studied on Star One. It was one of the reasons Julie had originally been recruited to work on the ecological habitats. It made feasible what Steve proposed to do, but would require a Herculean effort on everyone's part to complete.

Dryson and Stoler had designed a heavy cutting laser powered by the station's fusion reactor. They had used the laser specs that General Young had sent as the basis for the design. Under the watchful guidance of the two scientists, Lieutenant Emerson and Captain Gerald over the course of two long years had focused the laser on the asteroid. They had smoothed down the outside of the asteroid into a cylinder shape. Then they had started on the inside. Carefully using the laser and occasional explosives, including four tactical nukes, they had hollowed out the inside of the asteroid. They created a massive cavern twenty-four miles long and eight miles in diameter.

Once the cavern was completed, they had resealed the ends of the cylinder and installed massive airlocks to accommodate shuttles and other work craft. The FarQuest, due to its size, was left on the Space Platform.

By rotating the cylinder, they managed to create Earth normal gravity on the inside. Then they began the long, arduous task of establishing plants, animals, streams, lakes, and housing for the crew of Star One. Julie Gray recruited over 1,000 people to help in establishing a new world of plants and animals in the massive habitat.

General Karver had helped with all the organizing and getting people assigned to the right jobs. Once again, Captain Gerald's marines were a godsend as they were used to help direct all the different projects. Things Julie had only dreamed about started to become a reality. Julie could be found everywhere in the new habitat, directing people and explaining why this stream had to go here and that lake over there. It was aggravating and difficult at times, but with the talented people she had working for her, the job had been accomplished.

Steve and Christy Larson along with John and Julie Gray stood looking out over their new home. It was finally time to transfer their living quarters from Star One to the habitat. While Star One and the Space Platform were both fully operational and would remain manned with skeleton crews at all times, they had served their primary purpose. They had brought them safely through the wormhole to their new home.

The air was sweet and clean with the sound of birds singing in the distance. There was no pollution and no traffic noise. It was the kind of world that people had dreamed about creating back on Earth. Occasional butterflies were visible amongst the plants and trees. They watched as a honeybee flew by on its way to collect more pollen to take back to its new hive.

"I can't believe it's actually done," breathed Christy holding her husband's hand.

Looking toward the far end of the cylinder, she could see white, wispy clouds floating high up in the sky. Under the right conditions, Christy knew that Julie could even create thunderstorms in the habitat.

"It's quite a sight isn't it," Julie Gray said looking proudly at the world she had created for them. "Kathleen would have loved it here."

"Yes she would have," John replied with a sad smile.

"I wished she could have lived to see this," Christy added somberly.

As far as the eye could see, their new world was green and blue with a scattering of other colors. Of course, they would all have to get used to the fact that the gently sloping sides of the cylinder allowed people to live anywhere, including straight up above. Looking up you could see what looked like small dwellings, ponds, streams, and farmland seemingly hanging above their heads.

"Just think Steve, we can actually fish in the streams without getting yelled at," John said grinning remembering an incident from years back on Star One.

John had already discussed this with Ty. Looking down the gently sloping path that led to a small group of nearby dwellings, he could see their two teenage children talking to other kids close to their age.

They could see Teela and Todd Williams along with Jennifer and Ty Erin walking along one of the paths that led towards the comfortable bungalows that were nearby. Teela was obviously pregnant, and they could all hear her excited laughter in the distance.

"I was speaking to Teela the other day. The modifications to the FarQuest are almost complete," commented Steve looking over at John.

"A faster than light space drive," John spoke with an excited glow in his eyes. "We might actually be able to return to the Solar System and discover what happened after we left."

"All because of what Teela learned in the wormhole," Christy added as she watched the Gray's children in the distance.

"It also helped when we discovered we were only 118 light years away from our Solar System," John spoke with a nod of his head. "If Teela's theories about this new space drive are correct, the flight to the

Solar System will only take about two months."

"The drive uses gravity to distort space in front of the ship," Julie said evenly not understanding how this was done. "Teela learned the secret in the wormhole."

"Plus a lot of other things," Steve added. He could still remember the shock he had received when Andre Matheson had shown him all the new information Teela had placed in the computer core of Star One. Information she had learned during the transit of the wormhole.

"General Karver will be returning to the Solar System on the FarQuest when we launch her," Steve spoke wondering what the crew would find. "If there are any survivors, the general may know their leaders."

"Are we certain the new space drive is safe?" Julie asked with a frown.

"Dryson and Stoler have confirmed all the math," Steve reminded her. "They feel confident it will work as Teela has claimed."

"The Solar System will be an alien place now, with the passing of the neutron star-black hole binary," Julie pointed out. Then gazing across the world she had designed and created she continued. "This is our world now. Ours and our children's."

"It's a beautiful world," Christy said with a pleased look upon her face. "A good place to raise our children and to start over."

She looked down at her own stomach, which was swelling nicely. Doctor Wruggi had told them that their son would be making an appearance in another three months. Taking Steve's hand, she led him down the path into their new world and a new beginning. Julie and John followed close behind.

Teela looked up as she saw the commander and the others walking down the small hill toward them. She smiled to herself feeling extremely pleased with the way everything had turned out. She felt her baby kick and her hand went automatically to her stomach. Todd grinned recognizing what had happened.

She reached out with her mind and checked the computers on Star One. She had added this ability to her new body when she created it. There were other abilities also, which for the most part, she kept hidden so as not to make people feel uneasy. She checked the files in the computer making sure they were secure. Some of the files she had been opened for study by the scientists aboard Star One. However, a large number of files remained locked. No one was granted access. These files contained information she had learned in the wormhole that she didn't feel the human race was ready for yet.

Her daughter would be born in a few more months, and she would have the same hidden abilities that Teela did. Perhaps someday in the future, her daughter would open the locked files when humanity was ready.

Teela breathed out a deep sigh of satisfaction. Todd reached over and placed his hand over Teela's on her stomach. Teela still marveled at the feeling of being able to touch someone.

"I love you," Todd spoke softly with tenderness in his voice.

"I love you too," Teela replied, her dark blue eyes seeking and finding his. That was the most remarkable of all things. The ability to love and to be loved. It was what made her human.

The End

Website: http://raymondlweil.com/

Other Books by Raymond L. Weil

Dragon Dreams: Gilmreth the Awakening
Published October 2011

Star One: Neutron Star
Published May 2012

Star One: Tycho City: Discovery
Published August 2012

Dragon Dreams: Snowden the White Dragon
Coming October 2012

Star One: Tycho City: Survival
Coming January 2013

Dragon Dreams: Firestorm Mount
Coming May 2013

# Dragon Dreams:
# Gilmreth the Awakening

Currently available as an e-book and as a paperback.

# Gilmreth

Deep below the snow-covered mountain, the ancient dragon stirred lethargically in its cold, dark lair beneath the mysterious towering mountain called Firestorm Mount. Upon the high, stony ceiling of the dragon's lair dripping water had leached lime from the ancient stone of the mountain forming grotesque and distorted stalactites. Upon the tips of these, water condensed into small droplets to plummet away into the blackness below.

The occasional falling water drops echoed in the vast chamber as they struck the small pool on the cavern's floor. It was the only sound other than the shallow breathing of the sleeping dragon. Upon the surface of the pool, shallow ripples raced as they formed after each splashing droplet.

Small white fish, which had adapted to feeding in the dark, prowled the coal black water. The small turbid fish spent their lives feeding upon the few sparse aquatic plants and microscopic organisms that thrived in the pool's dark depths.

In ancient times, the sleeping dragon had been the largest and most fearsome of its kind. It was a specter of deadly power with flame spouting from its mouth to scorch the helpless earth below. The dragon's flame turned everything it touched into black, smoldering ashes leaving behind an unearthly, sterilized wasteland.

For untold centuries, the ageless dragon spread fear and death as it ranged the world searching for sustenance to feed an ever-growing ravenous appetite. Defenseless village after village fell victim to the dragon's unending hunger. The villages were burned to the ground with their populations decimated leaving the survivors fleeing in small groups, in unashamed terror and shock.

The dragon was all-powerful, and no power upon the Earth could threaten or stop it. Anyone that stood in its path met a horrendous and agonizing death from the dragon's unforgiving fiery breath or its deadly talons.

Other dragons had once existed, but these Gilmreth had killed one by one feeding on their powerful life force. Even this hadn't satisfied the dragon's ever-growing craving for sustenance. A life extending force that humans seemed to satisfy more than any other creature upon the Earth and then only briefly. For that reason, Gilmreth fed in an uncontrolled frenzy upon humans. Gorging himself on the life force, he desired so fervently.

A faint rumbling reverberated through the immense cavern, an indication of an avalanche of loose dirt, rock, and snow upon the steep, frozen slopes above. Sluggishly forcing open one large yellowish red eye, its horizontal pupil a dark slit of the deepest black, Gilmreth shifted his ponderous weight before succumbing back into a deep nearly dreamless slumber.

For a brief moment, the dragon's massive evil heart had beaten a little faster. Its cold blood had pumped through its veins a little quicker. A partial thought had formed in the dragon's ravaged, demented mind before everything returned to never ending unconquerable darkness. Inside the creature, the deep burning fire had briefly flared then lessened. The fire had never been completely stilled. Gilmreth's dark, grayish wrinkled skin had the look of coarse, dry leather. The dragon's massive wings lay folded about the great sleeping beast. Its tail with poisonous twin red barbs was laid out behind ready to strike at any danger.

For over two thousand years, the dragon had slumbered quiescently. Gilmreth was held captive by an incantation cast upon the deadly dragon by the world's last great sorcerer. The ancient enchantment was finally beginning to weaken. When it weakened sufficiently, the dragon would awake and rise to feed.

Up above, only in fading legends were dragons still remembered. Their stories told quietly, almost hesitantly around a late night campfire, or whispered nervously between weary travelers staying at the small inns in the few remaining villages and towns. Most of humankind questioned dragons ever existing, and the mastery of sorcery had become a myth a mere legend.

The greatest of these ancient legends was the story of Gilmreth, the most deadly and the last of the immortal dragons. Over the fleeting centuries, even that fearsome legend had gradually dimmed. Gilmreth had become a fairy tale. A fairy tale that, unknown to most of humankind, slept in the dark protective depths of Firestorm Mount waiting to awaken. That time of awakening was growing near. Sometime in the near future, the sleeping spell would lose its powerful hold on the great dragon. When that happened, Gilmreth would be free once more.

# ABOUT THE AUTHOR

I live in Clinton Oklahoma with my wife of 38 years and our three cats. I attended college at SWOSU in Weatherford Oklahoma, majoring in Math with minors in Creative Writing and History.

My hobbies include watching soccer, reading, camping, and of course writing. I coached youth soccer for twelve years before moving on and becoming a high school soccer coach for thirteen more.

I am an avid reader and have a science fiction / fantasy collection of over two thousand paperbacks. I want future generations to know the experience of reading a good book, as I have over the last forty years.

Made in the USA
San Bernardino, CA
16 September 2016